KINGDOM LOST

The Lost Stones of Argonia:

Book 1

ENDORSEMENTS

In *Kingdom Lost*, Dawn Shipman has penned an epic tale of adventure, mystery, and betrayal in an imaginative storyworld with magical stones and skyways. Readers will root for Princess Lyric as she strives to unravel the mystery and calling facing her. This fantasy debut will create new fans clamoring for the next book in the series. An absorbing adventure!"
—**Jill Williamson**, award-winning author of *By Darkness Hid and Thirst*

I enjoy reading speculative fiction, and Dawn Shipman's Lost Stones of Argonia series does not disappoint. A distraught princess, a handsome knight sworn to protect her, and the intrigue of battling the schemes of a dark prince and the wizard who empowers him keep the reader immersed in the story. You'll lose yourself as you meet the characters from the different peoples living in Argonia where *Star Wars* and the *Lord of the Rings* intersect.
—**Julie McDonald Zander**, award-winning author and publisher, *Chapters of Life*

Prepare to be swept into the magical world of Argonia! This brilliant debut captured me from the first page. The danger. The romance. The quest of Lyric to save her lost kingdom. Enjoy this magnificent adventure with its stunning scenery, fierce rivals, and all the unexpected characters along the way.
—**Melanie Dobson**, award-winning author of *Catching the Wind* and The Magic Portal series

KINGDOM LOST

The Lost Stones of Argonia: Book 1

DAWN SHIPMAN

ELK LAKE PUBLISHING INC
PUBLISHING THE POSITIVE
Plymouth, Massachusetts

COPYRIGHT NOTICE

Cover and Interior Design: Derinda Babcock
Editor(s): Mary W. Johnson, Deb Haggerty

PUBLISHED BY: Elk Lake Publishing, Inc., 35 Dogwood Drive, Plymouth, MA 02360, 2021

Library Cataloging Data

Names: Shipman, Dawn (Dawn Shipman)

KINGDOM LOST—The Lost Stones of Argonia: Book One / Dawn Shipman

362 p. 23cm × 15cm (9in × 6 in.)

ISBN-13: 978-1-64949-431-3 (paperback) | 978-1-64949-432-0 (trade paperback) | 978-1-64949-433-7 (e-book)

Key Words: YA Medieval Fantasy Quest; Sword, sorcery, magic, evil wizard; Princess heroine fights for kingdom; Intelligent non-human species, friend and foe; Ancient prophecy, powerful talisman; Warm romance, love story; Coming of age

Library of Congress Control Number: 2021948972 Fiction

DEDICATION

To my dad, Al Price, who first taught me the love of story and instilled in me the belief that I could do anything I wanted in life—if I was willing to work for it. I finally did it, Dad—I wrote a book! Thanks for all you gave me. I'll never forget it or you.

ACKNOWLEDGMENTS

Thanks so much to all the people who have believed in me and in this book. Some are already gone from this world. I hope they knew how much they meant to me. Others are still here and have been constant sources of encouragement.

My sister, Angel Collins—what would I do without you? You've been in my corner every step of the way.

My awesome critique partners—Melanie Dobson, Nicole Miller, Tracie Heskett, Julie Zander, and Ann Menke. You ladies are the best! You helped me stay on track so many times when I was tempted to wander off!

To Pat Bynon, who read an earlier version of the manuscript on her vacation to Hawaii and interrupted her time on the beach to say "Dawn—you need to publish this book!" Thanks for giving me that shove, friend.

To the good folks at Elk Lake Publishing. So glad we found each other!

And finally, to the Computer Guy, who, though he doesn't necessarily understand why young girls might want to read such things(!), still stays home caring for the critters and paying the bills while I race all over the country on writerly adventures. Hugs and kisses, forever and ever!

Looking back—

I see how little prepared I was for what happened that
day ...
The only child of a widowed king in a small, isolated
land,
I received everything I desired—often, as soon as I
desired it.

On that day, everything changed.
Those things I thought I could rely upon most
Were torn from my grasp.

I didn't know my necklace was anything more than a
family heirloom.

I didn't know there were sentient, intelligent beings in
my world
who were not human.

I didn't know that overnight
I would be pressed into a role
I had never before dreamed of.

I would soon learn.

CHAPTER 1: UNWELCOME GUEST

She had to get away.

Lyric slipped through the maze of dancing couples, relieved to have escaped the visiting prince, hoping he did not see her. Did not follow. Clenching her teeth, she held fast to her aura of royal control even as she fled the crowds in the Great Hall. Two of her court ladies giggled together in the corridor, but she did not wait for them to curtsy or acknowledge her as they should.

Sweeping past them, she aimed for an adjoining hallway that would take her far from the festivities. A high, shrill voice stopped her.

"Princess Lyric! Look!"

A child, a wide grin on his freckled face, jumped in front of her. He twirled in a circle before her, arms outstretched. "My grandmom made me this new tunic so I could serve tonight at the Solstice Ball. Isn't it handsome?"

Lyric lifted her hand, covering her wildly pounding heart, pausing for this one short instant. She forced a smile.

"You look amazing, Colin, as well turned out as any of the grown-up servers. But I must leave now—I will see you soon." She tousled the boy's mousy hair, stepped around him, and hurried down the corridor. She passed several closed doors, then ducked into a passageway that veered off to the left. She didn't go far before stopping and pressing back against the cool stone of the castle wall.

Behind her, the music of the Summer Solstice Ball thundered on, but she pushed it from her thoughts. She pulled her pendant from under the bodice of her sapphire gown and stared at it. She'd been dancing with the prince, despising the insolent, possessive way he held her, and the gemstone had come to life—throbbing, burning. Heat from the gem still radiated against her palm and like a burning ember, the stone glowed red.

Sucking in a breath, she couldn't believe what her eyes so clearly showed her. Clutching the pendant to her heart, she shrank against the wall, willing her breathing to return to normal.

Her pulse was still racing when the sound of marching booted feet echoed along the corridor. Prince Ralt of Malacar strode past, peering from side to side like a prowling beast. He'd been hunting her all week—ever since he and his entourage arrived at her kingdom.

He stopped short when he saw her, and after a quick glance back toward the Great Hall, he turned and stalked toward her.

A silver circlet rested atop his golden hair, and his burgundy military dress uniform was richly ornamented and perfectly tailored. He was not a big man, just a few inches taller than she, but he was fit and carried himself with unmistakable authority. When he'd first arrived in Tressalt, she'd thought him quite handsome.

Not anymore.

He stopped in front of her and gave an abbreviated bow.

"Your Highness. We had just been dancing, and lo! I looked away for an instant, and when I turned back, you had vanished. I wondered where you'd run to."

Gripping the pendant, Lyric pushed away from the wall and squared her shoulders.

"Run, my lord? I am at home in my own castle. Why would I run?"

The prince's lips tipped up at the corners, and he gestured with one hand, then the other, indicating the deserted hallway.

Lyric lifted her chin and stared into the mocking eyes. "It is hot, my lord, and I find I am feeling faint." She inclined her head. "If you'll excuse me—I believe I shall retire for the evening."

She made to move around him, but he stepped in front of her, blocking her escape.

"Not just yet, if you please," he said smoothly. "I've been hoping to speak with you privately for some time, so I find this meeting ... serendipitous." His eyes ran down her front, following the chain holding the pendant in her clutched hand. His eyes widened. "But what is this, Your Highness? May I see?"

He reached for her hand. She quickly stepped back, dropping the opal under the neckline of her gown. "It is nothing, my lord. Just a family heirloom given me by my mother. Now, truly, I must be going." She tried to go around him, and again, he blocked her.

"An heirloom, you say?" He eyed her speculatively. "I have a friend who's told me to search for just such ... heirlooms. But if you won't allow me to see it, perhaps you'll tell me how you came by this scar, instead? Not a birthmark, I trust?" He ran a finger over the rough skin of her cheek.

She flung her arm back to strike, but he was faster. Grabbing her hand, he held it over her head, pinned against the stone wall behind her. He chuckled, ice-blue eyes glinting, and leaned in closer. His breath reeked of wine, blowing hot against her face, gagging her. "You're going to fight me, are you? Splendid."

She'd never been afraid of anything inside her own castle, but she trembled now.

"Let me go," she ground out, fury uniting with her fear.

Out of the corner of her eye, she saw movement in the adjoining corridor. The serving boy, Colin, carrying a heavy tray of dishes, stared at her, eyes wide. Slowly, he backed out of sight.

Ralt followed her gaze, then stepped away, releasing her hand. He planted himself firmly between her and the corridor and brushed imaginary lint from his impeccable uniform.

"Now, Princess, it seems we may have gotten off to a bad start. Let's begin again, shall we?"

Hands clenched at her side, she longed to run, to shove past this beast, but she'd never get away. Wine-impaired or not, he'd have her in an instant.

Where were the guards? She could scream. Why didn't she?

She took a deep breath but couldn't make herself scream. This was her castle, her home—she must handle such trivialities as drunken guests herself.

Mustn't she?

Ralt ran his eyes up and down her quivering frame and smirked.

"Surely you know why I've come this long way to visit your lovely kingdom, do you not? A bargain is a bargain, you know, and I've determined now is the time to set the details in motion."

Bargain? Her disbelief must have been etched on her face because he laughed, a guttural sound devoid of humor.

"I don't know what you're talking about," she growled. "There is no bargain."

"Your father didn't tell you?" He tsked. "He must have wanted to surprise you." He pressed in closer. "But make no mistake, sweet Lyric. Sooner or later, you will be mine." He grabbed her, yanking her into his powerful arms. "Perhaps it will be sooner."

"Stop it! Let me go!" Her breath swooshed from her lungs as he crushed his body to hers.

"Princess Lyric?"

With an oath, Ralt shoved her against the stone wall and whirled to face the man standing at the end of the hallway. "Get out of here!"

Gasping, Lyric tried to see who was there, hoping, praying whoever it was would not leave her. He was tall, dark-haired, dressed in the ebony and silver of the King's Guard.

Her heart quailed even as relief flowed through her.

Marek. Captain Gareth's second-in-command.

He didn't move. He didn't look at her but stood at attention, hand on the hilt of his sword, facing the prince.

"Forgive me, Your Highness. King Sander has sent for his daughter. I am to escort her to him immediately."

"The king went to bed an hour ago," Ralt spat out.

The guard inclined his head politely. "Nonetheless, my lord."

Lyric grabbed her chance. "I must see what my father requires, Your Highness. Good night."

Ralt growled something incoherent as she slipped past him, but she kept going, head high, as calmly as she could, to her rescuer's side. He bowed to her as she approached. She nodded but refused to make eye contact.

They left the fuming prince and strode back toward the Great Hall, where the music still blared and couples still danced. They passed the doors silently, the other guards straightening to attention in the presence of their liege lady and their commander. She had nothing to say, and thankfully, neither did he.

She was desperately cold. A tremor shook her from deep within, and all she wanted was to return to her room and sob into her pillows until no tears were left. She shuddered and stumbled.

Marek grasped her arm. "Here, my lady, let me help."

She jerked away and resumed walking. "I'm fine."

They continued along the cobbled floor, down one torch-lit corridor and then another, leaving the Solstice Ball with its noise and peril far behind. When they arrived at the stairway that led up to the king's rooms, Marek kept walking.

Lyric stopped. "Aren't we going to my father?"

He turned and came back to her, brow creased. "I am sorry, my lady. I'm afraid I wasn't overly truthful. The king did not call for you." He shook his head back, flinging his dark hair away from his face. "Saying that he did was all I could think of to ... disentangle you and avoid a brawl with the prince. I hope I was not out of line."

Heat rushed through her. "How long were you watching?"

His jaw tightened. "I had just arrived, my lady. Colin, the serving boy, was concerned you were in distress and needed assistance. I came as soon as I heard."

And she'd be grateful forever he had, but she only nodded. It was all she could do. Any words she might have said stayed lodged in her throat.

She turned from him and paced down the wide hall toward her rooms. But another, horrifying thought intruded, forcing her to a standstill. *He hoped he wasn't out of line?* She whirled to face him.

"You don't think I lured the prince to that hallway, do you? That I wanted him to join me? Because I didn't. I tried to get away from him, but he followed me and—"

He reached out a hand as if to touch her, then dropped it to his side. "I believe you, Your Highness. And I'm sorry you were exposed to such treatment. But you're safe now. Let's get you to your chamber."

There was nothing left to say. Mutely, she resumed her pathway along the hall and up the stairs to her room, fighting the tremors that now shook her from head to foot. Marek pulled open the heavy oak door, and she slipped gratefully inside. Candles glimmered in their sconces, and a fire burned low in the hearth. Her bed with its quilts and cushions beckoned to her.

Marek poked his head in and scanned the room. "Where's Rowana?"

She shrugged tiredly at the mention of her maid. "Off dancing, I suppose."

He frowned. "I don't like to leave you alone. Shall I call someone for you? Mistress Mari'el, perhaps?"

She stood straighter, trying to meet his steady gaze with her own defiant one. "No, I don't need anyone. Good night." She made to close the door but he stepped forward, blocking it with one booted foot.

"Perhaps you don't need anyone," he said kindly, "but I need you to bolt your door. I'm going to post someone outside, just in case your prince comes calling, but until then—"

"He is not my prince!" she flared. Unruffled, he remained where he was, silent, waiting. She wilted. "Fine. I'll bolt the door."

He stepped back, and she slammed the heavy door, then, sighing, slid the bolt. He'd probably stand there all night himself if she didn't. And if the prince did come looking for her ...

She sagged back against the door, and pulled the pendant from under her gown. The opal stone was cool now. It had returned to its normal milky-white color, its sparkles of coral and gold gleaming from the center. No heat, no fiery red color.

But she knew what she'd seen. What she'd felt.

Shivering, she kicked off her dancing slippers and padded across the room to her bed. Prince Ralt had hunted for her. He had held her against her will, mocked her, threatened her. Hot tears flooded her eyes. She'd always known she might one day have to marry a man who cared for her no more than she cared for him, but surely her father wouldn't promise her to a man like Ralt.

She sat atop the ivory bed coverlet, facing her reflection in the gilt-edged mirror on the opposite wall. Setting aside the braided gold and pearl circlet—it had belonged to her mother—she unpinned her hair, and let the mahogany silk fall about her shoulders. Memories of the evening scrolled behind her eyes—the touch of Ralt's hand upon her skin, the scorn in his eyes, his savage presumption as he crushed her to his body. She shuddered and wrapped her arms around herself. If Marek hadn't appeared when he did …

Marek. She lifted her eyes to face the scarred, pale-skinned girl in the mirror. Marek had saved her from that horrible man, and she hadn't even acknowledged what he'd done.

She could have at least thanked him.

CHAPTER 2: ESCAPE

The morning began as badly as the night had ended. The seemingly endless memories of Ralt's menacing assault had wrenched Lyric from rest every time sleep tried to claim her. Finally, just before dawn, exhaustion won and she slid into a deep, dreamless slumber, only to be pulled to wakefulness mere hours later when the sun streamed through her window. Groaning, she forced herself out of bed. Mid-morning was well underway, and if she wanted to speak with her father she'd better hurry. Not waiting for Rowana, who should have come hours earlier, she pulled on a pale-yellow day gown, ran a metal comb through her tangled locks, and rushed for the door, only to nearly bounce off the solid form of the guard posted there.

"Oh, I'm sorry," she said breathlessly. "I'd—I'd forgotten you were here." She drew herself up and strove to speak with authority. "Thank you for attending me. You may go now."

The guard, an older man named Helmsmith, inclined his head. "You're most welcome, m'lady, but the commander ordered me to stay here until relieved by another and to stay by your side if you was to leave your chamber."

Lyric felt the heat rise in her cheeks. Marek had given that order? She clenched her teeth. This was her own castle—she did not need a guard with her wherever she went. Last night had been an ... aberration. But she sighed, letting it go. Good form dictated she not argue with a soldier following orders. She would speak with Marek later.

"Very well," she said with as much dignity as she could muster. "I am on my way to the king's apartment." Turning on her heel, she strode down the corridor, the guard at her side. Their footsteps echoed in the stone hallway, and her mind turned to her meeting with the king. Surely he hadn't promised her to Prince Ralt. He couldn't have.

Could he?

Cold stole over her as they neared the staircase that led up to the king's solar. She paused, rubbing her arms against the chill, and stared out a mullioned window. The summer solstice fair was in full swing in the village on the plain below the castle. She frowned. People came from miles around for the annual fun, but she didn't recall seeing so many in the past.

Shrugging, she hurried on. A guard at the foot of the stairs jumped to attention, and she brightened when she recognized him. "Rigel! How are you this morning?"

"F-fine, my lady. Very well, that is," the young man stammered. "And you, my lady?"

"Very well, thank you." She liked this young soldier. With curling red hair, freckles, and a ready smile, he made her think of the brother she didn't have but had always wanted. On the other hand, she also enjoyed flirting with him, shaking his hard-won soldier's composure.

"Is my father receiving visitors this morning?"

"Yes, my lady. Master Grimstead is with him now."

She smiled, trying to catch his eye, but he steadfastly refused to cooperate and stared at the wall just over her head. She sighed. "I believe I'll run up to see him for a moment then, as well."

"Of course, my lady."

Lyric stepped toward the stairway, paused and glanced over her shoulder. "I hope to put a riding party together this afternoon. Perhaps you will join us?"

The soldier's face reddened. "If my lord Gareth gives me leave, I will certainly be honored to be part of your escort."

"Wonderful. I look forward to it." *As if Captain Gareth would override her direct request on anything.* Triumphant, she swept up the wide stairs and along the hall toward the king's sitting room, the guard Helmsmith at her heels.

As she approached, Master Grimstead, the palace steward, came through the door and closed it softly behind him. An elderly man who had run the business of the castle since before Lyric's birth, Grimstead paused to greet her warmly before hurrying on his way.

A second guard bowed as she approached and opened the door for her.

"I will speak with my father in private," she said to Helmsmith, stepping through the doorway.

The King of Tressalt sat at a table, mug in one hand and a quill in the other, inspecting a thick sheaf of papers. Behind him, woven tapestries decorated the walls, some depicting scenes of horrific mythical battles, others with peaceful pastoral scenes. She'd always loved this room.

He looked up as she entered. "Good morning, my girl," he boomed. "This is a pleasant surprise. Come and give your old father a kiss."

Lyric stepped across the bearskin rug and kissed the top of his head. "You're not old, sire," she said, tousling the bronze royal mane. "Not a gray hair in sight."

"No?" He stood and hugged her. "But age is shown by more than gray hair, and these days—" He gave her a final squeeze and stepped back. "Well, these days I feel old all the time, gray hairs or no."

"I'm sorry, Papa." Lyric eyed him closely. "What is troubling you?"

"Not to worry, sweetheart," he answered, retaking his seat. "Just the usual business of state. Strange sightings on the borders, murmurings among the peasants, irritating neighbors. Oh, I don't suppose you'd want to marry that rascal Ralt, would you?" He peered up at her. "That would remove one burr from under my saddle."

She caught her breath and stepped away, hand to her heart.

Bursting into laughter, the king stood again, pulling her into a rough embrace. "I'm sorry, my love. I suppose I could have broached the question more gently. I assume that means *no*?"

At her mute nod, he sighed, then pressed his lips to her forehead. "Are you sure? He's been pestering me the entire time he's been here. Coming for an answer this afternoon."

Lyric found her voice. "Father, the prince spoke to me. He insisted there was already an agreement in place. Is it true?"

The king slumped into his chair, a belly-deep sigh escaping his lips.

"Long years ago, Ralt's father King Torian and I spoke. We discussed a match between you and Prince Ralt, but nothing was settled. Then your mother and so many others fell ill with the plague." He shrugged, his gaze far away. "We never returned to the discussion."

Relief left her weak in the knees. She leaned over and embraced her father again, tried to keep her voice steady. "I'm very glad to hear that. He's not a nice man."

He pulled back and peered up at her, brow furrowed. "Did something happen? Something I should know about?"

"No," she lied. No reason to add to her father's burdens. The prince would be leaving soon—without her—and if she was lucky she'd never see him again. "I just don't like him. I'll be glad when he's gone."

The king sighed again and slid the sheaf of papers closer.

"Truth be told? I don't like him either, but I had to ask. He's not going to be happy when I tell him, but I'll deal with it." He looked back up at her. "I feel that I've failed you, though, my darling. I should have made arrangements years ago to see you safely wed, but between that dratted plague and my own selfishness—well, I've not done it."

Lyric narrowed her eyes. "What do you mean? When have you ever been selfish?"

"Many times, my darling, but thank you for pretending not to notice." The king grinned, the forest green of his eyes lightening. "No, I speak of not making the effort, in spite of the plague, to allow you to meet the appropriate young people of other lands. But after we lost your mother ..." He broke off, his gaze focused on the open window. "Well, Ralt is not the only one who might have made a suitable match for you, but I didn't want to lose you to another land. I still don't. I want you to stay here, to be Queen of Tressalt when I'm gone."

He turned back to her—gaze still distracted. "But we can speak of that another time, after our cranky prince leaves. Is there anything else you want of me this morning? I wouldn't hurry you, but I have Duke Solano coming soon, and I promised him a full hour."

She gulped, overwhelmed by the turn in conversation. "Yes, sir. I was hoping I might have some time away today. I'd like to escape the castle. It's been a long, trying week."

He nodded. "That it has. What did you have in mind?"

"To go for a ride, perhaps?" The words tumbled out quickly. "I would so love to take Moon Song out and be away from all the festivities for a few hours."

The king stared out the window, thrumming his fingers along the table top. "Yes, it will be best if you're not around after I speak to the prince. A ride away is a splendid plan—I wish I could go with you. I don't suppose you want any of the court ladies along? No?" He blew out a breath. "Well, at least get one of the maids then, and I'll speak to Gareth about sending a guard as escort. No—*not* that young Rigel." His eyes twinkled. "You'd have him doing your bidding at every turn, just as you do me."

He reached for her hand, and his eyes softened. "You needn't pout like that. I know what I'm about. Those violet eyes could twist the heart of any man. You're smart, headstrong, and so very beautiful, despite your concern about that silly scar." He ran his knuckle gently under her chin. "You'll make a wonderful queen someday, but today, my darling, you'll need an escort who will keep you out of mischief."

She threw her arms about him. "Thank you, Papa. You know me too well. I'll try to be good."

He returned the hug fiercely. "I know you will. But have a pleasant day, too, sweet one. We all need a nice day now and again."

Planting a kiss on his cheek, she wiped a wayward tear from her eye and fled.

She rushed down the stairs, Helmsmith hard at her heels. She didn't want to add to her father's worries. Why couldn't that awful Ralt have stayed in his own land and left them alone?

Hurrying into the hall that led to her rooms, she bumped into one of the newer maids, a sandy-haired girl from the country.

"My apologies." She bent to pick up the linens she'd surprised the girl into dropping.

"Oh, no. Let me, my lady." The girl scrambled to straighten up the mess.

Lyric stood and peered at the maid. She appeared to be about sixteen, perhaps a little younger than Lyric herself. Her hair was in braids and she had the freckled, healthy look of one who'd spent a lot of time outdoors. "Becca, isn't it?"

"Yes, my lady." The girl ducked her head self-consciously.

"Can you ride, Becca?"

"My lady?" The girl's blue-green eyes widened.

"Can you ride a horse? Fast, possibly?"

"I rode a bit as a child, my lady," the girl said. "My father did a special service for a nobleman and the gentleman gave him his old warhorse as payment. My brothers and I had quite the time with old Banner. Why, I remember one time—oh!" Becca's hand flew to her mouth, her cheeks flaming.

"Excellent," Lyric said. "Run down to the stables and tell Master Kedrick to saddle Moon Song for me and to find a suitable mount for you. We are going for a ride. Tell him to have the horses ready as soon as may be, then come back to my room. I'll find you some garments and speak to Mari'el about your change in duties this afternoon."

"Yes, my lady, of course." Becca gathered the tousled linens in her arms and hurried away down the corridor.

Lyric strode the last few paces to her room and flung open the door. Her golden-haired chambermaid Rowana was straightening the heavy curtains that enclosed Lyric's bed.

Lyric marched across the room to her desk, pulled paper and quill out of a drawer and dashed off a quick note. She handed it to Rowana. "Take this to the housekeeper, please."

The chambermaid sighed dramatically as she took the note and sauntered away. Ignoring her, Lyric strode to her huge oak wardrobe and flung open the doors.

A timid knock sounded at the door twenty minutes later. Lyric yanked the door open, grabbed Becca's arm and pulled her into the room. She tossed a split skirt, an undershirt, and a tunic to the maid and gestured to the decorative screen in the corner of the room. "You can change back there."

Becca disappeared behind the screen.

"Did you have trouble finding the stable?"

"I did, my lady. I'm sorry. I took right turns when I should have gone left, but eventually I found it. Master Kedrick will have Moon Song ready for you and will pick a nice beast for me, just as you ordered." The girl stepped from behind the screen, and Lyric handed her a pair of her old riding boots.

As Becca pulled the boots on over her hose, the door swung open, and Rowana shouldered her way in, holding a wrapped parcel and four wine skins.

"Mistress Mari'el had Cook put this together for you, my lady. For your midday meal. Is there anything else I can do for you?" She glanced darkly at Becca.

Lyric looked around the room. Her clothes lay strewn everywhere. "You can put my clothes away, I suppose. And I lost a button on that gown. See if the dressmaker has a match."

"I'll see to it, my lady." Rowana curtsied, still scowling. Lyric ignored her. Rowana had been her maid for the past two years—the niece of one of her father's advisers—but Lyric had never liked the girl. She was a beauty and usually competent in her work, but she had a mean spirit. She also wasn't shy about visiting the bedchamber of whatever man caught her interest, and later enthralling the other female servants with the details.

Lyric really needed to speak to Mari'el about finding her a different maid.

But not today.

Dragging Becca in her wake, Lyric rushed down the corridor. Helmsmith was gone, but a younger guard Lyric didn't know had replaced him. He followed as they descended the first flight of stairs, and she was glad he did when she saw who waited at the bottom.

Ralt of Malacar watched her approach through narrowed eyes.

Against her better judgment and the triple-time beating of her heart, she stopped, inclined her head. "Your Highness."

He bowed stiffly. "I had hoped to speak with you this morning. After last night—"

"Yes," she said curtly, holding onto what remained of her civility. "Last night happened and will not happen again. Now if you'll excuse me. I have pressing business."

His face darkened. Ignoring his displeasure, she whirled past him, as if his very presence might contaminate her, and marched away, the guard at her side.

Her heart still raced after several turns and another flight of stairs. They passed through the castle's back doorway and across a cobblestoned courtyard to the royal stables. In front of the low brick building waited Kedrick, the gray-bearded stable master, holding the bridles of two horses. A groom stood a few paces away holding a third horse—her escort's mount, she assumed.

Lyric stepped up to the black mare prancing next to the stable master.

"Good afternoon, Moon Song. Are you up for a little run today?" She kissed the horse's velvety muzzle and ran her hands along the sleek neck. "She appears to be in fine condition, Master Kedrick."

"She is, my lady. As fit as may be," the stable master said. "And quite full of herself, as always. You be careful, now. Shall I help you up?"

"Yes, please." Lyric placed her left foot in the stable master's cupped hands, allowing him to lift her, then swung her right leg over the horse's back. She settled onto the saddle, gathering the reins, and Moon Song sidled away from Kedrick, shaking her head impatiently. "Patience, silly girl," she murmured to the excited horse. Glancing back, she saw a stable boy packing their lunch into the saddle bags of the quiet chestnut gelding she assumed Becca would ride.

A door slammed in one of the outbuildings next to the stable and a tall man in riding gear strode toward them. He wore chain mail over his shirt and a sheathed sword at his side, and a bow and quiver of arrows hung over his shoulder. Dark hair edged out from the light helm on his head.

Lyric looked more closely at the third horse and understanding dawned, even as her heart sank. She knew this horse and its rider. The big bay was as tall as Moon Song but powerfully built and looked just as ready to burst with energy.

Why *him*, of all people? And after last night ...

She glanced at Becca, now astride the gelding. "Are you ready?"

The girl looked nervous but spoke quickly. "I think so, my lady."

"Good." She turned to the man who had stopped in front of Moon Song. "So, Marek," she said silkily. "Here you are again. Did you lose at cards last night?"

"My lady?" The soldier dipped his head deferentially.

"You seem to have drawn nursery duty again today. That could only come of extremely bad luck, I'm thinking."

The soldier was silent a long moment. "I would not put it in such terms, my lady."

"No?" she said wickedly. "Well, good, because I'm in no mood to be coddled, so try and keep up." She turned Moon Song toward the gate, clapped both legs against the fiery mare's sides, and the horse was off like a black-tipped arrow, streaking across the cobblestones.

From behind her, she heard Marek shout her name.

She grasped the horse's mane and raced on.

CHAPTER 3: BATTLES

Servants leaped out of their way as she and her horse clattered out the gate and over the drawbridge that covered the moat. She didn't know what had gotten into her, but she didn't care. Once out in the open, Lyric turned Moon Song toward the Old Forest Road a mile away and urged the mare on to greater speed. Behind her, she thought she heard Marek calling her, but she didn't look back. Only her horse understood her fully today. They had both been penned up too long.

And she needed to get as far away from Prince Ralt as a horse could take her.

Moon Song was bred for the race; her sire had never been defeated and though the mare herself had never raced, the lust for speed ran through her blood. Stretched out, ears flat back, the black mare flew along the path that led to the last bridge and the forest's southern boundary.

The horse's powerful muscles churned beneath her, and the wind that sought to unseat her filled her nostrils and her soul with the heady fragrance of summer.

And freedom.

Guards jumped back as she and the horse raced toward the Silver Leaf River bridge. Grasping the reins in one hand, she gave the guards a triumphant salute as she flew past them. Her father would receive a report of her recklessness within the hour, she supposed. For now, she didn't care.

They plunged into the shadows under the summer-green oak and maple forest and ran until Lyric became aware of her horse's faltering strides. Frowning, she sat up in the saddle and pulled on the reins, allowing the mare to slow. Awash with guilt, she reined the sweat-drenched animal to a stop and slid off. Moon Song trembled, and her breathing sounded like the bellows at the blacksmith's shop. Out of the corner of her eye, Lyric saw Marek's horse gallop into view.

She'd been riding since childhood and knew better than to run a horse that fast for so long. What had she been thinking? A horse like Moon Song would run until she dropped. Shame throbbed through her in time with the mare's breaths.

Marek stopped next to her and sat quietly on his horse a long moment before speaking. "Is she injured?"

Lyric didn't want to face him, didn't want to see his accusation, but all she heard in his voice was concern.

"I don't know," she said miserably. "I lost track of how far we'd come." She was close to tears and she just couldn't allow that, but this—this was her horse, her lovely, feisty Moon Song, who loved to run. What had she done? The mare's beautiful head hung low, her sides heaving.

"If she's not injured, she should recover soon." He dismounted and stepped over to take the horse's reins. "Let's loosen the girth and walk her a bit. Shall I do that for you?"

She wheeled on him. "You think I'm a fool, don't you?"

"What I think," the soldier said, his expression unreadable, "is that if we don't get this fine animal moving, her muscles will stiffen and her recovery will take much longer."

Humiliated, she stepped back. Could she not do one thing right today? He loosened the saddle's girth, then Lyric took the reins from him.

"I'll walk her." She looked up the grassy road they'd just raced down. "Where's Becca?"

"She'll be along," Marek answered. "I spoke to her as I passed, and told her to just follow as she could. Her mount is an old timer. He'll take care of her."

Clucking to the mare, Lyric began walking down the path, back toward the castle. Marek strode along beside her, leading his own horse. A few minutes later, they saw the chestnut gelding trotting around a bend in the trail in front of them. By the time they reached Becca, Moon Song had recovered some of her usual vigor, lifting her head and neighing softly to her stable mate.

Now what? Lyric groaned inwardly. In ten short minutes, she'd managed to ruin the whole day. "I guess we'd better go back," she said to no one in particular.

"So soon?" Becca asked. "But we've just started." Her hand flew to her mouth, her eyes wide. "I'm so sorry, my lady. Whatever you think, of course."

Lyric looked uncertainly at Moon Song and down the path longingly. There was a lovely little meadow she'd discovered in early spring. Without putting the thought into words, she realized now that was where she'd wanted to go all along.

"If you'd like my opinion, Your Highness," Marek said, "your mare appears to be sufficiently recovered that a bit more time out should do her no harm."

She wanted to go on, but humiliation still throbbed through her. How could she, when she'd already proven true whatever bad things Marek probably already thought of her?

When she didn't answer, the soldier stepped over to the mare. "Let me check her for you." He slid his hand under the loosened girth and listened a moment before pulling his hand away and patting the mare's shoulder. "Her heart rate is almost back to normal—thanks to excellent bloodlines and conditioning. If Your Highness can be content with a moderate pace," he added, giving her a kind smile, "I believe we could ride on awhile."

Lyric wanted to take offense but found she couldn't. She was too disgusted with herself and grateful Moon Song would be all right. Maybe the day wasn't completely ruined.

She sighed. "Let us go on, then."

Marek tightened Moon Song's girth and held cupped hands to assist Lyric onto the horse's back. He stepped smoothly up onto his own horse and the three turned back toward the wilderness trail.

They rode on in silence under boughs of massive oak and willow. Sunbeams filtered through the branches to leave dappled patterns on the forest floor. Green, gold, and speckled butterflies performed an erratic dance across the path before them while invisible woodland birds whistled, chirped, and trilled in the branches above. She inhaled deeply, and for the first time in a week her nerves begin to unwind.

The Old Forest Road had been abandoned by all but the hardiest of travelers, having been replaced in her grandfather's time by the Merchant Way that ran from the castle south to the sea and north through the fertile plains of Tressalt's famed horse lands. It avoided the treacherous passes of the Grimwood Mountains where the Old Road wandered, and took a more circuitous but safer route to the neighboring kingdoms of Malacar, Graceen, and Parsiway. Though still wide enough for two to ride side by side, the Old Forest Road was quickly becoming overgrown and would no longer support wagons or larger transports. And already it had begun to climb.

It took longer to find her remembered meadow than she'd thought it would. She was beginning to think she'd imagined the place when she ducked beneath a low-hanging branch on the trail, then straightened to see a clearing through the trees on her right.

"Stop," she called to the others, reining Moon Song off the road onto what was no more than a deer path. She ducked under another branch and when she sat up, found herself sailing on her horse through a veritable ocean of tall, feathery ferns. If there was a trail, she couldn't see it, but Moon Song pushed through and the ferns parted before her. Lyric looked behind to see Becca and Marek emerging from the forest and into the sea of bracken.

The ferns petered out and knee-high grass replaced them in a meadow dotted by ivory, violet, and brilliant yellow wildflowers. Immense, wide-leafed trees surrounded the clearing. From its far side, she heard the burble and chatter of a mountain-fed brook.

"I was here once before," she told the others. "Let's stop here."

She guided her horse across the meadow toward the brook and dismounted near a stand of cottonwoods. Becca joined her and climbed stiffly off the gelding. Marek remained mounted and rode the perimeter of the clearing, peering under the trees and up and down the creek bed before returning to them.

"Is there a plan, Your Highness? Now that we're here?"

Lyric looked up at him and found her earlier irritation returning. "Not really," she said. "I would like to relax awhile and enjoy the sunshine and fresh air."

"We have the lunch Mistress Mari'el sent," Becca offered. "I can set it out here on the grass for us to share."

"That's a wonderful idea," Lyric said. "I'll pick some wildflowers for our table." She looked back at Marek. "And what will you do, Sir Knight?"

He dismounted and took all the horses' reins. "If you have nothing else for me, my lady, I'll tend to the horses." She nodded, and he led the animals to a stand of maple trees and pulled a coiled rope out of a pouch on his saddle.

Lyric wandered through the meadow, stopping from time to time to pick handfuls of the tiny purple and white flowers that dotted the grassy clearing. She held them to her nose, closed her eyes, and inhaled deeply, hoping the sweetness would permeate every part of her and push away the fear still gripping her. What if her father gave in to Prince Ralt's request? No, he had promised. She opened her eyes, shuddering.

She strolled to the stream and looked across to the thick cottonwoods on the far bank. Nothing moved under the dark shadows, and she remembered the last time she'd ridden this way. She'd beguiled several of the noblemen's daughters to join her and they, accompanied by Rigel and two of the older knights, had found this place.

The other girls quickly tired of the quiet beauty, contenting themselves with inventing stories of what terrors might come out of the thick woods at them—bogies or giants or wolves crazed with the frothing sickness. The spritely creek would be no protection, they'd emphasized in knowing horror. *Silly things*, Lyric had thought then and still thought now. So much more interest in the *what-ifs* than in the beautiful reality all around them.

"If you please, my lady," Becca called from across the meadow. "Your luncheon is ready."

Lyric wandered back to where Becca had spread a brightly-colored table cloth and a meal of bread, cheese and dried meat on the grass beneath a graceful maple tree. Marek had tied the horses to three separate trees on the edge of the clearing and all three were contentedly grazing. Saddles and bridles were set neatly a short distance away, and the soldier himself, she noted, was brushing the dried sweat and scruff from one of the horses.

Her horse.

Guilt once more washing over her, she lowered herself to the soft grass. Becca took a wine skin from the pack Mari'el had sent and handed it to her. Lyric took it and drank gratefully. It was the cider the castle cook was becoming famous for, made of apples from the king's own orchards. Leave it to the beloved housekeeper to think of everything. Lyric looked back at the maid. "Is there more to drink?"

"Yes, my lady. Mistress Mari'el sent three skins of cider and one of wine," the girl said, reaching into the pack. "Are you ready for more?"

"Oh, no. I'm sure she sent those for you and Marek. Will you see if he would prefer cider or wine? And offer him some of the bread and cheese as well."

Becca obeyed quickly and was back in a moment. "He says to tell my lady thank you, but he does not require refreshment at this time."

Lyric sighed. "Then you sit and eat, please."

After the meal, Lyric strolled back to the brook. She rinsed her hands in the icy water, then sat on a grassy knoll overlooking the stream. On a whim, she pulled off her boots and leggings and pressed her bare feet into the mud that bordered the swiftly moving water.

She sucked in her breath and closed her eyes in delight as the sun-warmed mud oozed between her toes. Bees buzzed around her and the ever-present song birds trilled gently in the trees. Could anything be more decadent? She could almost hear her old nurse's words.

For pity's sake, child! Grubbing about in the mud like a commoner? What's come over you?

Lyric shook off the accusing words and climbed to her feet. Pulling her riding skirt up to her knees, she stepped into the frigid water. She gasped, waited a moment, then moved carefully along the water's edge, watching for sharp rocks. A memory was working its way into her mind and she stared into the stream, unseeing, trying to remember. There had been a similar incident many years before. She had not been alone on the outing with the sharp-tongued nurse—her mother had been along, as well.

The very young Lyric had been abashed at the criticism and jumped out of the water, prepared to dry her feet and allow the nurse to replace her sandals. But her mother— her beautiful, loving mother—had laughed and said, "If commoners can have such pleasures, why can't we?" And she'd pulled off her own boots and hose and joined Lyric in the mud.

A lump rose in her throat. She hadn't cried over her mother in a long time. Truth be told, she hardly remembered her. She'd been only eight when the plague blazed into Tressalt, ravishing the castle as well as the peasants' cottages. The fever struck countless dead, commoner and royal alike, including the queen and the loyal cantankerous nurse. But for those left behind, life had gone on. Soon—too soon perhaps—the memories began to fade.

Lyric swished through the water on her now numb feet, then back to the spot where she'd left her boots and leggings. She sat, her feet still dangling in the stream, and yawned. What she wanted right now, more than anything, was a nap. Her very short night's sleep had caught up with her. Not pondering long, she pulled her feet out of the creek and lay back on the fragrant grass, staring up into the robin's-egg blue sky. Perhaps she would search the puffy clouds to see what shapes she could discern in their wind-swept beauty ... or perhaps not.

Yawning again, she gave up and closed her eyes.

She was torn from her rest by something hot, something burning against her chest. She sat up, confused, pushing her loosened hair out of her eyes. She cried out and grabbed the gold chain that held the gemstone around her neck. Yanking the pendant free from her garments, she stared at it in horror.

The stone blazed red and tiny images raced across its surface. She gasped, mesmerized by what she was seeing. A castle—no, *her* castle—with the flag of Tressalt and the banner with her father's coat of arms flying from its highest watchtower was under attack. Men swarmed the walls, outside and along the battlements. Armed men, some on horseback, others on foot, clashed on the fields surrounding the fortress. Swords flashed, arrows flew.

The scene changed to inside the keep. Armed figures fought at the bottom of a stairway, then rushed up the stairs and broke down the door that led to the man on the throne. Despite the minuscule size of the images, Lyric had no doubt the man she saw—the man besieged by attackers—was her father.

"No!" She scrambled to her feet, gasping.

Marek was at her side. "What is it, Your Highness?"

Lyric sucked in a breath, aghast at what she was seeing, but afraid to look away.

"My father. They have my father." She tore her gaze from the stone and turned on the soldier. "We have to go back. The castle is under attack. Look!" She pulled the chain off her neck and threw it at him, but even as she did, the images faded.

He stared at the stone, eyes narrowed, then back at her. "Is this a seeing stone?"

"It's just a necklace," she cried. "But I saw something in it—the castle, with attackers everywhere. They have my father." She bolted away from him and ran toward the horses.

Marek caught up and pulled her gently but firmly to a halt.

"I saw no images clearly, my lady, but I saw *something*. Please calm yourself and tell me about this necklace."

She placed one hand on her chest, trying to slow the ferocious beating of her heart.

"There's nothing special about it," she wailed. "I've had it for a long time, but until yesterday nothing like this has ever happened." She looked up into his worried dark eyes and for a moment forgot that she was a princess and he her servant. "Please," she whispered. "I don't know what's happening, but we must go back. Now."

Marek nodded and placed the chain back around her neck. "Get your clothing." He gestured toward the brook where she'd left her boots and leggings. "I'll see to the horses."

It took only minutes for Marek to saddle and bridle the three horses, but it seemed like hours. Lyric paced, rubbing her palms against her arms, trying to create a barrier between herself and the chill that engulfed her. What was happening at the castle? What was happening to her father? She lifted the gemstone, staring into its gleaming surface, but it stayed the same cool, milky color it had always been.

"We're ready, Your Highness," Becca called.

They mounted and headed out the way they'd come. When Lyric pushed Moon Song to the front, Marek intervened.

"Let me, my lady. You stay in the middle and let Mistress Becca follow." Lyric wanted to argue, but she saw the determination in the knight's eyes. Arguing would only delay their journey.

"You said something unusual happened with your gemstone yesterday," Marek said after a moment. "What was it?"

Lyric blinked, pulling herself from the fog that had claimed her thoughts. She told him about dancing with the prince, and the gemstone's heat and raging color.

"You saw no images on the stone?"

"No."

"And nothing like this has ever happened before?"

"Never."

What he thought of that, he didn't say, and she didn't ask. She just wanted to get home.

They'd ridden for perhaps an hour at a steady trot when Marek pulled off the widening Forest Road onto a little-used trail on the right.

"What are you doing?" Lyric demanded. "This isn't the way back."

Marek didn't reply, just signaled for them to follow. Impatiently, Lyric turned Moon Song onto the path. A few minutes later they came to another clearing, much smaller than the one they'd spent the afternoon in, but more secluded.

Marek turned in the saddle to face her. "I need you and Mistress Becca to stay here while I go on, Your Highness. You'll be safe while I see what's happening."

Lyric stared at him, disbelieving. "No," she finally said. "I give the orders and I'm not staying behind." She turned Moon Song back toward the Forest Road but Marek kicked his horse forward and caught her reins.

"Forgive me, my lady," he said, and though his words were polite, his voice held an edge of steel. "Ordinarily that would be the case, but my orders today are from your father. My task is to ensure your safety, whatever the cost. If there is indeed a battle at the castle, as the stone showed you, I cannot take you into it."

"But—but—" Lyric sputtered, rage engulfing her.

Marek held up his hand. "If you misread what the stone showed you, I'll be back within the hour and take you immediately to your father." As Lyric made to argue again, his face hardened. "That's the best I can do, my lady. You must stay here."

He looked at the maid. "If Her Highness makes any effort to follow me, do whatever it takes to keep her here. I will make it right with the king, if it comes to that." He turned back to Lyric. "And you, madam, please do not put your servant in that uncomfortable position. I will return soon, no matter the situation I find."

He refused to look away until her eyes and a brief nod told him she would obey. "Thank you," he said, his voice softer. "I know this is hard for you."

"Just go," she growled.

He nodded and with a touch of his heels, his horse leapt into a gallop. Moon Song reared onto her hind legs and plunged forward, trying to follow. Lyric reined her back.

"If I have to stay here, so do you," she said bitterly.

CHAPTER 4: BETRAYAL

Marek pulled his horse back to a slower pace once he reached the main road, and he moved ahead cautiously. He didn't understand what had happened today, but neither was he ready to discount it. He'd heard of seeing stones, but the stories were old and never consistent. The existence of such things smacked of a magic that people these days didn't understand or want to think about. The days of the wizards who'd used such power, if the old stories held any truth, were long past.

But something was wrong. The princess, though headstrong, had never been given to flights of fancy. She had seen something.

He had ridden several miles into the waning afternoon when he noticed the first oddity. Silence. Complete silence. No swooping birds, no chittering squirrels. And a scent that was out of place.

Smoke.

He swept his gaze from one side of the road to the other. There were no cottages in the area, and they'd seen no travelers earlier who might have started an early cook fire. He was still two miles from the castle and its village, and it wasn't windy. Smoke from there wouldn't reach this far.

Unless, of course, it was a large fire.

He rode farther, and the smoke grew thicker. Then a sound caught his ear and he reined his horse to a stop. A crashing through the underbrush ahead on his right, as of a large body, running, falling. He wheeled his horse about and rode swiftly back to a deer path he'd just crossed. He followed the path until he was sure no one on the road could see him and dismounted. Tying the horse to a tree branch, he crept carefully back to the road.

Once there, he stayed close to the trees and made his way to where he'd heard the commotion in the underbrush. He stood motionless behind an immense oak and listened. For several minutes he heard nothing. Then, a groan.

A man—not an injured animal—but friend or foe?

He left the road's edge and worked his way carefully in among the trees. No other sounds split the eerie silence. He stepped behind another oak and paused. Nothing. He waited another long moment, then peered around the tree and saw what he'd feared to see.

A man in the colors of the Guard of Tressalt lay face down with an arrow in his side. The man's back rose and fell with his labored breaths. He was not yet dead.

Marek clenched his jaw, fighting the urge to rush to his comrade's aid. Whoever did this might still stalk the woodland, hunting the injured man. He scanned the forest. Nothing but trees, no sound but the wounded soldier's strangled breaths. Finally, crouching low to the ground, he crept to the man. The turf around the soldier was bathed in blood. Working around the arrow, he gingerly turned the man over. His heart sank.

Rigel. Favorite of the Princess Lyric, not yet nineteen summers old.

The boy groaned and his eyelashes fluttered open. He tried to speak but could manage only a hoarse whisper. Marek bent closer.

"Tressalt has fallen," he wheezed. "Prince Ralt's men. Hundreds of them." He paused, struggling for air. "They were in the village, disguised as ... peasants at the Solstice Fair." He grabbed Marek's arm. "They have the king. Looking ... for the princess."

"The Princess is safe," Marek told him.

"Good." Rigel's hand fell back to his side. "Good." His breaths gurgled and rattled. He wouldn't last much longer. Hating to do it, Marek leaned closer and asked a final question.

"The king, Rigel. Is the king still alive?"

The boy's drooping light blue eyes opened wide. "I think so. Ralt wants the Princess. He's holding the king ... until she comes."

Once again, Rigel grasped Marek's arm. "My mother ... in the village," he whispered. "If you see her ... tell her—"

The words died in his mouth, and the blue eyes stared unseeing into the summer sky. A final rattling breath escaped his open mouth.

Marek placed his hand on the boy's forehead and gently closed the staring eyes. "I'll tell her," he promised. He sat for a moment, head bowed. He'd seen men die before, but it was hard, *hard*, when it was one so young.

He stood, waging war with himself. He'd wondered about the large numbers of peasants at the Festival of the Summer Solstice this year. He'd mentioned it to Gareth, but the captain had waved him off. There had been no attack on Tressalt in nearly a hundred years. "It's one of the few times a year the commoners get together," Gareth had reminded him. "They come from leagues away."

Marek looked down at the dead boy at his feet, sickened. Obviously they'd been wrong. He should go back, find any survivors, and mount an assault to rescue King Sander.

But those were not his orders, and his duty was clear. He must take Princess Lyric to a place of safety. Only then would he be free to rescue his king and seek revenge upon Prince Ralt of Malacar.

He knelt beside Rigel's body. It galled him to leave his comrade like this in the forest, unburied and alone. But he could do nothing more. He closed his eyes and offered a quick prayer, committing the spirit of the young soldier to the One. Then he rose to his feet. He'd done all he could.

He turned toward the road and froze as a twig snapped somewhere behind him. He flung himself to the ground just as an arrow whizzed past and struck the big oak with a resounding thud. Before the archer had a chance to fit another arrow to the string, Marek rolled to safety behind the tree.

Scrambling to his feet, he unsheathed his sword, back pressed to the oak. Would his attacker leave his cover and risk close-range combat, or stay where he was, patiently awaiting another chance to strike from a distance? Several moments passed and another twig snapped, this one much closer.

The attacker was not patient.

He braced himself, sword at the ready, careful to stay hidden behind the oak's girth. In one-on-one combat, his chances with the sword were better than average. He'd never bested Thomas, the sword master, but it had been a near thing on a number of occasions. No one else could stand against him for more than a few minutes. Still, it took only one mistake, one error in judgment, and even the best could be beaten.

He hazarded a quick glance around the tree. There he was, a black-garbed man, moving cautiously through the undergrowth, bow slung over his shoulder, sword in hand.

Foolish, Marek thought with grim satisfaction. Foolhardy as well as impatient. A smart fighter who had the advantage of seeing his enemy first would stay in hiding, bow ready, waiting for his foe to make the first mistake. Though cautious, this man walked openly into danger. It made no sense. Unless ... unless he had companions.

Marek crouched behind the oak, ignoring the approaching assassin, scanning the forest around and behind him for what he felt sure must still lie in wait.

There. Sunlight filtered through the boughs of the leafy forest a hundred paces away and glinted on something that should not have been there. Metal. Chain mail.

Scowling, Marek now understood his enemy's strategy and despised him for it. Send the younger, less-experienced soldier into the woods to draw the enemy's fire. Then, possibly when the soldier was injured or dead, his superior would know from which direction the killing blow had come, thus increasing his own chances of victory.

He ground his teeth, thinking of his bow and quiver of arrows strapped to Dragon's saddle. There was nothing he could do about it now. His sword would have to do.

Thankful for the oak's great bulk, Marek searched at its base and found two rocks, each the size of a large man's fist, buried under the dead leaves and lichen. A whistle pulled his attention back to the clearing. The soldier had discovered Rigel's body.

Marek palmed one of the rocks, then turned and threw it hard toward the road.

The enemy soldier dropped to the ground, as Marek had done, and scrambled behind a tree. After several moments, he crept out and made his way cautiously toward the road.

Marek listened until he could no longer hear the man, but he never took his gaze from the far tree where he knew the other soldier kept watch. After a few moments, a large man, mail-clad, disentangled himself from the ferns and vine maples and stepped carefully into the open.

Anger coursed through Marek as he recognized the scarred face of Lord Kent, Prince Ralt's second-in-command. The Malacarians had come to them under the guise of friendship, had partaken of King Sander's hospitality, only to turn sword and bow upon them. Marek hated few things more than treachery.

Gaze darting from tree to tree, Kent held his sword before him, marching slowly through the tiny clearing. Without a second glance he stepped over Rigel's body and continued toward the oak where Marek waited, stone in one hand, sword in the other. When the Malacarian was within ten paces, Marek stepped out from behind the tree and hurled the stone.

The rock hit Lord Kent square between the eyes, and he dropped without a sound to the forest floor. Marek leapt forward and drove his sword between the rings of the mail shirt and into his enemy's heart. The older man gasped once, eyes wide, then went still. Pulling his bloodied sword free, Marek whirled just as an arrow whistled from out of nowhere and struck him full in the chest. The impact knocked him off his feet, but his armor stopped the arrow.

He ripped the arrow away and flung it from him as a third attacker rushed into the clearing, sword flashing. Lunging to his feet, Marek blocked the first blow and stumbled backward, struggling to retain his footing. It took only a moment to regain his balance, and he took the offensive, driving the man back in an onslaught of slashing strikes. The man tripped over a downed log, lost his footing, fell back—

Marek felt white-hot pain slice into his side. He jumped away and whirled to see the first soldier pulling his sword back and bearing down on him with ferocious glee. As Marek lifted his own sword to block the assault, out of the corner of his eye, he saw the other soldier climbing to his feet.

Thomas had always said the only way to win a two-against-one fight was to quickly dispatch one of the two. He knew the truth of this, but he was losing blood. If he didn't stop them both quickly, he'd never leave these woods.

Grasping the sword with both hands, he hurtled forward, hacking, feinting, blocking, never forgetting his other foe was somewhere behind him. With a crushing blow, Marek knocked the blade from his opponent's hand, kicked it away, then whirled as the second man launched himself back into the battle.

Marek ducked under a strike that could have removed his head and sliced upward with his sword. The man was dead before he hit the ground. Marek ripped the blade out of the Malacarian's body and turned just in time to see the final soldier retrieve his blade and leap toward him. With his last strength, Marek hurled his sword, and the weapon impaled itself in the man's chest.

Gasping, he stumbled to his fallen enemy, removed his sword from the man's heart, and pressed his hand against his own wound, trying to stanch the flow of blood. Using his bloodied sword, he sliced a length of fabric from the man's tunic and did his best to wrap it tightly around his middle. He took the unspent arrows from each man's quiver and lurched back toward the road. Stepping out of the cover of the trees, he glanced up and down the road, and seeing no one, moved as quickly as he could back to where he'd left his horse.

CHAPTER 5: KINGDOM LOST

Lyric paced back and forth across the small clearing, frantic and furious. Sunset approached and Marek had not returned.

"Where is he?" she demanded, knowing Becca had no more answer than she. "He said an hour. He should have been back long ago." She stood for another moment, hands on hips, then strode purposefully toward the horses.

"No, my lady." Becca got up from a fallen tree she'd been sitting on. "We must wait. Master Marek said so."

"We've waited long enough." Lyric reached for Moon Song's bridle. "We must get back to my father."

"But my lady," the maid offered timidly, "what can we do if something bad has happened? We must wait for Master Marek."

"Urghhh!" Lyric leaned back against the saddle, clutching her hands to her head. "I *hate* this! What is happening?"

She'd examined the pendant countless times that afternoon, hoping to see something new, yet dreading another vision. The gem had remained its maddening bland self.

Why had no one told her of its power? She'd scoured her earliest memories for any clues but came up with nothing. She'd asked her father about it once. He'd said only that it had been in her mother's family for generations, passed down from mother to daughter or daughter-in-law. Some talisman from an earlier time, he'd said vaguely, then looked up at her and ruffled her dark curls. "Your mother received it from her mother on our wedding day and wore it until ... well, when your mother passed, it became yours."

This had surprised young Lyric. "But I thought I'd worn it always."

"No, love," her father had said affectionately. "An old priest, the last of his kind, took it from your mother's neck and placed it on yours when she died. You don't remember? That's all right." He'd reached over and drawn her into his comforting embrace. "I don't remember a lot of that time, either."

Pulling herself to the present, Lyric saw that night was filtering in through the trees, settling in the clearing. *Where was Marek?*

Moon Song lifted her head, ears pricked, then whinnied softly. A moment later, Marek's bay horse pushed his way into the clearing.

Lyric let the breath she'd been holding escape in a rush and ran to the knight, prepared to vent her frustration upon him, but came to an abrupt halt. Marek sat hunched over in the saddle, clutching his right side with his left hand. The horse stopped in front of her, and then Lyric saw the blood. A lot of blood.

She caught her breath.

"Becca," she shouted. "*Hurry!*"

The maid ran to her side as Marek lifted his head.

"Quiet," he whispered, swaying in his saddle as he spoke. "Enemies."

Becca stepped forward. "My lady, hold the horse, if you please." She moved to the horse's side. "Master Marek, let me help you." She patted the soldier's leg, then held up her arms.

Lyric wasn't sure how much Marek understood, but she did know the maid, strong as she might be, couldn't carry the man alone. Shaking herself, she plucked the reins from Marek's loose fingers and pulled them over the horse's head.

"Whoa," she ordered the animal, and she moved next to Becca. "Marek, you have to dismount." She said the words forcefully, hoping the semi-conscious man would understand. "We're going to try and help, but we can't do it all."

He shook his head. "Can't ... stay here." Squaring his shoulders, he looked down at Lyric and spoke slowly but clearly. "Prince Ralt has taken Tressalt. We must flee."

The world tilted.

Marek was speaking again, barely above a whisper, his tone urgent. "The battle is close behind us." He paused, as if speech was taking every ounce of his strength. "We must leave, but I am injured. Is there water?"

"I have some, sir," Becca said. "I filled the skins at the brook this afternoon. There is also one skin of wine left— should I bring that?"

Marek shook his head. "Just the water. Save the wine for later."

Becca ran off and was back in moments with one of the water skins.

Marek drank deep and long, then sat up straighter in the saddle. He handed the skin back to Becca with a nod of thanks. "My wound will need tending soon, but we must leave now. We are too close to the castle." He sucked in a deep breath, then looked down at the women. "Please—get your horses ready."

Becca hurried to obey, but Lyric did not move. "How do you know this? And the king? What of my father?"

"He was still alive when ... the guard I spoke to saw him last. That's all I know, my lady. Now please get your horse."

Lyric hadn't the strength to argue. Or to move. Her father. Her land. It couldn't be.

Becca retrieved both horses and held Moon Song for Lyric to mount. She did so, then Becca mounted as well.

Marek lifted his head. "Can you find the place we lunched this afternoon?" he asked Lyric. "In the dark?"

Lyric stared at him uncomprehendingly.

Becca looked at Lyric, then back to Marek. "I can, sir."

Marek nodded. "Then lead on, mistress, if you will. I will ride in back ... in case we are followed. And once we get there," he said, and shuddered, "I hope you have some skill with healing."

"A little, sir," the maid said. "I'll do what I can."

He nodded again, glanced at Lyric, then turned back to the maid. "Ride on, then. As quickly and quietly as you can."

Darkness covered the trail under the thick trees. Lyric remembered little of their journey that night, away from the castle, away from her father. Tressalt had fallen; her father was captive. Home was no longer home.

But one thing she knew with certainty—she was to blame. She had rejected the prince's suit and the king, loving father that he was, had accepted her decision. He had met with the prince, told him the news, and soon afterward, her home was aflame.

People were dead and it was her fault. She tried to push the thoughts away but they lay heavily upon her, smothering her with their truth.

Somehow they made it safely back to the first meadow. She was vaguely aware of Becca unfolding a saddle blanket on the ground for her to lie on and pulling out the table cloth from their lunch for a light coverlet. "It's the best we can do, my lady," the maid whispered.

The girl ran off, and Lyric understood on some level that she was tending to Marek. The summer night was warm, untouched by the troubles of her world. Resting in the clearing, on a horse's sweaty saddle blanket, under a stained table covering and the vastness of the starry heavens, she slept.

CHAPTER 6: JOURNEY NORTH

When Lyric awoke, it was still dark, but the stars had shifted and Becca was calling her.

"Please, my lady, you must get up. We must leave this place."

Cold enveloped her. Her light coverlet was drenched with dew and the cold and damp had soaked into her clothing. With a gasp, she threw the cloth off and struggled to her feet.

"I'm freezing." The words came out as a demand and were directed at Becca.

The girl looked at her, eyes wide. "I'm sorry, my lady. I'd give you my garments, but they are also wet."

"Here." A deep voice spoke quietly from the edge of the meadow. Marek moved stiffly into view holding a gray fold of cloth. He extended it to her. "It's an extra shirt I had in my pack. It's still dry."

Lyric took the garment, then wrinkled her nose. The material was coarse and prickly and smelled strongly of horse.

"Shall I help you, my lady?" Becca reached for the shirt. "Of course, it's not what you are accustomed to, but we have nothing else."

Lyric bit her tongue and submitted while the maid pulled the homespun shirt over her head and arranged it over her damp tunic. The sleeves were too long and the shoulders hung loosely below her own, but she felt warmer.

"Now, lady, we must be going." Marek turned toward the horses.

"Where?" She demanded. "I assume we are returning to the castle to help my father?"

He grimaced, and only then did Lyric remember he was injured.

"No, my lady. We must get as far from Tressalt as possible. I had thought to take you to Graceen, where you will be safe in the care of your mother's people."

"Graceen?" Lyric felt her fury rise. "It will take days to get to Graceen. In that amount of time, Prince Ralt may decide my father's life no longer has value. We must go back *now*."

"Madam." Marek's voice was quiet but determined. "That is not possible. There are three of us against a garrison. How do you propose to get into the castle?"

"There are secret entrances. I know them. We can sneak in after nightfall, and—"

"And what, Your Highness?" he interrupted. "Again, I will say it—there are three of us. Prince Ralt's men are even now scouring all areas surrounding the castle, looking for you. The young soldier I spoke with told me this. Forgive me, my princess, but can you not imagine why he searches for you? What he will do, once you are in his power?"

Lyric stepped back, her anger giving way to sudden cold.

"I am sorry to tell you these things, but you must know," Marek went on, his tone relentless. "If the king still lives, it's because the prince hopes to use him to lure you back. Once he has you in his power, he has no reason to keep your father alive. He can force you to marry him and set himself up as the rightful king of the realm. Do you understand?"

"Yes." Her rage had returned. "Yes, I understand. Let's go, then. We have to do *something*." Her grandfather was close to the King of Graceen. Would they be able—or willing—to help?

Marek rode ahead to the Forest Road, glanced to the right and left, listened a long moment, then signaled for them to follow. They turned northward and began the trek toward Graceen just as the sun rose glimmering in the east. They soon rode on pathways Lyric had never traveled. She'd been to Graceen a number of times, but always with a large group and always on the Merchant Way, many miles to the west.

Marek set the pace at a brisk trot. It wasn't long before Lyric no longer needed the warmth provided by the extra shirt. They had gone several miles by that time, and when they slowed to rest the horses, her rumbling stomach reminded her of another need. She turned to Becca, who rode her chestnut gelding just behind Moon Song.

"Is there any food left?"

The maid shook her head. "No, my lady."

Marek reined in his horse and looked over his shoulder at them.

"There is a village not far from here. I have a little coin. I hope it will be safe for us to go into the village for food."

Soon the woods on their left thinned, and sunlight filtered into the dim forest. Marek stopped his horse and raised his right hand, signaling them to halt. A moment later they could all hear what had caught his attention. A rhythmic, ringing clash of iron on iron—not far from the edge of the forest.

"A blacksmith," he whispered. "The village is nearby." He turned his horse and they retraced their steps before stopping once again. He faced Lyric and in the morning light she could see the lines of pain and weariness that etched his face.

"We have five days before we cross into Graceen, if we keep up a good pace and the road isn't held against us," he said. "We need food, and it will be safest if only one of us goes into the village. I'm afraid it will have to be Mistress Becca. You and I are too easily recognized. Do you agree?"

She nodded.

He turned to the maid. "Can you manage, do you think?"

Becca gulped, looking from Marek to Lyric and back. "I, I think so, sir."

"Good." Marek nodded. "You'll have to go on foot—the horse would attract attention—and you'll have to be careful. Look for groups of people you can blend in with, and get as much food as you can without being noticed. If you can, find out if Ralt's soldiers have come this far, or if people here have heard of what's happened at the castle."

Marek climbed slowly off Dragon and reached into a small leather pouch attached to his saddle. He withdrew two coins from it and handed them to Becca. "The village is just over that small hill. Keep your eyes down. If anyone asks you who you are, tell them you're traveling with your family and your mother has taken ill. Can you remember that?"

The girl looked up at Marek and blushed a bright crimson. "Yes, sir. I can remember."

He smiled wearily. "If you come by some wine and extra linen, they would also be most welcome. If there is any trouble between here and the village, call out. Loudly. I will come."

"Yes, sir." Becca handed her reins to him, then turned and scurried down the trail toward the village.

Marek watched until she vanished around a bend in the path. "I hope all goes well."

Lyric inhaled sharply, fear taking hold. "I hope so, too." If Ralt's soldiers, using the wide, well-traveled Merchant Way, were already in the village, what might happen to the cheerful peasant girl?

She shivered and glanced back at Marek. Attempting to throw off her dark mood, she said the first ridiculous thing that popped into her head.

"Well, whatever happens, I think you're in a fair way for making the poor lass fall in love with you."

Marek scowled and turned to loosen the girth of Dragon's saddle. "That certainly isn't my intent."

Regretting her comment, Lyric dismounted and followed Marek to a spot off the trail where flattened grass and the charred remains of a fire showed that other travelers had stopped here to rest. Lyric hoisted herself onto a fallen fir tree near the path to wait, hoping Becca would return soon.

Marek tied the horses, then positioned himself against one of the trees and crossed his arms, his gaze roving continually along the trail and into the forest.

Lyric's stomach growled. She was sore from the long hours in the saddle and sleeping on the ground, and already tired of her perch on the log. After several minutes, she slid down and began pacing along the trail, stopping once to stroke Moon Song's nose, another time to pick a tiny purple blossom that grew among the bracken and wood sorrel.

She breathed in the blossom's sweet fragrance, then tucked the flower into her hair. Suddenly self-conscious, she shot a furtive glance at Marek, but he was staring down the trail in the direction Becca had gone. As she watched, he turned back and leaned his head against the tree, closing his eyes. A grimace marred his lean features and moisture dotted his brow.

Frowning, she forced herself to speak. "Are you in very much pain, Marek? Is there anything I can do for you?"

He opened his eyes and turned to her. "I thank you, my lady, but no. There is nothing you can do."

He hadn't answered her first question, but as she continued to watch him, she realized he didn't need to. The answer was obvious and added to her sense of helplessness.

So many things she had no control over. She hated it.

She resumed her pacing, worrying about Marek, worrying about her father, and wishing desperately for Becca's return. On her third pass of the tree that Marek leaned on, he gestured for her to stop.

"Tell me, my lady, if you don't mind. I've always wondered why you stopped your training sessions with the King's Guard. You were showing promise with both bow and sword."

Her earlier compassion roiled away.

"You didn't think I showed promise." She stood squarely in front of him, hands on hips. "You found it amusing that I trained with the guard. You laughed at me."

Surprise washed over his tired features. "Forgive me, my lady, but I did no such thing. Why would you think so?"

"I saw you," she said, remembering the incident as if it had happened last week. "I was sparring with Master Thomas in the practice court. I was doing well—or rather," she faltered, "I thought I was doing well. He was probably just letting me—"

"You *were* doing well," Marek interrupted.

She paused, hearing conviction in his voice, but hurried on. "I lost focus, and Thomas took the advantage, and I was forced to surrender. When I looked to the side, I saw you and Radoff and Charn. You were laughing." The remembered humiliation blazed through her.

"I am very sorry, my lady, if that is how it appeared to you," he said softly. "I do not know now what we would have been laughing at, but I can assure you—it wasn't you. I pray you will believe me."

She stared at him a long moment, seeing both truth and kindness in his eyes, but unable to reconcile what she'd just heard with what she'd believed for nearly three years. Pivoting away from him, she stomped down the trail, not stopping until she reached Moon Song. Resisting the urge to bury her face in the horse's mane, she contented herself with stroking the glossy shoulder and trying to order her thoughts.

She'd been thirteen when she'd convinced her father to let her train with the guard. It wasn't real training, of course. At least, not at first. Captain Gareth had no doubt been told to humor the king's daughter. To let her feel as if she was truly a part of it all, but to handle her carefully, until she got bored and went on to her next obsession.

But Lyric never got bored. She'd loved it—the archery, the swordplay, the running, riding, and climbing. She was never happier than when physically active. She'd been furious when the king drew an unwavering line preventing her from practicing hand-to-hand combat with the soldiers. She'd thought he might let her practice with the younger squires, at least, but he'd been adamant. No daughter of his was going to wrestle in the dirt with the boys.

Shortly after the match with Thomas, she'd turned fifteen and her lessons with the guard ended. She'd missed them desperately.

She walked back to where Marek stood and planted herself in front of him. "You really weren't laughing at me?"

He met her gaze steadily. "On my word, my lady. I thought you were courageous to keep coming back, day after day. We all did." He paused. "Did you quit training because you thought we'd laughed at you?"

"No." She stepped away from him. "I would never have quit."

The soldier's dark eyes held hers and she realized there was no criticism in them, no censure. All this time, she'd thought he'd mocked her, scorned her weakness, only to discover it wasn't true.

"Why did you, then?"

She crossed her arms and turned her scarred cheek away from him, looking down the path to where the horses grazed. "Some of the ladies of the court came to my father. They told him I was too old for such things, that it was unseemly for the female heir to be cavorting with soldiers. People were talking, they said." She looked over her shoulder at him, bitterness coloring her words. "I was unable to convince him otherwise."

Marek took a quick, sharp breath, then drew a hand across his brow. After a moment, he returned his gaze to her. "I have no doubt the king wished only the best for you. But truly, you were becoming adept in your training, and we were all sorry when you did not return."

She knew she should reply but couldn't find the right words. This man she'd been angry with for so long was looking at her with kindness in his eyes and talking to her as if they were friends.

She'd never had a real friend before. She'd learned early that people often sought her out because they hoped to benefit in some way from their relationship. To use her.

She'd understood this for years, but she'd never gotten over the hurt.

Arms still crossed, she once again turned away and strode down the path. She stopped by the horses and stared unseeing into the thick forest behind them. After a time, she peered over her shoulder at the soldier. "Thank you. I wish I could have continued with the training."

He nodded once, understanding and sympathy in his eyes. "Perhaps you can start your lessons again one day. If you desire it, and I am present at that time, I would be honored to share what I have learned."

She tore her gaze away from him and forced herself to speak calmly. "I would like that."

CHAPTER 7: GRIM DISCLOSURES

Marek took a deep breath, then exhaled slowly, trying to stay on top of the pain lancing through his side. The girl, Becca, had done her best to help last night, dousing the wound with what was left of the wine and wrapping it tightly with strips of cloth, but by this morning blood had soaked through the bandages and his undergarment. That wasn't good, and he didn't like the fuzziness that made his mind feel like breakfast mush. He needed to keep his wits if he was to see the princess and her servant to safety in Graceen.

If he didn't recover soon, there wouldn't be much chance of helping the princess with that training he'd promised. What he desperately needed was a trained healer. He shook his head, trying to clear the cobwebs.

"Marek?"

He lifted his gaze and found the princess scowling at him from where she leaned against a tree opposite him.

"How is it," she said, "that our forces in Tressalt were overrun so easily?"

He'd been considering the same thing and hated to admit what he believed to be true. "I do not know for certain, my lady. Prince Ralt brought many men with him, disguised as peasants coming to the Solstice Festival. Our fighters, while skilled, were too few."

"But *why* were we too few? Why were we not prepared?"

Marek hesitated, gritting his teeth against the throbbing in his side. There was a new comfort in his relationship with the princess, and he was glad. He'd always admired her, appreciating especially her gutsiness when she'd trained with the guard, but then she had quit and seemed ever after to be angry with him. He'd never known why until now, but she appeared to believe what he'd told her. Even so, she wouldn't want to hear his thoughts on their defeat.

"Well?"

He roused himself. "Peace has ruled our land for a long time, my lady. It is expensive to feed and house a large army."

"What does that have to do with anything?" she demanded, her violet eyes flashing. "We had a kingdom to defend. Who made that decision?"

It was as he'd feared. She wasn't going to be satisfied with anything less than the whole truth. He sighed.

"My understanding is that the king did not believe it necessary to do so. Other than the castle guard, we have only small numbers of soldiers throughout the land—just enough to keep the peace in the villages and settle local disputes."

She stared at him a long moment, but, to his relief, she didn't flare up, accusing him of treasonous words. Neither did she erupt in a furious defense of her father's decisions. Instead, she crossed her arms and looked down at the ground before her. Her rich dark hair was disheveled, her expression pensive.

"Do you think they're all dead?" she finally whispered. "All the guard?"

He'd been asking himself the same question since hearing Rigel's report and watching the young soldier die on the forest floor. Did any of his comrades yet live?

"I know not, my lady. We can only pray it is not so."

She looked up at him, tears shimmering in her eyes. "Who was the soldier you spoke to? The one who told you of the battle?"

He hitched a breath. Another question he'd hoped she'd never ask. But she had, and he must answer. He looked her steadily in the eye. "It was Rigel, my lady. I'm sorry."

She closed her eyes, a new layer of agony etched on her lovely features. "It's my fault."

He frowned. "Of course it isn't. How could you think such a thing?"

"It is," she insisted. "The prince wanted to marry me. He was coming to seek my father's permission but I—I couldn't. You saw how he was that night." She shivered, then swiped at the tears with the back of her hand. "I told my father *no,* and he accepted my decision. Then I ran away, to ride, to enjoy the day, and ... my father stayed behind and told the prince *no.*"

She swallowed and looked away. "If I'd stayed home, agreed to marry the prince, as my father asked, done my duty, maybe none of this would have happened. All those people—"

"Your Highness, you can't let yourself think like that." He pushed himself away from the tree, took a step toward her. "This attack was planned. If you had ... sacrificed yourself to Prince Ralt, most likely all that would have happened would have been a delay in his ultimate plan. He would have had Tressalt and you. Your father would not have wanted that."

He knew what he said was true. He didn't know if she believed him. She had turned away, crossing her arms against the rough trunk of the tree, pressing her face against them. Her slender shoulders shook but she didn't make a sound.

He stepped toward her, reaching out a hand, but then stopped and let his hand drop. He clenched his fists. It was not his duty to comfort her. His only job was to protect her, to take her to safety. Comforting her would be the task of another.

Lyric had taken to pacing again, unable to sit idly by while her stomach growled and her fears grew. Where was Becca? The sunlight, as it filtered through the trees, had been directly overhead when she left. Now, it slanted low in the west, and the evening chill crept through the forest. Marek had said the village was no more than a quarter-hour's walk from the trail. Becca had been gone for hours.

Lyric heard a noise behind her. Marek trudged toward her, grimacing with each step. It wasn't like him to move in that slow, ungainly manner. And what was that? She gasped. A dark stain spread across the material under his chain mail shirt.

"I'm going to look for her." His voice had none of its usual vigor. "Something must have happened."

"You can't," she began, but as she did, one of the horses nickered softly. The chestnut gelding stood with his ears pricked forward, looking down the trail that led to the village. A moment later, Becca hurried into view.

Relief washed through her but quickly dissolved to frustration. "Where have you been?"

"I'm so sorry, my lady." The girl ran the last steps, panting. "I had to hide. There are soldiers in the village, but they're not ours. Prince Ralt's."

Fear slammed down Lyric's spine.

Marek stepped forward. "Are you sure?"

Becca put a hand to her heart, still gasping. "Yes."

"Tell us everything," Lyric ordered.

"I found an inn and spoke to the innkeeper about what I needed. The inn was crowded, but the innkeeper's wife was readying a parcel for me and then—" Becca's face blanched and her throat bobbed. "Two soldiers came in and they had this *thing* with them, a creature of some sort—I've never seen anything like it." She focused on Lyric. "It stood upright on two legs and was taller than the soldiers. It wore clothing, but it had hair all over its face and arms. I didn't think it was human, but then it spoke."

Lyric narrowed her eyes. "What *was* it?"

"I don't know," the girl almost wailed. "I was so afraid, I ducked into the kitchen and hid. The people in the inn were all afraid too, and the innkeeper told the soldiers to get out and take the creature with them. But the soldiers just laughed. They said people better get used to seeing such creatures in Tressalt, and then, they *struck* the innkeeper and said if he didn't want worse to happen, he better hurry and bring them food and ale."

Becca's voice faltered. "I hid in a broom closet off the kitchen. I could hear the soldiers talking to that creature. When it spoke, it was like a—like a *growling,* but if I listened hard, I could understand its words."

Lyric crossed her arms, shivering. "What did it say?"

Becca took a deep breath. "One of the soldiers asked it when the rest of its people would be coming. I think the creature laughed—it made this rumbling noise, anyway—then it said '*My people?*' and it laughed again. Then it said they would be coming soon."

"More of these creatures are coming to Tressalt? Why?"

Becca looked at her with large, grief-stricken eyes. "For the war, they said. To aid Prince Ralt and someone named Lothar."

"What war? They already have my land."

And who was Lothar?

"I don't know, my lady. That's all I heard. They started ... carousing after that. Drinking and shouting—I couldn't understand anything else they said."

"It sounds like a Borag," Marek said heavily.

"A *what?*" Lyric spun to face him. "You know of these beasts?"

"I've never seen them myself, but I've journeyed some distance in your father's service. Some of the mountain people in the eastern highlands speak of such folk. I didn't believe them, but neither does one call the mountain people liars." He grimaced. "Mistress Becca's description sounds like the creatures they call Borags." He turned back to Becca. "Speak on, mistress. What else happened?"

The girl shivered. "The soldiers said they'd just come from the castle. They said Prince Ralt of Malacar was now in charge and you'd been kidnapped, my lady. They said you had a servant with you, and it was one of King Sander's guards who had taken you." She looked up at Lyric, lips trembling. "There is a large reward being offered to anyone who finds you and brings you back."

Lyric rubbed her arms against the chill that overtook her and cast a sidelong glance at Marek. There were creatures out of ancient legends walking among them, and her people were being told she'd been kidnapped. If the people believed this story, Tressalt was not a safe place for any of them. And Marek was in more danger than she.

"How did you get away?" Marek asked.

"I hid in the closet till after they left, sir, too afraid to go out lest they see me. Then one of the servants found me and dragged me out to the innkeeper. He remembered me but looked at me very strangely." She turned terrified eyes to Lyric. "I thought he was going to call the soldiers back, because"—she gestured to her rumpled riding garments—"he didn't know me and I wasn't dressed as a house servant."

Lyric grabbed Becca's hand. "What happened?"

"He set me free." Becca spoke as if she still couldn't quite believe it. "He gave me the dried meat and pack of bread and cheese I'd asked for and added a small jar of wine and told me to wait. He sent one of the kitchen lads to see where the soldiers were. When the boy came back, he told me the soldiers were camped on the west side of the village and this was the safest time for me to go, unless I wanted to wait until dark."

She glanced at her hand that Lyric still held, then up into her mistress's eyes. "But I needed to get back, and I was afraid to be out after dark." She looked at Marek and spoke more boldly. "I was very careful, sir. I left the village on a different path than the one I'd come in on, then doubled back through the fields until I found this trail. I don't think anyone saw me."

"The innkeeper didn't ask you any questions?" Lyric asked.

"No. I thought he might, but he never did. And he told the others to leave me alone."

"I know this innkeeper. He's a good man," Marek said. "Loyal to the king and no one's fool." He turned back to Becca. "You did well. I must know more about this creature—this Borag—but you can tell us while we ride."

"Yes, sir." Becca rummaged under her tunic and withdrew a wrapped parcel. "But first, both of you must eat something. I've already eaten—the innkeeper's wife gave me a mug of stew while we waited for the kitchen boy to return." She unwrapped the package and handed a piece of bread to Lyric, then another to Marek. "I'm sorry, sir, but I was not able to get any clean linen."

"We'll have to do without, then," he said, drawing a hand across his brow. "We have no time for medicating now, anyway. We need to be as far away as possible, as soon as possible."

"Your wound must be tended," Lyric said.

He nodded. "As soon as it's safe."

Within moments, they were all astride, jogging along the trail to the north. It had not escaped Lyric's notice that Marek had mounted his horse with unusual stiffness.

What would happen to her and Becca if they had to travel on without him?

CHAPTER 8: DARKNESS AND LIGHT

They pushed the horses on until well past dark. Lyric didn't know how Marek could see, but maybe it wasn't Marek at all but his horse who found the trail. Dragon strode on tirelessly. Moon Song followed behind the big war horse, and Becca's gelding Arrow never strayed far from Moon Song's flank.

Disquieting thoughts tormented Lyric as they rode through the gloomy forest. Ralt's forces must have raced north to be settled in the village so quickly. The overthrow of her land must indeed have been a planned venture. And if that was his ultimate plan, why did Ralt go through the motions of seeking her as a bride? Was it, as Marek believed, just a ruse to get her people to accept him more readily as their king?

And her father? Did he yet live? Shuddering, she tried to push the fear away.

He must still live. He simply must.

Hours after they'd left the village behind, Marek reined Dragon to a stop. "I hear a brook nearby," he said, voice raspy. "We need water, and we must stop for the night. The horses need rest."

As do the humans, Lyric thought. Gratefully, and stiffly, she slid off Moon Song. Each muscle and joint in her body cried out in pain. She'd always considered herself an excellent horsewoman, but never in her life had she spent so many unending, grueling hours in the saddle.

Her discomfort must be nothing compared to Marek's. He'd scarcely been able to remove his saddle from Dragon's back, and Lyric found herself doing something she'd never done in her entire life—trying to unsaddle her own horse.

But it was hopeless. A gleaming half-moon sailed high overhead but little of its light reached through the trees to the forest floor. In the almost total darkness, she couldn't tell where one saddle strap began and another ended. Marek lurched over.

"Let me," he said thickly, and she stepped away, burning in humiliation.

Becca had managed to pull her saddle from Arrow's back and now knelt a few paces away, rummaging through her pack.

"I'll go for water." Grasping the water skins, she crept into the bushes toward the trickling brook.

Closing her eyes, Lyric crossed her arms and leaned back against a looming fir tree. The nighttime air was cool around her, heavy with the fragrance of the forest. The tang of pine needles and sap, the musk of the earth and decaying underbrush—it all swirled about her. An owl's mournful hoot echoed through the trees.

Her eyes flew open. She mustn't sleep, not yet. There were things that must be discussed. She turned to where Marek sat hunched against another of the trees, a dark shadow among the other shadows. The time for decorum was past.

"How bad is your injury, Marek? Tell me truly."

She heard him shift against the tree but it was a long moment before he replied. "It is not good, I'm afraid."

She inhaled sharply. "What can we do?"

"I have been unable to stanch the bleeding. That must be done. The wound must be cleansed and re-bandaged."

"Being on horseback all day is not helping," she murmured.

In the darkness she heard him shift again. "It can't be helped."

He needed rest and a healer's care, but with Ralt's men on their trail, they had to keep moving. Never in her life had she felt so helpless.

"I am sorry," he said a moment later. "My preference would be not to trouble you with this, but I am concerned. If I am unable to fulfill my duty, I fear what could happen to you and Mistress Becca out here alone."

Anxiety rolled over her like heavy fog and her stomach spasmed.

"I need you to listen to me carefully," he said. "This path we're on will bring you to Graceen's border. If something happens to me—"

"Nothing's going to happen to you!" She stepped away from the tree, furious and frightened.

"Probably not," he agreed, "but on the chance that it does, I need you to listen to me. Will you do that?"

Her heart pounded, drumming against her rib cage. She didn't want to have this conversation. She didn't want to have to think about this.

"Your Highness? Are you listening?"

"Yes," she whispered, knees weak.

"Stay on the trail. It will become more faint the farther north you go, but you shouldn't lose sight of it. Move as quickly as you can. If you can find food along the trail, do so, but don't take time to look for it. You'll be hungry but you won't starve. Get to Graceen as fast as you can. Find your grandfather. You'll be safe there."

A thickness lodged in her throat and hot tears threatened. Her mind whirled with the awfulness of his words. He couldn't leave them. She wouldn't let him.

What if she had no choice?

A soft rustling in the brush told her Becca had returned. The darkness was suffocating and she was cold and afraid.

She wanted a fire. Light and warmth to bolster her courage against the dark. But it was out of the question— Marek would never allow it. She shook her head and wrapped her arms about herself, trying to forestall the cold. They were still too close to the village, to Ralt's men and that creature. How quickly could the enemy travel if they learned of Becca's presence in the village and guessed her identity?

"Master Marek?" Becca called timidly. "Are you ready to have your wound tended?"

"I am, mistress," he replied. "Though I'm not sure how much can be accomplished in the dark."

"Can we—" Becca began, then hesitated. "Is it possible for us to start a small fire, do you think? Just so I can see to clean the wound?"

Lyric's heart leapt. When Marek didn't answer, she broke in, hoping she wouldn't regret the decision later. "Yes, let's have a fire. Long enough for the wound to be tended, at least."

In the darkness, Marek sighed but didn't argue.

"I'll gather some wood and brush," Becca said, and set off down the trail.

After a moment's hesitation, Lyric stepped toward the path. "I'll look for firewood, too." Another thing she'd never done in her seventeen years. With foot and hand, she felt around the clearing, searching for anything that would burn. Soon she and Becca had a small but usable pile of branches, pine cones, and dry underbrush near the center of the clearing.

"I have flint and steel in my saddle bag," Marek said in a low voice. "Do you know how to use them, Mistress Becca?"

"Of course, sir," the girl said almost gaily, and ran to retrieve the tinder box.

She was back in minutes and set about striking the flint against the steel. Sparks flew immediately, but it took a number of attempts before one of the sparks flared up enough to set the small stack of dry grasses to smoldering. Becca blew carefully on the tiny blaze, adding more bits of brush, then some larger twigs, coaxing the flames until they finally took hold. After several minutes a small fire crackled merrily.

Lyric knew they couldn't keep the fire going long, but for now she knelt before it, holding her hands above the dancing flames, delighting in the cheery warmth. She looked across the blaze at Becca. "Well done."

The girl beamed. "Thank you, my lady." She pushed a few of the larger branches into the flame, then turned to Marek. "If you please, sir," she said, gesturing to the saddle blanket she'd spread on the ground next to the fire.

Marek pushed away from the tree and trudged to the fire. He turned his gaze to Lyric, his dark eyes clouded with weariness. "You don't have to watch, my lady. It won't be pleasant."

Lyric shook her head, not knowing what to say or if she needed to say anything. He nodded and turned back to Becca.

"Can you remove your tunic, or do you need help?" she asked.

"I can manage." He unclasped and removed the mail shirt, then slowly pulled the stained tunic over his head.

Becca gasped and Lyric, when she followed the maid's gaze, felt her stomach buck like an unbroken colt. Dark blood soaked through the garment beneath the tunic.

"Oh, sir," Becca moaned. "I didn't know it was so bad. Riding has made it worse. Sit here and I'll do the rest."

Marek clenched his jaw and lowered himself onto the saddle blanket.

Though the sick feeling remained, Lyric couldn't tear her gaze away as Becca helped Marek remove the bloodied undergarment. The shirt stuck to his skin where the blood had dried and Lyric knew she must get away or chance losing what was left of her meal.

"I'll get more wood," she said, jumping to her feet and retreating to the darkness. She leaned back against a tree and forced herself to breathe in and out slowly, letting the cool air clear her head and calm her stomach. After a few minutes, more branches and pine cones in hand, she returned to the fire and crouched down across from Becca and Marek.

Becca had removed the bloodied strips of cloth that had worked as a wrapping for the wound and now tore a section of the old table cloth into rags. She poured water from one of the skins onto it, then offered the dripping cloth to Marek.

Wordlessly, he took the rag and began rubbing it over his torso, scrubbing carefully at the wound. As the rag became dark with his blood, he handed it back to Becca, who rinsed it out with water from the skin, then gave it back to him. They repeated the process several times and Lyric, having gained control of her roiling stomach, found herself fascinated by the sight of Marek's naked flesh, even while repulsed by the blood.

"Turn this way, now, sir," Becca ordered. "And lift your arm."

Marek did so and Lyric sucked in her breath. The wound was as long as a man's hand and gaped in the middle, below the rib cage. Blood still oozed from it and she felt her stomach whirl again.

"I was bent over when struck," he said, seeing Lyric's expression. "Otherwise the mail would have protected me."

Becca rinsed out the rag once again, then dabbed carefully at the wound. Marek winced, then gritted his teeth and closed his eyes.

Murmuring apologies, Becca worked steadily until the wound was as clean as she could manage. "Hold on, sir, we're almost done." Lyric hadn't noticed the small jar, but Becca reached for it now and splashed it onto the open wound.

Marek swore and scrambled to his feet before mastering himself and sinking back on the saddle blanket, panting.

"I'm sorry, sir!" Becca cried out. "But it had to be done. The wine will help with the cleaning. Your skin around the wound is an ugly shade."

Marek gasped, holding a hand to his forehead. "Don't blame yourself. I was just … startled." He sat back, and despite his words, Lyric couldn't miss the trembling that racked his shoulders or the bright sheen of sweat coating his face.

"Here, sir." Becca held the jar out to him. "There's at least one mouthful left, maybe two. It will help." He took the jar gratefully and drained its contents in one long swallow.

Lyric had jumped to her feet when Marek did, and for the second time that night she felt as if her heart would slam out of her chest. She wanted to scream, to run away from the gruesome sight and the awful stench of the blood, but she couldn't. She was the princess. She was in charge. She must be calm and lead by example.

And the words were as hollow as the way she felt inside. Useless.

She watched through narrowed eyes as Becca tore more strips from what was left of the table covering and wrapped them tightly around Marek's midsection. Then all was done that could be done, except ….

"You'll need this," Lyric said, finally thinking of one thing she could do to help. She pulled the borrowed shirt over her head and held it out to Marek.

"No, my lady," he and Becca said as one.

"Don't be foolish," she snapped. "You need it more than I do."

They both eyed her closely, neither speaking. Then, coming to a decision, Marek reached for the garment. "I thank you, my lady."

Lyric stared at both of them, these people who lived to serve her, and was ashamed of herself. Their surprise at her wanting to help, her desire to put their needs before her own, gave her much to think about.

And possibly to repent of. But not now. Other issues pressed harder.

"You're welcome." She turned to Becca. "If you'll show me where the food is, I'll try to get it ready while you wash out Marek's garments."

She refused to meet their gazes and pretended not to notice the glances that passed between them, but busied herself pulling items from Becca's pack. After a moment's consideration, she put another handful of brush and branches on the small fire. She was the princess, after all. If she wanted to keep the fire a little longer, well, that was her right. And she was going to exercise that right because she was cold and unnerved and far from home.

She hoped it was a decision she wouldn't regret.

CHAPTER 9: END OF THE TRAIL

When the cold of dawn awoke her on the third day after Ralt had torn her kingdom away, Lyric found Becca kneeling beside Marek. They'd made good time yesterday, covering many miles on the journey north, but Marek had moved slower and slower as the day had passed. He'd drunk some water when they stopped for the night, but spoke little and only picked at his food. His wound still seeped and looked nasty around the edges. Becca had re-wrapped it in what was left of the table covering.

The wine was gone. There were no more villages. There was nothing else they could do.

Now, the knight tossed and turned on his saddle blanket bed, muttering words that made no sense. He sat up, staring back and forth between them with wild eyes, eyes that didn't know them. Then he collapsed back on the blanket, unconscious.

Becca glanced at her mistress, then leaned over to place her work-worn hand on Marek's forehead. She pulled it back immediately. "He's burning, my lady. This is very bad."

Lyric knelt next to the prone man, staring. She had no knowledge of the care of illness or injury. Why had she never learned? "What can we do? How can we make the fever stop?"

Becca bit her lip.

"All I know is to try and cool him down with water, and get him to drink as much as possible. Sometimes it helps, but ... not always."

"Let's get water, then," Lyric said. "We'll do what we can." Without waiting for Becca, Lyric found the water skins and crept away through the woods to the brook. She took the briefest moment to splash the icy water on her face and arms, drying them off with her rumpled riding skirt. Then she filled the skins and returned to the campsite. Marek was still lying down but was conscious and appeared to be speaking to Becca.

"I'm fine," he told Lyric as she drew near, but his eyes were not his eyes. The glassy stare belonged to a thief—someone who had stolen her guard—and she wanted him back. She stepped around Becca and knelt beside him.

"Here, Marek. I've brought you some water. Drink it, please."

He collapsed back on his bedroll, then looked up at her, his expression puzzled. "I don't want to drink. I want to sleep."

"Well, I want you to drink," she said firmly. "And I'm the princess, so you have to obey."

"The princess?" His confused gaze narrowed in consternation. "She's just a little girl."

"No, she's not," Lyric said. "I am the princess, and I'm all grown up. When I command you to drink, you must do it."

Looking as if he didn't completely believe her, he took the water skin from her and sipped slowly. When it was empty, Lyric took it from him and gestured to Becca. "Now. This lady is going to wipe your face with more water. You let her do her job or I shall report you to Captain Gareth."

Marek's eyes widened at the threat, but he submitted to Becca's ministrations. After several minutes he yawned, and without asking leave, turned over on the smelly horse blanket and fell instantly into sleep.

She stared down at the unconscious man. They couldn't stay—even now, that horrid Borag thing might have found their trail and be closing in on them.

Becca raised worried eyes to her. "What shall we do? Do you think we two together can get Master Marek up onto Dragon? Tie him on somehow?"

Lyric lifted her shoulders and dropped them in a hopeless gesture.

"I don't know how." Marek, while not huge, was a good-sized man, and Dragon was a large and willful animal. She couldn't imagine any way she and Becca could get him onto the horse.

She shivered, then sat on the ground beside Marek while Becca went to the brook to refill the water skins. When the girl came back, amazingly, she had a broad grin on her freckled face.

"Look what I found!" She held out her hands to reveal several large red berries. "Wild strawberries! I found them growing in a meadow near the brook. Won't they go wonderfully with the last of our bread and cheese?"

Her enthusiasm was catching. "They will indeed," Lyric said, reaching for one and biting into it. The sweet juice exploded in her mouth, and at that moment, tasted better than anything she'd ever eaten in the king's castle. "Are there more?"

"Not a lot more. It's still early in the season, but I'll go back and get what I can."

Lyric ate a piece of cheese and then some bread, interspersing the staples with the fruit. The sun rose behind her and slanted through the tree trunks, luscious warmth creeping up her back as she broke her fast and watched over her injured, dozing guard. She was being chased by evil men, they were at least a three-day ride from safety, and her guard was dangerously ill. But for this moment, she would revel in the warmth of the newly risen sun, listen to the small, twittery birds as they heralded a new day, and savor another berry.

Becca returned with enough berries that they'd be able to have some for lunch, if they weren't crushed in the saddle bags. Now they had to deal with the problem at hand.

"I still can't think of a way to get him onto Dragon," Lyric admitted.

"Get who on Dragon?" a muffled voice asked.

Lyric whirled. Marek was still flat on his back but his eyes were open and he stared at them both.

Becca clapped her hands. "Master Marek! You're feeling better!"

Lyric was skeptical. This was just a bit too much of a miraculous healing to her mind. She was afraid he was still partly hallucinating.

She crept closer and looked carefully into his eyes. They were still glassy, but she could see more of the real man in them than she had earlier. "We were afraid you couldn't get on Dragon by yourself. Do you think you can?"

He focused on her and tried to smile, but it was a pitiful attempt. "I'll give it my best effort, my lady. More water would help, and ... are there really strawberries?"

"There are," she said, thrilled he was at least part-way back. Unthinking, she reached forward and grasped his warm hand with her cool one. A wave of heat rolled over her and she sucked in a breath, staring at her hand holding his. She raised her eyes to his and found him staring back, forehead wrinkled. Not angry, she thought, but perplexed.

Confused.

She released his hand and slapped it playfully. "Well, it's about time you do something for yourself. Becca and I are tired of doing all the work."

His lids drooped closed.

Becca hurried to the brook to fill the water skins and returned with those and another handful of berries for Marek. He sat up, drank more water, and ate the berries and a hunk of cheese while Becca and Lyric broke camp.

Lyric managed to saddle Moon Song, and Becca did the same for both Arrow and Dragon. Bridling the horses was more complicated but eventually all three were ready to travel. Lyric led Dragon close to a broken tree stump, while Marek, leaning on Becca, climbed onto the stump, swung his right leg over the horse's back and settled onto the saddle.

She gave a sigh of relief. She and Becca mounted and they set off, once again, on the trail north to Graceen.

Her relief was short-lived. Marek still led the group, while she rode in the middle and Becca brought up the rear, but by mid-morning she knew it was all he could do to stay on the horse. He slumped dangerously from side to side, almost falling several times.

Lyric took to ordering him in her sternest voice, as she had that morning. She told him to wake up, to pay attention, to stay on his horse. For a time it worked.

The sun climbed high and Lyric knew they must stop soon. The horses needed to graze and the humans needed food also, but if Marek managed to get off his horse, they'd never get him back on.

Their journey would be over.

In the end, the horses decided. When the trail left the forest and wound through a grassy meadow, Dragon, apparently determining his rider wouldn't care, simply stopped where he was, dropped his head to the earth, and began ripping up the succulent greenery.

Following their leader's example, Moon Song and Arrow pushed forward into the meadow and plunged their noses into the lush feast. Lyric couldn't bring herself to force Moon Song one more step. With a weary glance at Becca, she dismounted, looped her reins around the saddle's pommel, and walked over to Dragon. Marek was unconscious. Only years of habit had kept him in the saddle.

Becca joined her and moaned. "Oh, my lady—what now?"

Lyric glanced around the clearing. Giant firs stood like sentinels. It was a spectacularly beautiful day. The sky—pale blue behind the blazing summer sun—was dotted by high, wispy clouds that seemed put there for decoration only. A light breeze, warm and smelling of summer, swept across the meadow and rippled the grass like waves on water.

A beautiful day. A beautiful place.

And a dangerous place. They had no defense, but it didn't matter. They simply couldn't keep going.

"We let the horses eat." She shrugged and looked back at Marek. "And we try to find a way to keep him in the saddle."

Becca discovered a length of rope in Marek's saddle pack and used it to tie his leg to the stirrup on one side, then ran the rope under Dragon's belly along the girth, and did the same with the man's leg on the other side. They looped the rope around his waist, then around the cantle and pommel of the saddle, and knotted it as tightly as the two of them could muster.

If Marek was aware of what they were doing, he didn't show it. He sat limply in the saddle, eyes closed, leaning forward against the binding rope.

They rested for an hour, taking turns holding onto the horses and nibbling on the bread and cheese. Lyric set aside the last of the berries with a small hunk of bread for Marek, hoping he'd eventually regain consciousness and want to eat.

"We've got to go," she finally said, knowing there was only one way to force Dragon to leave his feast. "You'll have to lead Moon Song from Arrow," she told Becca. "I'm going to walk and lead Dragon."

"Oh, no, my lady! Let me," Becca said, horror in every word.

"We can take turns," Lyric retorted. "I'm saddle-stiff. The walking will be good for me."

The horses were not at all happy about leaving their bit of paradise, but with much urging Lyric got Dragon and his unconscious rider moving forward. The others fell into place behind. They'd scarcely entered the forest on the north side of the meadow when Lyric felt the trail begin to climb. She knew from her geography studies that this approach to the border with Graceen led through the Grimwood Pass, high above the plain where the Merchant Road took most travelers. They might yet encounter snow, even this time of year, but they had no choice but to keep going. She trudged on, all the while listening for the thunder of hoof beats.

The path continued to climb.

She and Becca traded places several times, and it was again Lyric's turn to walk and lead Dragon when the sun dropped behind the coastal mountain range far to the west. Fog descended like a great blanket. It blurred her vision of the uneven footing and muffled the sound of their breathing and the horses' plodding hooves. With the night and the fog came the cold.

In her past life, her normal life, Lyric was not a girl given to tears. She'd cried more these last days than she had in years, and she was now close to weeping again. Her body ached. She was cold, and the night was dark. When she sensed, more than saw, the trail leveling out and leading through a treeless area, she stopped. She desperately hoped there was water nearby but she didn't know and it didn't matter. They could go no farther.

Dread stabbed her when she and Becca went to untie the ropes that held Marek in the saddle. What if he'd died during their long march? But his body still radiated warmth—too much warmth. When he began to slip from the horse, he regained consciousness enough to keep from crashing to the ground. Once on his shaking legs, he leaned against Dragon, gasping for air, then pitched forward. Lyric caught him, staggering under his weight, and Becca jumped to help. Together, they settled him on the ground and moved the horse away.

Lyric sat in the grass in the dark beside him, resting first one of her ice-cold hands and then the other against his burning forehead. Becca unsaddled the horses and brought the saddle blankets to her. Lyric shook one out and laid it over Marek, tucking it around him.

In unspoken agreement, they scavenged in the dark for wood and brush. Becca retrieved Marek's tinderbox and started a fire near the unconscious man. Lyric was glad. This bit of light and warmth was all that stood between them and the horrors of the night.

Fear gripped her, smothering her like the heavy fog that blanketed their campsite. She had found some large leaves, wet from the mist, and arranged them on Marek's face, but she knew it wasn't enough. The fever was winning, and the infection was out of control. He wouldn't survive another day.

Despairing, she wrapped herself in Moon Song's blanket and lay down by the crackling fire, knowing its cheery warmth could not protect them from what awaited in the morning.

Only one thing was certain. They'd run as far as they could.

CHAPTER 10: IMPOSSIBILITIES

Words swirled through the fog in her head.

Her name, and other words, murmured by voices she didn't know.

Who?

Fear stabbed deeper than her exhaustion, dragging her from sleep. She jerked upright and scanned the outer rim of their tiny campsite.

Her breath lodged in her throat.

Tall, silent people surrounded the site, staring at her impassively. There were both men and women, clad in tunics and breeches in shades of green and brown, armed with long bows and daggers. Some moved among the horses, stroking them softly. Someone had built up the fire.

From the blaze's far side, Marek slept on, his breaths coming in labored, fitful gasps. Becca stared wide-eyed at the newcomers, clutching her saddle blanket about her. Their only weapons were Marek's sword and bow, both out of reach. Lyric sucked in a breath and lifted her chin, trying to prepare herself for what was to come.

A woman stepped forward. Her hair was silver, but no wrinkle marred her perfect features. The eyes that gazed steadily at Lyric were also silver, clear and untroubled. She dipped her head courteously.

"Princess Lyric," she said, in a voice low and melodious. "I am Amira of the Akyldi people. I am gratified to find you alive and free."

Lyric gulped, trying to calm her thundering heart. "I thank you for your concern, Amira, but ... how do you know me?"

Amira inclined her head. "The Akyldi have eyes and ears in many places, and the purpose behind your flight is known to us, Princess of Tressalt. It is for this reason we have left our homes in the deep forest to meet with you here."

Lyric clenched her teeth. "Are you ... are you in league with the Malacarians, then?"

There was a murmuring among the assembled Akyldi, but Amira lifted her hand to silence them.

"If that were so," she said kindly, "could we not have captured you while you slept? Put the sword to your dying guard and given you over to Ralt of Malacar?"

Lyric pulled the saddle blanket tightly around her shoulders, trying to understand.

"What is it that has brought you to me, then? If you know the reason for my flight, you also know that my only goal is to find safety until I determine a way to return to Tressalt and reclaim my land."

Amira nodded. "I assumed that was your plan. We are here to offer such aid as we can."

Lyric peered closely at her. "Why would you do that? What have the Akyldi to do with those of Tressalt? Do you live within our borders?"

The Akyldi woman's lips crept up at the corners and a light shone in her silver eyes. "Some would argue that the people of Tressalt live within the borders of the Akyldi, but perhaps now is not the time for such disputes."

Lyric narrowed her gaze. She was cold and hungry, tired, far from home. No, now was not the time for boundary disputes. She shivered. "You said you want to help us. What help can you offer? Do you have soldiers? Men-at-arms who can ride to the aid of Tressalt?"

The woman's expression softened. "The power of the Akyldi is not in arms, Your Highness, and for that I am sorry. But there are other ways in which we might be of assistance. As to why, that is best discussed away from the roads and ways of men." She looked from Lyric to Becca and to Marek, then back to Lyric.

"I will also tell you, Your Highness, that you are being followed, and all roads to Graceen will soon be held against you. You cannot go farther on the Forest Road. Will you come with us to a safe place? You will be able to rest, as I believe you have not since you began your journey. And our healers can see to your man." Amira cast a glance at Marek. "I fear he will not live long otherwise."

The cold that had been seeping into Lyric's heart the last four days was now close to enveloping her completely. Who were these people? How was she to decide what to do? She rubbed her hands across her eyes and tried to think. She didn't know these Akyldi. Normally, she would have nothing to do with such strangers, especially alone and defenseless as she and Becca were. But if they could be hidden from Ralt, even for a short while ... if these Akyldi could help Marek....

Her shivers turned into shudders. What choice did she have?

The silver-haired woman spoke again. "I know this is difficult. After you've heard my tale, if you prefer not to accept our help, I give you my word to return you to this spot, unharmed and unhindered. Whether you come with us or not, however, we must go." She turned toward the trail that led down to the Forest Road and cocked her head. Frowning, she looked back to Lyric. "Prince Ralt's men will be here by morning. Will you come with us?"

There were no other choices. Climbing to her feet, she faced Amira. "We will come with you, but I want to know how you know what has transpired in Tressalt. It is far to the south and west, and we have come with as much haste as my injured guard could manage."

Amira nodded. "It is a good question, and perhaps the answer will give you comfort." She reached inside her tunic and pulled out a fine chain. At the end of its golden length sparkled a stone, similar in size and shape to the one Lyric bore, but a deep, burnished red in color.

"This is Midara, brother of Menjar, the stone you wear next to your heart."

Lyric reached for her pendant, dismayed to find it had slipped from under her tunic.

Amira smiled. "Do not fret. I have known of Menjar long before now." A light glinted in her eyes. "Menjar has been silent for many years. He stirred to life when Prince Ralt arrived in your land, and came fully awake and spoke to you four days ago. When this happened, Midara heard, and therefore I also heard."

Lyric found herself swaying. Rocks that spoke? People living in the northern mountains of Tressalt she'd never heard of? She tried to speak but found her lips growing numb. "I don't understand any of this."

"All will be explained soon, but not here," Amira said kindly. She signaled to one of the Akyldi men standing nearby. "Quinn, will you see to the princess and her servant?"

The man came to her on feet as silent as a cat's, and for an instant Lyric had the distinct impression that everything about him, and all the Akyldi, was catlike. They were lithe, enigmatic, and they moved with feline grace. Two of the women bent over Marek, one holding a hand to his forehead while the other held a tiny glass vial to his lips. Two others bridled the horses.

"My lady," the man beside her spoke, his voice soft as a summer breeze. He held out a traveling cloak of deep forest green. She stared, uncomprehending, then in exhausted embarrassment disentangled herself from the sweat-stained saddle blanket and exchanged it for the cloak. The man went to Becca next, offering her a dark blue cloak. The maid followed her mistress's example and wrapped the cloak around her shoulders.

Marek's labored breathing had eased, and he lay quietly by the fire while the Akyldi prepared the horses. With brisk efficiency, some of the men cut two saplings and attached a heavy blanket between them, forming a makeshift stretcher. They placed Marek on it, and Lyric and Becca mounted their horses.

When all was ready, Amira led the way from the tiny clearing and into the forest. Lyric's last image of their camp was of one of the Akyldi blotting out their footprints with a leafy tree branch and kicking dirt onto the fire, plunging them into darkness.

The earlier fog had lifted, but thick clouds covered the moon and stars. The Akyldi held no torches but walked without hesitation or stumbling. They did not speak, and there were no night sounds of owls or other nocturnal hunters, just the squeaks of the saddle leather and the horses' plodding hooves.

Lyric didn't know how long they rode. It was hours, or perhaps days. She drifted in and out of sleep, jerking awake when her body told her she was about to fall. At last, Moon Song's steps slowed, then stopped. Lifting her head, Lyric saw that the trees had ended, and they'd entered a clearing around which torches and small fires glowed. A voice spoke at her side.

"If you will dismount, Your Highness, a meal and a bed await. I will tend your horse."

Lyric obeyed, sliding off Moon Song, landing on feet that seemed as dull with sleep as the rest of her. She could hear bustling around her as their guides spread throughout the camp. Becca joined her, rubbing the sleep from her eyes. Moments later, one of the female Akyldi stood before them.

"This way, Your Highness." She led them to a campfire where a delicious odor wafted from a bubbling pot. "Enjoy your meal," the woman said softly, indicating a rough-hewn bench holding bowls and cutlery. "We hope it is to your liking. Lady Amira will attend you as soon as she is able." She turned to go but Lyric stopped her.

"Where has our guard been taken? The man who is sick?"

"To the healers' tent, Your Highness." The woman pointed toward the trees behind her where Lyric could see shapes moving about in a dull light. "Lady Amira will explain all when she returns."

Trying to shake off her fears, Lyric turned to the meal and ate ravenously. The venison stew was cooked to perfection, with large chunks of turnips and carrots swimming in the rich sauce. As her hunger abated, she looked about their surroundings with more interest. The area appeared to be a temporary camp with no solid structures, though several tents dotted the landscape. It was impossible to tell how many people were there.

Amira stepped out of the shadows into the flickering light of the fire. "Would you like to be shown to your quarters now, Princess?"

"How is Marek? Is he being tended?" Lyric flushed. Her questions had come out as demands, an undeserved rudeness in light of their situation. "Forgive me," she said, lowering her gaze. "You have been nothing but kind to us. My father did not raise me to repay courtesy with such behavior."

Amira nodded in acknowledgment, her face, as usual, impassive. "You are tired beyond your limitations. All is being done for him that may be done."

"Will he live?"

Amira lifted one shoulder in a delicate shrug. "It is too soon to know. He appears to be a strong man, but nothing is certain with such a wound."

Lyric gazed into the fire's dying embers. "It is my fault he is injured."

Amira raised both silvery brows. "He is your protector, is he not? He did his duty."

"Yes, but ..." Lyric wasn't certain what she wanted to say. She'd been taught since earliest childhood that her life was of more value than the lives of other people, yet these last days, Marek—Becca, too—had given more than any person should have to give for another. She glanced over her shoulder to see the maid slumped against a tree, eyes closed, deep in slumber.

She returned her gaze to her hostess. "Thank you for assisting us. You cannot know how much I appreciate it, but will you answer some of my questions now? I know it is late but there are things I must know. I will sleep later."

Amira nodded. "As you will."

"I want to know about the gemstones—Menjar and Midara. And how the Akyldi can help my father and Tressalt. But first ..." She looked closely at the other woman. "First, I need to know who the Akyldi are. We are still within the borders of Tressalt—my own nation—but until a few hours ago, I had never heard of you."

Lyric saw what may have been a smile flit across the face of the silver-haired woman. "You have many questions, but I will begin with the last." Amira stepped away from the fire and stood for a moment, hands on slender hips, looking up into the cloudy night sky. "The Akyldi are—it is difficult to describe oneself, is it not?"

She hazarded a glance at Lyric and tried again. "The Akyldi are an ancient people. We dwelt in these woods long before the people who now inhabit Tressalt came to this land. We are a peace-loving people, but in the Great War with men and the non-human denizens of Argonia, we were forced to fight." Amira paused and stared into the darkness, as if remembering those long-ago days, but Lyric's attention had been captured by her words.

"Non-human denizens?" Lyric asked. "What do you mean? Animals?"

Amira looked back at her with both kindness and sorrow. "No, not animals. I have heard it said there are no lore masters left in Tressalt, but I did not believe it. Are there truly none who remember the tales of ancient times?"

Scowling, Lyric folded her arms across her chest. "No one speaks of the ancient times—we have plenty to do in the current day. We have no lore masters. There were priests long ago, I'm told—those who taught of the Creator of all—but the last died when I was a child." Lyric shrugged. "My nurse told tales of dark creatures that haunt the forests." She hesitated, remembering the creature Becca had seen in the village. A creature Marek had heard tell of. A *Borag*. Was this one of the non-human denizens Amira spoke of?

No. She refused to believe it. Becca had been alone and frightened. She had seen only a man in the village—a large and frightening human male.

She turned her gaze back to Amira and found the woman quietly observing her. Lyric lifted her chin. "There was no truth to that old woman's tales. Just stories meant to frighten me into obedience."

"Not all strange tales told to children are fiction," Amira said. "Tell me, Your Highness, do you suppose the Divine One was so limited that he could create only one intelligent people in this world? Do you suppose I am human?"

The hair on the back of Lyric's neck prickled. She looked at the slender woman and wanted to shrink back, to run away as she had as a child. To hide under the bedclothes until the fear and darkness left her. This could not be, could it?

"You ... you look human." She gulped. "If you are not human, what are you?"

Amira dipped her head, pondering. "I am ... Akyldi." She stepped closer and Lyric had all she could do not to flinch away.

"Look," the Akyldi woman said, holding out her hands to reveal four fingers and a thumb, each with short talons instead of finger nails. Lyric looked up at her, bewildered.

"And see," Amira continued, and for the first time she opened her mouth widely enough to display sharp predator teeth. Before Lyric could respond, she lifted the sleeve of the garment she wore to reveal pale skin covered by light, silvery fur. Then, as if in final display, she scanned the small campground, then raced toward a tree on the edge of the campfire light and vaulted upward, grabbing hold of a lower branch—a ten-foot jump. She scrambled up onto the branch then sat, gazing down at Lyric.

"The Akyldi are not human, Your Highness, but we are good people. A people who want to see peace rule the land as much as you do. In this, we must both stand against people such as Ralt. Are we agreed?"

Lyric stared at the woman—the creature—she'd been conversing with, assuming she was human. Assuming she was … normal. Why would she have thought otherwise? Her heart slammed against her rib cage, even as Amira gazed at her from her perch in the tree.

"Set aside your fear," the Akyldi woman said soothingly. "I know this is difficult for you and certainly there are those in the world you should beware of, but truly, it is safe to trust me. You will not come to harm while in our care."

Lyric looked deeply into the strange silver eyes, and though she knew this woman was powerful—dangerous, even—she saw truth in those eyes. Truth, and compassion.

But intelligent—*speaking*, human-like creatures who were not human? The words rattled inside her muddled mind. How could it be possible?

But Amira was before her. Beautiful, intelligent, and caring—but not human.

"I don't know what to believe," Lyric finally whispered. "But you seem like a friend, so I shall try to be a friend in return."

"It is an important first step." Amira dipped her head. "Thank you."

CHAPTER 11: WITH THE AKYLDI

When Lyric awoke the next morning, the details of the conversation she'd had with Amira blurred with half-remembered childhood stories. Even the reality of her father's imprisonment and the overthrow of Tressalt seemed feeble in comparison. Ancient, deadly wars. Enchanted gemstones that communicated with one another. Intelligent, non-human races—some who flew, others who lived under the sea. Mythical prophecies. Things beyond her most daring imaginings.

She pulled her coverlet close about her shoulders and looked up at the cloth walls that had been her bedchamber. They undulated slightly where they stretched across the wooden framework, and she surmised a breeze had sprung up with the morning. Outside a fire crackled and snapped, and behind that, the symphony of early morning birdsong.

Across the narrow space of her chamber, the mat where Becca had slept was vacant. She yawned, wondering where the maid had gone but unable to worry much. She was still bone-tired and there were strange, amazing things she needed to consider.

According to Amira, long before the Great War she'd spoken of, the six intelligent races of Argonia had intermingled freely. After the war, with their numbers devastated, the races had been splintered. The survivors had fled to far reaches of the land, in hopes such isolation would allow them to rebuild.

What Lyric desperately wanted to know was how such things could have happened, even a thousand years ago, with no record left.

"It was a terrible time," Amira told her. "Many died, and among them, many of the scribes who could have written the tale. But for those who lived, even among the humans, there was no desire to remember—only to scrabble out a bare existence, hoping to live long enough to produce offspring, to rebuild their people."

Amira had told her about the Borags. They were just as Becca had described—hulking, manlike creatures. They'd retreated to the far mountain reaches after the War but had always been a vicious, mercenary people. Amira spoke of them with distaste. Lyric didn't know exactly why—perhaps she just wasn't ready to share her own information—but she did not tell Amira of the creature Becca had seen.

The Sheevers were winged wanderers who studied the stars and could travel great distances faster than the fastest horse. "But," Amira had said sadly, "only one of the Sheevers has been seen in many years, and she only rarely. It is believed the rest have died or left Argonia. No one knows for certain."

There were others, Amira said, the Vala and the Remnan, but even less was known of them. As the night swept on, Lyric had listened to the tale, entranced, but had been brought back to the present by the sound of a groan from the healers' tents. "But what has all this to do with me?" she'd asked. "I need to rescue my father and wrest my land back from that thief Ralt. How can this information help me?"

Amira had not answered. She'd claimed fatigue and told Lyric that the rest of the story would be best told in the light of day. She'd bid them good night and called for servants, who led Lyric and the drowsy Becca to the cloth-covered lodging among the trees.

She heard a rustling behind her and turned to see Becca push her way through the flap that covered the door. The girl reddened when she saw her mistress.

"Begging your pardon, my lady," she said, ducking her head. "I went to the healers' tent to see how Master Marek fares this morning."

"How is he?" Lyric sat up, drawing the coverlet close about her.

The maid's face clouded. "The healer says he's better, but he's white as white can be, my lady, and he still hasn't awakened."

Lyric's eyes misted, and she lowered her lids, struggling for control. At least he'd survived the night. "We must trust the healers and be thankful we found them. Or rather, they found us." She looked over at the slim girl who stood near her pallet, a pensive expression on her face. "What is it?"

The girl jumped, then looked guilty. "I'm sorry, my lady. I was just thinking about Tressalt. My sister Emana lives in the village, you know. She's married to the weaver's son, Spence. And Mistress Mari'el at the castle—she's been very kind to me." She raised her eyes to Lyric's. "I hope they are all well."

Lyric nodded, trying not to imagine what might be happening at the castle and in the village with Ralt's men running wild and unrestrained. And yes—Mari'el! The dear housekeeper had been both mother and grandmother to Lyric after her own mother died. What might be happening to her, to young Colin and others of her people, even now? How many had survived?

A soft footfall sounded outside, and Becca stepped quickly to the door. She pushed aside the flap, spoke briefly to someone, then came back in, holding a bundle of neatly folded clothing.

"Look!" Becca's eyes sparkled. "Those Akyldi people brought us new clothes. Do you think they'll fit?"

"Oh, I hope so!" Lyric scrambled to her feet and they divided the garments between them. The tunic and breeches were woven of soft but hardy fabric and fit almost perfectly. There was even underclothing—praise the Maker! Lyric wanted to laugh out loud. Clean clothing—who would have thought such a simple thing could make a person so happy?

Probably anyone else who'd worn the same clothing for five straight days.

Smiling foolishly, she pulled on her riding boots and allowed Becca to fashion her wavy locks into a sort of order.

"The Akyldi girl said if we put our own things outside the tent, they'll wash them for us too. Isn't that wonderful?" Becca's smile was radiant. "She also said that breakfast would be ready as soon as we are."

Lyric scrambled to her feet. "I'm ready *now*."

They pulled the tent flap aside and found the morning still cool beneath the thick trees. Strolling through the edge of the forest, they followed the sound of the crackling fire to the clearing where they'd sat the previous night. Other than the women who brought hot dishes to the rustic table at the fireside, they saw no one.

"Your Highness." One of the women bowed. "My Lady Amira bids you to eat and be refreshed. She will attend you when she returns."

"I thank you," Lyric said politely. "May I ask where the Lady Amira has gone?"

"I do not know, Your Highness. I am sorry."

"Sit, my lady," Becca said. "Allow me to serve you."

Lyric sat, unsettled by she knew not what, then realized it was the same thought that had plagued her ever more persistently these last days. She was the daughter of a king, in line to be the next ruler of Tressalt. By rights, she *should* be served, yet Becca and Marek had stood with her without complaint these last days, suffering the same pains and indignities. Marek bordered on death, and surely Becca was just as sore and tired from the long days in the saddle as she.

This was how her life was, though, how it had always been, and when Becca brought her food, then stood behind her as she ate, Lyric said nothing.

A short time later, movement under the trees caught Lyric's eye. Amira and two of the Akyldi guard strode into the clearing. All three were armed with long bows and wore the same travel-stained clothing as the night before.

Amira paused, speaking a word to the guards. They nodded and set off toward the tents on the north side of the clearing. Amira joined Lyric.

"Did you sleep well, Princess?"

"I did. Thank you." She glanced at the other woman's clothing. "It appears you have not?"

"I did, actually. For perhaps two of your hours. But a report came that required investigation." She lowered herself to a cushioned seat on the far side of the rough-hewn table. A moment later a servant stood at her side, holding a mug of something steaming and fragrant. The Akyldi woman took it and sipped carefully but gratefully.

"What was it?" Lyric asked. "The report, I mean. What has happened?"

"It appears to have been a false report," Amira said. "We were afraid we had been followed from the place we met you. Ralt's men were only three hours behind you, it seems. They found your campsite but have returned to the road toward Windewere."

Only three hours behind them? Her stomach clenched. If Marek hadn't forced them on despite his own injury, if the Akyldi hadn't found them when they did, they would have been captured. Even now she would be on her way back to Tressalt, a captive to Prince Ralt.

The memory of his leering face made her shudder. She glanced over her shoulder at Becca. "I want you to eat now."

The servant girl lowered her eyes. "I'm to eat when you are finished, my lady."

"I'm finished enough. It's time for you to eat."

"As you will, my lady." Becca bobbed a curtsy and crossed the meadow to the cook's tent.

Amira spooned porridge into her mouth and chewed thoughtfully. "You do not appreciate being served?"

She shook her head. "I don't know what I appreciate anymore, but time is passing. You told me last evening that I must hear the rest of your story so that my way will be clear before me. You spoke of a prophecy, and why there is more to fear than Ralt and his malcontents."

"Yes," Amira said. "Ralt and his malcontents, as you call them, are a problem, but I think more is happening than you know. We have watched him from afar and have seen the quest for power growing in him. For long, we believed him just a petty discontented princeling, drawing to his side those who shared his ambition. But something has changed. For one thing, King Torian, the prince's father, has disappeared. No one knows what has become of him." She sighed and lifted her cup, peering at Lyric over its brim. "My fear is the welfare of all Argonia may be at stake. What you decide here today may affect us all."

Lyric shivered. "I did not know King Torian was missing. I'm sorry to hear it." She leaned forward, resting her elbows on the table. "But I don't understand why what I decide could have such broad implications. All I know is I must rescue my father and rid Tressalt of our enemy. What I don't know is how I am to do this."

The Akyldi woman set her mug upon the table and stood, placing her hands in the small of her back. She stretched backward, far beyond the reach of humans, then straightened and withdrew a scrap of parchment from the folds of her cloak.

"This is a copy of a prophecy from one of our most ancient documents. As I told you last evening, Menjar and Midara are but two of the stones the Divine One gifted to the nations of Argonia, to help rule and protect the people. The prophecy came into being after the Great War and the wizard Lothar's overthrow."

Lyric took the parchment, then stilled and stared into Amira's eyes. "Lothar?" Icy fingers of fear wrapped around her throat.

"Yes," Amira replied, eyeing her closely. "Is something wrong?"

Lyric gulped, trying to remember everything Becca said after she'd returned from the village. Shamefaced, she lifted her gaze to Amira's. "I didn't tell you ... but Becca saw a Borag with some of Ralt's soldiers. They mentioned someone named Lothar."

Amira's brows jammed together. "Where was this?"

"In a village about a day's ride from Tressalt on the Old Forest Road."

"What did they say about Lothar?"

"That the Borags are coming south to join Ralt and Lothar in their war."

Amira sighed. "It is as I feared, then. We must move quickly."

Lyric looked down and scanned the parchment with its strange characters. She looked back to Amira, grimacing. "I can't read this."

Amira pursed her lips. "Of course not—I'm sorry. I'll try to translate into the common tongue." Standing, she took the parchment back, glanced over the lines, and read aloud.

> Five stones are given those of the land,
> To defend their homes—water, sky, and sand.
>
> Five stones will rise when souls agree
> To stop the dark—make evil flee.
>
> Five stones there are: onyx, jade,
> jasper, opal, amethyst.
>
> Five stones as one, will might call forth
> From earth itself—the power's source.

Amira turned her silver gaze back to Lyric and stared at her a long moment.

"The prophecy was written by one of the Sentinels—those beings the Divine One sent to help lead the peoples of Argonia in the beginning. Lothar was one of them—the

Sentinel of the Borags—but he turned away from the light and led his people against the rest." She paused, clenching and unclenching her jaw. "Ultimately, he was put down, and the prophecy was recorded in case he ever arose again."

She peered into the sky beyond the forest a long moment, then turned back to Lyric.

"I am the niece of Carnosh, king of the Akyldi, who rules far to the east in the forests of Skanzon. For millennia, the Akyldi have been the lore masters of Argonia. For us, wisdom has not died. Your legends and myths are our history. You must know these things, Princess. Only then will you be able to make the choices that will save—or doom—us all."

Lyric shivered. "Just tell me."

Amira returned to her seat by the fire. "There is a great library in the hidden city of Ashkyld. The original city of the Akyldi kings was destroyed during the Great War, but many of the scrolls and parchments were salvaged and secreted away. They are kept and protected in Ashkyld now. I wish I could take you to my uncle and he could explain, but that is a far journey and I fear ..."

"What? What do you fear?"

Amira's gaze narrowed in a very human gesture. "I fear there is no time to return to Ashkyld and read to you all the history. Lothar has returned to these shores, and apparently, Ralt has struck a bargain with him."

"But how can this be, if he died all those years ago?"

"I did not say he was dead. When he was finally defeated, Lothar was not killed but banished. To an unknown and unknowable place, it was said. To live alone for eternity, remembering the grief he caused."

Lyric snorted. "Well, obviously, it wasn't an unknowable place, if he's alive and back to his terrible ways."

"Agreed," the Akyldi woman said.

Lyric threw herself down in the shade of a large maple tree, its graceful boughs laden with leaves larger than a man's hand. For her entire life, Tressalt had been the center of her world, all that was important. And now to find out how insignificant it was—a small, remote land on the edge of a wide and dangerous world. What was she to do?

She covered her face with her hands. "What is it you want of me? Isn't it enough that Ralt has taken my kingdom and imprisoned my father? That he won't release him or stop hunting me until I give myself over to him?"

"I am sorry," Amira said, her tone soft. "But I think you can see this is much bigger than one kingdom or one king, no matter how much he is loved. Each of the peoples of Argonia was given one of the gemstones. The gem you hold is the opal stone of prophecy. I hold the jasper stone. The scholars interpret the prophecy to mean that when all the people come together and the five stones are united, power will arise that will bring about Lothar's ultimate defeat."

Lyric drew a hand across her forehead. "So what now? We need to find these other gemstones and ... connect them somehow?"

Amira nodded. "My uncle, the king, believes it's the only way to destroy the wizard. None of us has the power to do this on our own. If Lothar is stopped, Prince Ralt will also be defeated."

Overhead, the maple's pale green leaves fluttered gently in the morning breeze. Beams of sunlight floated down around them, filling the meadow with the warmth and glow of early summer. Lyric leaned her head back against the tree, trying to make sense of all she'd heard, but another thought intruded. "Wait. You said last night there are six species of humans, er ... peoples in Argonia. But the prophecy only calls for five stones. Why?"

Amira sighed, her slender brows knitting together. "The Borags also had a stone, but it obviously is not part of the prophecy."

Lyric frowned. "So the Borags have a stone, too, but we don't care about it?"

"We do not."

A dismissive answer, Lyric thought, but many of Amira's ancestors had been killed by Borags long ago, so perhaps unsurprising. "Well, how do we go about finding the others?"

"We must look for those who hold them," Amira said simply. "We search for them and when we find them, we convince them to help. The races have been sundered for millennia, so it may not be easy. But we must try."

Marek had a plan. Lyric hadn't much liked it, but at least it had made sense. They were fleeing to Graceen to implore the king to come to their aid, to send an army. But this? The beginning of a headache pulsed behind her eyes. She turned to Amira.

"We're supposed to go off into the wilderness, looking for people who may not even exist anymore, hoping they'll help us fulfill an ancient prophecy?"

Amira's nostril's flared. "If Lothar is not stopped, what happened in the last war will be as nothing compared to the destruction he will wreak now. His fury has had a thousand years to grow." A line creased her forehead. "He only ever wanted power, and he will do anything to get it."

Her new friend's patience apparently had its limits, but Lyric forced herself to speak anyway. Softly.

"If Lothar is back and he's so powerful, why hasn't he already destroyed us? Why does he need Ralt?"

Amira drained her cup and set it on the table. "It is the one limitation he has. He is very powerful, but he must work through others who willingly give him that power. Apparently Prince Ralt has done this."

She rose gracefully to her feet, eyes dark with worry.

"I will make you a bargain, Your Highness. As I said, the roads to Graceen are held against you. I ask that you go with me to search for Venuzia—the Sheever I told you about last night. She is the nearest of those rumored to carry a stone of prophecy. To find her, we must travel toward Graceen through the forest on paths the enemy does not know. If we cannot find her, or we do find her but she cannot or will not help us, I give you my word I will bring you safely to Graceen."

Lyric expelled a deep breath. It was as good a deal as she could hope for. And yet ...

She looked into the silver eyes of the other woman—this woman who was not human—then lifted her hands and dropped them in a helpless gesture.

"Thank you. I appreciate the offer. But what if, while we are on this quest, Prince Ralt decides my father's life no longer has value? How am I to make a decision that may cost my father his life? I must have time to consider."

Amira dipped her head. "Of course. We don't have much time, but we have some. I must meet with my people. You may stay here or walk about the grounds. Please don't go far." She cocked her head to the side, gaze narrowing. Then she sprang away and raced to the far side of the grassy clearing. A moment later, an Akyldi male loped into the meadow.

Lyric climbed to her feet but did not follow.

Something was wrong.

CHAPTER 12: DECISIONS

Moments later, Amira waved the newcomer toward the cooking tent and jogged back to Lyric, a frown on her face.

"My scout has informed me that Ralt's men went on to Windewere as we thought, but they're now returning with a forest tracker and his dog. They have not yet arrived at your campsite from last evening, but they are only hours away. I must meet with my people. I am afraid I cannot now give you the time you requested."

Lyric clenched her teeth. "What do you mean?"

"If the trackers are this close, we will need to leave even sooner than I'd anticipated. I cannot speak further until I talk to the others. I'll return soon."

"Wait—" But the Akyldi woman was already gone, streaking across the meadow with the speed and grace of a bird in flight.

Lyric rubbed her hand over her aching head and began walking. She'd just begun her second circuit around the circumference of the encampment when Becca found her.

"All the Akyldi have gathered in the cooking tent. Do you know what's happening, my lady? They seem very upset."

"Prince Ralt has sent trackers after us. Apparently they are not far away."

Becca clapped a hand over her mouth and joined Lyric's anxious circling of the campsite.

How was she to decide what she must do? She had only two choices—to go with Amira into unknown lands to fulfill a prophecy that might or might not help her father, or to insist they be taken immediately to Graceen.

The answer seemed obvious, but on deeper thought she realized it wasn't. There was no guarantee the King of Graceen would help them. Their countries had always been on good terms, and her family on her mother's side hailed from Graceen, but why would the king jeopardize his own people for them? There was no pact or treaty between the lands.

For generations, there had been no need for such a thing.

But to go off on this quest with Amira? It was madness. How could she even consider it? And what about Marek? He wasn't fit to travel.

But those stories Amira told—

Yes ... the stories. As she and Becca strolled under the sun-kissed trees on the edge of the Akyldi encampment, Lyric realized that despite the utter strangeness of the tales, something about them resonated with truth. Amira herself, Lyric had no doubt, believed the stories and the prophecy.

What it came down to was whether or not she believed Amira. The woman was amazing. Beautiful, kind, powerful.

And not human.

Did it matter?

Unthinking, Lyric pulled the opal stone from under her tunic, fingering it as she continued to walk. Of another thing she was completely sure—her gemstone had behaved in a manner no gem should. She'd seen the change in color, beheld the images, felt the heat.

And the Borags? Amira spoke of them. Becca had seen one. Marek knew of them.

She shivered, rubbing her hands on her arms to warm them. The world she lived in was not as she'd always believed.

They'd finished their fifth circuit of the grassy meadow when the Akyldi began exiting the cook tent. Moments later, Amira stepped out of the tent, saw them, and jogged to meet them.

"It is as I suspected, Your Highness. I'm sorry, but we must leave immediately."

Lyric shook her head. "We can't do that. Marek can't travel."

"There is no time for further discussion." Amira's words were soft but the authority in her voice was unmistakable. "My people have not been seen or recognized by humans in unnumbered years and I deem now is not the time for this to change. We must leave this place within the hour. Sooner, if possible."

"But—"

"I am sorry these things are happening so quickly, but you must decide at once. If you will have me, I will go with you to search for Venuzia," Amira said tersely. "Your guard and your servant I will send with my people. They will carry the man until he is able to carry himself. We must also send the horses with them. They will journey to Skanzon and then to Ashkyld. If they make a good escape now, they won't be caught."

Lyric caught her breath, a roaring sound filling her ears. "No. The horses? What do you mean? I can't—"

"You can't leave me, my lady!" Becca screeched, then dropped her gaze to her feet, her face reddening. "Please, Your Highness. My place is with you."

"Someone needs to care for Marek."

"The Akyldi can do it, can't they, Lady Amira?"

Amira didn't answer Becca but slanted her gaze to Lyric. "You must choose now, Your Highness. Your guard cannot travel with us in his state. He must stay with the healers. The horses leave a trail that will be easy for the tracker to follow and they will be of no help through the forests that we must travel. I would rather not take your maidservant." She turned an apologetic glance to Becca. "But that is your decision. We will travel fast. Decide quickly. I must see to my people."

Lyric watched Amira stride away, her thoughts chaotic. Her belly clenched at the thought of leaving Marek, of being without Moon Song. And what was she to do with Becca?

"You should stay with Marek," she said. "He'll need a familiar face. And I can't have you slowing us down."

"Begging your pardon, my lady," the girl said with unusual boldness, "but I think I can keep up as well as you. And Master Marek would want me to be with you. I know he would. Someone needs to watch out for you, since he can't."

"And how do you propose watching out for me?" Lyric asked, exasperated. "Are you a trained archer? Did they teach you swordplay on the farm?"

"No, my lady. I can't do any of those things." Becca blushed and turned imploring eyes on her mistress. "But I can help. I know I can. Don't leave me."

Lyric opened her mouth to argue, then stopped as Akyldi from all sides of the encampment appeared. With quick and quiet efficiency, they began taking down everything that would give a clue to the identity of those who had used this site.

Amira hadn't been exaggerating. They were leaving *now* and Lyric was sure of only one thing.

"I have to talk to Marek."

She hesitated outside the healer's tent, steadied herself with a deep breath, then pushed the flap aside and stepped in. Marek lay on a mat on the earthen floor on the far side of the tent, an Akyldi woman kneeling beside him. The woman turned to look as she entered, and Lyric saw Marek's eyes were open. Relief surged through her. She hurried to his side and knelt down next to the healer. "You're awake."

A flicker of a smile crossed the soldier's gaunt face. "So it appears." His words rose scarcely above a whisper.

The healer stood and stepped away and Lyric scooted closer, weak with gratitude. There were so many things she wanted to tell him, to ask him, but now that she was here the words fled from her, and there was no time to waste. "Do you know what's happening?"

"A little." His voice was unsteady but the gaze that held hers was clear-eyed and unwavering. "I've awakened a few times and gathered that these people are helping us, but that's about all. Who are they?"

"They're called the Akyldi, and I was hoping you'd heard of them. But there's no time to talk now. Ralt's trackers are coming after us, and we have to leave this place right away."

She paused, trying to order her thoughts, to tell him the most important of all the things she'd learned in the last twelve hours. "The road to Graceen is held against us, so we can't go that way. The Akyldi leader has told me things I've never heard before, about my stone pendant, and ancient prophecies, and other people—like the Borags—who aren't human." She shivered and met his gaze. "There is much more at stake than Tressalt, and I don't understand most of it. But I think I must go with their leader to find those who can help and ... and you can't come with us."

Marek's gaze narrowed, and he tried to sit up, but Lyric put out a hand and pushed him back down. Easily.

He closed his eyes and grimaced.

"I'm sorry," she whispered, looking away from his quiet form. "I have to go with Amira and you need to stay with the healers until you're well. Then ... I hope we will meet again."

She heard a muffled sound and looked down to see her dark-haired guard, pale as he was, grinning at her. "You could just order me to stay, you know. Then order me to find you."

"Oh!" She scrambled to her feet and didn't know whether to laugh or cry. She heard noises outside the tent and knew she had to leave, but found herself rooted to the spot.

"My lady?"

She looked down at him.

"You don't have to order me. When I'm able to travel ... nothing will stop me from finding you. I promised your father, and now I promise you."

She gulped and blinked away the tears before they could fall. "That is well, then. I will see you at that time."

"And my lady? You will take Becca with you, won't you? It would be a sore trial for her to be separated from you."

Lyric sighed. "Yes. Becca will come with me." She stood a long moment, thoughts still chaotic, before glancing back at the wounded man. His eyes were closed, his breathing deep and steady.

"Farewell, Marek," she whispered. "I hope to see you soon."

CHAPTER 13: SKYWAY

"Look up, Princess. What do you see?"

One short hour later, Lyric followed Amira's instruction and turned her gaze skyward. All she saw was the understory of the great forest, branches of the tall firs and cedars weaving into those of the next tree as far as her eye could see. She shook her head. "What am I looking for? I don't see—"

"Neither will the tracker," Amira said with a grim smile.

She gestured for Lyric and Becca to follow as she walked around one of the mammoth trees. She tilted her head back and gave a low, lilting series of whistles. A moment later, something hurtled down toward them. Before Lyric could think to jump away, the end of the object stopped its descent and banged against the tree trunk in front of her.

It was a rope ladder unlike any she'd seen before. This one was made of a green material, vines of some sort, segmented into steps by short pieces of wood, each about a forearm length from the one above it. Her gaze followed the ladder until it disappeared into the branches high above.

"My people have created, along the forest heights, a road of sorts," Amira explained. "We call it the skyway." She gestured to the ladder. "We do not normally need assistance to reach it, but we keep these on hand in case one of us is injured, or in this case, to aid those who do not have our skill in climbing."

She looked between Lyric and Becca, her gaze narrowing. "I have been told that some humans cannot abide heights—that they are terrorized by them. I trust this is not true of either of you?"

Both humans shook their heads.

"That is well. Our journey through the forest would be far slower and more difficult if we were not able to use the skyway." She turned to Lyric, gesturing to the vine ladder. "Princess, if you will go first, please."

Lyric shot a quick glance at Becca, then shifted the rucksack Amira had given her to carry and stepped toward the ladder. Grasping the parallel, vertical vines, she placed a booted foot on the first wooden rung and began to climb. Up and up she went, wondering how far before she reached the skyway.

At twenty rungs, she looked over her head but saw nothing save the ladder stretching upward before her, the trunk of the tree, and endless branches she must maneuver around as she reached them. At thirty rungs, there was still nothing new to see, but as she approached the fortieth, she saw what appeared to be a wooden platform directly overhead. The ladder continued upward through a round hole in the platform.

Knees aching, Lyric continued to climb, forcing herself up the last twenty rungs until her hands, then her head, passed through the hole in the platform. An Akyldi man stood there.

"Your Highness," he said, reaching out a hand to steady her as she stepped onto the platform.

She took his hand and looked closely at him. "Thank you. Quinn, isn't it?"

"Yes, my lady." He inclined his head.

"Will you be traveling with us, Quinn?"

"I will, my lady," he replied, then returned to his post by the ladder.

Lyric scrutinized her surroundings. It was both warmer and brighter up here in the trees than on the forest floor.

The platform she stood on was square, made of rough-hewn boards lashed together, ten paces across. It reminded Lyric of the rafts on Lake Sindish, just to the south of her castle.

There were no railings on rafts, and neither were there any here. At sixty paces above the forest floor, she was very thankful she did not fear heights.

As she looked around, she saw that the platform appeared to be a way station of sorts. Swinging bridges, hanging from even higher branches, led away from it in three different directions.

The bridges were made of lengths of thick boards, perhaps two feet long and one foot in width, tied together with the tough green vines. There were railings on the bridges, but only of the same vines, suspended about three feet above the planks.

She gulped and stepped away from the edge of the platform, heart pounding. How were they to travel on those narrow passageways with only ropes for handholds?

A few minutes later, she sensed movement below the platform opening and heard quick breathing. Soon, she saw hands on the ladder. Then Becca's head with its sandy braided hair emerged through the opening. Quinn stepped forward, as he'd done for Lyric, and reached out to assist the servant girl.

Becca thanked him, adjusted the pack on her back, and moved over to stand beside Lyric. Her eyes were huge as she scanned the platform and the off-shooting bridges. She gave a little gasp. "Is this the skyway?"

"I assume so," Lyric murmured, knowing Becca's feelings mirrored her own. Perhaps the Akyldi—graceful, lithe, and feline—could skip heedlessly along this highway through the trees, but it would be much more difficult, as well as dangerous, for the humans to attempt it.

They would be better off on the ground.

Then Amira was on the platform and she and Quinn were hauling the vine ladder up, and Lyric knew going back to the ground was out of the question. Still, she had to ask. If either she or Becca placed one foot wrong, they would not survive the fall.

"Amira?"

"Yes, Princess?"

Lyric gestured toward the skyway. "Is this how we are to travel through the trees?"

"It is."

Lyric drew a deep breath. "I ... *we* are concerned that—"

"The planks are solidly attached, Princess," Amira said, "as are the vines. They will hold. Keep your eyes up and a light hold on the vines, and all will be well."

Lyric nodded, digging deep to find the confidence Amira obviously felt. She glanced at Becca and gave her the smallest of shrugs. It didn't appear they had any choice in the matter.

Amira chuckled and when Lyric turned to look at her, the silver-eyed woman winked. "No daydreaming, though. You must pay heed to where your feet go with every step."

The two Akyldi finished their careful stacking of the ladder, and then Amira stepped to the edge of the platform to look back in the direction of the camp. She whistled again as she had when she signaled Quinn to drop the ladder, but this time with a more complex series of notes. Moments later, an answering call floated through the trees. Amira listened intently, then sent out one final short musical note and turned to the others. "All is well. The others are breaking camp. Let us go also."

Gulping, Lyric followed Quinn out onto the skyway. The planks were very solid and as long as she put one foot carefully in front of the other, slid her hands lightly along the taut vine railings, and avoided looking down, it was not difficult to keep her balance. Only thirty to forty paces separated each towering tree from the next and Lyric took to pausing at each one and leaning briefly into its solidity before venturing onto the next section.

Quinn led the way, his longbow slung over one shoulder, a quiver full of arrows over the other. He also carried a pack on his back, and a sword hung at his side. Becca walked behind Lyric, and Amira brought up the rear.

Lyric's steps soon fell into a rhythm and she forgot her fear and began enjoying their sky-high journey through the trees. She wondered when the Akyldi had built the skyway and how extensively it ran throughout the forest.

Small, brightly-colored birds flitted around them, filling the forest with their song, and gray squirrels scampered through the trees, stopping occasionally to sit up and chitter insults at the large strangers who trespassed on their paths. Lyric felt herself smiling and breathed deeply, filling her lungs with the rich woodsy air, then gasped as her leading foot landed on the edge of the plank rather than the center. She lurched forward.

"Oh, my lady!" Becca called from behind her. "Are you—"

"I'm *fine*."

Heart thudding, she clung to the vine railing and pulled herself upright. Her legs trembled, but she took another deep breath, pushed the terror away, and marched on.

Carefully.

They'd traveled along the skyway for perhaps an hour before encountering the first platform they'd seen since beginning their trek. They paused for just a few minutes, and Lyric was happy to relax and stretch her legs a little without fear of falling.

They'd just begun moving again when Quinn stopped and raised his hand for silence. The three women halted and Amira slid carefully around the humans to join Quinn at the front. Both Akyldi crouched low, peering down to the forest floor.

Amira stood and rejoined Lyric and Becca.

"It's the tracker from Windewere with his dog and two of Ralt's men. They can't see us but we don't want them hearing anything that might encourage their looking up." A scowl crossed Amira's fine features. "This tracker has been working this side of the forest for many years. He is a good tracker, if not a good person. He may have suspicions of our existence. I do not want him to learn the truth."

She signaled for Becca to turn and lead them back to the last platform. When they reached it, Lyric and Becca sat down, leaning against the trunk of the reassuringly solid tree. Lyric drew her knees up to her chest, wrapping her arms around them, while Amira stood watch. Quinn appeared shortly after.

Soon the sound of men's voices and a dog's eager whine floated upward. Even high in the tree as they were, Lyric's nerves were taut. The thought of being captured, being taken back to Ralt, made her stomach churn.

"What's that mongrel's problem now?" a voice demanded.

"Oh, nothin', good sir," another more rustic voice replied cheerfully. "Ol' Rooster thinks he's heard something, is all. He gets distracted now and again, but once he picks up a trail, he follows it until we find what we're looking for. This dog has quite a nose on him. He'll even follow a scent over water."

"Well, get him going," the first speaker grouched. "We've been at this for hours, getting deeper and deeper into the forest, and no sign of them."

"No sign?" the tracker exclaimed. "What do you call that campfire back yonder, and the hoof prints? And Rooster's eagerness on the trail? Oh, no. There's plenty of signs, sir, we just have to catch up with them that made 'em."

Lyric heard a slapping sound, as of flesh on flesh, then the tracker complaining. "Hey—watch it. What was that for?"

"That," a third voice said coolly, "is for your quick tongue and your slow pace. We'd already found the campfire and the hoof prints before we hired you. You are being paid for results. Now get us results, or I'll put an arrow in both you and that worthless hound."

"Ya didn't know your party had been joined by a group of others," Lyric heard the tracker mutter. "Someone that's leading 'em into the deep forest. I had to tell ya that. I don't know who they be or how many they are, but there's lots more than the two of you. What are ya gonna do when you find 'em, that's what I want to know."

"That's none of your affair," the cool voice said. There were more sounds of scuffling and another noise, one that made Lyric cringe.

"Awright, awright. You don't need that sword," the tracker whined, and then they heard a soft thud and the yelp of the dog. "Get on, Rooster, you lazy cuss! You heard the boss."

It was several minutes before the sound of the hunters crashing through the forest faded into the distance. Lyric saw a flicker of a smile pass between Amira and Quinn, and she thought she knew what they found amusing. If the tracker and his employers continued making that much noise, the large Akyldi group had little to fear.

Marek would be safe.

"They should have listened to the dog," Amira said after a moment. "It either heard us or caught our scent. We'll have to be more cautious."

CHAPTER 14: IN TREES AT NIGHT

They waited a half hour, giving the trackers time to get well away before resuming their own path through the trees. The skyway veered north sometime later, long before it reached the Old Road, and Lyric felt a surge of relief. She did not want to encounter any more humans. At the front of their small party, Quinn continued to set a quick pace, and Lyric thought they must have covered several miles before the sun disappeared in the west and dusk filtered into the forest.

Ahead of her in the growing darkness, Quinn ducked under a large branch and disappeared. As she approached the branch, she, too, ducked, took another careful step forward, and found they'd arrived at another platform. She stepped off the skyway's last plank onto the platform, then stood aside to make room for Becca and Amira.

The platform was the same as all the rest they'd passed that day, between eight and ten feet square, built around the trunk of the massive tree. An opening in the platform near the trunk created space for an Akyldi traveler to slide through.

There were no railings.

"This will have to do," Amira murmured to Quinn, as if continuing an earlier conversation. Quinn nodded and shrugged out of the pack he'd been carrying. Amira turned to Lyric.

"It will soon be too dark for you and Mistress Becca to walk the skyway. We'll be spending the night here."

Lyric cringed as she looked around at the tiny space. "Here?"

A smile flickered across Amira's face. "It's safer than on the ground. We are deep in the forest. Wolves, large cats, and other night predators roam these parts."

Lyric nodded. "I understand about the night creatures and the dangers on the ground, but my concern is with plummeting to my death." Then, because she wanted to make sure she was clearly understood, she added the obvious. "There are no walls."

Before Amira could reply, Quinn stepped over from where he'd been going through his pack and for the first time, she saw a trace of a smile brighten his lean features. He held a coiled length of the vine rope out to her.

She pursed her lips, uncertain what he was suggesting.

"If you like, my lady," the gray-eyed scout said softly, "we can tether you and your servant to the tree when you're ready to sleep, so you'll not fear falling in the night."

Before Lyric could tell whether he was serious or not, Amira broke in. "A good suggestion. I had not considered your fear of falling while you sleep. Another difference between our kind and yours."

Lyric narrowed her eyes. "The Akyldi do not move around in their sleep?"

"We do," Amira conceded softly, her silver eyes sparkling. "But we are always well aware of where we are—even in sleep. We do not fall."

Hmm. Lyric had no answer to that. She looked at Becca, but the servant just shrugged, uncomplaining, her blue-green eyes wide. Impulsively, Lyric reached for her hand and gave it a quick squeeze, feeling pride in this farm girl who'd gotten herself into so much more than anyone could have foretold when she went horseback riding with the princess. Lyric turned back to Amira and nodded. "As you deem best, then."

Soon the darkness was complete. A light breeze sprang up and Lyric shivered. Becca wasn't the only one who'd gotten more than she'd bargained for when she'd asked that her horse be readied that day. She, a Princess of Tressalt, was about to sleep in a tree sixty feet above the ground. And who knew what the morning would bring?

She shivered again, then remembered the extra tunic Amira had given her this morning before they'd left camp. She knelt and opened her pack, rummaging through it before finding what felt like the garment. Then her hand stilled as it bumped against something else in the pack. Something unexpected.

Carefully she pulled out what her hands had already recognized as a long dagger, positioned safely amidst her clothing in a finely tooled leather scabbard.

"Amira? When did this—" She turned to face the Akyldi woman and almost dropped the dagger. Amira held a tiny glowing object in her hand. "What is that?"

"A glow-stone from the fire mountains of the Vala." Amira looked at her curiously. "You don't have them in your land?"

Lyric stepped closer, intrigued by the light that did not flicker, a light that was not flame. "No."

Amira smiled. "So many surprises for you on this journey. Would you like to keep this one? I have another."

Mesmerized, Lyric reached out for the stone. She flinched, expecting it to be hot when Amira dropped it onto her palm, but the small rounded rock was cool to the touch. The glow it produced was piercing white, fringed by orange and yellow. Lyric tore her gaze away from it and stared at Amira. "Thank you."

For the first time since Lyric had met the Akyldi, Amira burst into laughter—a joyous, lilting sound, the noise a shallow rill makes as it rushes over rocks in its path. The sound made Lyric want to laugh too.

"You're very welcome, Princess. Many of my people have them—we keep them to use when lighting a fire is not advisable. I believe you wanted to ask me about my other gift?" She gestured toward the dagger.

"Yes." Lyric returned her attention to the blade. "This was unexpected."

"I have one as well." There was wonder in Becca's voice.

"Neither of you had weapons, and where we're going, we're likely to need them. I trust you will not be afraid to use them?"

"I've been taught to use a sword," Lyric said, "but not one of these." She handed the glow-stone back to Amira and pulled the dagger carefully from its sheath. The blade was long and wicked-looking and glinted in the light given off by the stone. It looked sharp enough to gut a fully grown boar.

Becca shivered. "If I'd known this was in my pack, I'd have been even more scared of falling off the skyway."

Lyric smiled, even as she shuddered. That thought had occurred to her as well.

"There's no time for training now, and we can't do it up here in any case," Amira said. "About midday tomorrow, we must leave the skyway and go forward through the forest. Quinn or I will show you the rudiments of dagger use then."

Lyric looked around, realizing she hadn't seen the scout since he'd offered her the vine rope. "Where is Quinn?"

Amira nodded toward the skyway. "He's gone ahead, to make sure the way is clear for us and to listen."

Lyric slid the dagger back into its sheath. "What is he listening for?"

"Not *for*. *To*. He will listen to the forest. To the trees and the creatures of the night." She handed the glow-stone to Lyric.

Lyric digested this bit of information. It had never occurred to her that one could listen to the forest. Or rather that one could listen and learn something from the forest. Shaking her head, she returned to another thought. "Why will we have to leave the skyway?"

"We are nearing the northern boundary of our forest," Amira said. "My people have covered much of the forest with the skyway, but not all. We are nearing that border."

Lyric nodded, watching as Amira glanced toward the skyway in the direction Quinn had gone, her gaze intent.

"You and Quinn ...?" Lyric began, then stopped.

Amira looked back to her, a silver brow cocked upward. "Yes?"

"You ... work very well together," Lyric said lamely, glad of the excuse to reach down and put the dagger in her pack.

"Yes," Amira agreed.

Chiding herself for her nosiness, Lyric lifted the pack and removed the extra tunic. Shaking it out, she pulled it over her head and shoulders, grateful for the added layer.

Looking around, she saw that Amira had moved to the edge of the platform, again gazing to the north.

"As you have guessed," the Akyldi woman said, "Quinn and I are life-mates. We have been together for many years, but that is not the reason I asked him to accompany us. He is the best for what we need on this journey—the best scout, the best fighter. And he has considerable healing skills. I trust him with my life."

Lyric pondered this. "And it seems I have trusted you both with our lives."

Amira turned to her, eyes thoughtful. "So it seems."

Becca stood from where she'd been searching through her pack. "Should we have dinner, then? You must be starving, my lady."

Lyric pulled her gaze from Amira's. "I am indeed. Dinner sounds wonderful."

Using the tiny light from the glow-stone, they soon found the dried meat, cheese, and bread that was spread throughout the four packs. Lyric sat with her back against the tree and was just wishing for water when she heard a quiet scrabbling from the tree trunk below them. She looked at Amira in alarm, but the Akyldi woman was untroubled.

A moment later, hands reached through the opening in the platform, and Quinn pulled himself lithely the rest of the way up. Two bulging water skins were attached to leather thongs about his neck. He handed one of the skins to Lyric and one to Amira.

"All is well, then?" Amira asked.

He nodded, his eyes never leaving hers. "All is well."

Lyric drank from the skin and passed it to Becca, considering. This was what love looked like, then? Two strong people, working together as a team, but caring for each other more than they cared for others. She knew her father had loved her mother, but it had been long since her mother died, and she had no memory of how the king and his queen had acted toward one another.

She leaned back against the tree that would be her sanctuary for the night and gazed up through the many branches to the bits of starry sky she could see above. She had known other married people, of course, and at times true affection existed between them, but other times there appeared to be no special feeling at all.

And sometimes all the feeling seemed bad.

She'd known since childhood she might one day be required to marry a man in order to form an alliance between her country and his. Or the son of one of her father's more powerful noblemen. Or the nobleman himself, no matter how old. She grimaced, remembering Lord Dalton of Bridlewood, who had approached her father last year, hoping for her hand. He was older than her father and his breath reeked of garlic and pipeweed.

And yet, if her father had asked it of her, she would have married Dalton. It was a daughter's duty, a princess's duty, after all. But her father had not asked, and even when Ralt pushed his suit, her father left the choice up to her.

Which was one of the reasons she loved him so. A lump rose in her throat.

I must find a way to save him.

Perhaps once this was all over—Ralt dealt with, and her father back on his throne where he belonged—she would look to her future and consider if there was any man in the kingdom who might one day look at her as Quinn looked at Amira.

Unbidden, her thoughts strayed to Marek. She swallowed hard, remembering how she'd watched his every move when she was a girl of fourteen training with the Guard. How crushed she'd been—how angry she'd become—when she thought he'd laughed at her.

Only he hadn't laughed. And now ... now he was wounded and ill and far away, and she didn't know if she'd ever see him again.

"Princess?" Amira's voice called softly from the far side of the huge tree trunk. "Would you like to join me in a task?"

"Hmm?" Lyric blinked. Had she dozed off? Shaking her head, she tried to clear her mind and make sense of Amira's question. "What kind of task?"

The Akyldi woman stepped around the tree trunk, holding a second glow-stone. The light cast eerie shadows on Amira's face, and the cool evening breeze ruffled her pale hair.

"I thought if we combined the forces of the seeing stones—of Midara and Menjar—perhaps we can reach Venuzia. Tomorrow we will arrive at the place where one of my clan-mates last saw her several years ago."

Reaching under her tunic, Lyric pulled out her gemstone—Menjar—and slid over to make room for the slender woman next to her. Becca sat on her other side, watching them both.

"What are we to do?" Lyric asked.

"According to the lore masters," Amira said, "there is power when even two stones of the prophecy are united. Put Menjar next to Midara. Do they fit together?"

Lyric lifted Menjar, and as the two stones touched, a sharp hiss sounded and a tiny flash of light erupted between them. Lyric gasped and jerked back, dropping the opal stone and its chain onto her lap. She stared at Amira. "What was that?"

Fine lines furrowed the Akyldi woman's forehead. "I do not know. Did you feel anything?"

Lyric shook her head. "No. But that sound? The spark?"

Still frowning, Amira held out Midara. "Let us try again."

Lyric took a deep breath, exhaled, then tapped the rose-hued, milky stone against the orange-red jasper. Again there was a brief flash, and the sibilant sound hissed through the night. Lyric bit her lip and forced herself to hold the gemstone steady against the other. After an instant the sound died away, but a throbbing sensation between the connected stones continued. She looked at Amira.

"Do you feel that? Do you know what it means?"

Amira nodded. "I feel it, but I do not know its meaning. None of the prophecies speak of such a thing. Perhaps the connection between the stones is expressed in this way. Let us try once more. Only this time, let us see if the two fit together."

Steeling herself against the spark and the hiss, Lyric set her gemstone next to Amira's, but however they turned the stones, the jagged edges did not correspond with one another.

Amira sighed. "This means that when the five stones of the prophecy are united, Midara and Menjar will be interspersed between the others. There will be less power than if they were immediate neighbors, but two together are still stronger than one alone. Or so the legend says."

"We have the opal and the jasper," Lyric murmured. "Which means we still seek the jade, the onyx, and...." She cast about in her mind, trying to remember the final stone.

"The amethyst," Amira supplied.

She nodded, recalling another of the many questions she'd hoped to ask this morning before being forced to rush from the encampment. "Who of the—the *non-human* denizens—has the other stones?"

"We believe Venuzia has the stone the Sheevers were endowed with." Amira stared into the ruddy surface of the jasper stone. "If she does not, we hope she knows who possesses it and where it can be found. Legend says the Sheevers had the amethyst. As for the others, we think the onyx—the black stone—is held by the Vala, those who live under the earth."

Lyric looked up with interest. "The Vala? Those with the glow-stones?"

"Yes. The people of the Fire Mountain trade with others occasionally. They will sell the glow-stones to those who can afford to pay, or who have something of value to trade for them."

Lyric digested this bit of information. So the Vala were merchants of a sort. Still, she'd never heard of them. "And what of the last stone? The jade?"

"The jade stone belongs to the Remnan, the sea-dwellers."

"Sea-dwellers?" She vaguely remembered Amira mentioning this but was still surprised. "How can anyone live in the sea?"

"Fish live in the sea," Amira said, smiling faintly, "as well as other strange creatures. I have never met any of the Remnan, though my uncle did when he was young, before he took the throne in Ashkyld."

"But how," Lyric began, then faltered. "I don't understand. How can those who live on land have any ... relationship with those who live under water?"

"The Remnan may leave the sea and stay on land for a short while before they must return. Of us all, they are the most separate, the most isolated. For obvious reasons."

"Were the Remnan a part of the Great War you told me about? The one that destroyed so many and divided all the peoples?"

Amira nodded. "Yes, but they were the first to pull back, to return to their homes under the waves. Unlike the rest of us, they had a place they could escape to." She paused. "Though, if Lothar had won, I don't believe it would have been long before he reached into their watery homes as well."

Amira fell silent and Lyric tried to push the doors of her mind open a little wider, to absorb this information that even yesterday would have made her scoff.

"My lady," Becca said softly. "You know what this reminds me of?"

In the darkness, Lyric shook her head. She was too tired for guessing games.

"The tapestries in the Great Hall." Becca answered her own question. "When I was helping clean and decorate the hall for the Solstice Ball, I was amazed by the tapestries. Don't you agree? Some are of battles—most of soldiers on foot or horseback. But some show winged creatures and others of people coming up out of the sea to fight. You must know the ones I mean."

Lyric sat up, eyes wide. The tapestries were spread throughout the castle. She'd seen them every day of her life and never given them more than a passing thought. They told stories of ancient myths she'd been told as a child, entertaining and beautifully woven, but that was all.

Wasn't it?

There was one near the third-floor stairway that showed people she now recognized as Akyldi. Slender and fine-featured with no facial hair. Archers, most of them, ferocious. They wore armor unlike anything the humans had worn.

And Borags, certainly. Wolfish but on two legs. The winged Sheevers, and fierce warriors—the Remnan—arising from the sea.

The truth had been before her eyes all along and she'd never seen it.

CHAPTER 15: ATTACKED

Lyric bent low to avoid striking her head on the trunk of a half-fallen fir that lay across the miserable forest track. Straightening, she saw Amira disappear around a standing tree ahead of them, and she scurried to catch up. Her foot caught in a thorny bramble and she pitched forward, saved from striking the ground only by Quinn's swift strong arm.

"Carefully, my lady," the scout murmured, setting her back on both feet.

"I never thought I'd miss the skyway," she whispered to Becca as the maid caught up with her. Gritting her teeth, she moved on after Amira, being mindful once again to place each foot with care.

That part at least hadn't changed.

Amira and Lyric had spent more than an hour the night before trying to reach out to Venuzia with their gemstones. Bracing herself against the spark as the stones brushed against each other, Lyric sat shoulder to shoulder with Amira. The thrum of the stones' connection remained steady as Amira murmured words in a language Lyric did not know.

Neither apparently did anyone else, because nothing happened. As the evening grew cooler and Lyric's yawns became more pronounced, the two finally gave up.

They awoke with the dawn, alive and still on the platform, thanks to Quinn's vine rope that linked her and

Becca to the tree. After eating a quick breakfast of dried meat and berries, they began the final portion of their journey on the skyway. When they'd come down out of the trees just before noon, Quinn and Amira spent several minutes showing them how to hold and use their Akyldi-made daggers.

It wasn't terribly different from the short sword Lyric had learned to use when practicing with the King's Guard, except of course the enemy would be much closer. The dagger could be thrown as well, but that tactic would require skill that neither girl possessed.

Becca voiced Lyric's own thoughts as they began their march along the forest floor. "Maybe I'll get better at this one day, my lady, but I hope we are not beset by enemies any time soon."

As the afternoon wore on, heat set in, and soon they were besieged by buzzing, biting insects. As Lyric slapped what felt like the hundredth bug that landed on her exposed flesh, she was struck with an overwhelming desire to sit down on the forest floor, and cry. But of course that was ridiculous. Just the sight of Amira marching on ahead, back straight and uncomplaining, drove all thoughts of temper tantrums away.

Besides, what would such behavior say to Becca, after Lyric had so ungraciously suggested that the maid wouldn't be able to keep up on this journey? And what would Marek say, if he was here to observe?

He wouldn't say anything, Lyric thought miserably. He would be as he always had, helpful and kind, but in her heart she was certain he would be disappointed with her, and she couldn't stand the thought.

So she kept going, slapping at the bugs, ignoring her hunger. She didn't cry.

She'd just untangled herself from yet another encounter with some especially spiky brambles when she saw Amira jerk to a halt and spin around. Lyric looked over her shoulder to see Quinn staring down the trail they'd just made through the thick undergrowth. Lyric saw nothing but the endless forest. She turned back to Amira. "What?"

Amira put a finger to her lips, then tipped her head to the side, listening.

A moment later, Quinn leaped over the small bushes between them and grasped Lyric and Becca by the hands. "Hurry!"

They didn't need to be told twice. She and Becca raced beside Quinn as fast as their legs would take them, tripping and thrashing over the bushes. Amira stepped behind one of the massive pine trees, pulled an arrow from the quiver on her shoulder and fit it to the longbow.

"Go!" she ordered as they drew near. "Get them to safety. I'll hold them off."

"What—?" Lyric tried again, but Quinn's pace never slackened. They crashed through the vine maples, ivy, and nettles, and all Lyric could think of was Amira facing something terrible behind them by herself.

The farther they ran from the danger, the more Lyric knew they shouldn't.

"Quinn!" she demanded. "Stop! We must stop!"

"We cannot," he answered, still dragging them forward. "We are being pursued. They are moving swiftly."

They burst through the thick forest into a large clearing made, it seemed, by a forest fire from years past.

"Stop, Quinn!" she cried again. "Go help Amira. We'll hide until you come back."

Quinn slowed his pace, stopped, and dropped their hands. He whirled around, indecision flickering in his strange, otherworldly eyes. Blackened tree trunks stood among the shattered sections of burned logs that littered the area, while new grass and fast-growing shrubbery attempted to reclaim life from the desolation.

Lyric looked across the clearing and spied what appeared to be large standing stones amidst a huge, misshapen stack of rocky rubble, overgrown with ferns and mosses.

"Go back for her, Quinn," she gasped. "We'll be all right. We'll hide over there."

Quinn saw the rock and his indecision faded.

"Quickly, then." He led them across the clearing and around to the far side of the standing rocks. "In here," he said, pointing to a small alcove between the rocks. "Get your daggers out and be ready. Keep very quiet."

Without another word, he leapt to the trail they'd just made and raced back in the direction where they'd left Amira.

Lyric put her hand to her chest, feeling that her heaving heart was about to burst through her ribs. She looked at Becca and saw fear in her eyes. What was back there in the forest? Would Quinn and Amira be able to hold them off?

"Come." Lyric led the way into the space Quinn had pointed out. As she eyed the rock around them more closely, she realized it wasn't *rock* she was seeing, but rock-work. These were ancient stone walls, crumbling, fallen, leaning against one another in the midst of the deep forest. She sucked in a breath. *What was this place?*

The opening was narrow between the two main walls, but once they'd squeezed through, they found they were in a flattened area almost completely enclosed by the immense, jagged remnants of what might have been a stone tower, perhaps thirty feet high.

The girls looked at each other, then shrugged out of their packs and found their daggers. Fastening the leather belts that held the scabbards around their waists, they slid the sharp blades into the scabbards and sat down to wait.

All was silent around them. It was warm on the edge of the clearing, but no birds sang, no squirrels scolded and skirmished. It was as if the forest itself held its breath.

Waiting.

Lyric shivered, and her arms crawled with gooseflesh. As she rubbed them furiously, she also realized the forest wasn't as silent as she'd thought. In the distance, back the way they had come, she could hear the muted sound of shouts and something else. Something howling.

"What *is* that?" Becca whispered.

Lyric tried to swallow her panic. "I don't know."

And then the forest truly was silent.

Minutes later, she heard hurried footsteps approaching. She scrambled to her feet and pulled out the dagger, clenching it in both hands, facing the narrow opening between the old rock walls. Becca copied her, and though the girl's eyes were wide with terror, the hands holding the blade did not tremble.

"Princess!"

Quinn.

Weak with relief, Lyric stepped out of their tiny fortress, then froze. Quinn was supporting Amira, who was white as death and bleeding from a gash on her forehead. Blood oozed from several other wounds as well, and her left arm hung limply at her side. Her quiver was empty and the sword she held in her right hand was bloodied.

"Borags," Quinn reported grimly. "A large group. They have pulled back, but not for long."

"We must find a place of safety," Amira said, her voice raspy.

Lyric scanned their surroundings. The fallen shards of what had once been walls—possibly a small castle's walls—littered the countryside, along with the blackened leftovers of the fire. There was nothing else but trees. If there was safety in their path to the north, it wasn't visible. Looking at Quinn's worried face, she saw he agreed.

"I fear this is the best we can do," Lyric said. "At least here we have the old walls to hide behind." She pointed to the space where she and Becca had hidden. "Take Amira in there and help her if you can. We'll go to the front and keep watch."

Quinn nodded. "If you see anything, anything at all—call for me." He slung Amira's uninjured arm over his shoulder, wrapped his arm around her waist, and led her into the shelter. Amira's eyes were half-closed, but she still managed to carry most of her own weight.

Lyric crept to the front of the ancient shelter, her gaze on the far side of the clearing. Becca followed. No tower-wall alcoves here as in the back, but the crumbling walls offered support for their backs and chunks of the fallen rock-work on the ground before them were large enough to stand behind. They could only hope they saw the enemy before they themselves were seen.

She glanced at the dagger in her hand. At best, she might be able to stop one attacker with it before they were overrun.

"I'll be right back," she whispered to Becca. "Shout if you see anything." Not giving the other girl a chance to reply, she slipped away to the alcove in the back.

Amira sat on the floor, her back pressed against the rock wall, while Quinn wrapped a cloth around the laceration on her head. Both Akyldi stared at the door as she entered.

"I can shoot," she said. At their bewildered looks, she hurriedly added, "I've been trained with the bow. I can shoot." She held up the long knife. "I don't know how helpful I will be with this, but if someone lends me a bow and some arrows, I can help hold them off." She tried to control the trembling that suddenly seized her voice as she realized what she was saying. Her skill with the bow was good, but she'd never shot at anything but a stationary target.

Her gaze flickered to Amira, to the blood she had already shed trying to defend them all. If it weren't for her and Becca, the Akyldi could have been far out of harm's way by now. She thought of Marek and her father and others who had suffered for her, and sudden determination lanced through her. She lifted her chin defiantly.

"I can kill, and I will, if I have to."

CHAPTER 16: TO LIVE OR DIE

The Akyldi looked at each other, then Quinn reached for Amira's bow that stood propped against the rock wall. He handed it to Lyric, then pulled a handful of arrows out of his own quiver and held them out to her.

"Call me the moment you see them," he murmured, and turned his attention back to Amira.

Lyric nodded and left the alcove. Blackened earth surrounded the remnants of the ancient structure. By the looks of the re-growing shrubbery, though, it was apparent the fire had been more recent than the fall of the building. Perhaps a lightning strike? She didn't know and couldn't fret about it now. The forest itself lay about two hundred paces from the fallen walls. If they were overrun by the enemy, could they reach the trees and whatever feeble safety the woods could provide?

No.

Amira couldn't run, and they wouldn't leave her.

She returned to the far side of their rocky fortress. Becca crouched behind one of the crumbling fragments of fallen wall, peering across the scorched open space that surrounded the ruins of whatever this place had been.

If time could be measured in heartbeats, it seemed a lifetime before Lyric heard a sound, but when she did, it came from behind her. She whirled to see Quinn picking his way around the rocks. His bow was slung over his shoulder next to the quiver, and he carried both his and Amira's swords.

"Mistress Becca," he said softly. "Would you stay with Amira and do what you can to protect her, if it comes to that? I believe your lady and I have the best chance of stopping the enemy from this quarter."

Becca opened her mouth to protest but Lyric caught her eye and nodded.

"It's all right," she whispered. "Do what you can for Amira. Go on, now."

Blinking away tears, Becca grasped Lyric's hand. "Be careful, my lady." Sliding her dagger into the sheath at her side, she hurried back to the alcove.

"How bad are Amira's injuries?"

"Her arm is broken. The Borags attacked in force and she'd used all her arrows by the time I got to her. She killed or injured many."

Lyric couldn't miss the pride in the scout's voice as he described his mate's skill. Even in this terrible situation, when there was every possibility that none of them would survive the coming assault, she was comforted knowing at least these two had found love.

"She climbed into a tree and shot from there," Quinn went on, his gaze never leaving the forest from where the enemy would soon come. "One of the Borags threw a large rock and it struck her in the head. I saw her fall. She landed on her arm, but was on her feet and slew the Borag with her sword before I could reach her."

"How many Borags are there?"

"I am not sure," he said, shaking his head. "Ten or more were injured or killed. At least that many still live. They are good fighters, but their greatest strength is in their numbers."

"Do you think they'll keep coming? Is it possible they'll just give up, since they've lost so many already?"

He must have heard the hope in her voice. The ghost of a smile flickered across his pale face. "That is not the way of Borags. They have a sort of mindless rage that does not allow them to turn back. Unless someone in authority orders them to stop, they will keep coming until there are none left to come."

He turned to her and quirked an eyebrow in a gesture that reminded her of Amira. "You had better get an arrow out. It won't be long now."

She did as she was told and, despite her terror over the coming assault, was pleased she had the strength to draw the string back. She hoped she'd keep her wits. She inhaled deeply, exhaled slowly. It was possible, even probable she would die this day, but she was the daughter of a king. If she was to die, she would take as many of the enemy with her as she could.

She peered out from behind the tallest section of the wall's rubble. Three upright figures, covered in short fur but also clothed in rough shirts and pants, moved stealthily from tree to tree. They had dog-like muzzles and sharp teeth she could see from here.

As they worked their way closer to the edge of the clearing, Lyric was struck with their similarity to the images stitched into the tapestries throughout her castle. She shook her head. If she'd only known ….

"Do you see them, Princess?"

She nodded.

"Can you shoot that far?"

She nodded again.

"On the count of three, then," Quinn said. "Step out from behind the rock. Take the one on the left and I'll aim for the one on the right. Don't wait to see if you've hit him— step back behind the rock, nock your next arrow and shoot again."

Lyric drew the bowstring back, taking careful aim at the creature approaching on the left, the creature she was about to kill without his ever seeing the death that came for him.

"One," Quinn whispered.

She willed herself to hold the bow steady.

"Two."

She focused her gaze on her enemy.

"Three."

She stepped out, released the arrow, and an instant later both Borags pitched back to the forest floor. The third jumped forward, and he, too, went down immediately, a feathered arrow in his throat. Lyric was bewildered. What ...?

Quinn pulled her behind the standing stone. "Set another arrow, Princess."

Yes. Yes. She wasn't supposed to watch. She was supposed to ready another arrow, shoot another enemy, the way Quinn just had. Quickly. *Stop them before they stop me.*

She whipped another arrow out of her quiver, nocked it and drew again. But when she looked toward her next target, there were none to be seen.

Quinn stood beside her, keen eyes searching the forest.

"That was just the advance party," he murmured. "Now they know where we're defending from. I think you killed your Borag. At any rate you slowed him down. Very good." He gave her the briefest of smiles.

"I don't understand," Lyric said. Despite her best efforts, she couldn't keep the tremor from her voice. "Why do they keep attacking when their people are being killed? Why don't they just go back? Why do they want to kill us? We've done nothing to them."

"I don't know," he said softly. "I only know I would rather kill then be killed."

"I don't want to do either," she choked out, trying to speak over the lump that clogged her throat.

He looked at her with his alien gray eyes, then reached across the space separating them and gave her shoulder a quick squeeze. Then he turned back to stare across the clearing.

"Sometimes we are given no choice."

They had not seen anything move across the clearing for some time. Lyric hoped that Quinn had been wrong—that the Borags had indeed given up and gone their way—and when the attack came, it did not come from the direction they'd expected. The Akyldi scout had tilted his head to the side, listening intently, but even he had not sensed the movements of their enemy until almost too late.

"Over there!" he cried, pointing into the woods on Lyric's side, then turned and shot at a Borag rushing toward him from the right who swung a battle ax. Lyric let fly an arrow that struck an attacker barely fifty paces from her and immediately whipped out another arrow. She would not repeat her earlier mistake.

The Borags had circled the clearing and were attacking from both sides. There were far more than Quinn had estimated. They raced out of the forest toward the two defenders, roaring as they came, heedless of their fallen comrades. Lyric fired and fired until she reached for another arrow and found the quiver empty.

"The sword!" Quinn ordered, as he continued to draw arrow after arrow from his quiver and shoot with mind-numbing speed.

Lyric dropped down behind the rock she'd used for protection and clasped Amira's sword, knowing she was about to die, knowing there was nothing to do but fight until she could fight no more. Lifting the sword, she stood and faced the enemy, struck by the sudden silence. The Borags were no longer roaring and rushing at them. The creatures stood in place scarcely thirty paces away, glaring at them with toothy, carnivorous glee.

She glanced at Quinn and saw why. He, too, was out of arrows. He stood beside her with sword drawn, watching the circle of their enemy closing in.

"Aha," one of the Borags growled. "Your arrows are gone. How unfortunate." His voice was both snarling and guttural but, as Becca had said, understandable. He stepped closer, pointing at them with the long pike he held. "You have killed many of my people and that makes me angry. Now it is your turn to die." He took another step toward them.

"Why did you attack us?" Lyric screamed, unable to stop herself. "We have done nothing to you!"

The Borag leader turned his gaze upon her. "Is this a human female? I had thought you were all foolish tree-climbers. Come out to us, missy, and we will answer all your questions." He beckoned to her with his free arm and smiled, exposing jagged yellow teeth. The dozen or so of his remaining followers howled in laughter that sounded like wolves descending on a wounded deer.

As a group, they moved closer. Lyric's gaze focused on the pike. It would skewer them to the rock wall at their back long before the Borag came within sword's reach.

"Do what you can," Quinn said to her, his voice soft but resolute.

She found herself wondering if her father was still alive, and if he was, if he would ever know what had happened to his daughter in this far-off forest. She thought about Becca and Amira, sad that they would die soon after Quinn and her. Then she shook herself and stood taller and gripped the Akyldi sword for the final assault.

"I will," she murmured, more to herself than to Quinn.

The Borags continued their snarls and wolfish howls and stepped forward, brandishing spears and swords, pikes and battle-axes.

The shadow of something immense darkened the sun and floated over the ground between them. A keening wail shivered the air. The Borags stared up in surprise, then disbelief. Some at the back of the circle turned and ran to the protection of the trees, yipping like terrified hounds.

Lyric didn't want to look away from the death she had already accepted, but something was happening. She stood frozen, half-aware of her surroundings, and stared at the horrified Borags.

The leader roared at his followers, ordering them to stand their ground and fight. He held up the pike, jabbing at the sky, defying whatever was coming. The last Lyric saw of him, he was slammed aside, along with several of his followers, by something large and brilliantly feathered. Massive talons reached down to snatch up the leader, and the giant bird flew skyward, forty, then fifty feet. At sixty feet, the bird's talons opened and the Borag fell roaring, only to smash into a cluster of downed trees and rock at the edge of the burned clearing. He did not move again.

The rest of the Borags dropped their weapons and fled. The bird plummeted to the earth again, its high-pitched wail sending shivers down Lyric's spine. It grabbed two more of the retreating Borags, flew up with them as before, and flung them to the earth. The remaining Borags disappeared into the forest.

Then the great bird arced around the clearing, soaring lower with each circuit, finally landing some twenty feet from where Lyric and Quinn stood. The creature's head was ten feet above the ground, and everything about its appearance and bearing screamed *bird of prey*. Everything except its plumage. Feathers in brilliant reds, golds, blues, and greens covered the immense beast. No hawk or eagle had ever had such bright plumage, or reached a quarter of its size.

As the bird settled on the ground and gathered its wings to itself, Lyric could see what she'd not been able to see before. On top of the huge bird, at the point where the powerful neck slid back to meet the enormous wings, sat the wildest-looking woman Lyric had ever seen. Her hair was the red of deep sunset, shot through with gold, and it billowed about her bare shoulders. She was muscled and powerful, and the garment she wore matched the plumage of the bird.

The woman turned fierce dark eyes to survey them. She unstrapped herself from the bindings holding her on to the bird's back and tossed one end of a rope ladder to the ground. Then she threw one leg over the feathered back and scampered down the ladder. Dropping the last few feet, she lost her balance and landed on her backside.

Lyric gasped.

Climbing to her feet, the woman brushed dust off her clothing that was now the plain brown of peasant garb, then whirled to face them. Wrinkled and aged—not the muscular, powerful form on the great bird—the woman's watery blue eyes darted rapidly between Lyric and Quinn.

"Someone was looking for Venuzia," she said, her voice as dry as fallen autumn leaves. Throwing her scrawny arms wide, she cackled and gestured to the giant bird. "We are here."

CHAPTER 17: VENUZIA

Lyric gawked at the ancient woman. "You're Venuzia?"

"That's what I said, isn't it? It *is* what I said—ha!" The crone cackled, clearly enjoying her own wit. "Who are you? And where's the one I saw in the stone?"

Lyric found her voice. "I am Lyric dru' Septim, daughter of King Sander of Tressalt. This is Quinn, of the Akyldi people."

"A princess, eh?" Venuzia ran her bright, bird-like eyes up and down Lyric's form. "You don't look much like a princess. Don't they know how to dress royalty down there in Tressalt? And what's a princess from the southlands want with Venuzia, other than rescuing from those wretched dog-men?" She slapped her hand on her thigh, chortling, then turned and looked over her shoulder. "Though that was the most fun we've had in ages, wasn't it, Zia, my girl?"

Lyric followed the old woman's gaze and gasped. Venuzia's huge mount's brilliant plumage had faded to browns and grays, just as her human counterpart's clothing had done. The bird had lost nothing of its proud, predatory bearing, though, still looking every inch the raptor. Lyric looked over her shoulder at Quinn and saw he was as stunned as she.

Venuzia turned back to them. "I can see you're both a bit addled, but are you able to answer my question or not? Where's that female who was calling to me with the stone? She, at least, seemed to have some sense."

Lyric caught her breath, deciding the woman was right about one thing—she felt completely addled. So who was Venuzia? The woman, the bird, or both together? She shook her head. That was an answer she'd probably have to wait for. "She's been injured. Come, we'll take you to her."

Lyric stepped out from the shelter of the boulders and found that Venuzia, the woman, stood only as tall as Lyric's shoulder. At least *this* Venuzia did. It was difficult to erase the vision of the warrior woman astride the great bird from her mind. Leading the way, she strode around the piled rocks and debris to the tiny alcove on the far side.

As they neared the entrance, Becca jumped out and grasped Lyric's hand. "Oh, my lady—we were so worried! All that noise and—" She stopped, eyes wide, looking over Lyric's shoulder.

"Becca," Lyric said, squeezing the girl's hand. "This is Venuzia. We all owe her our lives."

"So," Lyric said later that night, trying to understand. "A Sheever is not one *being,* then, but two. Together?"

"That's right," the old woman said, stirring the contents of a kettle over the crackling fire. "Two that become one and are more powerful than either by themselves. My name was ..." She paused, tilting her head to the side. The hand that held the spoon stilled. "Before I met Zia, before the ceremony that bonded us. Oh, I remember." She cackled and resumed her stirring. "Venas! That's who I used to be. A long time ago."

Lyric sat cross-legged on the earthen floor of the Sheever's cave, high among the eastern peaks of the Grimwood Mountains. Once Venuzia had met Amira and was convinced they were telling the truth about their mission, she'd offered them better shelter than that provided by the forest or the castle ruins.

"You're all pretty scrawny," the old woman had declared. "Zia can take three of us at a time. Who's going first?"

Lyric had eyed the raptor with doubt, and Zia seemed to know she was being scrutinized. While the others discussed how their transport would best be managed, the bird turned her scornful predator eyes on Lyric, stared a long moment, then blinked once and turned away.

Lyric gulped.

"Stop that, Zia!" Venuzia swatted at the bird. "You're upsetting the princess!"

In the end, it was decided that Becca and Amira would go first, so the injured woman would not be alone while awaiting the rest of them. Quinn stayed behind with Lyric, in the unlikely event the Borags returned.

Becca had yelped with glee, her eyes ablaze, when Zia launched into the air, but that had not been Lyric's experience. If she lived a century of years, she knew she'd never forget sitting astride the giant bird when it was her and Quinn's turn to be carried away. The wind buffeted her like the worst of hurricanes, tearing her breath away. If she hadn't been strapped on, if she hadn't had Venuzia's warrior presence to cling to in front and Quinn's strong arms holding her in back, she was sure she'd have plummeted to her death. Her stomach she'd left far below in the soot-blackened clearing.

Since childhood she'd dreamed of flying, but she'd never once imagined the dream would come true. And she wasn't sure she ever wanted to do it again.

"But how did it come about?" she asked now. "This connection you have with Zia? Did you grow up together?"

"Don't they arrange marriages down south in Tressalt? Well, it's like that. Only these *marriages* last a whole lot longer." Venuzia chortled, then reached up with the hand holding the stirring spoon and scratched her head. Lyric looked away, trying not to think of hair, dirt, and pine needles landing in the soup.

Venuzia went on as if nothing out of the ordinary had happened.

"The human side of the Sheevers have looked after the birds since ... well, since the beginning. Whenever that was." The old woman shrugged her frail shoulders. "In the spring of the year—the fourth full moon after the winter solstice, to be precise—was when they formed the partnerships. All the clans flew in from the far corners and met in a wonderfully huge meadow high in the mountains south of here. There was singing and dancing and eating and flying—such a fine time it was." Venuzia sighed and once again stopped stirring, her pale eyes seeing things Lyric could not.

"Anyway, that's how it happened. The keeper of the birds brought in the ones who'd come of age that year, and we children who'd turned twelve came, too. They lined us up across from each other, us little kids and those big birds. Then the names of the matches were announced. And there I was, looking up into the eyes of my Zia." The aged woman sniffed, ran a hand across her eyes. "She was the most beautiful thing I'd ever seen."

A log on the cook fire cracked and split apart. Lyric sat back, trying to envision those long-ago festivals, happy times when children ran playing in meadows and great birds and their riders swooped through the purple twilit sky. A deep stillness filled her heart, and it was a long moment before more questions pressed in. "But how do you—?"

"How what?" Venuzia asked, shaking dried herbs from a small clay vessel into the kettle.

"You ... change," Lyric said tentatively. "You and Zia, both. When you're together—"

"We're amazing, aren't we?" The old woman's eyes lit up. Then the light dimmed and she turned back to the fire. "And when we're apart, we're ... old. Yep, that's it. We're old and gray and feeble."

"But how—?"

"How should I know *how?*" the old woman snapped. "It just is, that's all. It's how it's always been. It's the way the Creator wanted it, I suppose. Zia and I have been together for more than a hundred years and we've seen a lot in this world. But it won't last forever. Nothing does."

Lyric didn't know what to say and decided that perhaps she needn't say anything. She leaned back against the ancient tree trunk that supported the cave's roof, savoring the light and warmth of the fire and the tantalizing odor of the cooking soup. She pondered all she'd learned in the days since she'd left her castle to go for a carefree ride in the country, about all the things she'd never known as the daughter of a king.

"It's funny when you think about it," Venuzia said in a less-than-amused tone. "People thinking—the people who knew anything about us at all, anyway—that we Sheevers were singular winged creatures. My people used to have such fun laughing at the joke. But there's nobody left to make the jokes now, and no one to enjoy them either."

Lyric wished she could say something to bring the smile back to the odd little woman's face, but found she couldn't. "You are the last, then?" she finally asked.

"Yes," Venuzia replied, not turning from her task. "Zia and I, we're the last of the Sheevers. Not a lot of us survived the Great War. We built back up after that, of course, but never to what we were before the war, if the stories can be believed. Chicks died in the egg that shouldn't have, and there were fewer matches for the children. Rumor had it that some grew up and left the Sheever villages, joining the humans on the plains, pretending to *be* them. They never came back." She shook her head, causing her flyaway white hair to wave and fall against her pink scalp.

"But these last sixty or seventy years have been the worst. The plague that killed so many humans? It hit us Sheevers, too. We had even less defense against it than the humans. My mother, father ... all my sisters. Gone." The old woman paused, swiped the back of her hand over her eyes. "There were only thirty or so of us left when the last plague hit. Zia and I went looking for them after things settled down, and they were gone—all of them. Zia and I were the only ones spared. I've asked the Creator *why* every day since then, but he's never answered me."

Lyric heard a rustle behind her and turned from the bleakness in Venuzia's voice to see Becca entering the cave from a small side cavern. "How is Amira?"

"Better, I think. Quinn has medicines. He dressed her wounds and gave her a drink that makes the pain go away and helps her sleep." Becca frowned. "I've never heard of such a thing, my lady. Have you? I wish we'd had something like that for Master Marek."

"He's able to receive it now, if he needs it," Lyric said. "And yes—the Akyldi seem to know far more about healing than we do. We must learn all we can from them."

"Master Marek?" Venuzia said, still stirring the simmering brew that was causing Lyric's stomach to rumble. "Who's he?"

Lyric stared at her interlocked fingers, wondering how to describe the soldier to whom she owed so much, the one she'd despised for so long and now found herself missing every day.

"He was a member of the king's palace guard. My father sent him with Becca and me as escort on our day trip away from Tressalt."

"And that's when that scoundrel Ralt and his folk struck your castle?"

Lyric nodded. "Yes. Marek was attacked and injured later that day, trying to discover what had happened at the castle. He got us away and kept us safe until the Akyldi found us."

"Sounds like someone you'd want to keep around," Venuzia said gruffly. "Where is he now?"

"With the Akyldi healers. On their way to Ashkyld."

"Will he rejoin you when he's healed?"

"I hope so." The words spilled out with more feeling than she'd expected. She looked up into the knowing gaze of Venuzia, and lifted her chin, embarrassed. "He will come when he can. He loves Tressalt and my father as much as I do."

"I doubt that." Venuzia turned back to her kettle. "A soldier's loyalty is very different from a daughter's love. Still, loyalty is not to be scoffed at in days like these. Food's ready. Somebody get Quinn. He can eat while his lady rests."

"I am here," said a soft voice.

Lyric glanced over her shoulder. As usual, she hadn't heard Quinn's approach. Lines of care etched the pale skin around his gray eyes, but when he felt her gaze upon him, he looked up and a fleeting smile lightened his countenance.

Just hours earlier, she'd been about to die, shoulder to shoulder with this man— someone she'd only met days ago. And it occurred to her, as she thought of Amira resting in the back cavern, and glancing from Quinn to Becca to Venuzia, that even without Marek's presence, she had more friends—true friends—than she'd had in her entire life as princess of a realm.

She wished her homeland had not been overthrown. She hoped, more than anything, that her father still lived. But she wasn't sorry she was in this place, near the top of the world, in the company of these allies.

CHAPTER 18: WITH THE HEALERS

Marek pushed himself up to a sitting position and scanned the forest about him. He had little memory of the last days' journey—sleep holding him captive both morning and night. He was jolted to wakefulness only when the men carrying his stretcher stumbled over the uneven ground, or when the pain from the wound in his side returned with unbridled ferocity. At those times, it was only moments before a quiet-footed healer appeared and poured a bland-tasting liquid down his throat. And soon the pain would recede, and with it his ability to remain conscious.

As if in response to his thoughts, one of the healers appeared out of the woods to his left and moved through the ferns toward him.

"You're sitting up, master." The soft-spoken girl with silky bronze hair was the younger of the two healers. "You are feeling better, then?"

Marek smiled at her. "Yes, thanks to you and your people. Isme, isn't it?"

The girl nodded gravely. "Yes, sir. We are pleased to have been of assistance."

Marek looked around the meadow. "Where are the others? Why have we stopped?" Though the sun itself could not be seen under the canopy of the dense forest, the deep green shadows were shot through with gold light from above. Still daylight, then.

The healer knit her dark brows together, looking troubled. "Our scouts say we are still being followed. There are not many of them—only three and a tracking dog. We had thought to be far away by this time, but ..." The young woman stopped, seeming unsure what else to say.

Marek grimaced. "But you're being slowed down by an invalid."

The girl looked at him and smiled ruefully.

"It is as you say, sir. But you are not a burden to us. You, too, are trying to stand against what is evil in the world."

"Trying, yes." He blinked and shook his head, attempting to push away the returning weariness. "What are we doing now, then? Waiting for the trackers to catch us?" He smiled, not wanting to distress the girl more than she already appeared to be.

"In a way, yes," she murmured, her smile disappearing. After a moment's seeming indecision, she sank to the forest floor next to him and looked back the way she had come. "It is not the way of the Akyldi to attack unannounced, but these trackers must be stopped. We cannot allow them to follow us deeper into the forest toward our home."

"I'm sorry," Marek said. In his brief moments of clarity, he'd appreciated what he'd seen in the Akyldi. They were unlike any people he'd ever encountered, and he didn't know what to make of them, though he was certainly grateful for their care. Hoping to avoid killing was something he could appreciate.

Sometimes, though, it could not be avoided. It was the way of the world they lived in.

Isme kept her eyes on the far woods. "My betrothed is one of those sent to stop the trackers. He will do his duty, but it is hard." She was silent a long moment, then turned back to him. "It will be over quickly. They will not suffer and are unlikely to know what struck them."

Marek nodded but said nothing. There was little left to say, and nothing he could do. He lay back on his mat, looking up to where the towering evergreens touched the pale blue of the sky. A summer breeze whispered through the pine-scented branches and played across his face. Mesmerized by the sight, sound, and touch of the living forest, he slid back into sleep.

When he awoke, the darkness was deep, but he heard muffled words and then the soft voice of someone nearby, holding something cool to his lips, instructing him to drink. He drank.

It was still dark when, despite the power of the Akyldi elixir, he was awakened again. A whining sound and something cold and wet touched his hand, pulling him from his sleep. Then a gruff voice issued a command and he was vaguely aware of something receding into the brush before sleep claimed him once again.

Light had begun to seep down through the trees when next he woke. Except for the morning fanfare of birdsong, all was quiet. Uncomfortable on the thin mat, he tried to shift his weight, then realized something pressed down upon his feet. Groggily, he opened his eyes and lifted his head. All his dreams of late had been disturbing and confusing and completely unmemorable once he was awake. This felt different.

At his feet—no, *on* his feet—lay a brown and white mixed-breed hound. As he stared at the dog, it lifted its head, yawned widely, then climbed to its feet. It shook itself vigorously, then trotted up toward Marek's head, wagging its brush of a tail, grinning.

No, Marek told himself, slumping back on his mat. *Dogs don't grin.*

This one did.

Not only did it grin, but it apparently had no intention of letting him go back to sleep. The instant his eyes closed, the dog whined and thrust its cold nose against Marek's jaw.

"Stop that," he muttered, pushing the hound's face away. "I don't have anything for you. Go away."

The dog sat back on its haunches and panted happily. Then it raised a spotted foreleg and pawed at Marek's shoulder.

Yawning, Marek sat up and stroked the dog's head. "Where'd you come from?"

The dog thumped its tail in delight and turned its head to lick Marek's hand.

"Oh, I'm so sorry, sir!" Isme hurried toward him, a mug gripped in one hand and waving wildly at the dog with the other. "Shoo! Go away, you!"

"It's all right," he assured her. "He's not hurting anything."

The healer slowed her steps, eyeing the dog warily. "Are you sure, sir? I can call someone to take him away."

The dog turned his happy face toward her and waved his tail uncertainly. Isme's expression softened.

"No," Marek said. "He's fine. Where do you suppose he came from?"

"He belongs—" Isme hesitated, then, narrowing her eyes, corrected herself. "He *belonged* to the tracker who was following us. When our men returned ... from their task last night, they discovered he had followed them."

Marek caressed the dog's floppy ears, then examined the creature more carefully. Ribs protruded from the short, dappled fur and the hound pulled away, whining, when Marek found a swollen spot on its side.

He looked up at the healer. "Do you think you could spare a piece of bread for him?"

Isme hesitated, then nodded, holding the mug out to him. "And here is your breakfast."

Marek took it, eyeing the contents dubiously. It appeared to be a grain mush with wild berries mixed in. The odor rising with the steam from the mug caused his stomach to give a loud rumble. Still, he hesitated. "You haven't put any of that sleeping potion in this, have you?"

Isme raised a slender eyebrow. "It's not a sleeping potion. It aids the body in its own healing efforts and helps with the pain of injury. Sleep is simply ... an extra benefit."

"Whatever it is has worked well." Marek smiled, hoping to take the sting out of his words. "But I am feeling better now. I prefer to stay awake."

The young healer lifted her delicate chin and glared. "Nothing has been added to the porridge but some honey and berries for added flavor. I will speak to my mother about your desire to no longer partake of the medication."

And with that, she turned and flounced away, as much as flouncing was possible in a forest with abundant underbrush.

He grinned and ran his fingers over the hound's broad forehead. Though they looked nothing alike, the girl's spirit reminded him of Lyric. His smile faded. Where was the princess now? Was she safe?

For seven years he'd been sworn to protect the royal family of Tressalt, and now, both the king and his daughter were beyond his aid. Duty demanded he find the one and devise a way to save the other.

As quickly as possible.

CHAPTER 19: DECISION

Lyric pulled a handful of huckleberries off the bush and dropped them into the woven basket Venuzia had provided.

"It's true then? About Lothar?"

Venuzia sat on a nearby tree stump, a floppy hat sitting askew on her head. "That he's back and stirring up trouble just like he did a thousand years ago? Yes, it's true. Did you think the cat-woman lied to you?"

The old Sheever had awakened her and Becca this morning just as the sun crested the far eastern mountains, saying if they wanted breakfast, they'd need to help provide it.

"Well, no, I don't think she lied," Lyric mumbled, scanning for more huckleberries. "It's just that I've never heard of any of this, and I didn't know what to think."

"It's true," Venuzia said again. "Lothar was the wizard-leader for the Borags. He led them into revolt way back then against us other folks and our wizard-leaders—the Sentinels. I've had the amethyst stone since my mother passed it down to me, but I don't usually spend a lot of time looking into it. Still, I've seen some things lately. This Lothar is surely the same one, and he's connected with that nasty prince Ralt. Hurry up, now," she admonished. "Can't you pick and talk at the same time? Your basket is only half full. Look at Becca's."

Becca stood at an adjacent bush, her nimble fingers flying, her basket nearly full. Lyric considered pointing out that Becca was far more practiced than she at such tasks but decided against it.

"Wait." Ignoring the laden bush, Lyric stared at Venuzia. "*Other* wizard-leaders? There were others?"

The old woman scowled. "We all had one—you humans, the Sheevers, Akyldi, Remnan, Vala, and Borags. Back in the beginning, the Maker sent them to help us all find our way in the world. Didn't Amira tell you?"

Lyric tried to remember that day in the Akyldi camp. "I think she did, but I didn't give it much thought."

"We all had one, and, far as I know, they all did a fine job … until Lothar wanted more than his fair share and decided to take over." She shrugged. "At least, that's the story I was told when I was a youngling."

"What happened to the rest of the Sentinels?"

The frail shoulders rose and fell.

"Don't know. They gathered together, dispatched Lothar, wrote the prophecy, and went their way. A lot of things changed after the war. Many things were destroyed that have never been rebuilt, and there are still a lot of questions no one can answer."

Lyric peered at Venuzia, remembering something that had bothered her earlier. "Yes—that place where you found us—it looked like castle ruins, but it was so old. Do you know who built it?"

The old woman shrugged once again.

"Men. From I don't know how long ago. Before the war." She shoved her hat back and scratched her pale forehead, leaving a blue smear of berry juice. "The lines where people lived were all different then. Most of the humans lived in villages scattered around the area now called Graceen. That old fortress was about as far south as they had any permanent dwellings. The war started, and the Borags under Lothar killed all the people and tore the castle to pieces." She snorted, spat.

"Then the forest grew up around it, as forests do, until a big storm hit about ten years ago. Lightning struck, and the fire was a bad one." She popped a berry into her mouth.. "Now it's all re-growing again."

She paused, glaring at Lyric. "You gonna pick those berries or just dawdle around the bushes?"

Lyric sighed and reached for the nearest cluster of fruit, returning to her earlier thoughts. "So you think the best thing to do to help my father and Tressalt is to find those who have the other gemstones and try to fulfill this prophecy?"

"How should I know what the best thing for you is?" Venuzia pulled berries out of the full pouch at her side and popped more into her blue-stained mouth. "You have to decide. What are your choices?"

Good question. She mulled her options over and found them lacking. Going to Graceen, begging their larger, better-defended neighbor to help them.

Or do nothing at all. Hide. Wait out this horror. Hope there was a place to call home when all the battles were over.

She had no way to know whether Graceen would help. But she knew she couldn't do nothing.

"I do know my people believed that prophecy," Venuzia said. "I was told as much when I was old enough to understand about the amethyst stone. All my kin just hoped nothing would come of it while they lived." She scowled and reached into her pouch for another handful of berries. "I guess they got what they wanted."

Lyric sighed and turned back to the heavily-laden bush but couldn't focus on the tangy fruit. It was true, then— Lothar, the prophecy, everything. She couldn't deny her opal stone was unusual. It had warned her of danger, shown her visions, seemingly contacted Amira, but the rest of it? She'd not been convinced before. But now?

She'd agreed to come with Amira, agreed to seek further evidence of the need for this quest, and now she'd found it. Or at least, she'd found another non-human who told the same tale.

"Come on, Princess," Venuzia ordered. "Stop that daydreaming and pick. Huckleberry cakes for breakfast when we get back to the cave, but at the rate you're going, we'll never get there!"

Becca handed her full container to Venuzia, moved over to Lyric's bush and started picking, adding the berries to the princess's basket. Under the guise of reaching for a lower branch, Becca leaned toward her mistress, whispering. "Are we going on with Amira, then? To find those stones in the prophecy?"

Lyric dropped her berries into the basket, eyeing her juice-stained fingers, her mind far away where her father was held captive in his own castle.

"Yes," she said at last. "Yes, we are. I don't see that we have any choice."

The idea of pursuing this quest even farther into the unknown was terrifying, but she had decided. She would do what she must to save her land.

And pray that her father survived until then.

"You what?" Lyric stared at Venuzia, horrified.

It was the evening of their third day with Venuzia. Their small company sat together outside the cave's entrance amidst ferns and blue and white lupines. Venuzia straddled a small boulder and sharpened a large, wicked-looking blade against a foot-long whetstone. Becca sat near Lyric's feet, and Amira and Quinn leaned against the cave's outer wall.

"You heard me." Venuzia knit her frosty brows together in a fierce scowl. "You all need to be journeying north soon, but I won't be joining you."

"But—" Lyric shook her head, shocked and furious, because she could see that nothing she could say would change the woman's mind. Finally, bleakly, she looked into the old Sheever's watery eyes and said the only thing left. "Why?"

"Look at me!" The old woman waved the big knife around her head irritably. Dangerously. "Do I look like I could keep up with you?"

"But—" Lyric began.

"You're thinking of the Venuzia in the sky," she snapped. "Do I look like her? Your road leads into the deep forest. There are trails and passageways on the ground for humans and horses and the like, but Zia and I can't walk those paths."

Lyric turned to Amira for support, but the silver-eyed woman shook her head. A bandage covered her forehead and her arm was in a sling, but her eyes were bright once again.

"That's right." Venuzia set the blade aside and folded her hands together to crack her knuckles. "Listen to your friend there. She knows what's what."

Lyric shivered. In the west, the summer sun dipped below the horizon in a blaze of red, gold, and streaks of violet, but she was finding it impossible to appreciate the extravagant beauty. A cool breeze sprang up with the setting of the sun, but it wasn't the dropping temperature her body resisted. Venuzia was an invaluable resource. She had to come. If she didn't …

The sound of immense wings pulled her from her dark thoughts. Zia, returning from hunting, landed on the hill that loomed over Venuzia's cave and set about preening her dull brown feathers.

"I didn't say I wouldn't do anything to help." Venuzia's nostrils flared as she returned to the rhythmical grinding of the knife blade against the gritty whetstone. "I know what the prophecy says. I'm the only Sheever left and I have the amethyst stone, so I'm part of this whole thing, but I can't go on foot through the forest with you."

"What Venuzia says is true," Amira said softly. "It would be foolhardy to waste what strength she has when her gifts are better used in other ways." She caught the old woman's eye. "I assume you will pass us messages via the stones, and come to us at need?"

"Yes, of course," Venuzia said irritably. "And if you find the Vala and the Remnan and convince them to help, we'll come with the strength of the Sheevers' stone and do our bit."

If, if, if.

Lyric buried her face in her hands and tried to think. She knew she should thank Venuzia for this—it was certainly better than nothing—but there were so many *ifs*, and so few of them fighting this battle. How were they supposed to save her kingdom—much less all of Argonia—with just four of them?

Venuzia cleared her throat. "You said this Marek fella was steering you toward Graceen, right? That your grandsire is there and has the ear of the Graceen king?"

Lyric nodded.

"Well, that seems like a sensible plan. Graceen has an actual army—not huge, mind you, but a good many more soldiers than what you lot down in Tressalt had the sense to keep."

Lyric felt her anger rising at the insult but before she could speak in defense of her father, Venuzia pushed on.

"The day after the moon rises fat and full, I'll take the four of you to the border of Graceen. We'll avoid Ralt's men on the main roads, and I'll set you down about an hour's walk from the capital city. Border guards will find you long before you get that far, I'll warrant. You tell them who you are and they'll take you to your grandsire."

Lyric threw her arms up in exasperation. "And how long until this fat full moon you speak of?"

Venuzia eyed her thoughtfully, then shook her head and sighed. "Five days."

"All right," she burst out, shaking in frustration. "But if we're going to do that, I don't want to wait another five days. We'll go in the morning." A thought broke through her ire and she turned to the two Akyldi. "That is, if you're up for travel, Amira?"

Venuzia spoke again. "I suppose that'll work if you don't care to know what's happening in Tressalt."

Lyric wheeled to face the querulous old woman. "What?"

Venuzia shrugged and returned to sharpening the blade. "Zia and I can fly over there after dark, when no one can see us. She'll hide out in the forest and I'll get myself down to that village of yours in the morning, and see what I can find out. But of course, if you can't wait ..."

Lyric exhaled, her frustration draining away with the possibility of hearing news from home, of knowing for a fact that her father still lived.

As if from a great distance, she heard Venuzia still speaking, something about flying over Akyldi land. Lyric forced her mind back to the present.

"Would the king of the Akyldi welcome us?" The question was put to Amira. "Or would your people shoot us down? Does the king remember the Sheevers?"

"He remembers," Amira murmured. "He would be glad to see you and receive word of our journey."

Lyric's heart beat faster. If Venuzia went to the Akyldi capital, perhaps Marek and his group would have arrived also. If she could hear word of him, too ...

"Well, Princess?" Once again, Venuzia's raspy voice pulled her from her reveries. "Will it be worthwhile to delay your journey a bit if it means receiving news from home?"

"Yes." She looked from Becca to Quinn and then to Amira before turning back to Venuzia. "Yes, of course. I can't think of anything I'd want more." She let her words trail off, then looked into the eyes of the aging Sheever. "Thank you. And I'm sorry for—"

Venuzia cut her off with a wave of her scrawny arm. "Never you mind. You're young and don't know any better. Impatient. Wanting everything yesterday. I used to be that way, too. Most young people are. Well, not Amira, probably." The old woman cackled. "I can't imagine her ever being restless and impatient. Quinn either, for that matter."

She struggled to her feet and brushed the dust off her backside. "And now I have a request to make of you, Princess."

Lyric looked up at her expectantly.

"I want to take your girl along with me. I think she can be of help."

Her girl? For a moment, she was completely baffled.

"Me?" From her side, Lyric heard Becca's astonished voice. "You want me to come with you?"

"Yes," Venuzia said to the bewildered girl, then turned to Lyric. "Yes, I do. It'll be for just a few days. You can manage without her that long, can't you?"

"I—" Lyric turned to Becca.

"My place is with Princess Lyric," Becca said staunchly, but Lyric had seen it—the light that gleamed for an instant in the girl's eyes when she realized what Venuzia was requesting. And she remembered the pure joy in Becca's face when riding the great bird with Venuzia on the day of their rescue from the Borags.

As the daughter of a peasant farmer, Becca had undoubtedly had little opportunity for pleasure in her life. Only hard work and more hard work, until one day she would catch the eye of another peasant's son. Then she would work even harder trying to maintain a household in a harsh world while bringing a new child into that world every year.

Becca deserved a chance to be young awhile longer. To enjoy her life.

Lyric turned to Venuzia.

"Yes, I agree. Becca should go." Behind her, she heard Becca's yelp of surprise and delight, but Lyric looked at Venuzia through narrowed eyes. "You do promise to bring her back safely?"

Venuzia chortled. "She'll be as safe as Zia and I can keep her. Get what you need, girl," she ordered Becca. "I need to talk to Zia."

Lyric watched, lost in her own thoughts and in the happiness in Becca's eyes, as the old woman clambered up the hill behind the cave to converse with the giant bird—her other half—in their own indecipherable language.

An hour later, Lyric's heart slammed in her chest and her stomach clenched as Becca and Venuzia flew southward into the graying sky.

CHAPTER 20: NEWS FROM HOME

A keening wail cut through the close air in Venuzia's cave and brought Lyric to her feet. Without waiting for Amira and Quinn, she dropped the tunic she'd been trying to mend and raced out the cave's entrance.

Looking skyward, she sought proof of what her heart scarcely dared hope for. Venuzia and Becca had been gone four days with no word sent through the amethyst stone. Each of the twenty-four hours they were gone beyond the seventy-two Venuzia had anticipated had felt like torture, and last night had been the *fat full moon*. What if they'd been hurt or captured, or worse? She'd been unable to sleep more than a few minutes at a time the entire night.

She shaded her eyes with one hand while holding the other against her chest, trying to quell the furious beating of her heart. What if the woman and her avian steed brought bad news? Her troubled mind had been unable to dispel that thought. What if her father—?

She heard the wail again and whirled to the south. A dark form with huge wings skimmed just above the neighboring ridge top. Once again, the bird screamed, then it arced toward her, the rays of the setting sun glinting against the brilliant plumage.

Amira and Quinn joined her as Venuzia soared over their heads and circled, coming closer and lower with every circuit. The warrior Venuzia—for so Lyric always thought of her when she was astride the bird—caught Lyric's eye as she passed and thrust her fist into the air, an unmistakable sign of triumph. Behind her, Becca waved ecstatically, her face wreathed in smiles.

Moments later, the great bird glided to a landing just feet from where the three friends stood. From her perch above them, Venuzia looked down at Lyric, and in a deep, mannish voice, declared the words she'd longed to hear.

"King Sander of Tressalt still lives."

Lyric choked back a sob.

"He is not well," Venuzia added, "but he is alive."

Lyric turned to Becca and stared, stunned. For a brief moment, she saw a blurred image of the girl, looking radiant and powerful with fierce, shining eyes, much as Venuzia looked when she rode upon the great bird.

"I saw Mistress Mari'el, too," the girl chattered, unstrapping herself from her place behind Venuzia. "She is well, and—"

Unable to shake the vision, Becca's next words were lost on her. Then the moment passed, and when Becca scrambled down the rope ladder and turned to her mistress, she was the same earnest, bright-eyed servant Lyric had grown to love these last few weeks.

Lyric shook her head, undone by the vision, and Becca ran to her and grasped both her hands. "Did you hear us, my lady? The king is alive and Mistress Mari'el is attending him!"

Lyric took a deep breath, steadying herself. "Tell me everything."

"Supper first," Venuzia called, climbing down from her mount, transforming as she did. "I hope the lot of you saved us something to eat. I've not been this hungry since Bondasai II ruled the Sheevers."

"I hope you royal folk can find it in your hearts to forgive us the delay," Venuzia told them later over a meal of venison and greens. "It took us longer to find out about the King of Tressalt than we'd hoped."

They ate their meal sitting on the stitched-together bearskins that covered the earthen floor of Venuzia's cave. The Sheever had a small table, but it wasn't large enough for five of them, and in any case, there were only two rough-hewn logs in the cave that served as chairs. In the days they'd been Venuzia's guests, Lyric had often wondered who the extra chair had been made for, but she'd never asked.

"We went to the land of the Akyldi first." The old woman picked up a large strip of venison with her bare hands and ripped a piece of flesh off with her yellowing teeth. "We met with King Carnosh, and you were right, Amira—we were well-received. He'd heard about the fall of Tressalt and was glad to hear that you're still alive and aiding the princess."

"What of Marek?" Lyric burst in. "Had he arrived in Ashkyld yet?"

"I was coming to that, if you please, ma'am," Venuzia growled. "King Carnosh had received word that a group of his people were returning with horses and an injured Tressalt soldier. If they continued as they were, horses and all, he believed they were still several days from the city."

Lyric lifted a leaf of wild lettuce to her mouth, trying to hide her disappointment. She'd been so hoping for better news of Marek, but at least, as with her father, he was still alive.

"Your king will continue to have the borders watched," Venuzia said to Amira, "and he will gather such fighters as can be mustered." She paused a moment. "Carnosh also asked if I would be willing to bring news, as I hear of it. I told him I would do so."

Amira inclined her head. "This will be of great aid. Even with the swiftness of our people, sometimes it is days or weeks before news of the outside world reaches our land."

Venuzia shrugged. "The least I can do. More than any of the other peoples, the Akyldi were always welcoming to us Sheevers. And as it turns out, your king sent a message for you." She fished into her grubby tunic, pulled out a folded piece of parchment, and handed it to Amira. "And now," she said, turning to Lyric, "on to Tressalt, where we've been forgotten or ignored for centuries."

Still lost in her own thoughts, Lyric refused to be baited. It wasn't her fault her people had forgotten the others.

"At first, we couldn't find anyone in the castle village who would tell us anything," Venuzia said. "And most of them were afraid to say what they thought. Malacarian soldiers everywhere, you know. And a whole crowd of those stinking"—here the old woman launched into a colorful description that burned Lyric's ears before she was done—"Borags!" Venuzia spat on the floor. She picked up another large hunk of venison and sank her teeth into it.

"We went into the village after finding a place for Zia to hide," Becca explained. "We had to be careful, because people in the village know me. We were afraid someone might recognize me and tell the soldiers."

"I wish you had let us know," Lyric interrupted, remembering last night's sleeplessness. "You were supposed to return yesterday—you could have used the stone to contact us."

"Yes," Venuzia replied slowly, forehead wrinkled. "Well, as for that, it seems that I left the amethyst stone here in the cave." She shrugged, refusing to meet Lyric's gaze. "You can hardly blame me, can you? I told you. I haven't done much with the stone for nigh on twenty years. I just forgot it."

She turned to Quinn, shoving yet another large piece of venison into her mouth.

"This is great," she mumbled, trying to talk around the juicy morsel. "I don't get meat much anymore and I never was a good cook. Sure going to miss you all when you're gone."

Lyric forced herself to concentrate on her own meal, though the richness of the venison was lost on her for the moment. How could Venuzia *forget* the stone? What else might the aging woman forget once they'd separated from her?

"We hid out at night, then wandered through the village during the days, pretending I was a blind beggar from the country. Becca here was my doting granddaughter. It was the end of the second day when Becca saw—"

"I saw Mistress Mari'el!" Becca burst out, then looked at Venuzia and turned scarlet. "Sorry, ma'am."

"Don't worry about it, girl," Venuzia said, her mouth full of red meat. "Go on, tell the story while I eat."

"I saw Mistress Mari'el," Becca repeated, this time in calmer tones. "She was at the market and I was so excited, I almost ran right to her, but Venuzia stopped me."

"Young people," Venuzia muttered, shaking her head and chewing vigorously.

"We were finally able to get close to her, and when I was sure no one was watching, I pulled my head scarf back so she could see it was me. Her eyes lit up, but then she looked around, and she was looking for you, my lady. I just know it."

Lyric felt a lump rise in her throat as she realized how much she wished she could have been there, too. Mari'el had looked after her when her mother and old nurse had died. She dearly missed the aging housekeeper.

Becca went on. "I whispered to her that you were safe but we needed news of the king. Then she reached for a length of cloth and acted like she hadn't heard a word I'd said. I looked and there was a Malacarian soldier standing nearby, watching her."

"Eat something, child," Venuzia ordered Becca. "I can tell the tale from here. So this Mari'el of yours is pretty sharp, it seems. She pretended she didn't know us, paid for her goods, and when her guard was distracted, whispered for us to meet her at the southwestern castle gate early the next morning."

"With all the soldiers standing by?" Lyric said, aghast.

"It was fine," Venuzia said, waving her arm in the air, as if by doing so she could push aside Lyric's fears. "I just showed up as my blind-beggar self, seeking handouts. Nothing unusual about that. One of the scullery maids came to the door and we asked for the housekeeper. A bit later, here she came."

"How did she look?" Lyric turned to Becca. "Is she well?"

"I think so, my lady," the girl answered. "She said the king had been injured, and they'd thought he would die, but he's been getting better. No one knows why Prince Ralt is allowing him to live, but she thinks it might be to lure you back. She said the king—" Becca's voice hitched. "She said your father thinks that's why, as well."

Oh, Papa ... She set her plate on her lap and shifted on the bearskin, leaning against the table leg. How could he endure this, knowing his people were suffering and he was powerless to help them, that at any moment his enemy could end his life?

"Mistress Mari'el told him that you are free and well, my lady. He was so happy to hear it." She gulped and reached out a hand. "He wanted you to have this. She said to tell you 'with all his love.'"

Lyric took the object Becca held and choked back a sob. Her father's signet ring—in all its ebony and golden splendor. She pressed the fingers of one hand to her eyes, clutching the ring with the other.

He was saying goodbye.

Her companions sat quietly beside her, leaving her to her own thoughts. Finally, Becca spoke.

"And another thing—Amira and Venuzia were right. Prince Ralt is not alone. A wizard is with him at the castle. No one knows much about him, but he has powers that frighten everyone—even Prince Ralt's soldiers. Everyone who's still alive is doing the best they can to stay away from the wizard and not make Ralt angry." Becca's words stuttered to a stop and she clapped a hand across her mouth.

"*Everyone who's still alive?*" Lyric repeated, pulling herself from her pain, knowing she must ask the question but dreading the answer. "Who's gone, Becca? Who died? Did she say?"

"I'm sorry, my lady," Becca said wretchedly. "I didn't want—"

"Just tell me."

Becca glanced at Venuzia but the elderly Sheever kept her eyes on her food, chewing noisily.

"Master Grimstead and Captain Gareth. Master Kedrick," the girl recited dully. "Duke Solano. Many of the nobles, most of the guard, though not all are accounted for. Some escaped into the forest but if they are found, it is certain they will be killed."

Lyric closed her eyes, fighting not only the tears, but even more, the rage that coursed through her. She'd known Grimstead, Gareth, and Kedrick her whole life. They were honorable men, loyal to her father and Tressalt. Good men who didn't deserve to die as they had. And there were others—who knew how many?

Ralt must be stopped. And the wizard. And if they killed her father? She ground her teeth, staring at the flattened hair of the bearskin. There would be no place those men could hide. She would find them, one way or another, and they would pay. The fury in her would never be sated until those men followed the good ones out of this life, into whatever fate awaited evil ones in the next.

"There's one more thing, my lady," Becca said quietly.

Lyric focused once again on the servant.

"Mistress Mari'el said to tell you that no matter what, you are not to come back. Prince Ralt is looking everywhere for you, and she fears what he will do once he finds you.

Mistress Mari'el said your father would want you to find a place of safety and stay there, until others have come to the aid of Tressalt. Only when it's safe are you to return."

"And did you promise her I would do as commanded?" Lyric glared at the girl.

Becca's cheeks flamed as she looked down at her clenched hands. "I ... I told her I would give you the message, my lady. I made no other promise."

"Good," Lyric said. "This way you will not have to break your word." Jaw set, she looked around at the others. "Those of us who are traveling north leave for Graceen in the morning. Does anyone disagree?"

No one did.

CHAPTER 21: CAPTURED

The sun had scarcely pushed its way over the eastern hills when Venuzia swooped down from the gray-blue sky and landed in front of her cave. The Sheever had already delivered Amira and Quinn to a clearing only an hour's walk from Graceen's border and had now returned for the humans.

Lyric climbed up the rope ladder and settled herself behind the warrior woman. It still seemed beyond belief that the aging, almost crippled woman could transform into this ferocious being. When Lyric saw the warrior version, it seemed impossible that anything could ever be a threat to her. Then she remembered the human Venuzia, separate from her winged steed, with her flyaway white hair and creaky gait. If she'd been twelve when she'd bonded with Zia and that was a hundred years ago ... the woman was one hundred twelve years old.

How long could she continue to fly the world's azure skies?

Becca climbed up to her place behind Lyric, and both girls wrapped the leather straps around themselves and tied the ends to Venuzia's belt.

Lyric sucked in a breath as the great bird took flight, feeling, as before, that she'd left her stomach on the ground below them. Behind her she heard Becca's shout of exhilaration.

They flew north and west, the rising sun at times behind them, at other times to their right. Venuzia skimmed just over the top of the giant trees of the forest, hoping, as she'd explained to Lyric the night before, to stay out of sight of Borags or other keen-eyed wanderers of the woods. Between the flapping of the immense wings and the erratic wind that seemed bent on dislodging them, Lyric was grateful for the stout leather thongs that bound her and Becca to Venuzia.

The ground seemed very far below them.

In less than an hour's time, Venuzia began her descent. Peering out around the Sheever, Lyric saw the thinning trees and the emerald green of a small clearing. They circled the clearing, lower and lower, and then, with a jarring thump, hit the ground. The flight that had taken an hour would have been more than a day's journey on foot. Even so, she was thankful to be back on the ground.

Venuzia untied the rope ladder and tossed it down. To her left, Lyric saw Quinn and Amira emerge from the trees and stride out to join them. Lyric and Becca scrambled down the ladder, but Venuzia remained astride, her fierce eyes upon them. She pointed to the west.

"The road you call the Merchant Way is in that direction, about ten miles, but as the Akyldi reported, it is held by men of Malacar. What remains of the Old Forest Road is closer, perhaps three miles away, but I understand it is also held." She pointed to the north side of the clearing. "A footpath is there. A brief walk under the trees will bring you to a deep gully that marks the border between Graceen and Tressalt. You can enter your mother's people's land from the back. I wish you good fortune on your journey."

The warrior woman paused, looking over her shoulder to the north, then turned back to the small group. "On the far side of Graceen's city, about a day's journey afoot on what remains of the Old Forest Road, there is another clearing where I can come to ground safely. If you wish to meet with me, use one of your stones to call me. I will come with whatever assistance and news I can bring."

She looked at Lyric and a trace of a smile crossed the haughty features. "I will keep the amethyst stone with me at all times, Princess. You can count on that."

Lyric smiled in return. "Thank you, Venuzia. For everything you've done."

The bright eyes narrowed, and Venuzia seemed to be considering her next words.

"It was good to be with people again. I had almost forgotten entirely what it was like." She turned to Becca. "And to you, Mistress, take care of your lady, but do not forget our words in Tressalt." Leaning forward, she spoke softly to the bird, then turned once again to those standing before her. "Farewell. May the Creator himself light the way before you."

The bird unfurled its huge wings and launched itself into the air. Raising an arm in final salute, Venuzia circled the clearing once, gaining altitude, then flew over the towering fir trees to the south. Lyric stared into the sky until the Sheever was lost to sight. The forest around them suddenly felt very empty.

"Shall we go, Princess?" Amira said.

"Yes, of course." Lyric turned and faced the path to the north. Then, remembering, she whirled on Becca. "What was Venuzia talking about? What conversation did you have in Tressalt?"

Becca swiped her tears away and opened her mouth to answer, then looked past Lyric. She gasped.

Lyric spun around and to her horror saw soldiers emerging from the forest, bows at the ready. One man, dressed in livery of emerald and gold, walked ahead of his fellows and stopped a bow shot away.

"In the name of King Rasmus, Lord of Graceen, I order you to halt," he called. "Lower your weapons. Do not attempt to flee."

Glancing from the right to the left, Lyric saw armed soldiers closing in on them from all sides. She turned to Amira and Quinn, who also had arrows nocked and ready. "I don't think we have a choice," she murmured.

The Akyldi lowered their weapons, and Lyric turned to the soldiers in front of them, raising her hands.

"As you will, sir," she called. "We have business with the King of Graceen and will be glad of an escort."

She smiled to herself as, even from this distance, she could hear the soldiers muttering among themselves until a sharp look from their captain silenced them. Clearly they hadn't anticipated being treated as servants by their captives.

As the soldiers surrounding them came forward, tightening their ranks, Lyric kept her eyes on their leader, knowing their fate rested on his opinion. Ten feet from them, the captain signaled his men to stop while he came on another two paces. He was a big man, tall and broad, with hair that matched his ebony helmet. His eyes were dark, assessing and intelligent.

Frowning, he scanned each of her companions before returning his gaze to her.

"I am Captain Monteith, of the second border guard of Graceen City. And who might you be, lady, that you are delivered to our land by a giant winged creature, and claim you have business with our king?"

Lyric met his gaze steadily. "I will answer your question, Captain Monteith, if you will first answer one of mine."

The captain's posture stiffened, and behind him, his men moved restlessly. "Need I remind you, madam," he said, his voice respectful but firm, "that you are infringing on our land, and it lies with the interloper to first give an account."

Lyric inclined her head. "I understand, Captain, but we have come far and through much danger to arrive at your border. The question I have of you is, whom do you serve? The King of Graceen or the ruler of Malacar?"

Angry muttering burst from the surrounding soldiers.

"Peace!" Monteith ordered, and looked back to Lyric. "As you can no doubt tell, my men are not happy at your suggestion, madam. We serve none but Rasmus, King of Graceen, upon whose lands you are trespassing."

"As to that, Captain, there may be some disagreement. Do you recognize this?" Lyric held out her right hand, upon which the gold and black signet ring of Tressalt glimmered.

Monteith stepped forward and peered at the ring, then, eyes troubled, looked back at Lyric.

"I do indeed recognize the ring, lady. There is only one woman who has the right to wear it, but I have never seen her. Disturbing rumors have reached our land about that lady. How do I know that you are this ring's rightful bearer?"

Lyric considered a long moment before answering. "How many others would know the land well enough to question your claim that the ground on which we stand belongs to Graceen? If my information is correct, you and your men are actually on *my* land, and it is my prerogative to order you off."

Despite her haughty tone, the captain still hesitated. "The rumors—"

"Yes, the rumors!" Lyric interrupted. "The rumors say I was kidnapped by a member of my father's guard. The rumors are lies, Captain. Thanks to that palace guard, I and my maidservant escaped Malacar's deceit. We have come by a circuitous route to the land of my grandfather, Duke Foxmir, hoping for asylum. Will you take me to him or not?"

The big captain inclined his head but held his ground.

"Forgive me, madam, but it is my duty to protect the border. If I am not satisfied with your identity, we must take you to Graceen City as prisoners." He lifted his hand to forestall any argument. "Certainly, I would prefer not to have to proceed in this manner, but I will if I must." He turned to his men. "Are there any among us who has seen the Princess of Tressalt?" He scanned the group before one of the soldiers caught his gaze. "You, Danulf? Come forward."

Danulf, a gray-bearded soldier standing behind Lyric, stepped up to his captain, then turned to look directly at Lyric.

"Well, Danulf?" Monteith asked. "Is this the Princess of Tressalt?"

The old soldier squinted through deep-set hazel eyes at Lyric. After a moment, he nodded. "It's her, Captain. I was assigned to Duke Foxmir's guard last summer at his country estate. I saw the princess many times throughout her stay."

The captain thanked Danulf and turned his attention back to Lyric.

Lyric sighed, the effort of keeping up her arrogant demeanor wilting. "Are you satisfied, Captain? May we proceed?"

"I am satisfied," the captain answered, stepping back and bowing his head. "Forgive me, Your Highness. We will be most happy to escort you to our city."

"Thank you," Lyric said, relieved the verbal jousting was over. "And there is nothing to forgive. You are doing your duty, as you should." She lifted her chin, studying the captain. "Although I still claim this land belongs to Tressalt, not Graceen. What have you to say on that matter?"

The dark eyes crinkled in good humor. "I will tell you in full, Your Highness, but perhaps we may begin our journey and speak as we walk?"

"Of course." Lyric nodded. Monteith turned to the soldier who stood closest to him and quietly conferred with him, then stepped away from Lyric's small group, calling another soldier to his side. This man listened carefully, nodded, then turned and raced away toward the dark trees and the north.

Ah, Lyric thought. *The messenger.* Word of their arrival would reach Graceen City long before they did.

The rest of the men were quick to fall into place, some going on before them, the rest bringing up the rear, and moments later they began the march toward Graceen. Captain Monteith walked at Lyric's side, with Becca, Quinn, and Amira following closely behind.

"As to your assertion," Monteith said, "I confess that you are correct. We have indeed trespassed into Tressalt lands, but to explain our reason for doing so gives me the opportunity to ask a question of my own." He glanced down at her as they strode along the path toward the forest, but Lyric made no comment.

"We are but a half-hour's march to the true border, but our scouts will sometimes cross into neighboring lands in these less-inhabited areas. Especially in light of the rumors we've heard from the south. Early this morning, one of these scouts saw the great winged creature I spoke of earlier."

She could tell he wanted a response, but she had none to give.

"A huge flying creature, far larger than any bird we in Graceen have seen or heard tell of, landed in the clearing behind us. It stayed for only a moment, then flew off toward the mountains of the east. The beast left behind two people, both armed with bow and sword. The scout sent word immediately, and we crossed the border to investigate. We had just arrived when the creature returned with you and your servant."

They walked on in silence, leaving the clearing and the brilliant sunlight behind as they entered the shadowy forest. Lyric struggled with what to say, knowing she was not required to make any explanation. This man was a mere captain, but still … he had been kind to them.

"I accept your reasons for crossing onto Tressalt land," she finally replied, "and I appreciate your extra diligence, given what is happening in my land. But there is little I can tell you about the manner of our arrival in the clearing."

She hazarded a quick glance at him. "I can only say the creature has been a friend to us, and is no danger to any of Graceen who are loyal to their king."

The captain nodded, accepting her explanation. How satisfied he was with it, though, she couldn't tell. After a moment, she forced herself to speak again.

"I don't know whether it is possible or not, Captain Monteith, but I would like to request that the subject of our ... winged friend could perhaps remain between us for the time being."

The captain frowned. "I can order my men to speak no word, Your Highness, but you must know I am required to give a full report to my own superior. The king himself will want to know how you came to be among us."

"Yes." Lyric sighed. "Of course he will."

The soldiers set a quick pace, and they soon crossed a wooden bridge over the deep gully Venuzia had mentioned, arriving at the border encampment within thirty minutes. A half-dozen tents surrounded two wooden sheds, and behind those, an enclosure held several horses. A saddled horse tied to a rail outside the enclosure lifted its head and peered at them from under its dark forelock.

Captain Monteith turned to Lyric and smiled. "We cannot allow the princess of our friend and ally to enter Graceen City on her own two feet." He glanced at the rest of her party. "Unfortunately, we do not have enough horses for everyone. This is only an outpost, and I must leave horses for the scouts and messengers."

Seeing the horse made her think of her own lovely Moon Song, now far away. But as much as she longed to ride, she found she was loath to do so while her companions walked. They had been through much together. But before she could give voice to her thoughts, Becca spoke.

"He's right, of course, my lady. You must ride."

Monteith looked from Lyric to Becca and back again, surprise evident in his dark eyes.

"You should listen to your servant, madam. I am not jesting when I say Duke Foxmir will have my hide if I bring his granddaughter, the Princess of Tressalt, walking into the city."

Too true. The captain must know her grandfather well.

After that, there was nothing for it but to allow Monteith to assist her onto the horse. Half the men who had accompanied them thus far stayed behind in the encampment, turning to other duties, while the rest walked with them on this final leg of their journey.

Though much had happened that day, Lyric realized it was scarcely mid-morning when they left the forest and entered a broad, flat area, cleared of trees. A quarter mile across the plain towered the wooden palisades marking the entrance to Graceen City. Lyric had seen these on her yearly visits to her grandfather—though before she'd always come on the Merchant Way to the far side of the city. But only today did she realize how strong the defenses of Graceen were.

And how completely feeble Tressalt's had been.

As they approached the great walls, she heard the high, shrill blast of a trumpet. A moment later, the wide gate in the wall began to open.

"We are expected, I see," Lyric said dryly.

Monteith, who marched along at her side, looked up at her and gave a slight grin. "But of course, Your Highness."

Moments later, a mounted delegation came through the gate and trotted toward them.

Monteith raised one gloved hand, signaling for his men to stop, and with the other hand, grasped the bridle of Lyric's horse, pulling it to a halt.

"Wait here, please," he said to them all, then left her side and strode forward.

"What's happening, there, Your Highness?" Lyric followed Amira's gaze to a commotion at the gate in the palisade. Foot soldiers surrounded a single rider astride a rearing horse. Even from this distance, Lyric could hear a booming voice.

"Out of my way, you villains! That's my granddaughter out there!"

Pulling free from the guards, his silver hair flowing over his shoulders, Duke Foxmir raced his horse across the plain toward them. Sliding to a stop, he flung himself off his mount and strode toward her, arms outspread.

Squealing in delight, Lyric jumped off her borrowed horse, ran to him and leapt into his arms.

"Oh, my dear, my dear," he murmured, squeezing her so tightly she was soon gasping for air. "I've been so worried." He pulled back, holding her at arm's length, and gazed at her with love radiating from his keen blue eyes. "How are you? And how is your father? What is happening in Tressalt? You must tell me everything."

CHAPTER 22: REFUGE

Lyric sucked in her breath, unable to control her delight as she lowered herself into the steaming bath. How long had it been since she'd enjoyed such decadence?

Much too long.

Sinking into the rose-scented water, she closed her eyes and lost herself in the luxury, allowing the hot water to soothe her trail-weary body and overwrought mind. As they'd ridden across the burgeoning city from the north gate to her grandfather's palatial home on King's Row, she'd told him of all that had transpired in her land. Of Ralt's deceit and the overthrow of Tressalt. Of her father's capture and imprisonment. Of her escape and long journey north with Marek and Becca.

She did not tell him of the Akyldi or Venuzia. Those weren't her tales to tell.

Neither had she told him of the newfound talents of her opal gemstone, or of her mission to find the holders of the other stones. She loved him dearly, but she suspected he wouldn't believe the first part and would want to stop her from pursuing the quest.

Immediately upon their arrival at his home, her grandfather had handed her over to his housekeeper, ordering that she be given "absolutely anything she wants!"

Lyric's first request had been the bath.

"Yes, of course, my darling." The duke had pulled her into another rib-crushing embrace. "King Rasmus will want a full report of the happenings in Tressalt, but he is hunting today and has not returned. We had no knowledge of your arrival, of course, but I imagine he will want to meet with you as soon as possible. Today, though, we have to ourselves. I am so delighted that you are well. When I heard the rumors—" He stepped back then, his mane of thick white hair disheveled, a suspicious dab of moisture in the corner of each eye.

"You have that bath, dear heart," he said gruffly, "then join me for luncheon on the east deck." He gestured toward the regal-looking woman standing near the door. "And do order my granddaughter some appropriate garments, won't you, Celeste? She is a princess and must look the part when she meets with the king."

"Of course, my lord."

Lyric glanced at the woman, then frowned, turning back to her grandfather.

"What's become of Simone?" The elderly woman had been her grandfather's housekeeper as long as Lyric could remember.

"She's well and living with her daughter out east of the city." He smiled. "It was time for her to start collecting her long overdue pension, and Celeste came highly recommended."

"I'm sure." Lyric nodded at the woman, then returned her attention to her grandfather. "My friends—" she'd begun, indicating Amira, Quinn, and Becca.

"Of course," he'd answered. "Celeste will see that they are attended to, as well."

"But my lady—" Becca stepped forward.

"It's all right." Lyric lifted a hand to stop her. "Go with Amira and Quinn. You need to rest, too." When Becca opened her mouth to protest, Lyric spoke more firmly. "Do as I say. I will call for you later."

Only begrudgingly had Becca allowed herself to be led away with the Akyldi.

Lyric lingered in the bath until the water lost its heat, then reached for the thick towel a maid had left by the tub. The girl had assisted Lyric in washing her hair—another luxury she had missed these last days.

Sighing, she climbed out of the tub, trying to remember just how many days she had been on the trail. Twelve days? Thirteen? She frowned as she dried herself, then shrugged into a dressing gown the maid had left for her. Had it been two full weeks?

Leaving the bath chamber, she entered the adjoining room and found the maid awaiting her. Several lovely gowns lay across the bed.

The maid, a blue-eyed, chestnut-haired girl, curtsied. "My lady Celeste said Your Highness should wear the gown that fits best for your luncheon and meet with the seamstress afterward to have the others altered."

Lyric missed Simone, her grandfather's former housekeeper, but she had to admit—Celeste had wonderful taste in clothing. A half hour later, she followed the maid down the wide circular staircase in search of Duke Foxmir. Her mahogany hair had been plaited, and she wore a gown of soft forest green with matching calfskin slippers.

She smiled at her reflection as she passed an ornate gold-framed mirror. Even Venuzia would have to admit she looked fine now.

But the thought of the old woman—alone again except for her feathered counterpart—caused her smile to fade. What would it be like to be the only one of your kind left? She shivered, then tried to shake off the chill that snaked up her spine. There was so much grief in the world, so much more than she'd known.

"This way, Your Highness." The maid directed Lyric to the hallway on the right, at the end of which a doorway opened to an outdoor dining court. Lyric found her grandfather there, seated at a gleaming hardwood table.

"Ah, there you are, my dear," he said, rising to his feet. "You look radiant. Sit with me and help me understand what's going on in this world of ours."

She took the chair across the table from his and opened her mouth to reply, but was interrupted by a servant bringing in a tray with fragrant bread and a tureen of steaming soup. She waited until the servant left, then turned to the old man.

"I was hoping you could explain things to *me*, Grandfather. I never expected anything like what I've seen these last weeks. I am so worried about my land and my father."

"I am too, my dear." He shook his head and reached for a slice of the thick-cut bread. "The Malacarians appeared on the Merchant Way ten days ago, on the border between Graceen and Tressalt. They sent representatives to King Rasmus, saying your father fell ill while their prince was visiting Tressalt. They said you'd been kidnapped by one of the King's Guard. It all sounded very fishy—if such a thing were true, why wouldn't the men of Tressalt come?" He shook his head. "Rasmus is worried, but we've not been able to acquire any other information. The Malacarians are letting supply wagons through from the south but only after searching everything, supposedly for you."

"The prince desired my hand in marriage," Lyric said flatly. "My father refused him."

Foxmir's eyes widened. "Indeed? Is that what this is all about?"

"I don't know if it's what this is all about, but I know this is the third time I've heard he's searching for me, so I have to wonder."

He sighed and leaned back heavily in his chair.

"This makes no sense. We've never had a problem with Malacar before. This is completely unlike Torian. Has there been any word from him? Is he behind this attack?"

Lyric reached for her soup spoon, buying herself time to answer. If she said she'd heard King Torian had disappeared, her grandfather would want to know how she knew this. She was not ready to speak of the Akyldi.

"No one knows," she finally said, "but my father would agree with you about King Torian. He believed him utterly trustworthy."

"But what's the likelihood that Ralt would be acting without his father's knowledge and support?"

"I don't know, but Grandfather—" She reached over and grasped his gnarled hand. "Do you think King Rasmus will help us? Tressalt and Graceen have been allies for generations."

He turned her hand over in his and squeezed it gently. "I don't know, my dear, but I will go with you in the morning to make your appeal."

Tears filled her eyes. "Thank you. I am very afraid."

"I know you are, child, but lay your fears aside for this day. You have arrived here safely and that is much to be thankful for." He let go her hand to address the bowl of savory vegetable soup in front of him.

Lyric followed his example. It had been several long hours since she'd broken her fast in Venuzia's cave, and she was desperately hungry. She reached for her spoon, then looked back at her grandfather. "I have not seen my companions since our arrival. I trust they are being attended to, as well?"

He waved a hand in the air, dismissing the question. "Yes, of course. Celeste is seeing to their needs."

They ate in silence until both bowls were empty, and Lyric's stomach was happily full. Her grandfather pushed his dish away and peered across the table at her.

"Tell me about these traveling companions of yours. Becca, of course, is a servant, but these others—where did you come by them?" He sucked in a deep breath, frowning. "There's something about them that doesn't seem quite right."

His words caused a chill to edge up her spine, and she chose her words with care.

"They are part of a roving band of hunters from the mountains to the east of Tressalt. They came upon us along the Old Forest Road. Ralt's men were just hours behind us and my guard Marek was near death. He had been attacked by soldiers of Malacar and his wound festered. After hearing our story, they offered their aid. Their healers are tending to Marek. Quinn and Amira took his place as my protectors."

She lifted her chin. "I know it is not normal—nor safe—to align with strangers this way, but I was alone with Becca in the wilderness and felt I had no choice. I just thank the Maker Quinn and Amira arrived when they did. They have been faithful companions and have saved my life more than once." She leaned forward, eyeing him keenly. "They are good people, Grandfather. I would not have arrived here safely, were it not for them."

"Yes. Yes, of course," he agreed, nodding his head decisively. "And for that I owe them everything."

Desperate to turn his thoughts away from the Akyldi, she pulled the pendant out from under the bodice of the green gown and held it out for him to see. "What can you tell me about this? I believe it belonged to my grandmother at one time?"

"Ah," he answered, a smile creasing his regal features as he leaned forward to inspect the pendant. "I'd forgotten all about that. Yes, it was your grandmother's. She wore it every day of her life until our daughter—your mother—married your father. Of course, you would have it now. I'm thankful you have something of hers, since you never met her yourself."

"I'm thankful, too," she said, fingering the stone. "And I'm sorry I never met her. What was she like?"

He sat back in his chair, his smile widening.

"Now that is a tale that could take a year and a day to tell. She was ... well, she was amazing." His eyes lost their intense focus and turned dreamy. "She had a temper that could make a grown man run. And believe me, I almost did a time or two!

"But she was also most tenderhearted. She'd hear that a laborer's child was ill, and she'd be the first one down to the cottage to help. One of my best hunting bitches died whelping, and blast it if your grandmother didn't bring all the pups into the manor house—right outside our chamber. She got up three times a night for nearly a month, squeezing goat's milk from a cloth into their mouths." He sighed and shook his head. "She saved seven of them—only lost one, and it was the runt—but she still wept over that one. It was just her way."

He sighed again, lost in his memories, before turning his attention back to Lyric. "She was so happy when the news reached us that our daughter was to be a mother soon. And then ... she was gone from this world before you arrived in it." And suddenly her grandfather looked old. Old and sad.

She reached across the table and gripped his hand. "I wish I could have known her."

"I do too, sweetheart. You're much like her, you know. She would have been proud of the fine young woman you've become."

Lyric felt a lump at the back of her throat and the unmistakable threat of tears. She did not want to cry. She hadn't come here to cry. She needed help rescuing her father, to free her land, and to find answers to important questions. She looked up into his lively blue eyes.

"Grandmother was given the pendant by her mother, correct? Did she ever say anything unusual about it?"

He squeezed her hand, then released it. "Yes, she received it from her mother. Apparently it had been passed down through her family line for generations, no one knows how far back. But anything unusual other than that, I don't think so. Why?"

Lyric tried to swallow her disappointment, dropping the pendant back inside her bodice.

"Oh, sometimes I think ..." She hesitated, not sure how much to reveal, then decided to plunge on. "Well, there have been times that the stone seems warm to the touch, which doesn't make any sense, I know. I was wondering if Grandmother had ever spoken of anything like that."

"Now that you bring it up," he said slowly, "I do remember something. It was so long ago, I don't think I've thought of it even once since then. When your grandmother and I were first married, she showed me the pendant and mentioned her mother had told stories of seeing images in the stone, of all things. Your grandmother was hoping she might see such things, but if she ever did, she didn't tell me." He looked at her, eyes narrowed, but with good humor reflected in their blue depths. "Don't tell me *you've* seen images in the stone? Your grandmother would have been most disappointed to know the magic skipped two generations!"

Lyric chuckled with him, but again something within her warned against saying too much. "How I wish! I could use a little magic about now."

"You and me both, darling. But I'm sure King Rasmus will have some thoughts about dealing with those Malacarians. After that, we'll be able to see you safely home to your father." He looked over her shoulder. "Yes, Celeste?"

The housekeeper stood in the doorway. "My apologies, my lord, but the dressmaker has arrived and Princess Lyric is needed for her gown fittings."

"Of course, of course," the duke said jovially, climbing to his feet. "We mustn't keep the dressmaker waiting." He stepped around the table and enveloped Lyric in his warm embrace. "Off you go, then, dearest. I have business to attend to in my study, but I shall see you at supper."

Lyric followed the housekeeper into the hall where the chestnut-haired maid awaited. "Please accompany Her Highness to her room and wait upon her there," Celeste ordered and turned to go.

"Mistress Celeste," Lyric called softly.

The woman stopped and turned slowly to face her. "Yes?"

"I have need of your service and have not dismissed you. Certainly, this is not acceptable behavior in my grandfather's home?"

Lyric was tall, but Celeste was taller and for an instant the woman's expression bordered on anger, perhaps even defiance. But the moment passed, and Celeste gave a stiff curtsy. "Forgive me, Your Highness. I was ... distracted. How may I assist you?"

"I would like my companions brought to my room as soon I'm finished with the dressmaker. Will you please see to it immediately?"

The housekeeper stared at her a long moment. "As you wish. Of course." With a curt nod, she spun on her heel and stalked away.

CHAPTER 23: IN HER GRANDFATHER'S HOME

Lyric paced back and forth in her elegantly appointed chamber, arms crossed, fingers drumming against her arms. She'd still been reeling from her encounter with Celeste and was scarcely halfway through her dress fitting when the maid delivered a note from her grandfather. King Rasmus had returned, he wrote, and called him to an immediate meeting.

Lyric had not been called and there was no explanation as to why.

She was heir to Tressalt's throne and the only one in Graceen with direct knowledge of what had happened in her land. Shouldn't she have been presented to the king immediately?

True, she hadn't come of age yet, but if something happened to her father, it wouldn't matter. Eighteen or no, she would be queen.

The thought made her shiver. She strode to the bellpull next to the immense four-poster bed and gave it a savage yank. Her companions had still not come to her and the dressmaker had been gone an hour. Where were they?

A moment later, a soft knock sounded at the door and the maid stepped in. "Yes, Your Highness?"

"I had ordered that my companions be brought to me. Do you know where they are?"

"No, Your Highness." The girl curtsied.

"Then go find the housekeeper and send her to me immediately."

"Yes, Your Highness." The girl curtsied again and turned to the door, only to have it swing open just as she reached for the handle. Becca, Quinn, and Amira entered the room.

"There you are!" Lyric said. "What took you so long?"

Amira tilted her head to the side. "We came as soon as we received your message but our rooms are at some distance from this one."

Lyric frowned, then realized the maid was still waiting. "You may leave us."

"Yes, Your Highness." The maid curtsied. "Does my lady still wish to speak with Mistress Celeste?"

"No," Lyric began, then stopped. "I mean, yes. Please let her know I wish to speak with her immediately."

"Yes, Your Highness."

The door closed and Lyric gave a throaty sigh. She pulled an ornate armchair from in front of the dressing table and collapsed into it. They were housed in a beautiful, palatial home, but she was less at ease here than in Venuzia's cave. She gestured to the huge bed. "Sit. There's room for everyone."

Looking a bit taken aback, the others sat, gazing at Lyric expectantly.

"Is everything all right?" she asked. "Are your rooms comfortable? Have you eaten?"

"We have eaten and our room is quite comfortable," Amira said but something in the woman's eyes belied her words.

"But ... what?" She looked between the three but none offered further information. She focused on Becca. "Where is your room? Are you close to Amira and Quinn?"

"Yes, my lady." Becca's voice wavered and her eyes darted between the two Akyldi. "My room is right next to theirs, but I'd much prefer to be here, serving you. And as Amira said, we're on the very farthest side of the house, and it's a very large house." She hesitated, looking at her hands folded on her lap. "Couldn't you ask your grandfather if I could move here?"

"Yes, I certainly can." She turned to the others. "Now, tell me. What's wrong? I can see that you're bothered about something."

"Do not worry, my friend. It is most likely nothing." Amira pursed her lips. "We have been treated well and have no complaint. It's just that we have never stayed inside a human habitation so things feel ... unusual."

"Such as?"

"A servant of the house stands outside our door at all times. He is pleasant enough but we are not allowed to go anywhere on our own."

"It's like he's our jailer!" Becca burst in. "We'd been waiting to hear from you and when your message finally came, he followed us all the way."

"He probably just wanted to make sure you could find my room."

"We had a maid to do that. We didn't need him." Becca paused and lowered her voice. "He's probably standing outside the door now."

Lyric was tempted to look but before she could, a firm knock resounded on the door.

"Enter."

The door swung open and Celeste stepped in. The almost imperceptible rise of one finely sculpted brow was her only response to the sight of the Akyldi and Becca seated on the bed. She turned to Lyric and inclined her head. "You sent for me, Your Highness?" The words were properly polite, but her tone was cool.

Lyric raised her chin. "Yes. I would like my companions moved to this section of the house, closer to my room." She tilted her head toward Becca. "And I would prefer my own servant to one of my grandfather's household. Have a bed moved into the antechamber for her, please."

Celeste straightened her shoulders and stared directly into Lyric's eyes.

"If Noni has not provided fit service—"

"She has provided excellent service," Lyric interrupted. "I have no complaint. I simply want my own servant near at hand."

"Of course." The woman bowed her head briefly. "I shall make the arrangements by tomorrow."

Lyric sighed. "That will not do. See to it today, please. Before my grandfather returns from his appointment with the king."

The housekeeper narrowed her eyes but hesitated only a moment. "Certainly, Your Highness. I will see to it."

"Thank you," Lyric said, even though she didn't have to. Her mother had taught her to be gracious to all, including servants, but there was something rather unpleasant about this one. She gave a quick shake of her head. Perhaps she just missed the kindly Simone and her own Mari'el. "That will be all."

"Of course," the woman said and swept from the room.

"Ssss," Becca hissed. "You should report her to your grandsire, my lady. She acts like she doesn't want to help you at all."

"Yes," Lyric mused. "I wonder if she thinks she can bully me because I am young. Very odd."

She glanced at Quinn. An uncharacteristic grin colored the scout's usually enigmatic expression. "What is it?"

"I'm afraid the housekeeper doesn't think much of your choice of companions."

"I don't care what she thinks as long as she performs her duties and keeps a civil tongue." She pondered a moment. "I have a mind to call her back and insist you all join me and my grandfather at table."

"That would not be wise, lady," Amira murmured.

"Why not?" Lyric shot back. Now that she'd considered it, it seemed perfectly acceptable. "You are niece to the king of your people, Amira. Your station in life is very similar to my own. And besides, you are my friends."

"Thank you." Amira inclined her head gravely. "But you have struck on the most important point, I believe. Quinn and I are special to *our* people, but no one here knows of our people, and for the time being, we must keep it that way. Our king has so ordered it."

"What did you tell your grandfather about us?" Quinn asked.

She frowned. "I left it rather vague. I told him you were part of a roving band of hunters from the mountains of Tressalt. Which is true, of course. I just didn't say exactly where you had roved from." She bit her lip. "I hate to lie to him, though, or even to lead him astray. He loves me, and if ..." She paused, hating to say the words. "If my father does not survive this attack from Malacar, Duke Foxmir will be my only living relation."

She stood and moved restlessly to the wall and pulled back the heavy drape that covered the window. She looked down onto the cobbled street, where carriages and horsemen moved briskly about their business. Graceen was much bigger and more cultured than her small kingdom to the south.

She felt movement beside her and knew, without looking, that Amira had joined her.

"I do not think it wise to force us on your grandfather," Amira said. "He is not a foolish man, and his loyalties are with his own land, as they should be. If it comes to defending your strange companions or disobeying an order from his king, I think there is no question what he will do." She smiled sadly. "He might feel badly for you, but he will do his duty as he sees it. I wonder even if it was best for you to order the housekeeper to move us closer to you."

Lyric looked back out the leaded glass window into the busy street below. "Possibly. Possibly not. It's too late to change that now." She sighed and turned back to the others. "My grandfather thinks I am staying safely here until the Malacarians are all *sorted out*. Once that happens I will be put in a caravan and sent back to Tressalt."

"But—" Becca started.

Lyric lifted a hand. "I know. I am committed to the quest, and we have no time to spare." She suddenly felt a powerful urge to throw herself on the luxurious bed and pull the pillows over her head.

She resisted the urge.

A chill stole over her, and she crossed her arms over her chest and tried to rub warmth back into them while she thought. She knew the answer but that didn't keep her from speaking the question aloud.

"Why did we come here? And how can we possibly get away without notice?"

"We came because Graceen lies between where we were and where we need to go," Amira reminded her, smiling. "And to see if King Rasmus will help free your land."

And because Marek wanted to keep me safe, she reminded herself. As did her father and grandfather. And even Mari'el. But she had taken on the mission to find the missing gemstones, and she couldn't do that while sitting at ease in her grandfather's home.

After a moment, she turned to Amira. "When Venuzia returned from your uncle, she brought a message for you. Anything of importance?"

Amira's fine brows pulled together. "I don't think so. A party of scholars had just returned from exploring a site far to the east, where a large settlement of our people once lived. A number of parchments were discovered, different, they hope, from anything already contained in the Ashkyld library." She gave a faint smile. "They were beginning the translation work. He is looking forward to seeing the work when they are finished."

Lyric smiled too. "I'm sure that will be interesting. But for us—if King Rasmus does not call for me soon, I will demand to meet with him. I must." She paused, thinking.

"I agreed to help find the gemstones and to that calling I hold, but it would be foolish not to also gather as many fighting men as we can. The wizard may be unstoppable by normal human means, but Ralt can be killed and so can his soldiers. Even the Borags."

Quinn nodded. "You are right, of course. It would be wise to gather fighters of all kinds, if it can be done."

"I will try to convince him," Lyric said. "Then whatever the king decides, we will return to our mission as soon as we can."

King Rasmus sent word that he wished to meet with Lyric first thing in the morning.

"He has many questions that I could not answer," her grandfather told her when they met that night for dinner. He gazed at her over his wine goblet for what felt like a moment too long, then turned his attention to the stuffed pheasant adorning his plate.

This was what she'd wanted, of course, but now that the time was set, apprehension closed in. There were things she must say to this king—Tressalt needed his help. But there were other things she must be very careful about, things she herself had just learned in the past few weeks. And it wasn't just these that concerned her. Truth be told, she had never been the sole representative of her land before another king. Would she bring honor or disgrace to her father, her land?

Despite the wonders of the meal set before her, her appetite fled.

She longed to share her worries with her grandfather, to ask his advice, but he seemed distant this evening, distracted, concentrating only on his food. Finally she caught his eye.

"You will be accompanying me, won't you, Grandfather?"

"As it turns out, not this time, my dear. The king would like to meet with you privately, and my steward has discovered something that needs my immediate attention." He skewered a section of fowl with his carving knife. "You'll be fine on your own, won't you? You've been trained at court. Nothing to fret about, I'm sure. Just tell the king what he needs to know. Answer him honestly."

Was it her imagination, or had he particularly emphasized the word *honestly*?

CHAPTER 24: THE KING OF GRACEEN

"Your Highness?" A footman dressed in midnight-blue brocade held open the carriage door and stood aside. Lyric rose as gracefully as she could in the cramped carriage and allowed the footman to take her arm as she descended. The short journey from her grandfather's house to the palace had done nothing to alleviate her nerves from the previous night.

Three women, all of them royal from their appearance and each accompanied by a servant, stood together in front of the largest castle Lyric had ever seen. A dozen turrets rose sparkling into the sun-drenched morning sky, and atop them all waved the banner of Graceen—a great golden eagle in flight against an emerald background.

"Princess Lyric." The eldest, a regally handsome woman with silver-streaked dark hair, greeted her. "I am Queen Bethen, and I welcome you to Graceen."

Lyric took the Queen's gloved hand. "Thank you, Your Majesty. I am pleased to finally meet you."

The Queen smiled. "We did meet once before, but you were very small and wouldn't remember. Please allow me to present my daughters, the Princesses Carnelian and Demesne."

Lyric took one of the Princesses' hands, then the other. Carnelian was a statuesque dark-haired beauty who took after her mother in appearance and looked to be about eighteen. Demesne was a golden-haired, lively child of perhaps twelve. Her eager smile showcased twin dimples that could only be described as adorable.

"We heard of your meeting today with my lord the king," Queen Bethen said, "and I begged him to allow us to greet you and escort you to the throne room. I was appalled when I discovered you had arrived here under such disconcerting circumstances. Are you quite comfortable at Duke Foxmir's home?"

Lyric inclined her head. "I am. Thank you, Your Majesty. You are kind."

"I would be pleased to assist you in any way while you are here in our land."

"Thank you again," Lyric murmured. "You are most gracious."

"It's not gracious of us to be kind to you," Demesne burst in. "You're a princess just like my sister and me."

"Shhhh," scolded her sister Carnelian. "Mind your tongue, Demesne."

Rebellion creased the younger princess's brow, but their mother smoothly intervened.

"This way, my lady Lyric, if you please." She gestured toward the huge open doorframe behind them. The Queen and Princess Carnelian led the way through the massive door into the palace, while Lyric fell into step with Princess Demesne. The servants followed in their wake.

"I'm very happy to meet you," exclaimed Demesne. "I've never known any other princesses except my sister, and she's so *perfect*—" The child made a face as she dragged the word out. "She's no fun at all! Do you have any sisters? Oh, wait—I did just meet another princess, but—"

"Demesne!" Princess Carnelian interrupted, but Lyric was charmed by the younger girl's openness.

"No, no sisters," Lyric told her. "And no brothers, either. Do you have any brothers?" They'd reached an ornately-decorated curving staircase. The Queen and Princess Carnelian led the way up.

"Yes, but just one," Demesne confided. "But he's old—more than twenty! And we hardly ever see him anymore, which makes me sad, but no one cares about what I think. Why don't you have any servants?"

"Demesne!" This time it was the Queen who spoke.

Inwardly chuckling over the whirlwind change of subject, Lyric murmured quietly to the excitable young princess. "I'm sorry to hear about your brother. And I do have servants, but most of them stayed at my castle. I only have one who came with me."

"Well, where is she? Why isn't she here attending you?"

Lyric sighed, unsure how to answer the girl's complicated question. Technically, Becca was still her servant, but she was not a lady's maid, and after the time they'd spent together since their escape from Tressalt, the girl seemed much more a friend than a servant. Almost a sister.

Her grandfather had told Celeste to offer one of their servants to attend Lyric during her stay, but not wanting to offend Becca, Lyric had declined the offer. Now she wondered if that had been the best decision. It made her seem rather … less than royal, coming alone. And she feared she'd need all the royal finery she could muster to manage this day.

"I just arrived in your city yesterday," Lyric said to the younger girl. "My servant and I were not prepared to be visiting other kingdoms when we left our home, so we did not bring the proper garments." And with Celeste's attitude, Lyric couldn't bring herself to ask for clothing for Becca.

"But you—" Demesne gestured to Lyric's gown.

"Demesne," the Queen said sternly, "leave the princess alone. Here we are, Your Highness." She gestured toward yet another impressive doorway. A servant swung the door open, and Lyric followed the royal ladies into the throne room.

King Rasmus sat on his throne in quiet conversation with a gray-haired man, a retainer, Lyric supposed, or possibly an adviser. Upon hearing the door's closing, the king lifted his head and peered toward the ladies. Raising a hand, he signaled for the man beside him to wait, then nodded at the queen.

She stepped forward, then inclined her head to the king.

"Sire, may we present the Princess Lyric of Tressalt. She has come in answer to your invitation."

"Of course," the king said. Lyric was surprised to see that his hair was just as silver as her grandfather's. Fine lines ran across his brow and slanted down from his mouth. He was a regal-looking man, but seemingly much older than his wife. And judging by the scowl on his face, nowhere near as kindly.

"We will leave you now, Your Highness," Queen Bethen said to her, smiling. "It has been delightful to meet you once again. If time allows, I pray you will honor us with your presence for an evening meal soon. Duke Foxmir will be invited, too, of course."

"Thank you, Your Majesty," Lyric responded, dropping into a small curtsy. "That will be wonderful. Thank you for meeting with me and escorting me to the king."

"You are most welcome," the queen said, inclining her head. "We hope to see you again soon." Then she turned and swept from the throne room, both princesses at her heels.

Alone again, Lyric turned to face King Rasmus, who stared at her for a long moment. Then, to her dismay, the king dismissed the rest of those in attendance, except for a secretary at a table at the foot of the dais and a young sandy-haired man who sat just below and to one side of the king. With a regal hand, the king beckoned her forward.

And now Lyric was doubly sorry she'd brought no attendants. This man was of no higher rank than her own father, but without a word, he ordered her about as if she were a castle servant. Lyric advanced, stopping at the dark line engraved on the floor ten feet from the first of the marble steps that led up to the throne. She dropped into a curtsy, then rose to return the king's stare.

"You bid me come, Sire, and I have done so."

"So you have," the king said, observing her through shrewd, dark eyes. "Sander's daughter, eh? How old are you, girl?"

She blinked. "I am seventeen, Sire."

His gaze narrowed, and with a start, Lyric noticed how strange his eyes were. Almost black, with very little other color separating the black from the surrounding white. The king shook his head and sat back, jaw muscles visibly clenching.

"Duke Foxmir has reported to me all that you have expressed to him. We are most distraught over the current state of affairs in Tressalt. King Sander and I have long stood together, along with King Torian of Malacar, over the governance of southern Argonia. The news you have delivered to your grandfather is something that has never occurred during the past five centuries."

He leaned forward, his dark, deep-set eyes scanning her intently. "Even so, I desire to hear with my own ears what has transpired in your land."

Lyric dipped her head. "Of course, Your Majesty."

"Carlton," the king ordered. "Get the princess something to sit upon. This may take some time, and we can't have her falling into a faint."

Lyric glanced around to look for the servant. With some surprise, she noticed the slender, sandy-haired man sitting near the king rise to his feet.

"Certainly, Father." Carlton stepped behind one of the ornate columns that lined both sides of the throne room and reappeared a moment later, carrying a gilded armchair. He moved swiftly to Lyric's side and set the chair before her.

"My lady." He bowed his head, then returned to his seat near his father.

Lyric sat, pondering Demesne's much-missed elder brother being ordered about like a slave in the throne room he would one day inherit. One more odd thing to set aside, to consider another day.

"So. From the beginning, then," said the monarch, never allowing his gaze to stray from her face. "Tell me everything you know about the overthrow of your father's land by Ralt of Malacar."

"From the beginning," Lyric repeated, and began with the arrival of the delegation from Malacar for their so-called social visit. Both Rasmus and Carlton proved attentive listeners, stopping her only when clarification was needed.

"King Sander told you he would not force a betrothal between yourself and Prince Ralt?" Prince Carlton asked, leaning forward in his seat.

"That is correct." Lyric met his gaze steadily.

"And do you believe your father's refusal to Prince Ralt could have motivated Malacar's attack on your city?"

"I do not know, Your Highness. I was not there." At Carlton's quizzical stare, Lyric pushed forward. "What I do know is that Malacar had many more soldiers hidden among Solstice revelers than those within the castle or those who attended the prince. They could not have known whether my answer would be yea or nay when they planned their visit to my land."

"And how did you know these extra soldiers were in attendance?" asked the king. "Obviously your father did not."

She paused, confused by his reaction. Rasmus seemed inclined to be set against her, and she did not know why. She had to use caution and not let him overrun her. She lifted her chin and spoke with a confidence she didn't feel.

"My attendant, Marek of the King's Guard, spoke to a dying soldier of Tressalt. He is the one who told us about the extra soldiers." She looked directly into the king's age-lined countenance. "What my father knew or guessed, I cannot say."

"But Tressalt was ill-prepared for attack." The king ground his teeth and stared down his patrician nose at her, but she remained silent. He shrugged his silk-clad shoulders. "Obviously."

Rage hammered at her but she resisted its tug. What was wrong with this king? The interview felt more like an inquisition, and it seemed she was not the only one disturbed by the king's behavior. Prince Carlton glanced at his father more than once, concern etched on the younger man's face.

"We trusted Malacar and the long relationship with King Torian," she said simply. "My father and others have paid the price for our naïveté. I imagine no one feels as badly as he."

"If he still lives," Rasmus said coldly.

Lyric skewered the king with her glare. "Which I, for one, certainly hope."

"Father." Prince Carlton leaned closer to the king, his gaze remaining on Lyric. "Perhaps we can move on to Malacar's potential danger to Graceen. This is what you called Princess Lyric here to discuss, is it not?"

Rasmus cast an irritated glance at his son, then turned his attention back to Lyric.

"Perhaps. But I imagine the princess will simply tell us she doesn't know what Malacar's plans are, since she wasn't there to hear them."

"Indeed, Sire, you are correct in that," Lyric said, refusing to be manipulated. "But I have questions of my own, if you don't mind. What can Tressalt expect from its long friendship with Graceen? Will you send aid? No one knows what has become of King Torian, but all those I've spoken to believe this move does not sound like him. If Prince Ralt has stepped out on his own and overtaken the seaports, merchant roads, and horse lands of Tressalt, do you really believe it will be long before Graceen can expect a similar visit?"

She turned her attention to Carlton. "It is my understanding that Malacar has blocked the Merchant

Road from the south with a ridiculous story about me being kidnapped." She looked back at the king. "If the Malacarians are already lying to you, what can you expect in future dealings with them?"

"I have come to this understanding already, young Lyric." Rasmus lifted himself from his throne and stood shakily, glaring at her. "I am indeed concerned with Malacar and Prince Ralt's plans, but I have another concern that at the moment bothers me even more." He reached for his royal staff, took a step forward and stared at Lyric imperiously. "Why does the heir to Tressalt's throne stand before me and herself lie? The pot calling the kettle black when it is just as dark?"

"Father!" Carlton leapt to his feet. "Surely this is not—"

Rasmus waved the staff at his son. "Let the girl answer."

Lyric pursed her lips but remained seated. "I do not know what you are suggesting, Your Majesty. I have certainly spoken no lies."

"Ha!" Rasmus scoffed, striking the staff on the marble stair step. "Perhaps not in so many words. What about lies of omission? I have heard many things already that contradict the story you tell. Right now, I want to know why you have said nothing to either your noble grandfather or myself about the great bird of prey who delivered you and your companions to our borders."

He took another unsteady step toward her, eyes blazing.

"Did you think my guard would leave out such an important detail?" He slammed his staff against the floor again, voice trembling. "You come here under the guise of friendship, but you have your own plans, girl, and I'll not be pulled into them. The power of Graceen will not be sold to the highest bidder. Who is this that rides in out of our legends of old?" He gestured madly at the tapestry hanging from the wall behind the throne.

Lyric looked beyond the king and saw that the tapestry was of the same style and theme as those she'd seen all her life in Tressalt. A great winged Sheever flew above a pitched battle between human men, silver-haired Akyldi, and those she now recognized as Borags—human in appearance but with the snapping jaws of wolves. The Sheever extended its talons for the kill, the eyes of its human rider half-crazed with blood lust.

"Ah, you see now." The king's chuckle was devoid of humor. "You can keep no secrets from me, girl. Prince Ralt wants me to give you to him. You want my people to fight your battles, but you'll have nothing from me until I know the truth. Something is very wrong here. Tell me all, or—" He grimaced, as if in pain, shook his head and took another step forward—off the edge of the marble stair.

"Sire—*no!*" Lyric leaped to her feet but could do nothing. The king fell, arms windmilling in a vain attempt to save himself. Carlton threw himself forward, trying to soften the king's fall, but he was too late.

King Rasmus hit the marble floor with a sickening thud and lay silent.

"Father!" Carlton knelt at the king's side and shook him gently. No response. Looking up, he saw Lyric, but turned from her to the secretary who stood next to his table, eyes wide. "Get a healer," the prince ordered. "Hurry!"

The secretary ran from the room.

CHAPTER 25: AFTERMATH

In moments, the throne room overflowed with people. Lyric stood in front of the gilded armchair where she'd been when the king fell, serving as an unmoving rock around which a whirling stream of people flowed.

No one paid her any mind. Not until the white-robed healers pushed through the crowd and knelt beside the unconscious king did Carlton look away from his father and catch her eye. Stricken, Lyric could only return his gaze.

He stared at her a long moment, before nodding briefly and returning his attention to the king. In a matter of minutes, the healers pronounced Rasmus still alive and ordered him taken to the infirmary. Six burly guards stepped forward with a stretcher and four others carefully lifted the monarch onto it. Carlton called for a path to be cleared through the crowd.

Lyric was one of those forced to move, stepping aside with the castle residents, courtiers, and servants, while the litter passed by. She glanced at the king as he was borne past her. For all the world he looked to be sleeping, except for the large purple swelling on his forehead and the blood leaking from the gash at the center of the bruise.

She shuddered.

Carlton stopped when he reached her, telling the healers to go on.

"Your Highness," he said, dipping his head. "There is much I wish to say and to hear from you, but now is not the time. Please understand that I don't know what came over my father this day. He is not normally like this. I don't—" He dragged both hands through his hair and looked away.

"Now is not the time," he repeated, as if to himself. He turned back to her, hazel eyes reflecting his grief. "But if my father's condition improves, would you permit me to visit with you at your grandfather's this evening? There are things I truly must speak with you about."

"Certainly," Lyric said. "At your convenience, of course. And, Your Highness?"

"Yes?"

"Please know that I am truly sorry this happened to your father, and I wish nothing but the best for him—and for all of Graceen."

He nodded to her once again, then turned his attention to a servant who lounged against one of the columns.

"You, there. No duties at this time? Then make haste to the stable and call for Princess Lyric's carriage. And you, Lord Nix"— this time his voice was calmer—"if you will, please escort the princess to her carriage and stay with her until she's safely aboard."

The lounging servant raced away, and Lyric was joined by a middle-aged, bearded gentleman, dressed in the finery of nobility. With him came the man Rasmus had been talking to when Lyric had first entered the throne room.

"Dulain?" Carlton turned to the new man. "Please find the queen and tell her there's been an accident. Ask her to meet me in the infirmary."

"Princess Lyric?" He looked back at her and she could see the worry etched deeply in his rather plain but kindly face. "Please tell Duke Foxmir what has happened and ask him to come as soon as he can. I must meet with him and the other lords immediately."

With the duties of responsibility and hospitality set in motion, Prince Carlton of Graceen spun away and strode after the litter-bearers.

Duke Foxmir's carriage had barely come to a halt in front of his mansion before Lyric was out the door and hurrying toward the house as quickly as the tight skirt of her gown allowed.

"My lady!" the footman called.

She ignored him, hurried the last few paces and wrenched open the heavy door. She stepped over the threshold and, further ignoring decorum, raised her voice. "Grandfather!"

No answer. She tried again. "Grandfather!"

A moment later she saw movement from down the long hall to the right and took a joyful step forward, only to see it was not her grandfather who approached.

"What's the meaning of this?" Celeste demanded. She looked at Lyric as one might an urchin dragging mud in over a clean floor.

"I need my grandfather," Lyric said, refusing to be put off by the woman's officiousness.

"I'm sorry," Celeste said in a tone only slightly conciliatory. "I do not know where he is at the moment. Shall I take a message to his study?"

"I need to speak to him now. Personally." Lyric could feel the heat rising in her cheeks, and suddenly decided she'd had enough of this woman. It had been a very long day. "Find him for me immediately," she ordered quietly, "or I shall use every ounce of my influence to see that you are removed from your post before the day is over."

The housekeeper's lips pressed into a tight slash of red, then abruptly her face smoothed.

"Princess Lyric," she said, as if placating a tantrum-throwing toddler, "I have done nothing but try to see to your comfort while you have been with us. There is no reason—"

She stopped, seeing Lyric look past her down the hallway she had just come from.

Lyric had heard his footsteps. She pushed past Celeste, ran the half-dozen steps to her grandfather, and threw herself into his arms.

"Well, isn't this a pleasure," he murmured into her hair. "This is a greeting I could grow accustomed to—"

"Grandfather!" Lyric pushed back. "There's been an accident. You must go to the castle at once."

"What?"

"The king has been injured."

He stepped back and away from her, his face drained of color, eyes wide in shock. "What kind of accident? Is he badly hurt?"

"He fell, but I don't know how badly he is injured. He was unconscious when I was escorted from the castle. The queen and the prince went to him in the infirmary."

"This is dreadful news." He drew a hand across his forehead and Lyric saw that the hand trembled. "It's too soon," he whispered. "The prince isn't ready."

"Grandfather." Lyric grasped his forearm. "There is no need for such talk. The king was alive when I left, but you must go to the castle and speak with the prince."

He shook his head, as if the action itself could force away the dark thoughts.

"Yes, of course." He took a deep breath and exhaled slowly. "You're right, of course, dear one. I'll go immediately." He looked over her shoulder. "Celeste, get Horatio to bring the carriage around."

"Right away, Duke Foxmir," the housekeeper purred, and the tap-tapping of quick steps against the stone floor soon disappeared into the distance. How Lyric wished she could speak with her grandfather about the housekeeper, but as Prince Carlton would have said—*now is not the time*.

She stayed with her grandfather until a page came to inform him the carriage was ready. With a final embrace, Lyric reminded him once again that fretting would not help, and waited at the front door until the carriage disappeared around a bend in the cobblestoned drive.

She returned to the mansion, hurried up the marble staircase and to her room. She longed to tell her friends everything that had happened. She was still shaken by the king's rage before his fall. Granted, she hadn't been completely truthful with him, but she didn't have permission to speak of the Akyldi and the Sheevers. They had lived on in a world that had long forgotten them. Their choice was to remain hidden, only coming forward now in answer to the summons of the gemstones.

Keeping their secrets and communicating openly with a demanding monarch required diplomatic skills she'd never mastered.

Most disturbing of all, he'd known Ralt wanted her back.

She pulled open the door to her rooms but found them empty. The main room had been straightened. Her bed was made and the clothing she'd worn since leaving the Akyldi camp had been laundered and folded neatly in a stack near the hearth. But there was no sign of Becca.

Frowning, she left her room and strode across the hall to the room Quinn and Amira had been settled in the night before, much against Celeste's will. She knocked firmly, expecting the door to be pulled from her hand at any moment and to be greeted warmly by her companions.

It didn't happen. Neither the Akyldi couple nor Becca were there.

She returned to her room, trying to contain her dismay. *Where could they be?*

Perhaps it was something as simple as them going out to view the grounds.

She clamped her hands on her hips and glared at nothing. If they'd done such a thing, they would have left her a message. A quick glance around told her there was no message.

Her patience at an end, Lyric marched to the bell-pull and gave a vigorous yank. A quarter of an hour passed and no one came in answer to the bell. Lyric seethed. This would never happen to guests in her father's castle. *What was happening in this house?* She jerked the bell-pull again and after several long moments, the young servant girl who had assisted her yesterday quietly entered the room.

"Yes, my lady?" The girl's voice was mouse-like and tremulous as she curtsied.

"Noni, isn't it?" Lyric asked, reminding herself that whatever was amiss in her grandfather's house was not likely this girl's fault.

"Yes, my lady."

"Noni, do you know where my three companions are?"

The girl curtsied again. "No, my lady."

Despite herself, Lyric felt her anger rising. She took a deep breath and tried to speak calmly. "Will you send for Celeste for me, then?"

Noni's eyes grew wide in what looked like terror. "I will, miss, surely. But I'm ... I'm not sure where Mistress Celeste is, either."

Did the girl not recognize this was an order? Lyric used her most authoritative tone. "Find her or *someone* who can answer my questions. I need assistance *now*."

"Yes, miss," the girl squeaked and fled the room without pausing to curtsy.

It was another quarter hour before Noni returned. Lyric had been reclining on the bed but scrambled to her feet when Noni entered the room. "What did you find out?"

The girl curtsied. "Mistress Celeste says—" She paused, gulped, then went on. "She says she will attend Your Highness ... when she has time, my lady."

"She said *what*?" Her fury erupting, Lyric stalked over to the cowering servant, only to see what she hadn't noticed when Noni first entered the room. The girl's eyes were puffy from weeping, and a large pink mark stained one of her cheeks.

"Noni?" Lyric said, her heart sick with what she could not ignore. "Who struck you?"

CHAPTER 26: A CAMP DIVIDED

Marek leaned back against the gnarled trunk of the tree and ran his hand along the dog's spotted back. It was nearly sunset and the Akyldi had halted their journey for the day. He'd been walking on his own feet for the last two days, but when he offered to assist with the camp setup, Isme's healer-mother had waved him away and told him he should rest.

He was tired of resting.

His hand strayed to the still-wrapped wound on his left side. He was not back to full strength but was far closer to it than he had any right to expect. By all rights, he should be dead.

Would have been dead, if not for the Akyldi.

The hound lifted his head, ears pricked, and stared intently across the clearing.

Marek followed the animal's gaze.

"What is it, friend?" The dog stared into the forest a moment longer, nostrils quivering, then turned back to Marek and thumped his tail.

The Akyldi. Who or *what* were they, exactly? He'd never met anyone like them. They'd kept him alive, for which he was grateful, but that didn't answer his questions. What did they want?

Several of them, including the healers, spoke the common tongue, but others spoke only a strange sibilant language he'd never heard. They were stealthy and moved with a grace that he'd never seen. And there was something about their eyes that didn't seem quite right.

Why should they save him?

And more importantly, what had they done with Lyric?

He shifted against the tree, seeking a more comfortable position. They were not all happy to have him traveling with them. Language barrier or not, he couldn't miss the scowls and rigid shoulders of some of the men. As he'd grown in strength, he also became uncomfortably aware that he did not know what had become of his sword, bow, and dagger. He had no real reason to think he was in danger, but he'd learned one thing from watching his hosts—if he was ever in battle with them, he hoped they were on the same side.

Movement from under the trees across the clearing drew his attention. Quidar, the company's leader, and Remzold, Quidar's second, emerged from the forest. Both men were slender in the Akyldi way, but Quidar's hair was pale gold, while Remzold's was a shimmering light brown. Marek assumed Quidar was older, but he based his belief on their respective positions within the company, not by appearance. As with all the Akyldi, they looked young, their ages impossible to guess.

The two men picked their way through the ferns and over the downed trees toward him, purposeful, yet light of step. At his side, the hound scrambled to his feet and peered at the approaching Akyldi. A whine escaped the furry throat.

Marek put his hand to the dog's head. "Shh," he soothed. The two men stopped in front of him, and Marek tipped his head in greeting. "Good evening, Quidar."

Quidar nodded back, his gaze scanning both Marek and the dog. "It appears our enemy's hound has found a new master."

"Perhaps," Marek replied, keeping his hand on the dog. "Or perhaps he recognizes we two are the only outsiders among your people."

Quidar inclined his head in affirmation. "You have been walking with us the last few days. Sareta agrees that you are making your way back to health."

Sareta? For an instant, he was stumped, then memory returned. "Yes," he replied. "Thanks to her care and that of her daughter, I am doing much better. And for that, I thank them and all the Akyldi."

Quidar nodded acknowledgment, but at his side Remzold clenched his fists and fairly vibrated with tension.

Quidar spoke a quiet word that Marek did not understand, but its impact was immediate. Remzold dropped his gaze and stepped back half a step.

"I am glad your health is returning," Quidar said calmly. "This is why I come to you today. There are decisions that must be made. Indeed, they would have been made already if not for your injuries." He paused and looked around the tiny clearing. Spying a downed tree, he stepped over and lowered himself gracefully to its broad expanse.

Remzold, Marek noted, remained standing.

"It seems I have a dilemma," the Akyldi leader said. "Before she left us, my lady Amira gave me clear guidance about how you were to be cared for, and I have done my best to obey her commands. But some things were left unsaid, and I find myself uncertain as to how to proceed."

"I don't know what your dilemma is," Marek said after a moment. "But if you are free to tell me more and want my assistance, I'll help in whatever way I can."

Quidar gave a faint smile. "I have never met any of your kind before, but I am inclined to trust you. Perhaps because you fought to the death to save your lady." He shrugged. "I can appreciate such loyalty. But if I am wrong, I will pay for my mistake, as might others of my people."

Remzold bristled, muttering something under his breath.

Marek focused on Quidar. "If you are asking if you can trust me, it is easy for me to say yes," he said. "But I have no way to prove my words to you. And truthfully, I can make no promises until I know what the trust involves."

Quidar dipped his head. "Spoken as an honest soldier. We Akyldi have a way to travel that few outsiders know. My lady Amira took your princess and her servant on this pathway, but I was not given permission to take you. This is my dilemma."

Remzold now paced back and forth across the small clearing, muttering to himself.

Quidar scowled at him before turning back to Marek. "But I do have permission to use my judgment, and as I said, I believe I can trust you. We are able to move quickly, crossing the forest in half the time it takes on foot."

"Oh?" Marek asked, deciding levity was needed. "Do you fly?"

Remzold skidded to a halt. Both men stared at him.

"No," Quidar answered, drawing the word out slowly. "Why would you ask that?"

Marek grinned, glancing at first one man, then the other. "I was jesting," he said. "Do your people not make jokes?"

"We make jokes," Quidar said slowly, not removing his gaze from Marek. "It is just this is a matter most serious for us, so jokes do not seem appropriate."

"My mistake," Marek said. "Perhaps you should just tell me about this pathway through the forest."

Quidar inclined his head. "It has been nearly a week since we have been on this journey with you. We have gone slowly because of your injury and because of the horses. Now that your health is returning, we could leave the slow pathway behind, but the other path cannot be traversed by horses."

Marek frowned. "I am most curious about this, but I am even more curious about another matter. Where are we going?"

Quidar's silver eyes widened. "Forgive me—I thought you knew. The healers did not tell you?"

"The healers have done an admirable job tending me, but they are very tight-lipped. They've told me little of importance."

The Akyldi leader looked over his shoulder at his second-in-command. The younger man crossed his arms, his expression stony. Quidar spoke quietly but sternly in their own language and Remzold's face fell. After a moment, he nodded but refused to look at Marek.

Quidar turned back to Marek. "My apologies. We are on our way to our capital city, where the king of the Akyldi awaits our report. If we continue as we have, it will be another week before we reach our destination. If we switch to the quicker way, we can be there in three days. Things are happening in the outside world that suggest we should get to our home as soon as may be. My people ... grow tired of the slow path." He gave a wry smile.

"Must I accompany you to your capital city?" Marek asked. "As you have said, I am much healed and have my own tasks to return to."

"You wish to return to the aid of your princess," Quidar stated.

"Yes, but where *is* my princess?" Marek broke in. "She and her servant have gone into the wilderness with your leader, but I don't know where they are or what they're doing. My duty—" He stopped, surprised at the emotions flooding through him as he spoke. He took a deep breath, exhaled slowly. "My last orders from my king were to protect the princess, his daughter. As long as I am not at her side, I fail in that duty."

"I understand," Quidar said gravely. "But let me assure you of this. Your princess is in the care and guidance of Lady Amira and her consort, Quinn, of the mountain Akyldi. She could not be safer if she were in a stone castle, surrounded by soldiers."

"I am relieved to hear this, but what are they doing? How am I to find her?"

Quidar turned his silver gaze upon him, considering. "Your land has been overthrown by a neighboring kingdom. Enemies long unheard of are filling the lands of Argonia. I cannot tell you more because I do not know more, but I believe Lady Amira and your princess are seeking a way to stop these enemies."

Marek shook his head, frowning. "Princess Lyric is young—scarcely past childhood. How can she contribute in any way to such a task? I must find her."

"I do not know the answers to your questions, but I cannot allow you to leave us. My orders were, that should you survive, you were to be taken to our king. Perhaps he will answer your questions when we arrive, but that is all I can say." He paused, his gaze unwavering. "I'm afraid our contrary orders place us at odds with one another."

"So I am a prisoner?"

"Not as such." Quidar narrowed his gaze. "You are not bound. We have done our best to care for you. But you must stay with us. I am sorry."

Marek stroked the dog's head, considering his options. The truth was, he didn't have many, unless he wanted to take on these mysterious forest dwellers— the forest dwellers who had saved his life—without a weapon. He looked across the mossy pine-needle-covered space to where Quidar gazed intently at him. Even with a weapon, he would not wish to fight this man or any of his people. They had been kindly hosts, but Marek didn't forget that when it was deemed necessary the Akyldi had quickly and efficiently disposed of the tracker and his company.

"For the present," he finally said, "let's say that I go willingly with you to your king. What will happen to the horses? I am responsible for them and will need them when I take up my task to find my lady."

Quidar nodded. "I have given some thought to this. I can order some of my people to stay behind and bring the animals to our king's city. They will be at least three days behind those of us who go on ahead. We also have a settlement a half-day's journey to the north where the horses can be taken and kept safely until you come or send for them."

"And then you'll show me this mysteriously fast way through the forest?"

Quidar smiled, unfolding himself from his seated position on the log. He lifted his arms over his head, stretching with feline grace. "I can show you now, if you like."

Less gracefully, Marek climbed to his feet. "Lead on, then."

Quidar's smile broadened, and Marek realized the man's teeth were not rounded, like most people's, but ended in points. Before he could react, the Akyldi male spoke again.

"There is nowhere to lead—we are already there. You should step away from the tree." He turned to Remzold and nodded.

The younger Akyldi scowled, then launched himself toward the tree Marek had been sitting beside. Remzold's strides went off the ground and up the trunk of the tree. Then he leapt into the air, grabbing onto a branch far above the ground. He scrambled out of sight. A moment later, he dropped back to the ground with the end of a green rope ladder in hand. Grinning his own version of that strange toothy smile, Remzold held the ladder out to Marek.

"After you."

Marek took the ladder, struck by something he hadn't thought of in years. In his home village, an ancient, toothless woman sat by the town well, telling stories to any and all who would listen. Often, she spoke of folk who once inhabited the land, folk who walked and talked and looked human ... but were not. Along with all the children, he'd laughed, mocking the old woman's ailing mind and foolishness. Lyric, too, in his last meeting with her, had spoken of *non-humans*.

Could it be true?

What he'd just witnessed was not a human skill. But he said nothing to the grinning Remzold, merely stuck his booted foot into the ladder and began to climb.

He was breathing heavily when he reached a wooden platform built into the tree. He leaned back against the tree trunk, taking in the structure he stood upon and the swinging walkway that went roughly east and west. Both ends of the walkway disappeared into the adjacent trees, and he wondered how long they'd been marching through the difficulty of the forest floor when they could have fairly flown along this path.

No wonder Quidar's people were impatient.

He could just see the horizon where the fiery remains of the crimson and gold sunset flared against the darkening purple sky. When Quidar joined him on the platform, without looking away from the sunset, he addressed his host. "So the Akyldi don't fly?"

"No," Quidar said. Marek could hear the humor in his voice.

"Then what is that?"

Quidar followed Marek's gaze. Together the two men watched the huge, outrageously-colored bird as it winged its way over the treetops toward the Akyldi capital.

Unless his eyes deceived him, two people sat upon the great bird's back.

CHAPTER 27: BETRAYED

"This is not right, Noni," Lyric said, gripping the girl's shoulders and peering into her red-rimmed eyes. "My grandfather would never allow such treatment of his servants. Celeste did this, didn't she?"

The girl cried softly as she struggled to escape Lyric's grip.

"I can't say, Your Highness. Truly. It would only make things worse for me. I just need to go back to ... Mistress Celeste and tell her I delivered her message. Please let me go."

Lyric released her grip on the girl and stepped back. Noni couldn't have been more than fifteen, a pretty girl with soft golden brown hair and a milky complexion. Lyric was galled to see her abused, but she could see the girl's point. Until she could talk to her grandfather about Celeste's treatment of the lower servants, there wasn't much she could do to help. She didn't even know where her own servant was.

"All right," she said heavily, lowering herself to the bed. "I'll let you go, but I promise that when I see my grandfather, he will hear about this."

"Oh, no, miss. Please! She'll know—"

Lyric lifted a hand. "Hear me out. I will do what I can to help you, and I'll be very careful that no one knows how I got my information. But I need you to help me as well."

Noni wiped her leaky eyes with the back of her sleeve and focused her gaze on Lyric.

"I am glad to help you in any way I can, my lady. But you don't have to do anything for me."

"We'll discuss that later," Lyric interrupted, tired of the argument. "What I want to know is where my friends are. Do you know or not?"

Noni's eyes went wide again. "I don't know, miss. Truly I don't." She looked around as if to make sure no one could hear them, though it was obvious she and Lyric were the only ones in the room. Then, to her amazement, Noni put a finger to her lip, signaling for silence, and beckoned the princess to follow her into the alcove that had been set up as Becca's room the night before.

When they stepped through the curtain-covered doorway, Noni turned back to her and spoke just above a whisper. "It is not safe to speak freely in your room, Your Highness. There are small holes in the walls, where people can listen to what is said."

"What?" Lyric was aghast.

Noni held her finger to her lips again. "I don't think anyone is listening now. I believe everyone is at the noon meal, but I don't know for certain. I will tell you only this. People—I won't say who—were listening to you and your friends when you were talking together yesterday. They heard about your plans to leave, to go on some ... *mission,* and they told Duke Foxmir. He was very angry."

Lyric stared at her, unbelieving. "Someone was listening in on us?"

"Yes." Noni still whispered but spoke quickly. "I don't know if Duke Foxmir knows about the listening holes, but when he heard what they told him, he ordered your friends be taken away." She held her hand up to keep Lyric silent. "I don't know where. I just know that as soon as you left for the castle this morning, several of the king's guards came and took them. Duke Foxmir was going to talk to you about it when you returned, but then he had to go to the castle."

Lyric felt her knees go weak. She was being spied on in her grandfather's house and he had taken her friends captive? Of all the things that had happened since she'd left her home, this was surely the most appalling. She shivered, feeling the prickle of goose flesh spreading across her arms.

How could this be happening?

Noni reached out and tentatively touched Lyric's sleeve. "I am so sorry, Your Highness. I will try to find out where your friends were taken, but I will have to be very careful. Now I must go." She tried to step away, but Lyric grasped her arm and stared at her desperately.

"Do you think my friends have been harmed?"

Noni gave her a look of distress. "I don't know, miss. Your grandfather just said to take them, but some of the other servants thought the two from across the hall seemed dangerous. If they resisted the guards ..." She shrugged her shoulders, then hurried out of the alcove and away from Lyric's room.

Infuriated, Lyric paced back and forth through the luxuriant suite, searching. She found two holes in each wall, each covered by furniture or decorative fabric. She also checked her door, deciding that if it was locked she was going to do something truly violent. Fortunately, the door opened easily. She stepped out into the corridor, tempted to go rip one of the adjacent doors open and look for spies, but she knew giving in to her outrage would be pointless. She must calm herself and think things through.

An hour after her first visit, Noni returned, dutifully somber, bringing Lyric soup and bread for the midday meal. She listened to Lyric's request to be informed of her grandfather's return and carefully replied that she would relay the message to Mistress Celeste. Lyric understood, by Noni's attitude, that someone was at the listening hole in the adjoining room.

Determined to play her role convincingly, she smiled and dismissed the girl, knowing that Celeste would inform her of nothing that didn't directly suit the housekeeper's purpose. She supposed she should be grateful she was given something to eat. Wherever Becca, Quinn, and Amira were, she hoped they, too, were being fed.

Hours later, Celeste herself came to tell Lyric that Duke Foxmir required her presence in his formal sitting room. As a verbal response didn't seem necessary, Lyric rose wordlessly to her feet and followed the woman down the stairs to a well-appointed room near the front door.

"Here is Princess Lyric, Duke Foxmir," Celeste said cheerily as they stepped into the room. "Dinner will be served in an hour."

"Thank you, Celeste." Her grandfather had been sitting in a comfortable armchair near the hearth but rose to his feet as the women entered. Lyric did not miss the look of understanding that passed between him and the housekeeper.

"Sit down, my dear," he said affably, indicating a chair near his.

"Thank you, sir," she said, and took the proffered chair. She'd had all afternoon to think about this encounter and meant to make the most of it. The complication of being odd-man-out against the united front of her grandfather and the housekeeper was something she'd not considered. She'd have to add it to her list of obstacles to overcome. "How is the king?" she asked solicitously. "Is he better?"

"Oh, yes. Yes, my dear." The lines in his face softened, and he allowed a smile to touch his lips. "Thank you for asking. He regained consciousness this afternoon and was rather confused in his speech, but the healers think he will soon be fine. He will need to rest for the next several days. He took a nasty blow with that fall."

"I'm glad to hear he's doing better," Lyric said, nodding. "And who is in charge until the king is on his feet again? The queen? Prince Carlton?"

He cleared his throat and reached for the tankard of ale that rested on an ornate tea table nearby. "Well, as to that, nothing of any consequence should need tending in the next few days, but as the prince is the heir and is of age, he will officially be in command. I'm sure, though, that he will confer with the queen and the nobles, should major decisions need to be made."

"Such as answering the Malacarians who are still blocking the Merchant Road and are, in effect, cutting Graceen off from the ports and all traffic south?" she asked. "That seems rather major to me."

He looked at her sharply over the tankard's rim.

"Well, yes, I suppose it is." He took a long swallow before setting the tankard down. "That may indeed require a response soon."

The banality of the conversation seared a hole in Lyric's determination to remember herself and tread carefully.

"Grandfather." The word came out like ice. "Enough of this. What have you done? Where have my friends been taken?"

"Now, now," he harrumphed, pushing himself back from the table. "If you must know," he went on, closer to his usual stern self, "I received word that you and they plan to go off on some foolhardy quest, and I won't have that. It is not safe, and in your father's absence, I must decide what's best for you."

"Such as being spied on in my own room? Is that what's best for me? What is happening in Graceen, that I am treated in such a contemptible way in my grandfather's home?"

He narrowed his bushy brows. "What do you mean, spying? I know of no spying taking place in my home."

One thing at a time, she told herself, breathing deeply, controlling the rage that boiled within. "How did you receive word about these plans, sir?"

"One of the servants came forward. I assume she overheard you in the hallway or some such."

"So you maintain you know nothing about the listening holes between my room and those adjacent to it, where servants have been ordered to sit and listen in to my private conversations?"

"Listening holes?" He jumped to his feet, trembling in his wrath. "There are no such things."

"Would you like me to show you?" she asked calmly. "I've found four, just this afternoon."

He ran both hands through his wavy white mane. "I've lived in this house for forty years. I tell you, I know nothing about any listening holes."

"I'm glad to hear it," she replied softly, knowing she needed to get him back on her side. "But obviously someone knew, and I assume she ordered the spying. And determined, it appears, to put me in that particular room for this very reason."

He still stood, clenching and unclenching his fists, but he turned his back to her, and she knew he was trying to make sense of something he'd never expected to take place in his own home.

"I apologize for this invasion of your privacy, my dear, and rest assured I will get to the bottom of it, but—" He wheeled to face her. "Regardless of how I received this information, do you deny the truth of it? Were you or were you not planning to leave here on some sort of mission with that servant and those other two? Answer me truthfully."

Lyric inclined her head. "It is true that I have a task I have taken on. Prince Ralt of Malacar has plans much larger than overrunning Tressalt. He must be stopped."

"And we have an army to do that, should it be necessary," he broke in, his anger returning. "You are heir to the throne of Tressalt. You cannot go wandering off in the wilderness as you please. You should know that!"

"What I know, Grandfather," she said quietly, "is that I have already spent weeks in the wilderness, trying to escape those who would do me harm. I have come to your land and your home for refuge, and you have imprisoned the very people who have saved my life on this journey."

"They're not in prison," he said roughly. "They are comfortable and their needs are being met. But they will not be released—not until I have your word you will remain under my protection until this difficulty with Malacar has been addressed. Do I have your word?"

"Grandfather," she said, her voice very soft, "you have said it yourself. I am heir to the throne of Tressalt. How dare you do this? Release my friends immediately."

He waved a hand dismissively. "You are a child. When you were here last year, you were playing games with the servants. You don't know what's best for you."

Fury roiled through her, but she clamped it down and forced herself to speak calmly.

"I am not that child anymore. I am three months from coming of age. Release my friends."

He stepped back to his chair, slumped into it. "I will release them when you give me your word to abandon this insane mission."

"I have already given my word, Grandfather," she said softly. "It is to that promise I am bound."

"I see," he said slowly. "I am sorry, my dear, and I hope one day you'll forgive me, but you've left me no choice."

"People always have choices." She held his gaze until a soft rapping at the door broke the spell.

"Enter," her grandfather called.

One of the older maids pushed into the room. "Begging your pardon, your lordship, but there's been a message from the castle." She held up a folded parchment sealed with gleaming gold wax.

"Thank you, Gertie." He reached for the parchment.

"No, sir," Gertie said, lowering herself into a stiff curtsy. "It's for the princess, sir. From Prince Carlton."

Lyric stood and took the parchment. Breaking the seal, she opened the missive, read it quickly and handed it to her grandfather.

He scanned the letter, eyes narrowing, then looked at Lyric. "The prince wishes to come here for a private meeting with you? Why?"

"I do not know." Smarting from the overbearing treatment from this man she'd loved as long as she could remember, Lyric made little effort to mask her sarcasm. "I assume this meets with your approval?"

His face fell. "Of course." He handed her the parchment and turned to leave.

"Grandfather, please!" She stepped forward, grasped his arm. "Let us not be at war over this. I know what I must do."

He raised his bushy brows, regarding her sorrowfully.

"Then you have the advantage of me, my dear." He dropped her hand and stalked from the room.

CHAPTER 28: PRINCE CARLTON

The bells of the city pealed eight mournful times, echoing through the sitting room window. Lyric straightened a painting on the wall and sighed with relief. The colorful scene of a springtime country fair did not cover listening holes. She'd questioned Noni earlier about whether this room had the invasive holes, but the girl hadn't been sure. Lyric had to know. She didn't know what Prince Carlton wished to discuss with her but whatever it was, she didn't want Celeste listening in.

Dinner had been a quiet affair, and she'd excused herself as quickly as possible, both to prepare for the prince's visit and to escape her grandfather's brooding silence. She hated quarreling with him, but her anger at what he'd done was far from diminished.

The fire had been built up in the hearth, but its dancing flames did nothing to cheer her. Her grandfather had kidnapped her friends, and an unknown prince was coming to speak with her in private. The last time she'd been alone with a prince, she'd been assaulted. What did this prince want?

She released a gusty breath. He probably just wanted to take up the questioning where his father had left off. If so, she hoped it would be a less eventful conversation than that one had been. She turned to the last of the sitting room's walls. This one held a smallish tapestry and two paintings.

She stepped toward it, then jumped as a log in the fireplace cracked and splintered. Scowling at her frayed nerves, she reached for the first painting, then froze, her hand inches from the wall.

Voices in the corridor.

Spinning on her heel, she scurried to take her seat at the tea table. A moment later, the door opened and her grandfather entered the room, followed by Prince Carlton, and finally a guard, in Graceen's emerald and gold livery.

"Here she is, Your Highness," her grandfather said more jovially than she'd heard him speak all evening. "I'll be right down the hall in my study, if you should need anything." He gave a quick bow to his future sovereign.

"Thank you, Duke Foxmir." The prince was not as tall as the older man and more slender in build, but he carried himself as one of royal birth. "It's most kind of you to receive me on such short notice."

"Not at all, my lord. You are always welcome here." Her grandfather gave a final bow and exited the room. The prince's man took his place in front of the now-closed door, expression bland, right hand on his sword hilt.

"Welcome, Prince Carlton. I am glad to see you again." Lyric forced her voice to stay calm while her thoughts whirled. What if there were indeed listening holes behind the tapestry or the paintings behind her? There was nothing she could do about it now. She indicated a chair across the tea table from her own. "Please sit down."

"Thank you, my lady." He bowed courteously and sat. "Please forgive me for this intrusion, but as I said this morning, there are important matters I would like to discuss with you."

"Certainly." Lyric gave what she hoped was an encouraging smile, then lifted one hand, palm facing the prince. "But first, may I inquire as to the health of your father?"

He blinked. "Oh, yes, of course. Thank you for asking. He has regained consciousness several times since his mishap this morning. He is ... confused, but the healers believe he'll have a full recovery."

"Wonderful. I'm glad to hear it."

The prince stared at her, his gaze intense. "That's gracious of you, considering his rather poor treatment of you in the throne room."

Lyric considered her words carefully, hoping for a way to agree with the prince without insulting his father. "He is a king. Kings are not ruled by the constraints that others of us are."

"True." His sandy-colored brows knitted together in a frown. "But as I said earlier, this was very out of character for my father. I have been with him in many difficult situations, and I have never seen him show the fury he did today. Do you have any idea why your presence should excite such a spectacular change in his disposition?"

Her right hand flew to the bodice of her wine-colored gown, covering the hidden gemstone and her racing heart. "None at all, Your Highness. I was trying to ascertain that very thing before his fall this morning."

The prince leaned forward, eyes narrowed in a manner that reminded her of his father. "Forgive me, my lady. I am not suggesting that you'd done anything to bring on his behavior. Even before you arrived today, I had noticed something amiss in his attitude. I am simply trying to understand it myself. I was hoping perhaps you could help."

She pursed her lips. "I wish I could be more helpful. Of course, you are worried about your father. As I am for mine." She dipped her head toward him. "In this we understand each other very well."

"True." He pressed forward, bracing his elbows against the table and intertwining his fingers as he stared over them at her. "I am very sorry about your father. His predicament, that is—Tressalt's predicament—is one of the things I wished to speak with you about. I'm afraid we didn't get very far this morning." He gave her a wry smile. "All we in Graceen know is what the delegation from Malacar has told us. Neither my father nor I were convinced of their honesty, but until your arrival, we had no way to disprove their words."

He paused, turning away from her to gaze into the fire, a troubled expression marking his unlined face. After a moment he looked back at her, his expression resolute.

"Please tell me again exactly what has happened in Tressalt and how you came to be here. I believe you mean well," he said, his voice kind, "but as my father said, you haven't been completely forthright with us. You may have reasons for this, but I need to know as much as possible so I—and my father when he is well again—can know how best to judge this situation."

Her heart skipped a beat and she sat back in her chair, staring at the sandy-haired prince. She hardly knew him, but she liked what she'd seen so far. It pained her that he might think poorly of her. Even so, she had to be wary, both of telling him too much and of the possibility of a listening hole somewhere in the room. She lifted her chin.

"I will be as honest as I may be, Your Highness. But I have already told you, to the best of my ability, what happened in Tressalt. Prince Ralt came to my court as an invited guest, partook of our hospitality, then showed his thanks by overrunning my land and taking my father captive." Despite her best efforts, her voice trembled. She swallowed and forced herself to go on. "Many of my people are dead, people I have known all my life. The only reason I am not currently in Ralt's power is because I was away from the palace at the time of his attack. My guardsman learned of the attack from a mortally wounded soldier and then was himself gravely wounded before returning to warn me. I have been running for weeks, hiding in the forest, and have finally found my way here, to what I hoped was safety."

She saw compassion as well as caution in the prince's eyes.

"About this part of your tale," he said. "I can truly say I am sorry for the difficulties you've been through. My father didn't tell you this morning, but he sent spies out as soon as the Malacarians put up their blockade on the Merchant Road. They are going to both Tressalt and Malacar to see what they can discover. We have yet to hear back from them, but I trust we will soon." He leaned forward, holding her gaze. "If their story backs up your own, my father is prepared to send aid to Tressalt."

She hadn't realized she'd been holding her breath. She exhaled, almost dizzy. "Thank you, Your Highness. This is the best news I've heard since my arrival."

He smiled and the smile transformed his rather plain face into quite a nice one. "I'm glad I could help. Now that that's settled, I have some other questions. Do you mind?"

Her stomach knotted at the thought someone might be listening, spying on them at this very moment. Outwardly she stayed calm and shrugged. "I won't know until you ask them."

He smiled again. "True enough. The first has to do with my father's behavior this morning. As I told you, this was completely unlike him—to *harass* you the way he did." He sighed. "I'll start with what I already know. When my father returned from hunting yesterday and heard of your arrival, he was very pleased—happy you had survived the so-called kidnapping, and looking forward to hearing your report of the goings-on in Tressalt." He paused, peering closely at her. "Despite some of the things he said today, he does consider your father a true friend and a good king."

Lyric nodded gratefully. King Rasmus's cold comments about her father had been one of the things that disturbed her most in today's interview.

Carlton turned a faint smile upon her. "Then he received word of your, shall we say, *unusual* means of transport to our border. Even then, he was more fascinated than anything else."

Oh. She cleared her throat. "And then?"

"And then a delegation from Malacar arrived early this morning, demanding an immediate audience. It seems they'd also received word of your arrival."

She sat stone still, fear clutching at her heart. King Rasmus had said Ralt wanted her back, but how had the Malacarians known she was here? *Had someone listening to her in this house sent word to Ralt?*

Carlton met her gaze, but his expression told her nothing. "I do not know what was said in that meeting, but when I arrived I found my father in the state you saw him in later."

Surprising her, he jumped to his feet and paced across the room, whirled and strode back, spitting words out as though they were stinging him. "I believe something happened when he met with the Malacarians, but I do not know what. He was irritable and impatient, shouting at everyone. I asked him what was wrong just before you arrived. His only response was that he was king, not I, and I should stay out of affairs that didn't concern me."

Stopping his fevered pacing, he pivoted to face Lyric, running his hands through his hair. He took a deep breath, exhaled slowly, then reached into the pocket of his breeches. He lifted out a small, cloth-covered object and laid it carefully on the tea table.

"Have you ever seen this before?"

She leaned forward as he unwrapped the object. It was a miniature sailing ship, perhaps three inches long. The detail was impressive, from the stalwart masts to the billowing sails to the gilded prow in the shape of a wolf's head. She reached for it but he pushed her hand away before she could touch it.

Startled, she looked up quickly, but he didn't explain or apologize. Just stared at her, waiting for her answer.

"It's beautiful," she finally said, "but no, I've never seen it before. Where did you get it?"

Carlton's jaw was tight. "My father had it clenched in his fist when we took him to the infirmary this morning. When we tried to open his hand to see what he held, he thrashed and shouted like a wild man. Then he fainted again."

She frowned. "And you've never seen it before?"

"Never. I was hoping you knew something about it."

She shook her head. "Not I. Perhaps—" She stopped, thoughts racing. "You say your father's disposition changed after his meeting with the Malacarians?"

"Yes. Why?"

"What about his eyes?"

He sighed and sank into his chair. "You noticed them?"

She shivered. "I did. I thought his eyes were strange, almost all black, with no color, but I'd never met him before. I wondered if they were always like that."

"No," Carlton said heavily, leaning against the tea table. "His eyes are hazel, like mine. I asked him about them this morning because I thought they looked odd too. He refused to answer." He shook his head. "I don't know what's happening, but I'm worried that perhaps he's ill. That could explain the strangeness of his eyes and his odd behavior."

"Ralt has a magician." The words were out of her mouth before she realized they were in her mind.

Carlton's eyes widened. "He has a *what*?"

She gulped, furious with herself, but the words couldn't be unsaid. If there were listening holes under those paintings on the last wall, even now Celeste or one of her minions could be hearing everything.

She leapt to her feet.

"It is a lovely evening, Your Highness, don't you think? I would enjoy some fresh air. Perhaps you'll accompany me on a short stroll through the grounds?"

The prince climbed slowly to his feet, confusion in his eyes. "Yes, of course, my lady." He turned to his man at the door. "Hanseth?"

The prince refolded the cloth about the tiny ship and stuffed it back into his pocket while the green-clad guard pulled open the heavy door. He held it as the prince and Lyric passed through, then strode the dozen or so paces to the mansion's front door and opened that, as well.

Tremors ran through her. She needed to get out of this house. Away from rooms where no conversation was private. Leading the prince out the door, she turned onto a cobbled pathway that ran along the front of the mansion.

Tonight, just a few weeks past the longest day of the year, the night was not completely dark. A smattering of stars shone in the dusky twilight, and low on the horizon the Maiden cast her final brilliance before sinking into the west. The evening air was fragrant with the musky-sweet odor of the roses that lined the pathway. Lyric inhaled deeply, hoping this separation from the mansion and its secrets would calm her spirit. As they passed the corner of the building, she gestured toward a copse of apple trees that marked the border of a small private garden.

The prince and his man followed her into the garden. Lyric led the way to a wrought-iron bench next to the lily pond in the grassy area's center. A burning torch stood at the pond's edge, filling the garden with its flickering light.

She sat on the bench, and after a moment's hesitation Prince Carlton joined her. The guard stalked around the garden's edge, examining the whole area carefully before planting himself at the entrance, hand upon his sword hilt.

"I am sorry for the drama, Your Highness," Lyric began, "but I have reason to believe that words spoken in my grandfather's house do not always remain between the original speakers." She raised her hands and let them fall, trying to lighten the tension. "I may be wrong and it may be nothing, but if we are to speak of serious matters, I would prefer not to take chances."

The prince frowned. "I cannot imagine such a thing in Duke Foxmir's home but it is, as you said, a pleasant evening. If you are more comfortable speaking here, I have no complaint."

Lyric sighed gustily. "Thank you. Now where were we?"

"You were telling me about Prince Ralt and a magician."

She bit her lip. "I have met Prince Ralt, and I do not exaggerate when I say he is a terrible man, but from what I understand, the magician is worse. Since your father's character change was so dramatic and came about after his meeting with the Malacarians, I thought perhaps it had something to do with Lothar."

"Lothar?" The prince grinned and shook his head. "This is almost amusing. Some so-called magician in our time has named himself after the worst of all wizards in our oldest myths?"

"You know of him?" Was she truly the only one who had never heard of these things? Grimacing, she forced herself to go on. "I think it's the same person. At least that's what I've been told."

"That's impossible," Carlton said. "If the wars in the old stories ever actually happened, they were thousands of years ago. No one can live that long."

Lyric shrugged. "I've seen many things in the last few weeks I would once have said were impossible. If he's truly a magician, perhaps he can live for thousands of years."

She turned her gaze to him and spoke firmly. "What I *do* know is there is a magician named Lothar aiding Prince Ralt. I don't know how he could exert influence on your father from hundreds of miles away, but perhaps that is what happened. Prince Ralt wants me back because then his victory over my people will be complete. Maybe Lothar has cursed anyone who mentions my name. Or maybe it was as simple as a drug placed in the king's morning ale. Or perhaps that sailing ship has something to do with it."

The prince jumped to his feet and stalked to the pond's edge, then wheeled to face her.

"I would not give credence to any of these suggestions, Your Highness, had I not heard from reliable witnesses that you flew into our land on the back of a mighty bird. None of these things happen in the world I live in. It is difficult for me to accept their possibility."

Lyric met his gaze steadily. "Until two weeks ago, I would have agreed with you."

He nodded slowly. "Perhaps the king was correct when he accused you of riding in on the wings of legend. My father may or may not have been struck down by this Lothar, but what can you tell me about these impossible things you have seen and experienced?"

She pursed her lips, considering. "I will answer your questions if you answer one of mine. If you'd been sworn to secrecy by those who might be injured should their truth be known, what would you do? For that is what you're asking of me, Prince Carlton. I think you are an honorable man, but there are lives at stake."

The prince stared at her through the shadows of the early evening.

"I see I have put you in a difficult position," he said, his tone thoughtful, "as you have done to me. What if I tell you what I already know—or have guessed—and you can decide whether or not to tell me if I am hitting near the mark? I can say, in all truthfulness, that I will not knowingly cause harm to any innocent creature."

"And what of your man?" She gestured to the silent guard.

"I trust Hanseth with my life," Carlton said without hesitation. "He'll not say a word."

Looking at his youthful face but already kingly expression, Lyric found she believed him. He wanted proof of her honesty, which seemed only fair, and she needed his good favor if she was to have Graceen's help against Malacar.

"We can try that, if you like, but—" She held her hand out to him in warning, "—I reserve the right not to verify your guesses if ... if that seems best to me," she finished lamely.

His eyes brightened, and his teeth flashed in another transformative smile. "You are quite the crafty negotiator, Your Highness. I must remember this, should you and I ever discuss trade between our lands. I accept your conditions. Shall we begin?"

Heat flooded her cheeks but she forced herself to go on.

"Of course," she answered primly.

"Very well, then," he said, sobering. "I will tell you now my first vision of you and your traveling companions was yesterday, when you entered our north gate and your grandfather raced out to greet you. It was I who brought my father word of that happy occasion when he returned to the castle, but not before I took note of those who traveled with you. Two of them—the man and woman—the ones who never stray far from one another—carry themselves as warriors. I noticed, but thought little of it at the time. I assumed they were your guards.

"Later in the day, I was in the council chamber when my father and your grandfather met. My father had by then heard from the commander of our guard about the winged creature that delivered you to the clearing near our border. Your grandfather, however, had not heard of this. He was, I'm sorry to say, quite upset. He mentioned his concern with your traveling companions—the two I'd already noticed. He told us he would talk to you immediately and discover the truth about both the winged creature and your two friends."

He paused and let his gaze linger on her, but she turned away. No wonder her grandfather reacted the way he had. He'd had to hear the amazing news of her arrival from the sky from someone else. He would have been humiliated. And hurt.

"My father told him he would prefer meeting with you himself, and privately. I think your grandfather was not pleased but he agreed with the king's request. And then today ..."

"The Malacarians came," Lyric finished for him.

"Yes," he agreed.

They were silent for a moment, while the night wind whispered its own secrets through the trees.

"Setting aside," Carlton finally said, "for the time being, who or what is responsible for my father's uncharacteristic temper this morning, may I ask you another question?"

"You may as well." She sighed.

"What kind of education have you been exposed to in Tressalt?"

Her confusion must have been evident, because the prince continued without waiting for an answer. "Here in Graceen, I have worked with tutors for many years. I have studied mathematics and geography, literature, music, protocol, diplomacy, and economics. Archery, sword play, and horsemanship." He peered closely at her. "I trust your education was similar?"

She nodded, not wanting to point out that she'd had to demand to learn the defensive arts but was forced to endure the domestic ones of weaving and needlework.

"What about history?" he asked.

"Yes," Lyric said. "My tutor taught me history."

"How far back?"

"Excuse me?" she asked.

"How far back in time did your history lessons take you?"

She frowned. "To the beginning, of course. When our ancient fathers came down from the far reaches of northern Argonia to Graceen, and then to Tressalt."

"Nothing before that?"

"There was nothing before," she said in exasperation, mimicking the words, tone, and mannerism of her long-departed, unlamented tutor. She had once asked him the very same question. But he had lied to her—or not known the truth himself. She knew that now.

"Do you still believe your lessons?" the prince asked quietly. When she only stared at him, he went on. "The stories about things that happened before our own history are mostly forgotten, but I always enjoyed them. Myths and legends, my tutor called them. Did you never read such accounts?"

She shook her head. If there were such stories in the archives of Tressalt, she'd never seen them.

"I'm sorry to hear that," he said. "But unless I am much mistaken, I believe you now know more about these things than even those who, like me, have studied the scrolls. The impossible things you were referring to a few minutes ago. Am I right?"

Emotions battled in her heart. What exactly did he know? What did the scrolls say and why did he have access to them, but she herself had never seen them? On the other hand, if she had seen and read them, would she have believed them? Not likely.

He stood quietly, staring up into the darkening sky, and she was grateful for the silence. After a moment he stirred and looked back at her.

"I always liked the old stories, but I didn't believe them. Then the young kidnapped Princess Lyric of Tressalt arrives in our land on the back of a huge bird, accompanied by strange otherworldly companions, and I began to wonder. When your grandfather left us yesterday, I went directly to the palace library and after some digging, found what I was looking for."

He reached for the satchel he carried at his side. Untying the leather thong that held it closed, he pulled out a small faded, worn scroll. Sitting on the bench beside her, he unrolled the parchment and ran a forefinger lightly along its surface.

After a moment's search, he looked back up at Lyric, and his eyes blazed with excitement.

"I believe, Princess Lyric, that your two friends might be what were once called *Akeeldy, Akiildy?* A catlike people who lived in the mountains in the east between what is now

Tressalt and Graceen. And could it be true? Did you actually arrive at our border on the back of a prehistoric Sheever?"

She froze. Hearing the names spoken aloud by an outsider, even one as kind as this prince seemed to be, was unnerving. He stared at her, his face eager, awaiting her answer.

She spoke slowly. "I believe that is what they are called. I have only met them myself in these last weeks when fleeing from Ralt and the attack on Tressalt. Their people have been here all along, I'm told, but have had no interaction with humans for centuries."

He turned from her and leaned back against the bench, staring upward at the sky. "It's true, then," he said softly. "The old stories are true." They sat in silence for some time before the prince glanced her way again. "There is so much I want to know—about this and other things—but I must meet with the healers and my father in the morning, and then with leaders of the metalworkers' guild after that." His eyes lit up. "But would you consent to ride with me tomorrow afternoon? I can show you the city. Perhaps we can speak more of these things."

This was the last thing she'd expected to hear, and for the moment words failed her. Was this just a friendly invitation? The darkness was now complete but even with the torchlight, she couldn't see the prince's eyes well enough to guess his intentions. But she needed to respond.

"I would enjoy seeing the city," she admitted. "And I love riding, so I believe I shall say yes."

"Splendid." The prince rose to his feet. "I must be getting home to the castle. Come, I'll escort you to the mansion, and we can discuss the details."

CHAPTER 29: MENJAR—THE OPAL STONE

A quarter of an hour later, Prince Carlton strode down the walkway to Hanseth and their saddled horses.

Lyric waited until the rhythmical clopping of the iron-shod hooves disappeared into the night. Then she closed the door, turned, and slumped against it, her mind whirling. She was going on a tour of the city tomorrow with the prince. Their conversation had been fascinating. And overwhelming. He knew—had known—about the intelligent non-human inhabitants of their world since boyhood, while until recently she'd known nothing. She hoped his enthusiasm would translate into support for her mission to find even more of these ancient peoples.

Pushing away from the door, she slipped quietly back to the tearoom and pulled the bell for the servants. How she longed for Amira's advice. Was there a way she might get it?

Moments later, Noni hustled down the curving stairway and across the marble hall toward her. She dropped into a curtsy. "Are you ready to return to your rooms, Your Highness?"

"I am."

The maid accompanied Lyric back to her rooms, past the low-burning torches in the wall brackets. Lyric did not see her grandfather or anyone else of the household.

"Noni?" She kept her voice just above a whisper as they climbed the stairs. "That thing we were discussing earlier today. About my room?"

"Yes, my lady." Noni spoke just as quietly.

"Is someone in there now, in the adjacent room, do you think?"

"One person was sent up as soon as the prince left." Noni's voice was the ghost of a whisper. "She won't stay all night. If you are very quiet, you might hear her leave."

Noni opened the door to Lyric's chamber. The room was warm from the fire crackling in the hearth, and the lighted candles scattered about only added to the room's ambiance. It was a lovely room, but one with a secret. Lyric knew she'd never enjoy it again.

Noni closed the door behind them. "Shall I help you with your clothing and hair, Your Highness?"

"Yes, of course." Lyric absently turned so the maid could begin unfastening the many ties and stays on her gown, her mind on her meeting with Prince Carlton. Despite her growing conviction that he might be an ally, she'd remained careful during their time together. Too much was at stake for her to be free with her trust. He'd accepted her caution, and for that she was grateful.

Noni pulled the gown over her head and helped her into a linen night shift, then pulled the clips from Lyric's hair. She fluffed out the stylish up-do she'd labored over before the prince's visit and carefully combed through Lyric's mahogany locks with a boar-bristle brush.

"Will that be all, Your Highness? Do you need anything else for the evening?"

"No," she replied. "It's late. I believe I'll go straight to bed."

"Very good, my lady. Feel free to pull the bell if you need anything." Noni curtsied and let herself out of the room.

Eagerness gripping her, Lyric snuffed out all but two of the candles and climbed into her bed. She pulled the coverlet up to her chin but kept her eyes open, focusing on the patterns in the wall coverings.

After several minutes, she heard the tiniest rustle of movement, then a small creak—the opening of a door—and after that the quiet *snick* of the door latch closing. She wasn't certain if someone was indeed leaving the room next to hers, or if she'd heard only what she hoped to hear.

She forced herself to lie quietly for another ten minutes. After hearing no further sound from the next room, she flung the bedcovers aside and sat up. Picking up the candles from the table near her bed, she crept quietly to the maid's alcove next to her personal chamber.

After she placed the candles on a small oak chest at the foot of the narrow bed, she sat down and pulled the pendant from under her nightclothes. She brought the gemstone close to her face. She hadn't attempted to use the stone since their unsuccessful attempt on the skyway when she and Amira tried to reach Venuzia.

She hoped to do better tonight.

She stared at the creamy-misted opal, marveling that she'd worn it so long with no idea of its power. She'd been groggy that night on the skyway, but she remembered something about rubbing the stone, blowing on it. Using her forefinger, she stroked the gem's surface, then stopped and blew lightly upon it. Then she rubbed again, staring into the milky depths of the stone. *Menjar,* she reminded herself. She repeated the rubbing and blowing on Menjar's surface two more times, then whispered her friend's name. "Amira."

Nothing happened.

Gritting her teeth, she tried again. *This has to work.*

It didn't.

What had she forgotten? She pressed her fingers against her tired eyes. Was she supposed to rub a certain way? In a circular motion? Back and forth? She didn't think so, but then recalled Amira hadn't been successful in contacting Venuzia either. Or at least they hadn't thought so. Not until the wild woman with the flaming red hair sailed into their lives the next day on the back of her great bird.

What an unforgettable day that had been. And it turned out Venuzia *had* heard them. She'd just chosen not to reply.

A pang of loneliness clutched at her heart as she wondered how the crotchety old Sheever was doing. Sighing, she lifted the gemstone to try the ritual once more.

And gasped.

The pendant was glowing.

She held it to her face, seeing nothing but the soft golden glow.

"Amira," she whispered, "are you there?"

Suddenly, Menjar's glowing surface clouded over. Images appeared on it as she'd seen once before. Venuzia sat staring into a fire's dying embers, tears coursing down her sunken cheeks. Before Lyric could make sense of what she saw, the scene shifted.

A fluid, swirling surface bubbled and spat in shades of red, brown, and dark gold like a strange muddy lake, a steaming crimson lake. Then a figure rose from the simmering liquid. It paused for a moment, red streams running down its body, then strode purposefully toward her. It looked human, but somehow not.

She shrank away from the stone, but already the scene was changing again. Hues of blues and greens pushed the red away, and fronds of a plant she didn't recognize swayed gently back and forth across the stone's surface. A sleek, silver form slid among the fronds, swishing its tail fin calmly, its tiny, beady eyes focused fixedly ahead.

With a supreme effort, she pulled her gaze away from the stone. What was this? Why the underwater scene? And what was that glowing human shape she'd seen rising from the red lake?

Reluctantly she looked back at the stone. The fish and its underwater world had vanished. Now she saw nothing but darkness, but she heard a roaring like a raging voice shouting unintelligible words.

She pulled back, shuddering, then heard another sound. A different voice. The surface of the stone glowed and swirled once again.

"Princess Lyric? Are you there?"

The voice was tiny, remote, but she'd know it anywhere. She pulled the pendant close to her face and stared into the radiant surface.

"Yes, Amira, it's me. Can you hear me?"

And there was her friend. Her lovely face coalesced from the whirling streams of gold and white emanating from the gemstone.

"I hear you, Princess." Amira's brow had been furrowed in concentration, but the lines smoothed as her familiar wisp of a smile pushed them aside. "It is good to see you, my friend. And you have learned to use Menjar. That is also good."

"Oh, Amira," she said, weak with relief. "Are you all right? Is everyone there?"

"We are all well," Amira said in her calm voice.

"Where are you?"

"That is less certain." Amira looked away from the stone, spoke briefly to someone Lyric could not see, then turned back, her eyes crinkling, her delicate lips upturned. "Mistress Becca asks that I send you her greetings and wonders if you also are well."

"I'm fine," Lyric replied, surprised at the catch in her voice and the tears gathering in her eyes. She paused, cleared her throat. "Tell her I send her my greetings as well."

Oh, how she missed them all, but there would be time to think of that later. Right now, there were things she must know. "Tell me everything that's happened. How were you taken this morning?"

Soon after Lyric had left for the castle, Amira explained, a half-dozen armed guards arrived in their corridor. They had taken Becca from Lyric's room first, then held her captive while they knocked on Amira and Quinn's door.

"They told us that if we had any concern for her life, we would hand over our weapons and come quietly." Amira pursed her lips. "I don't know whether they would have actually harmed her, but we couldn't take the chance."

Lyric sighed. "Thank you. Were the guards of my grandfather's household?"

"Some were. They did not wear his colors, being dressed entirely in black, but Quinn had seen one of the men earlier in Duke Foxmir's home. However—" Amira lifted a hand, "—we are no longer in his home. We were bound and blindfolded, and then loaded into a conveyance of some sort and taken away."

"How long did you travel once you were in the carriage?"

"Nearly an hour, but we have not left the city."

Lyric frowned. "How do you know?"

"Because we were on cobblestone streets the entire time."

"Of course." She smiled, then grew serious again. "My grandfather says you are not prisoners as such. That your needs are being met. Is this true?"

"We certainly *are* prisoners," Amira said, her tone offended in a way Lyric had never heard from her. "We are being kept here against our will. But they have fed us and we are not being abused, if that is what you are asking."

Once again, relief flooded through her. If they had been injured in any way, she would not have been able to forgive herself—or her grandfather. She raised her eyes.

"I will do everything in my power to find you and secure your release, but there is another thing I must tell you, and I want your true opinion."

Amira inclined her head. "Of course."

"My grandfather declares he will release you as soon as I agree to give up the quest and stay quietly here in his home. What do you say to that?"

Amira's nostrils flared. "You cannot make such a promise. Is that what this is about? Your grandsire learned of our plans?"

Lyric nodded. "It is a very long story and only one of many, I'm afraid. I will tell you all when I can." She lifted her chin. "I will either see you rescued by this time tomorrow, or I will contact you again. Try to be patient."

A smile flashed across her friend's fine-boned face. "We Akyldi are always patient." She tilted her head to the side, listened for a moment, turned back. "Quinn is correcting me. He says to tell you that we Akyldi are *usually* patient."

Lyric smiled back at her, then sobered. "I also must tell you what happened at the castle today." Briefly, she ran through her interrogation by King Rasmus, his accident, and the news Carlton had given her later.

"So the Malacarians know you are here," Amira said, "and the king has possibly fallen under the wizard's power." She squinted, shook her head. "This is not good."

"I know," Lyric said, sighing. "And there is one more thing you must know—a thing I have found most surprising." She described her meeting with Prince Carlton and what he'd shown her in the scroll.

Amira narrowed her gaze. "This is surprising, but not impossible. The lore masters have long taught us that the old knowledge was eventually lost to humans, but trackers have come across human encampments over the generations. They declare that some still remember." She shrugged. "But as I say, it is unusual. What is he like, this prince? Is he trustworthy?"

Lyric considered a moment. "I think so. It's hard to be certain in two brief meetings, but I think he is."

"It would be most useful to have a prince on our side."

Lyric nodded. "It would indeed. I'll see what I can find out. We are meeting again tomorrow."

"Are you?" The question seemed to mean more than the words implied. Lyric was tempted to do something very unprincess-like, such as stick out her tongue. "Is this prince married?"

"I don't know." But she thought not. He didn't *act* married, though now that she considered it, she wasn't sure how a married man might act differently. She'd really not spent much time with men other than her father and the courtiers at the palace. Well, and the soldiers she trained with in the guard. And that dreadful Prince Ralt.

And Marek.

She shook her head, trying not to think of her lost guard, and returned to the task at hand.

"I see you are having a wonderful time teasing me. From what I've seen so far, Prince Carlton seems to be a good prince, and that's all I'm going to say now. Are you certain you are well? I wish I could do something to help."

Amira smiled. "You have done very well, and we are encouraged to know you have found us."

Lyric gulped around the lump swelling in her throat. "I haven't exactly found you, but I'll do everything I can to get you out as soon as possible."

"We know you will."

Amira's visage dissolved as the stone's surface shimmered for a moment, then went blank.

CHAPTER 30: A FRIEND INDEED

The next morning, Lyric squared her shoulders as she swept across the dining chamber floor to join her grandfather at breakfast. She *would* convince him to free her companions—she must. She couldn't get past the image of Becca, Amira, and Quinn imprisoned, held against their will, at his command.

She slipped into her seat, but before she could speak, he dove in first.

"Good morning, my dear. And how was your visit with the prince last evening? He stayed for quite some time, I believe."

She peered at him over the rim of her goblet. "We had a pleasant visit."

"Very good." He waited while a servant stepped in and poured the tea. "And did you sleep well?"

She glared at him. "Yes, exceptionally well, considering."

He wilted, turning his attention to his bacon. She blew out a breath. This was ridiculous—she hated being this way. *I am a guest in his home, and I love him, and this is all so wrong.*

She sipped her tea, set down her cup. "Prince Carlton has invited me to survey the city with him this afternoon."

"Is that so?" He beamed, then the smile faltered. "But I thought—?"

"You thought what, sir?"

"Nothing. Nothing." He looked away from her back to his plate. "That's most marvelous. I'm sure you'll have a delightful time."

She glanced briefly at him. He was a terrible liar. "What is it, Grandfather?"

"It's nothing, truly, my dear. Shall I have Horatio select a nice mare for you?"

Whatever he was hiding, he wasn't going to tell her. She sighed, returning her attention to her meal. "That won't be necessary. Prince Carlton is bringing along a mount for me."

"Excellent," he replied, still studiously avoiding her eyes.

Suddenly, his misery was too much for her to bear. Heart aching, she reached across the table and covered his large hand with her own.

"Grandfather, if only you'd—"

"I can't." The words were rough, but the gaze he lifted to her was full of pain. "I just can't, dear heart. If anything were to happen to you ... I'd never forgive myself."

And in his words she heard an echo of her own thoughts just the night before—how devastated she would feel if anything happened to her companions.

She'd known them only a few weeks, but he'd loved her for her entire life and even before, from the time he'd first learned that a grandchild was about to grace their family.

In that moment, she knew she and her grandfather had come to an impasse, a stone wall they would not easily breach.

Prince Carlton arrived with his entourage early in the afternoon. Six guards and two ladies accompanied the prince, and one of the guards led a riderless gray mare. As Lyric and her grandfather stepped out to greet the prince, she was delighted to see that one of the ladies was the effervescent Princess Demesne. The older woman was a servant sent along for propriety's sake, Lyric supposed, as well as to keep the young princess out of trouble. Demesne waved frantically when she saw Lyric, causing her stocky chestnut pony to sidestep and prance.

Lyric smiled. She turned to Carlton and inclined her head.

"Good afternoon, Prince Carlton. How pleasant to see you again. And you, Princess Demesne. I am pleased you could join us."

"When Carlton—I mean, *Prince* Carlton—" Demesne corrected herself with a dramatic sigh, "—when Prince Carlton told our mother you had consented to ride with him this afternoon, I *begged* Mother to let me come, and she said yes!"

"I see that," Lyric replied, shading her eyes against the afternoon sun as she looked up at the mounted princess. "I am very happy she said yes."

"I am too—" Demesne began, but was interrupted by her elder brother.

"Demesne, please. If we don't get Princess Lyric on her horse soon, we won't have time for our ride." He gave Lyric a conspiratorial wink, then turned to one of the guards. "Hanseth, if you'll assist the princess onto her horse, we can be on our way."

Lyric had already stepped over to the gray mare. "I rarely need much assistance," she told the guard, stroking the mare's dappled neck. "This sweet girl is a full hand shorter than my own mare. What is her name?"

"Moonbeam, Your Highness."

Lyric froze.

Hanseth turned the mare and after a moment's hesitation, Lyric put her booted foot into the stirrup. She leapt lightly up onto the mare's back, and settled into the seat of the hand-tooled leather saddle. Moonbeam tossed her head and sidled sideways, but stopped when Lyric lifted the reins.

Carlton noticed the expression on her face. "What is it, my lady? Do you dislike the mare? Is she too much for you?"

"Oh, no, she's fine." Lyric looked at the prince and smiled sadly. "My own lovely mare is named Moon Song. I'm just remembering how much I miss her."

Carlton smiled his understanding and turned to the white-haired gentleman who stood before the mansion's oaken door. "We'll be off then, Duke Foxmir. I expect we'll have her back to you in plenty of time for the evening meal."

"See that you do, sir." His voice was gruff, but a smile belied the words and tone. "I'm sure you young people will have a splendid time."

Lyric glanced back at her grandfather and saw the smile slide from his face as the prince turned his back. She sighed and moved her horse into place next to Carlton.

They left the circular drive through the ornate wrought-iron gate and turned onto the cobbled city street. Two of the guards rode at the front, one carrying Graceen's emerald flag with the golden eagle, and the other the blue and silver banner of the king's household. Two other guards rode on each side of Lyric and Prince Carlton, while the final two rode behind Princess Demesne and her lady-in-waiting.

A few scattered clouds sailed in the deep blue of the summer sky, and a light breeze wafted gently around them as they rode. Prince Carlton was good company, gifted with intelligence coupled with a wry sense of humor, and Princess Demesne was a sweet child who could be counted on to say the most outrageous things when least expected.

But as fine as the day and as pleasant the company, Lyric's thoughts never strayed far from her missing imprisoned companions. Where were they? The city was huge—so much larger than any town in Tressalt. They could be anywhere. How would she ever find them? And her father. Did he still live? Would she ever see him again? She blinked, trying to shake away the dark questions.

They rode for perhaps an hour through the city, the guards clearing a path before them through the busy streets, while Carlton pointed out such grand edifices as the theater, a concert hall, and guild headquarters. Lyric was enchanted and a little embarrassed. Imagine a building created just so people could come and listen to music or watch plays!

She felt very provincial but also determined. If she ever returned to Tressalt, if she ever sat upon its throne, she would see that some of these splendors were brought to her land. Her people deserved the joys of civilization as much as any.

They rounded a corner and meandered down a short avenue. Lyric lifted her eyes in surprise. Only two buildings graced each side of this street before it came to an end at a long wooden gate. As they rode closer, she saw on the far side of the gate a large greenway that spread out in both directions. A slender brook splashed along the length of the parkland and in the midst of it all lay an almost perfectly circular lake of sparkling sapphire blue. The entire area was fenced in and surrounded by buildings on all sides.

Lyric turned to Carlton, certain her face gave away her shock and amazement. "What's this?"

The prince beamed at her. "I thought you'd like it. It was built in my grandfather's day. A way for city dwellers to enjoy the country—without leaving the city."

Lyric looked back at the park and shook her head in wonder. "It's incredible."

"There's a riding track around the edge," he added. "Shall we go inside and let these horses out for a little gallop?"

Right now there were few things she could imagine wanting more, in spite of her fear for her father and her desperation to find her friends. She glanced over her shoulder at Carlton and nodded. "That would be lovely."

"Yay!" Demesne cheered, kicking her pony forward. "Shall we race, Princess Lyric? Golden Boy is short but he's really fast! He can keep up with Moonbeam."

"No racing," Carlton broke in before Lyric could reply. "You know how excitable horses are when they think it's a race. Mother would have my hide if you were to take a fall. And let's not even think about what Duke Foxmir would do to me if something were to happen to Princess Lyric."

"He wouldn't do anything," Demesne muttered, her youthful face in full pout mode. "You're the prince. And neither Princess Lyric nor I would fall, anyway. Would we?" She looked hopefully up at Lyric.

"I do like to race," she admitted to the younger girl, "but I cannot overrule your brother. He is responsible for our safety. We mustn't make his duty more difficult than it already is." Demesne scowled but Carlton looked over her head at Lyric. He smiled and mouthed a silent *thank you*.

They reached the long wooden gate and waited while one of the guards dismounted and slid the plank aside, holding it while all the riders rode through.

"I'm not up for galloping, Lord Prince," Demesne's nurse called out. "I'll just wait for you all right here, if you don't mind."

"That will be fine, Lasrae," Carlton answered. Then they were on the riding track and the guards at the front urged their mounts into a canter. Carlton's black stallion lunged forward, shaking his head ferociously at the prince's restraining rein, and both Moonbeam and Demesne's Golden Boy galloped along behind him.

Lyric couldn't help smiling. Indeed, she would sing for joy if she weren't surrounded by people she hardly knew. How she loved to ride, sharing the horse's strength and speed, feeling the wind whipping through her hair. She hadn't felt so free, so full of wild joy since the day she raced away from her own castle, scoffing at Marek, urging her own mare on too fast and too far. It was the same day her land was overthrown and her father taken captive.

The day her life had changed forever.

Cold swept over her and she sat up on her galloping horse, fighting the waves of emotion bombarding her.

"Ha ha, watch out, Princess Lyric! I told you Golden Boy was fast!"

Pulled from her disconcerting thoughts, Lyric glanced over to see Demesne, her pale blond hair streaming out behind her, as the chestnut cob pulled ahead of Lyric's mare. Ahead of them, Carlton looked back from his seat on the fiery black stallion.

"Have a care, Demesne. Do not pass the guards." Carlton was a kindly elder brother but the authority in his voice was unmistakable. The young princess sat up and pulled back on the pony's reins, giving Lyric an impish grin as Moonbeam caught up. The two girls finished the circuit of the park at a brisk canter, their horses matching each other stride for stride.

"That was fun!" Demesne crowed when the entire group pulled up next to the gate. Blue eyes sparkling, she turned to her brother. "You *must* let us race next time, Carlton. Lyric won't fall off—did you see her? She's a much better rider than Sharelle."

Demesne's tone of voice as she said the unfamiliar name caught Lyric's attention. She'd been patting Moonbeam's dappled neck but she glanced up and saw the prince's frown as he stared at his sister. She looked back and forth between the siblings before asking the question. "Who's Sharelle?"

Demesne opened her mouth to speak, but Carlton held up a hand to silence her. He turned to Lyric.

"Princess Sharelle Parsiwein is the first daughter of the king of Parsiway," he answered gravely. "She is also my betrothed. Our wedding is set for next spring."

"Oh." She continued to stroke Moonbeam's neck, not sure what to say. She hadn't known, but it didn't matter. She had only just met him. He was very pleasant, and she enjoyed his company, but that was all.

She returned her gaze to him to find he was still watching her.

She drummed up what she hoped was the appropriate enthusiasm, adding a smile at the last moment. "I am very happy for you, Prince. How splendid! I trust I shall be invited to the ceremony?"

"Of course." The smile he gave her showed his relief. "I am sorry you learned of it in this way, Your Highness. I assumed Duke Foxmir had told you."

She frowned, remembering the awkward breakfast conversation with her grandfather. "I believe he almost did, actually. I wondered what he'd been about to say, but let it go. Unfortunately, we've not been speaking much of late."

Carlton signaled the guards at the front to move on then turned back to Lyric. "You haven't been speaking with your grandfather?" He looked puzzled. "Why is that? Surely you have much to speak of."

"You would think so." She nudged Moonbeam forward so she could ride beside him. "But he has done something I can't quite forgive, and I'm not yet sure how that story will end."

"Duke Foxmir?" He shook his head. "I cannot imagine such a thing. What has he done?"

They followed a winding path that led to the shimmering blue lake at the center of the greenway. As she rode along beside the prince, she pondered how best to answer his question.

"You seemed very interested in my traveling companions last night," she finally said. "But you have not asked about them today."

He frowned. "No, I have not. Should I have?"

She sucked in a deep breath. She was walking a very fine line on this quest that had been thrust upon her. If she wasn't careful—if she stepped too far to the left or to the right—she might reveal more than she should, and people would suffer.

Amira, Quinn, and Becca had already suffered because of her unguarded words. It hadn't been her fault, of course, but still ...

She was alone, and she needed help. A chill ran through her. Time was running out for her father—maybe it had already run out. Could this prince give her the help she needed? Amira had been jesting but had nonetheless made a good point. Having a prince on one's side could only be a good thing.

She looked up and saw they were nearing the lake. Behind her, she could hear Demesne teasing one of the guards and the nurse admonishing the child to behave as a princess should.

"All right," Carlton said. "I will ask. How are your friends—your servant and the Akyldi pair? Are they enjoying their time in Graceen?"

"They are not," she answered softly. "They have been abducted and imprisoned by order of my grandfather. I do not know where they are."

Carlton pulled the stallion to an abrupt halt and turned blazing eyes on her. "Why? What have they done?"

"Nothing but help me on my journey."

Carlton narrowed his gaze. "Surely there is more to the story than this. I would very much like to hear it all."

Lyric nudged her mare on and Carlton followed suit. They reached the lake and she saw that a trail meandered along its edge both north and south. The guards in the front reined their horses onto the northerly path. Behind her, Demesne was still chattering nonstop, seeming to have no need to breathe while she spoke. The guards who had been riding alongside her and Carlton had dropped behind and were bringing up the rear of their party with the other two.

This might be the most privacy she could hope to have.

"In our conversation last night," she began slowly, "do you remember that I had certain ... reservations about some of the subjects we discussed?"

"Indeed," he answered, a smile playing on his lips. "I was flattered you told me as much as you did."

"I have a task that has been entrusted to me. I can't explain it all now. I *can* say that only I and a few others can accomplish this task. One of the others is among the group of people who arrived with me in Graceen. When my grandfather learned of our plans, he was very unhappy but rather than talk to me about it—"

"He took matters into his own hands?"

She nodded. "I know it's because he fears for me, and I understand that. But it can't be helped. I must go on."

"This task," he asked, his face serious. "Is it dangerous?"

She blew out a breath. Strange that after all they'd been through thus far, the question had never been put so directly. She'd never even put it that way to herself. But the truth was obvious—the quest had already proved dangerous, and surely would again before all was done.

"Yes," she finally said. "But I must go on, and for that I need my companions. They need to be found and released, but I don't know where they are."

"I know where they are," Demesne's bright voice chirped behind them. Lyric wheeled her horse and stared into the girl's laughing face.

"They're at the palace," Demesne said. "I saw them brought in yesterday."

CHAPTER 31: REVELATIONS

Carlton held up a gloved hand. "Stop, everyone. Gather around." The guards in the front bearing the banners turned their horses and rejoined the group. Those bringing up the rear came forward. All eyes were on the prince.

"My royal sister and I, along with the Princess of Tressalt, have decided to take a short break from our riding. We will leave the horses here with you and stroll along the lake on our own feet for a brief time."

With that he dismounted and held out his reins to the nearest guard. After a moment's hesitation, Lyric slid off her mare. An instant later, a perplexed-looking Demesne followed suit.

"But Your Highness—" Lasrae, the nurse, began.

"Do not fret, mistress," Carlton said. "I take full responsibility for my sister's well-being." In a lower voice he spoke to the guard closest to him. "Keep everyone here, Hanseth. We will not go far." Turning back to the girls, he gestured toward the lake, a scant fifty paces from where they stood. "Ladies, shall we go?"

Lyric and Demesne fell in beside him and together the three walked across the springy turf until they reached the lakeside. Lyric stepped back when her boot sunk a half-inch into the soaked and fragrant vegetation at the water's edge.

Carlton spoke. "We don't have much time so, Demesne, you need to tell us as much as you can about what you think you saw yesterday."

Demesne scowled at her elder brother.

"I don't *think* I saw anything. I know what I saw. Yany and Leeta and I were playing stickball in the east courtyard when one of Father's carriages was driven in. It stopped right next to the scullery entrance. Three men jumped out of the carriage, and a minute later three other people got out. They were blindfolded and had their hands tied." Demesne shrugged her slender shoulders. "They all went inside."

"Why do you think these people might be Princess Lyric's friends?"

Demesne rolled her eyes. "Yany's mother had been at the north gate when Princess Lyric and her friends arrived. She said it was them." She shrugged again and turned to Lyric. "I'm sorry. I was going to ask you about them but then I forgot."

"It's all right, Demesne," Lyric said. "I'm just glad you saw all this. I've been worried about them."

Demesne brightened. "What did they do? Were they very wicked? Shall your grandfather have them flogged?"

Lyric's hand flew to her heart. "Oh, no, they've done nothing. It—"

"Demesne," Carlton broke in. "It's very important that you not tell anyone else what you've told us today. Can I trust you to keep it secret?"

"Of course!" Another eye roll. "I'm very good at keeping secrets."

Carlton nodded gravely. "Excellent. Now, can you go fetch Hanseth for me?"

Demesne narrowed her gaze. "Why?"

Carlton sighed. "Just do it. I have a plan which I'm sure you'll like."

She stood, undecided for an instant, then dashed off to the larger group.

Carlton turned to Lyric, his jaw set. "I hope, Princess, that we will be able to get to the bottom of your mysteries soon. Please be prepared to tell me everything I need to know as quickly as possible."

Lyric's stomach knotted. She hoped she wasn't making a mistake.

Hanseth rode up. "Yes, my prince?"

"I need to speak with Princess Lyric in private. Could you go back and challenge Princess Demesne to a horse race? Tell her she has my permission but you think it's rather silly, because Golden Boy doesn't stand a chance."

A quizzical expression crossed the guard's face. "Well, that's true. He doesn't."

Carlton shook his head, a grin playing across his own countenance. "You and I both know that, but Demesne doesn't. Make sure she wins the first round—then challenge her to the best two out of three. Can you do that?"

Hanseth grinned. "Firebrand won't like it."

Carlton glared at Hanseth's restive chestnut. "Tell him I insist."

Hanseth dipped his head. "Yes, my prince."

"And Hanseth?"

"Yes, my prince?"

"Please don't let any harm come to my sister."

Hanseth nodded. "I'll do my best, my prince."

The guard rode away and Carlton wheeled about to face Lyric.

"And now, Your Highness, we have perhaps fifteen minutes. What is this mission that you have undertaken that has caused a well-respected noble to act in such a manner?"

Lyric lifted a hand to her heart, covering the opal stone.

Carlton's expression softened. "I am sorry this is so difficult. If we had time to get to know one another better, you might be convinced you could safely trust me. But time is the one thing it seems we do not have."

He was right. Time was running out and she had to choose. Behind her, she heard a squeal of pure glee— Hanseth must have delivered his challenge. This prince did indeed know his sister well. And he sincerely cared for her too. He was a good person and a kind one.

A prince one could trust.

He cleared his throat. "You should also know that my father's health is improving. We believe he will return to his duties soon—perhaps in the next few days. I still do not know why he reacted to you the way he did—whether it was because he was bewitched by the wizard's gift or something else completely—but it seems fair to surmise your chances of support are better with me than with him."

She held up a hand. "No need to go on, Your Highness. I also wish we had more time but sometimes we must trust quickly. Shall we sit?" She gestured to a drier portion of the wildflower-studded turf.

She stepped away and eased down into the sweet-smelling grass. As he joined her, she pulled the pendant from under her tunic and held it out for inspection. "You say you have studied the ancient lore. What do you know of the gemstones of prophecy?"

He squinted at the gem, then lifted his gaze back to hers. "Very little, I'm afraid."

Looking past him to the perfect, crystalline lake, she took a deep breath and began recounting the tale she herself had learned so recently.

Lyric waited that night in her bed until she heard the soft click of the door closing in the chamber next to hers, and then made her way silently to the adjoining servant's quarters. Apparently, her grandfather had yet to speak to Celeste about the listening holes.

She stroked and blew on the stone's unblemished surface, calling out Amira's name. This time, she saw no strange visions but was rewarded almost immediately with the Akyldi woman's visage in the stone's depths.

"Has Prince Carlton come to you?"

"Indeed, he has, lady." Amira smiled. "I must say I like your prince very much."

"He is not my prince," Lyric retorted. "What did you tell him? Will he help us?"

"As you instructed in the missive he delivered, I told him no less than he needed to know in order to reach his decision. He believes us. He has agreed to help."

Lyric exhaled gustily. "Thank the Maker! What is the plan?"

"Much depends on how quickly the king revives. The prince will return as soon as he can, order the guards off, and take us to a private hidden place until you are able to join us and we can resume our journey." She paused, her silver brows pulling together. "He is risking much to help us, you know."

Lyric sighed. "I know. We are fortunate to have found him."

"Indeed."

Another thought intruded. "Have you spoken with Venuzia?"

"Yes, she knows what to do. She awaits our word."

She tapped her fingers on the small table before her. Things needed to happen soon but instead, everyone waited. On the other hand, when the time was right, would all the details come together so they could escape quickly, cleanly? And if they did, how would it affect her grandfather? Until this week, he'd never been anything but good to her—kind, loving. He would see her actions as open defiance, as plotting behind his back.

She bit her lip until she tasted blood. Her grandfather would be crushed and angry, but her father's life, and so much more, was at stake.

Even for her grandfather's sake, she couldn't delay one instant longer than necessary.

The storm hit two days later. Lyric stood in the stable feeding apples to the carriage horses when she heard the roar.

"Where is my granddaughter?"

A moment later, he strode down the passageway between the stalls, a frightened-looking stable boy at his heels. He ground to a halt before her.

"Leave us," he ordered the lad. Rage radiated off every inch of his body. He skewered her with his eyes. "What have you done?"

She resisted the urge to shrink away. She'd never seen him like this, but she had to remember who she was and act accordingly. She lifted her chin. "I love you, Grandfather, but you may not speak to me in such a manner. If you want any information from me, you will lower your voice and ask in a reasonable tone. What is it you want to know?"

The duke put a hand to his heart and stepped back, breathing heavily. He stared at her as if he'd never seen her before, as if he didn't know her. "Your *friends* have escaped their captivity. I want to know where they are and what your plans are."

She met his gaze. Spoke calmly. "I do not know where they are and I have no plans to discuss with you."

The heat rose in his haggard face. "I am responsible for you—"

"No," she interrupted, "you are not. I am the princess of my land. If my father does not survive this, I will be queen. You cannot and will not tell me what I may or may not do. I am responsible for myself." Her heart pounded furiously, but she spoke the words with the absolute authority she knew to be hers.

He listened. His breath returned to normal. Then he shook the disheveled white hair out of his eyes and lifted his own chin.

"You are seventeen years old. Unless and until I hear from your father, or until you come of age, I will continue in my role as your guardian. If these friends of yours want to go on some fool's errand, that's up to them, but you, my granddaughter, will not go with them."

Disbelief coursed through her. "You intend to make *me* a prisoner now? How dare you?"

"I will do what I have to do to protect you." He turned his back and strode away.

He did not look back.

CHAPTER 32: LAND OF THE AKYLDI

"Griff-ah!"

The command tore through the forest, destroying the early morning calm. Marek jerked to a halt on the swinging skyway and hunkered down, scanning the area, searching for the speaker.

Ahead of him, Quidar froze. Hand raised, he replied to the invisible speaker in the sibilant Akyldi language, then whispered over his shoulder in the common tongue to Marek. "Wait here." He strode to the mammoth cedar looming fifty paces before them.

Two days earlier, three of the Akyldi had taken Dragon and the other horses to the spot where Quidar had told Marek they would keep them. The rest of the clan had gone ahead on the skyway, leaving Marek with Quidar to find their way to the Akyldi capital. There, whether he liked it or not, he would be presented to the king.

He'd hoped to survive the presentation. Now he hoped he survived the journey.

A moment later Quidar emerged from the concealed platform in the cedar and waved Marek forward.

Marek ducked under the heavy branch and found himself on an *enoch*—the Akyldi word for the wooden platforms—unlike any he'd seen on their journey thus far. It was much larger, and instead of bare wood, this one held two finely-crafted chairs and a low table. More furnishings stood on the far side of the vast tree trunk and on either side of it he saw reed baskets of food, rolled-up sleeping mats, tools, and water skins. Most amazing of all, beneath a wooden canopy upon a shelf lay stacks of scrolls and leather-bound books.

Beside him, Quidar chuckled. "Are you surprised? Did you believe us to be ignorant, unlearned folk?"

Marek looked back, only to be met with glowers from two strange Akyldi men wearing light armor and silver helmets. One had a longbow slung over his shoulder, while the taller, dark-haired man held a spear.

"These are Cardan and Simtani," Quidar explained. "Wardens of the First Gate."

Marek inclined his head but the two continued to glare in silence, much as Remzold had done days earlier.

The black and white hound he'd named Hunter shifted in Marek's pack. A deep, throaty growl sent the Akyldi guards jumping back, eyes wide. Marek bit back a grin. *Interesting.*

Quidar ignored the dog and spoke to the guards in their own language. Marek heard Amira and Quinn's names among the torrent of unfamiliar words. Finally, the shorter guard gave a curt nod and stepped aside. The dark-haired one lowered his spear and gestured toward the ongoing skyway out the eastern gate.

Once back on the aerial path, Quidar set a quicker pace. "Gate wardens are the first line of the city's defenses," he said. "They stay at their posts weeks at a time."

"We are close to the city then?"

"Yes."

Marek pondered a moment. "The gate wardens seemed unduly ... surprised when the dog growled."

"They did, indeed." Quidar chuckled. "We Akyldi know about dogs, of course, but have nothing to do with them. We don't keep them as pets or use them for hunting. We don't eat them." He wrinkled his nose. "You mustn't hold their surprise against them, though. Even if one knows about dogs, one does not expect to find one in a tree."

"I suppose not."

Since they'd begun their trek on the skyway three days earlier, they'd moved through ever deeper, denser forests. The trees were ancient and immense, bearing long curtains of gray-green moss. Their crowns soared out of sight into the sky and six large men with outstretched arms could not have reached around some of them.

The Akyldi had chosen their home well.

Now, as he and Quidar neared the end of the journey, the forest began to thin out. Steady streams of light filtered through the trees, and the breeze carried a fragrant mix of scents interweaving with the tang of pine and fir and the musk of damp earth.

Marek inhaled deeply, sifting through his memories. Wild roses, heavy with summer, he thought. Fruit trees. Ripening grain. In Akyldi land, then, as in his own, harvest approached.

Soon he could see land below them. The skyway had been on a downward slope for over an hour and they were now but a scant thirty feet above the ground. The woods diminished to scattered groups of the monolithic trees. Sunlight grew brighter, and small cottages appeared on the forest floor, with an occasional thin line of smoke curling from a stone chimney.

Then without further warning, the skyway entered a vast clearing. A number of the huge evergreens remained, including those that held their swinging walkway, but the brilliant blue of the sky now burst into view. Marek had to squint against the fullness of the morning sun. The skyway was lower, rising scarcely higher than the apple and peach trees he'd smelled earlier. As he glanced around, he saw that three other sky-paths also entered the clearing, all heading to the same central location.

Cottages with garden patches spread out about them, connected by rock-lined walkways meandering through verdant green lawns. Laughing Akyldi children, more graceful than their human counterparts, did back flips and scampered about the area, then stopped to point as he and Quidar came into view.

Marek looked ahead. All four sky-paths were about to touch ground in an open courtyard in front of a glistening wooden structure. The massive building rose four stories into the air but appeared as a child's toy compared with the giant trees that stood sentinel about it. A thick wall with jutting turrets at each corner surrounded the building. Armed sentries patrolled along the wall between the turrets.

The Akyldi castle, then, but quite different from the castles Marek had seen in Tressalt, Malacar, and Graceen. This one was made entirely of the gleaming, rich wood of the magnificent trees that both protected and led the way into the kingdom of the Akyldi. There were no banners or flags, but something that appeared to be a huge wood carving stood before the gates. From this distance he couldn't make out what the carving depicted, but small groups of people clustered before it, looking up.

Marek pulled his gaze from the castle and took in the courtyard before him. Scattered tables held colorful fruits and vegetables, baskets, pelts, tools, finished cloth, and much more. The enticing odor of cooking meat caused Marek's stomach to grumble. Many people, dressed in the greens, tans, and browns preferred by the Akyldi, milled about, examining the vendors' wares.

"Market day," Quidar said, beaming. "One of our women brews an ale so light it will lift your spirit and fill your human heart with joy. Come, I shall lead you to her."

The skyway ended at a small platform ten feet above the ground. A wooden ladder led to the ground, but they'd no sooner stepped off the final rung and onto solid earth, when a familiar scowling form stepped in front of them. Remzold inclined his head to Quidar.

"King Carnosh requires you to bring the human to him immediately."

"Immediately?" Quidar frowned. "Are you certain?"

"His very words, sir."

"Fine." He turned to Marek and gave an exaggerated sigh. "I'll have to take you to Madam Foyle's table another time, but you'll find it worth the wait."

Marek grinned. "I look forward to it."

Leaving the enticing smells of the market behind, Marek followed Quidar toward the castle. As they approached the gate, he saw he'd been right about the tall structure in front of it. It was a wood carving—a statue—of an Akyldi woman. Mounted on a huge plinth of dark wood, the figure was twice the size of a normal female. Slender and defiant, she held a book outstretched in one hand and a raised sword in the other. Words engraved in a stylish hand graced the plinth.

Marek stared at the carving a long moment. So many things about it tugged at him—the woman's stance, her expression. He gestured at the words. "What does it say?"

"'*From wisdom and strength come power.*' It is the maxim of my people." Quidar crossed his arms over his chest. "Great learning without strength leads only to impotence. But strength without wisdom makes us no better than the beasts."

Marek nodded. The woman held in her hands the symbols of her people's maxim, but her expression was where he most clearly saw its truth. Wisdom and strength, dignity and power—all shone out of the lifelike eyes, the set of the jaw.

And something else ....

Resilience. This woman and the people she represented had known defeat and had risen to fight another day.

"Come," Quidar said. "The king awaits."

Shaking off his reverie, Marek followed Quidar through the high wooden gate into the inner courtyard. They crossed it quickly. Quidar, all business now, strode toward the largest building—the castle close. A number of lesser buildings lined the inner walls—a bakery, the cookhouse, and laundry on one side, the armorer and fletcher next to the blacksmith's stall on the other. There were others, but they had no time now to stop and look.

Two liveried sentinels, hands on sword hilts, stood at the building's entrance and watched every move of their approach. Quidar stopped before them and spoke hurriedly. The guards turned narrowed gazes on Marek, and one directed a question to Quidar. He responded by removing his bow and quiver of arrows from his back and handing it to him. Then he pulled his dagger from its sheath and handed that over as well.

Marek bristled but said nothing. No one asked for his weapons, and once again he wondered where they were and when—if ever—he would get them back.

The guards signaled them to go on, then issued a sharp command as Marek passed. The guards spoke rapidly, gesticulated wildly. From his pack, Marek felt Hunter shift and growl. *Of course.* Quidar raised a hand, spoke in soothing tones to the guards, then turned to Marek. He grinned broadly. "I'm afraid your companion is not allowed into the close. He'll have to stay out here."

This turned out to be more difficult than Marek would have imagined. No one seemed to know what to do with the dog. After allowing the Akyldi to argue about it for a time, Marek intervened.

"Isn't there an empty store room or something nearby? If the cook can spare a bone or two, my friend here will be happy to lie down and gnaw on it until we're back."

Quidar translated the suggestion to the guards and one of them begrudgingly beckoned to a young page. The golden-haired child eyed the dog suspiciously but listened to the request, nodded, and raced away. In moments, he was back, bearing a deer's leg bone. The lad gestured for them to follow. Soon Hunter was happily housed with his bone in an empty broom closet.

Leaving the dog behind, Marek and Quidar stepped out of the morning brilliance into the darkness of the castle close. Even indoors, the influence of the forest lived on. Open windows let in drafts of the pine-scented air along with swooping birds, who brought their varied songs with them. Rather than the tapestries that decorated the halls in Tressalt's castle, the Akyldi center of power sported framed paintings of woodland and waterfall, cougar and bear, mountains and seas. Marek stopped in front of the seascape. The colors and sense of movement made him feel as if he were seeing it with his own eyes. He could almost smell the salt air, feel the crash of the surf upon the shore, hear the seabirds overhead.

A man stepped out of an alcove beneath a spiral staircase and moved silently toward them. He nodded at Quidar, then turned his piercing gaze upon Marek.

"I am Sagalay, steward of the House of Carnosh," he said in formal, unaccented Common. "In the name of Carnosh, king of the Akyldi, I welcome you, stranger. He awaits you in the throne room."

Marek inclined his head. "I thank you, Sagalay."

Quidar gestured toward the stairway. He murmured instructions as they began climbing the spiraling steps. "I do not know the customs in your land, but here we do not stand in the presence of our king until given permission. Enter and kneel. Speak to the king only when he asks a question or grants permission." He glanced back at Marek, narrowing his gaze. "Tell the truth. He will know if you do not."

The weight of responsibility and dread that had been plaguing Marek for days settled over him like a mantle. At the same time, Quidar's insinuation cut deep. He was an honorable man, a truthful one, but there were questions he hoped this king did not ask.

They reached the top of the stairs and strode along a tiled corridor, finally arriving at a gilded door. The design upon the door was of a majestic tree reaching into the night sky. The tree, the moon. and the stars were created from inlaid gemstones Marek couldn't identify. The guard on duty nodded at Quidar and pulled the door open.

Marek had only an instant to take in the room and its décor as they stepped inside. The wall behind the throne was covered with a scene of the forest at either sunrise or sunset. Colors of both dawn and dusk—gold, mauve, scarlet, and violet—filtered through the sky and into the trees. On both sides of the mural, against an ebony backdrop, glimmered the silver and gold motif of sword and scroll.

"My Lord King." Quidar stepped forward and dropped to one knee. Marek joined him. "In accordance with the command of the Lady Amira, I have brought Marek of the King's Guard in the land of Tressalt to you this day."

"You may stand."

They did, and Marek caught his first glimpse of the person who sat upon the throne. Carnosh was clothed in a stunning midnight-blue gown with tiny points of light gleaming across its folds, but that was not the first thing that grabbed Marek's attention. The king was old. In a land where most people appeared either young or ageless, Carnosh was ancient. Deep lines grooved the monarch's face—vertically between his eyes, curving around his mouth. His hair was silver-white and across his upper lip, where human males might have a mustache, individual strands of white hair—whiskers—arched to the side. Much about the Akyldi had appeared feline to Marek before, but never so much as now.

And the king's eyes—they captured him. Held him. Life and vigor emanated from eyes so blue they could have been chiseled from a mountain glacier. Marek doubted anything escaped the king's fierce gaze or the keen mind behind it.

"You have done well, Quidar," Carnosh said, his gaze never leaving Marek. "You may leave us now. Meet with Sagalay to see that suitable lodging is arranged for our guest. Come back to the hall afterward. I will call for you when we conclude our discussion."

"Yes, my Lord King." Quidar dropped to one knee again, inclined his head, then rose and left.

"So, Marek, King's Guard of Tressalt, do you know you are the first human to enter these halls in over a thousand years?"

Marek dipped his head. "I did not know that, Lord King."

Carnosh narrowed his gaze, the vertical lines between his eyes deepening.

"You are also the first human to venture much beyond the borders of our land who has been allowed to live. A good number of my advisers are not pleased about this."

Marek made no reply. He was not pleased about being brought here either, but he was thankful for his life. He hoped he would leave with it.

For the first time, Carnosh pulled his gaze away.

"Nevertheless, things are changing in the outside world, and I believe change must occur here as well." He stood, rolled his shoulders back creakily, then carefully lowered himself to his seat. He again fixed his eyes on Marek. "It is for this reason and others that I insisted you be brought to me. I am told you were the guardian of the princess heir of your land on the day Torian's son of Malacar overthrew Tressalt. How well do you know your princess?"

How well did he know her? Marek thought of Lyric's quick wit and sharp tongue. How her eyes sparked when she was angry. How much she loved her horse. He also remembered her cool hand on his when he lay sick in the forest, the concern in her eyes. He remembered their last meeting, when she asked that he return to her when he was well. There had been tears in her eyes. He shook his head.

"I have known the princess since she was a child, Lord King. Not well, of course. The lines between royalty and—"

The king waved him off. "I don't care about that. From what you know of her, do you believe she is the kind of person who will stay with a task she has taken on? Or will she quit when the task becomes difficult?"

His shoulders stiffened. He didn't like speaking of Princess Lyric's character. It seemed disloyal. He was a soldier, not a judge. He looked up to see Carnosh staring at him, his gaze so penetrating he wondered why the king needed to hear his words.

"It doesn't seem appropriate for me to speak so of my lady, Lord King. It is not my place—"

"Ordinarily, that would be true," Carnosh said. "But these are difficult days and such considerations must be set aside. Your lady has taken on a mission that will affect many more than the people of Tressalt. *My* people may suffer, and I must know if she can be relied on."

Marek lifted his chin in an unconscious imitation of the princess.

"I do not know what task my lady has agreed to, but if she went into it eyes open, she will do her best to complete it. She is young but strong-willed, the daughter of a king."

Carnosh nodded. "And what do you know of the gemstone your mistress wears?"

"I have seen it only once, Your Majesty. On the day Prince Ralt took Tressalt, Princess Lyric saw a vision in the gemstone. She was most distressed."

"Did you see the vision?"

Marek shook his head. "Just the remnants of it, but—"

"But what?"

Marek stood up straighter. "What my lady saw in the stone was true. Torian's son was indeed attacking at that very time."

"Of course." Carnosh stared at the signet ring on his right forefinger, appearing lost in thought. Without looking up, he asked, "If I were to order your weapons returned and sent you back to the borders of my land, what would you do?"

Finally, a question he could answer easily, but it bewildered him. Carnosh was trying to discover something, but he couldn't fathom what. "I would set about finding where my liege lady is, and return to her service at once."

"And do you know how she is occupying her time?"

Marek gritted his teeth. He did not know. Where Lyric was and what she was doing were chief among the thoughts that plagued him during the long nights when sleep evaded him.

The ancient king turned the power of his ice-blue eyes fully on Marek, who met and returned his gaze.

"All I know is what she told me the day she left. She said she was going with some of your people to find a way to stop Prince Ralt's assault on the lands of Argonia. I know nothing of their plan."

Carnosh stared at him, gaze narrowed, assessing. "What if, when you are reunited with your princess, you discover she is engaged in a task you do not understand or approve of? What would you see as your duty then? Protecting her from danger, or assisting her in the task she's taken on?"

He squared his shoulders. "I would like to think I could do both, Your Majesty. But I am, first of all, my lady's servant. It is she who commands."

"Agreed." Carnosh gestured to the door guard. "Let Quidar in."

Quidar joined him before the king, dropping to his knee.

"Stand," Carnosh ordered. "When this man has had the opportunity to refresh himself after his long journey, take him to the library. Show him the texts, explain the history of the last war, and answer his questions. Bring him back to me the day after tomorrow."

Quidar bowed. "Yes, Your Majesty."

The king stood and snapped his fingers. A woman in deep mauve robes stepped out from behind the throne and came to the king's side. Carnosh stared at Marek, his eyes now the color of blue steel. "And you, human, learn what you can. Be prepared to answer my questions." He tilted his head. "If you answer to my satisfaction, I have someone I'd like you to meet."

Without another word, the aged king took hold of the woman's arm, leaned into her, and left the room.

CHAPTER 33: DEATH IN THE CASTLE

"Princess Lyric, you must wake up. Please." The words swirled through Lyric's mind, intertwining with the dark images of a dream that refused to release her.

She felt a tugging at the sleeve of her night dress. "My lady, please," the voice called. "Wake up. Something terrible has happened."

Lyric sat bolt upright, shaking off the dream, looking into Noni's anxious eyes.

"What is it?"

"You must hurry, Princess." Noni used the candle she held to light the others throughout the room. "Your grandfather awaits you downstairs. Dreadful news has come from the palace."

Fear pushed the last cobwebs of sleep from her mind.

"What has happened? Tell me now."

Tears splashed from the girl's eyes. "Oh, Your Highness. King Rasmus is dead."

Lyric stared at her uncomprehendingly. "But he was getting better. I don't understand."

"Nor do I, Your Highness." Still sniffling, she handed Lyric a velveteen dressing gown. "Come, we must make haste to your grandfather."

Duke Foxmir was summoned to the palace immediately. Lyric, though not summoned, refused to stay behind. Noni accompanied her, as did two guards. Lyric assumed the guards were to keep watch over her. True to his word, her grandfather had not allowed her out of the mansion unaccompanied since her companions had escaped.

Her fury had not abated, either. She was princess heir of her land—he had no right to do this. This was a matter of state, but at present she had no one to speak for her. She'd considered talking with Prince Carlton, but he'd already helped her so much, and with the king injured, she'd decided to wait. Bide her time, put up with her grandfather's so-called protection for now.

But not forever.

And now this. King Rasmus was dead.

The sun was a brilliant sliver of orange rising from the dark eastern horizon when her grandfather's matching grays pulled the carriage past the gatehouse and into the palace courtyard. A high-ranking servant greeted them at the large oak door and escorted them to the Council Hall.

Scattered groups of somber-eyed Gracenians murmured quietly among themselves. Fires roared on the hearths at both ends of the large room, and torches blazed on all four walls. At a table on the dais at the front of the room, Prince Carlton conferred with several resplendently clad men and women. Lyric was surprised but pleased. She hadn't known women were part of Graceen's ruling class, but obviously these were. Carlton looked across the room, saw Duke Foxmir, and waved him forward.

"Stay with the princess," the duke ordered the guards, and pushed through the crowd to the dais.

Lyric glanced around the room, wondering if the queen and her daughters were in attendance. She didn't see them and hoped, probably in vain, that Demesne would be spared the news of her father's passing until she awoke. Poor child.

A change in the mood of the crowd pulled her back to her present circumstances. Surreptitious glances touched on her, then slid away. Words were whispered behind ladies' fans and noblemen's hands. *Princess ... Tressalt ... kidnapped ... Duke Foxmir ... granddaughter.*

She took a step closer to one of the ornate marble columns in the crowded room, ignoring the whispers. She'd been here a week but had had no formal presentation at Court. Of course people would talk.

A stirring at the table on the dais caused her—and everyone else in the Hall—to look expectantly to the front of the room. With a final word to the nobles, Carlton faced the crowd.

His sandy hair was disheveled and his face ashen. Dark shadows underlined his hazel eyes. He looked very young but very determined.

"Friends," he said, scanning the crowd. "Thank you for answering my call so quickly. This is a very sad occasion, something none of us anticipated. As you know, early this week the king took a bad fall and struck his head. He has been kept under observation by the healers and seemed to be improving. Then last night ..." He paused, staring beyond the crowd. Lyric glanced over her shoulder in the direction of his gaze. Another huge tapestry of the ancient inhabitants of Argonia covered the wall.

"Last night," he began again, and when Lyric looked back, she found his eyes resting on her. "Unbeknownst to anyone, my father left his bed and wandered through the castle. When the chief healer discovered him missing, I was notified, and we began an immediate search."

Carlton paused again, staring at the floor in front of the dais for a long moment before returning his attention to his audience. "His body was found at the bottom of the southeastern staircase. No one knows why he was there or what he may have been seeking." He sighed, and again his gaze drifted to Lyric.

"This is all I can tell you at this time. The queen has been informed of the tragedy, but my two sisters have not. I ask for your prayers and good thoughts for my family in the coming days. Duke Edmonds will speak to you now."

A lean, middle-aged man, sumptuously clad as the others, moved to the front. The duke began speaking about what the king's untimely death would mean to the people of Graceen, but Lyric no longer listened.

Her gaze followed Carlton as he rejoined the group of nobles. He'd acquitted himself well, she thought, in what had to be the hardest speech of his life, but now that he was no longer the center of attention, she watched as shock and grief overtook him. He leaned back against the heavy table, jaw clenched and arms crossed, lines of pain etched across his face.

Her heart went out to him. No matter her experience with the king, his son had loved him.

What had happened to King Rasmus? Why was he wandering the corridors alone in the middle of the night? Had he lost his mind and, addled as he was, fallen down that flight of stairs?

Or had someone pushed him?

She shuddered, the thought of murder too terrible to consider. Gradually, words spoken from the front of the Hall pulled her attention back to the dais.

"Prince Carlton will carry on in his role as Regent, supported by Queen Bethen," Duke Edmonds intoned. "The investigation into King Rasmus's death will continue as we plan for the coronation of King Carlton. A date for that event has yet to be selected, but it will be soon. It is our wish that life in Graceen City will go on in as uninterrupted a fashion as possible in this difficult time."

As the duke rejoined the nobles, the crowd throughout the Council Hall broke out in conversations of their own, the buzz becoming almost a roar. Lyric's eyes followed Carlton as he spoke to one noble, then another. Moments later, he turned away from the group and disappeared through a door behind the dais.

"Your Highness?"

A tall man, dressed in the garb of Graceen's palace guard, stood before her. She knew this man. Her grandfather's guards looked him over appraisingly but kept back, making no move to interfere.

"Hello, Hanseth. It's good to see you again."

Hanseth stepped between her and her grandfather's guards.

"As it is for me, Your Highness." He bowed, then held a rolled parchment out to her, speaking softly. "Prince Carlton asked that I deliver this to you and that you read it as soon as you can. In private."

Lyric grasped the parchment and slid it into the folds of her gown. "Thank you," she whispered. "I will do so."

Hanseth nodded and started to go but Lyric held up a restraining arm and spoke in a normal tone.

"Please tell the prince I am very sorry for his loss."

He nodded deferentially. "Of course, Your Highness." A moment later, he'd vanished into the crowd.

She felt as though the hidden parchment might burn a hole through her gown. Standing on tiptoe, she peered over the milling crowd until at last she located her grandfather. He was still on the dais, head bent in conversation with Duke Edmonds. She judged she had at least a little time before he returned to them.

"Noni, stand in front of me, please."

"Your Highness?" The girl turned bewildered eyes on her.

"Right here." She took Noni's shoulders and forcibly moved her between herself and the currently distracted gaze of her grandfather. "Tell me if Duke Foxmir comes this way."

Her grandfather's guards stood back from her, talking quietly, ignoring her, except for the occasional glance. Apparently, their only task was to keep her from running away.

Good.

With a quick look around to make sure no one else paid her any mind, Lyric turned her back to the guards and pulled out the scroll. Hands trembling, she unrolled the yellowed parchment and began to read.

My Dear Lady,

I am most sorry that we have been unable to meet again to further discuss your situation. I have been excited about the mission you are undertaking and had toyed with the idea that I might accompany you, but this, as you now know, cannot be. I must stay here and you must leave as soon as possible. Our spies have returned and things are just as you reported them. The banner of Malacar flies over both kingdoms and no one has seen your father or the king of Malacar in weeks. Word has just reached me that a large contingent of horsemen, armed for battle, is amassing in Tressalt and they are joined by creatures my men have never seen—manlike but larger, covered in fur, and vicious. Borags? What else from the ancient fables am I to see walking in the light of day?

I have debated with myself these last days about the advisability of helping you leave, contrary to the wishes of your worthy relative, but this latest discovery has decided me. Prince Ralt wants you—that is reason enough to send you away. I believe we have the strength to defend our walls, but if I am wrong, you must be far from here.

There is something else which you must know. When my father's body was found, he was clutching that object I showed you earlier—the statuette of the sailing ship. When my father was unconscious earlier, I had placed it in a drawer in an adjoining room. I don't know how he found it—did it 'call' to him? I do not know, but I believe this object drew my father from his sickbed, and eventually, to his death. Its image had been burned into his hand and was still smoking when we extracted it from him. If the Malacarians brought this token to the king on the morning you appeared before him, and if the wizard imbued it with some monstrous power, then two things are certain. This wizard is responsible for my father's death, and the Malacarians have access to far more power than we have anticipated.

You must leave, my lady, and quickly. If you disagree, let me know within the hour. Otherwise, Hanseth will bring a carriage for you at four this afternoon and take you to your companions. If you are questioned, tell any who ask that you have been called to the castle to grieve with my mother and sisters. I will provide horses and provisions for your journey and see that your relative is away from home, so your absence may go undetected as long as possible. If I may make one request of you—if your journey takes you that far north, try to meet with the king of Parsiway. Deliver to him the enclosed message—it explains our current situation. May the protection of the Maker be with us all.

Yours in haste—C.

She sagged against the marble column, heartbeat echoing in her ears. Only one thing was clear and unarguable—she was leaving Graceen today. Somehow.

"Your Highness?" Noni squeaked. "Duke Foxmir is coming."

Lyric re-rolled the scroll and stepped out from behind the maid. Her grandfather strode through the crowd, courtiers and townspeople giving way before him. He relaxed only a little when he stopped before her. "I didn't see you," he growled.

She blinked at him in feigned surprise. "Well, here I am. Just as you left me."

"Yes, well, you may go home now." His voice gentled. "There will be no further announcements at this time. I will stay here and meet later with the prince and nobles to hammer out the details of the funeral, the coronation, and everything else that must be done."

Lyric waved the scroll at him, making sure he could see the prince's seal. "I have been invited back this afternoon to sit with the queen and princesses."

He frowned. "Why didn't the prince speak to me of this?"

"I do not know. Perhaps he had other things on his mind."

He glanced back at the dais, gaze softening.

"Yes, of course." He turned to the guards. "Accompany the Princess of Tressalt back to the manor. Plan to return with her this afternoon when she comes to attend the queen." He leaned forward and placed a quick kiss on her forehead. "I shall see you at dinner, my dear." Then he turned and was gone.

CHAPTER 34: ARRANGEMENTS

Lyric paced circles in her chamber, rubbing her hands vigorously against her chilled arms. The city bells had just rung the noon hour, and she still didn't know how she was to escape her guards when the prince's carriage came for her.

She'd racked her mind for ideas since her return from the castle, but each thought seemed worse than the one before. What was she to do? Everything hinged on her escaping the guards' notice.

A soft knock on her chamber door stopped her frantic pacing. She grabbed her bed quilt and threw it over the rucksack she'd been packing. She turned to face the door.

"Come."

The door opened silently and Noni, carrying a tray with food and drink, shouldered her way into the room. She set the tray down on the writing desk, then gaped as she viewed the quilt-covered lump on the bed.

Lyric followed her gaze and saw the sheath holding her dagger protruding from under the quilt. She pressed a finger against her lips and shook her head.

Noni nodded and gestured to the food.

"I've brought your luncheon, Your Highness," she said in a sing-song voice. "Cook has outdone herself today. We have sliced ham, fresh oat bread, and clam stew. The wine is from last year's grape harvest, and I'm told it is delicious."

"Lovely," Lyric said, mimicking the servant's tone. She moved to the bed and shoved the dagger and her remaining clothing into the rucksack. She cupped a hand behind her ear as if listening closely to something, then pointed a finger toward the closest listening hole and looked at Noni questioningly.

Noni nodded, and Lyric scowled. Someone was listening from the room next door. Communication was going to be difficult. She sat at the desk chair and Noni shook out a napkin and placed it on her lap.

"Has Duke Foxmir returned from the castle?" She knew the answer but hoped an opportunity could be found in extended speech to both deliver and discover further information.

"No, Your Highness," Noni answered, pouring the wine into Lyric's goblet. "It is possible he and the other nobles will stay at the castle throughout the day. There is so much that needs to be decided. Poor King Rasmus's funeral must be planned, as well as Prince Carlton's coronation."

Perfect! "Yes," Lyric said, trying to sound dreamy and unconcerned. "You heard that the prince is to send a coach for me soon. He thinks it fit that I come to the castle and sit with Queen Bethen and the princesses in their grief."

"Of course, miss." Noni bowed her head then looked pointedly at the pile under the quilt on the bed. "You'll be needing an attendant. Shall I prepare to accompany you?"

"Oh, I don't think—" Lyric began. This was not at all what she'd planned, or what Carlton would be expecting.

"It would be most inappropriate for you to go to the castle unattended, my lady." The girl's words and tone were bland but the cornflower-blue eyes held a desperate glint.

Mindful of the listening ears in the next room, Lyric spoke carefully. "Of course. What was I thinking? Certainly I should be attended." She looked into the younger girl's eyes. "Do you think Celeste can do without you this afternoon?"

A look of panic crossed the girl's face, but she spoke boldly. "Oh, I'm sure she can, Your Highness. She knows it wouldn't do for you to answer a summons to the castle without an attendant. I shall inform her, of course."

"Of course," Lyric agreed, dipping her spoon into the thick clam stew. Her thoughts whirled. She didn't need this complication. If Noni went with her on her supposed visit to the castle, how was she to get away from her later? She was a sweet girl and had been most helpful, but Lyric needed to find her companions and flee Graceen City as soon as possible.

But what would Celeste do to the girl if Lyric somehow eluded her? Just thinking about it made her shudder.

She finished her meal in silence, scarcely tasting the delicious food. Just as she set the empty wine goblet down, Noni reappeared from the adjacent servant's quarters where she'd been tidying and placed a scrap of parchment on the desk next to the goblet.

Celeste has told us all to watch you. To report anything unusual.

Alarmed, Lyric stared up at the girl but Noni bit her lip and looked away. Lyric stood. "I have some clothing I would like cleaned. Will you take them to the laundress, please?"

"Certainly, my lady."

She gestured toward the servant's room. "They're in here."

Once out of range of the person at the listening hole, Lyric whirled to face Noni. "Why does Celeste want me watched? I'm already guarded."

"She thinks you're running away and doesn't believe the guards are ... enough," Noni whispered, her voice trembling. "She sends and receives messages almost every day from those people outside our gates. Those Malacarians. She's been doing that since before you arrived. Jiddy, the errand boy, told me Celeste thinks you helped your friends escape from Duke Foxmir and that you will be joining them soon to leave the city. She received a message back just last night saying that, no matter what, you were not to escape."

Lyric pressed her hand to her heart, covering the pulsing gemstone, and sank down onto the narrow bed. *Celeste in league with the Malacarians? How could this be?*

"And then, today—" The girl's eyes filled with tears and she pressed both hands against her mouth.

"Today what?" Lyric asked, only half-listening, trying to order her thoughts around this new complication.

"Today," Noni choked out, "no one has seen Jiddy all day. We think she found out he told, and she's done something to him. He's just a child, a sweet little boy."

Lyric shuddered, then reached out and grabbed her hand.

"I'm so sorry. I'll ask my grandfather to look into this, but that's all I can do right now. I have to get away from this house as soon as possible. Do you understand that? Prince Carlton knows what I must do and he is helping me. Do you think your prince would help me do anything that is bad or wrong?"

Noni sniffled and shook her head.

"Good." Lyric smiled encouragingly and squeezed the girl's hand. "Now, the first thing is, I have to get away from the guards. Do you know where they are? Will you help me?"

Noni's eyes widened. "Oh, my lady—if Celeste finds out—"

"It will be all right," Lyric said, reminding herself to keep her voice low. "She won't defy the prince's orders, will she? Besides, my grandfather gave permission for me to go to the castle. Prince Carlton is sending his bodyguard to fetch me, but I must escape my grandfather's guards."

Noni was still sniffling, but she nodded. "One of the guards is taking his midday meal now, and the other is at the front door. They will trade places soon."

Unable to sit any longer, Lyric jumped off the narrow bed and began pacing the circumference of the small room.

"The prince doesn't know my grandfather ordered the guards to accompany me to the castle. The carriage is to arrive at four. I cannot wait until I'm called for and hope to escape the guards." She stopped at the cot in front of Noni. "I've thought about this all morning, and I still don't know what to do."

"Perhaps the prince's bodyguard will simply tell our guards that they mayn't come?" Noni suggested.

Lyric sank back onto the bed. "I've thought of that. And if I can't think of anything else, that's what I must hope for. I don't know who Grandfather's guards are more frightened of—the prince's bodyguard or my grandfather. I don't want it to come to blows or bloodshed." She dragged her hand through her rumpled hair. "If only we could lock those guards up somewhere—throw away the key until I am far away."

Noni's eyes widened, and Lyric stared at her. "What?"

"I'm not sure, Your Highness, but we might be able to do that." She licked her lips, then clamped a hand against her mouth.

"What do you mean?" Lyric demanded. "How could we do this?"

Noni took several deep breaths. "One of the guards, Roger—he ... fancies me, I think. If I go to him, tell him and the other that Duke Foxmir wants them to do something—he might believe me." She squeezed her eyes shut, her breath coming in quick gasps. "I know where the keys are." She opened her eyes and stared at Lyric. "I could lock them in."

Lyric stared at the terrified girl. "Why would you do this? You are risking so much."

Noni swiped her hand across her forehead. "I must leave this place, too, Your Highness. Celeste is cruel but Duke Foxmir does not know. Jiddy has disappeared, and Roger is—very insistent." She gulped and lifted her chin. "I cannot stay here. Let me go with you, Your Highness. I will help you escape the guards and do anything else I can to serve you. Just take me away from here. Please."

Noni's situation, the complications, the need for hurry—all spun through Lyric's mind with bone-rattling speed. In the end, the last one decided her. She was running out of time.

"All right," she said softly. "I will take you with me. But we have to move quickly. The carriage will arrive in less than three hours."

"Yes," Noni said, her chin raised, seemingly determined now to do her part well. "You said you needed me to take clothes to the laundress. I'll take your bag, to pretend those are your soiled things, as if I'm going to the cleaning chamber. It will look strange if anyone sees you later, dressed for the castle, carrying it."

Lyric blew out a breath. She hadn't thought of that. "Good idea."

"I'll set it behind one of the bushes near the front door." Noni said. "I think Duke Foxmir's study is the best place to lock the guards. I'll need to get the key, and then find a way to make them follow me. I'll lock the door behind them." She looked at Lyric, biting her lip. "And hope they're too embarrassed to pound on the door until we're gone."

"Yes, perfect," Lyric said. "I can give you more time to look for the key if you send Celeste up here to speak with me. Can you do that?"

Noni's face flamed red but she squared her shoulders. "Yes."

"Very well. Tell her I need to speak with her, but not until after you take my—my laundry downstairs. Once you see her coming up the stairs, go look for the key."

"Yes, my lady."

They returned to the main chamber.

"I think this is all," Lyric said in a normal tone. "I'm sorry I spilled wine on the quilt. I do hope the laundress can get the stain out."

"She'll do her best, my lady." Noni picked up the rucksack, still wrapped in the quilt, and moved to the door.

When the door closed quietly behind the servant, Lyric collapsed on the bed, staring at the ornate ceiling. She'd been authoritative with Noni, trying to infuse the girl with courage, but in truth so many things could go wrong. What if Noni couldn't get the key, or the guards wouldn't go with her?

And what about Celeste? Did the woman really intend to stop her? Lyric had tried to pooh-pooh Noni's fears, but she'd been uncomfortable with the housekeeper since her first day in Graceen. She hadn't known until today that the woman might also be dangerous. If Celeste was involved with the Malacarians, that would explain how they knew Lyric had arrived in Graceen. And why she had been placed in a room where her conversations could be overheard.

Lyric rolled over on the comfortable bed, grasping the feather pillow in her arms, trying to control her rampaging thoughts. If only everything went well and they were able to escape this place, reunite with her friends, and leave the city! She needed to be calm, just as she'd ordered Noni. And she needed to be strong.

She closed her eyes, hugging the pillow closer. She was her father's daughter. If Ralt and the wizard were to be stopped, she must complete her mission. The lives of her people and those of other kingdoms would be affected—for good or bad—by what she did in the next hours.

The click-clicking of footsteps marching along the corridor outside her room sent her scrambling to her feet. At the instant the sharp knock came on the heavy door, Lyric saw Noni's scrawled note still resting on her midday lunch tray. Grabbing the parchment, she stuffed it into the bodice of her gown, next to the milk-white gemstone.

"Come," she called, sitting back on the bed and arranging her face into lines of boredom.

Celeste entered the room, her own expression unreadable.

"You called for me, Your Highness?"

"Yes. Prince Carlton has requested that I come to the castle this afternoon to sit with Queen Bethen. My grandfather knows and has approved."

Celeste's dark eyes narrowed into slits.

"I'm sorry, Your Highness, but I have not received such a message from Duke Foxmir. He has told me you are not to leave the manor without—"

"Without the guards?" Lyric waved a languid arm. "They are to go with me."

"I see. And will you need a carriage?"

"No. The prince is sending one for me. At ... half-past the four o'clock hour." Would the housekeeper notice her hesitation at giving the time? She didn't know but plunged on. "I shall need Noni's assistance with my hair and gown and, I assume, to attend me to the castle."

Celeste pursed her lips, gaze still narrowed. "You seem to have grown most fond of Noni. How nice for you both."

A chill ran through Lyric, colder than anything she'd felt since first sighting the Borags. This woman was both evil and dangerous. She shrugged, forcing bored casualness into her tone. "She's been competent. I've needed someone, of course, since I've been robbed of my own servant while in this household. But if you'd rather send someone else, it makes no difference to me." She ran her fingers through her silky, dark locks. "As long as she can fix my hair."

The woman nodded in what Lyric now recognized as an imitation of respect and turned to the door, then stopped, eyes focused on the luncheon tray left behind.

Lyric shrugged again. "I sent her with some laundry. I assume she'll come back for the tray." She waved her hand at the tray and gave a vapid smile. "She does need a lot of reminding. Perhaps you *should* send me someone else."

The housekeeper glared at her, then spun on her heel and strode from the room, slamming the door behind her.

Lyric blew out her cheeks and lay back on the bed. She hoped she'd given Noni enough time to find the correct key and she was suddenly, deliciously happy she'd agreed to take Noni with her. The girl would suffer dreadfully if Celeste had any inkling that she'd helped Lyric.

Soon they'd both be on their way.

CHAPTER 35: ESCAPE

Her breath whooshed out in relief when Noni pushed the door open a quarter of an hour later. For the sake of the listeners, Lyric greeted the maid querulously.

"What took you so long? The prince is sending for me soon, and my hair and gown still need tending. You left the meal tray as well."

Noni stared at her, eyes wide in astonishment, but Lyric put a finger to her lips and smiled.

The girl sighed and smiled back. "I'm so sorry, my lady. Shall we start with your hair or your gown?"

An hour later, Lyric was dressed in a formal gown of rose and cream, and her hair was glorious in ringlets and silver combs. Noni truly was amazing with hair. Their conversation would have sounded trivial to the listening ears, but even so, Lyric had learned that Noni possessed the key to her grandfather's study, and that her rucksack was hidden safely in the large shrubs near the front entrance. Celeste, surprisingly enough, had left the house soon after ordering Noni to continue waiting on her.

Lyric sighed, realizing only then just how worried she'd been that Celeste might try to stop her.

"It's time, my lady."

Shivering, Lyric rose to her feet and followed Noni to the door. When she turned toward the spiral staircase, Noni stopped her. "The guards will see us if we go that way," she whispered. "We must use the servants' stair."

Lyric followed the girl to the end of the long corridor, fear pumping through her body along with her blood. What if they ran into someone, perhaps another servant who was loyal to Celeste? But the hall was empty, and relief flooded through her when they ducked through the door that led to the servants' narrow, cobwebby staircase.

They crept slowly down the wooden steps, mindful of any noise that might alert someone to their presence. At the bottom, Noni touched Lyric's shoulder, then pulled her hand away violently. "I'm sorry, Your Highness," she breathed. "Please stay here until I see if anyone is about. I'll come back for you."

Lyric nodded and Noni pushed out the door. She was back a moment later. "The hallway is clear—only the guards are at the door. You can stand in one of the doorways while I speak to the guards. As soon as we go down the corridor to Duke Foxmir's room, you must get out quickly." The girl breathed in and out deeply. "If I don't come out right away, hide. Wait for the carriage."

Lyric took both the girl's shoulders, squeezed them.

"I will. Thank you, Noni, for all you've done. You don't know how much—"

Noni gave her a shaky smile. "You can tell me all about it later, miss. It's nearly four."

They stayed on the right side of the hall as they crept quietly toward the main door. Lyric could hear the guards speaking to each other, but the entrance was recessed between floor-to-ceiling columns, so the guards wouldn't see them until they were much closer. Or at all, when she and Noni ducked into the alcoves of the approaching doorways.

She hoped.

"Here," Noni whispered a moment later, directing Lyric into the doorway of a chamber near the sitting room where she'd conversed with Prince Carlton. "Remember everything I told you." Noni squared her shoulders and walked away.

Lyric hoped everything went according to plan for the girl.

She put a hand to her heart, clutching the message she'd earlier written to her grandfather while awaiting Noni's return to her room. She hoped he would understand and forgive her. She also hoped that one day she'd be able to forgive *him*.

More than anything, she hoped Celeste hadn't returned during the last hour.

From down the hall, she heard raised male voices.

"Well, hello, beautiful," one said. "What are you doing down here? Where's your princess? The carriage should be here soon."

"Oh!" Noni sounded surprised. "It's not four yet, is it? She told Celeste the carriage was to arrive at half-past the hour. She's mostly ready, but was napping when I left her. I'll have to re-do her hair, I suppose." The girl sounded irritated but then her tone changed. "But I was wondering, since we have a little time, perhaps you two gentlemen could help me with a small project."

Both men spoke at the same moment. "What project?" queried one, while the other—Roger, Lyric assumed—drawled, "Both of us?"

Noni giggled in a way Lyric had never heard her laugh before. "Yes, I think I need both of you. Mistress Celeste told me to retrieve Duke Foxmir's journal earlier, but it fell behind his desk and I couldn't reach it. I couldn't move the desk either, and I've only gotten away now to try again. Will you help?"

Lyric chuckled inwardly. The request was made so sweetly, she couldn't imagine any healthy male refusing.

She was wrong.

"Celeste wants the duke's journal?" said one. "That doesn't sound right."

Lyric couldn't see Noni but she imagined the girl shrugged. "I thought it sounded off, too, but you know how Celeste is when she's not obeyed. And it's not my place to question orders."

"Well, no," said the guard. "But still—"

"Please." Noni's tone turned whiny. "She struck me the last time I didn't do exactly as she'd said. Perhaps one of us can mention to the duke later that she asked for it?"

After a moment or two of grumbling, the men agreed and followed Noni down the opposite corridor toward Duke Foxmir's study.

This is it! Lyric counted to three, then left the protection of the doorway and raced to the sitting room. She'd leave her message here. Her grandfather would get it and maybe someday things between them would be healed. She pushed open the door, stepped into the room and froze.

Gertie, the ancient housemaid, was running a feather duster along the windowsill. She looked up in surprise as Lyric burst into the room.

"I, uh, have a message for my grandfather," Lyric stuttered, waving the parchment.

Gertie's surprise faded. "Why don't you leave it in his study? Or give it to Mistress Celeste?"

"Um, I don't know where Mistress Celeste is and I don't know which room is the duke's study."

"Shall I show you?" The old servant's eyes gleamed with something that could have been humor.

"No." Lyric couldn't keep the terror from her voice. "It's all right. I'll find another way to get it to him. Thank you anyway."

"Here." Gertie stepped forward, hand outstretched. "I'll see that he gets it." She took the parchment from Lyric, fixing her with a steady stare. "I am loyal to the duke—no one will ever tell you different—but I cannot abide Celeste. Now go. Quickly, before she returns."

Lyric stared, open-mouthed. "Thank you," she muttered, then turned and fled.

Tight evening gown notwithstanding, she raced toward the manor's oak door, only to see Noni running toward her from the far corridor.

"Why are you still here?" the girl asked breathlessly, but Lyric didn't answer. She pulled open the heavy door and both girls ran out, closing the door behind them.

No royal carriage awaited them. Lyric stood, gasping for breath, then ran to a large, spreading chestnut tree. She hid behind it while Noni hurried to where she'd stashed the rucksack, returning with it moments later. The broad thoroughfare in front of the mansion was cluttered with traffic and Lyric's nerves popped. The city bells tolled four.

Where was the carriage?

"The guards are locked up?"

Noni, eyes wide, nodded.

Lyric tried to smile. "I don't hear them pounding to get out."

"They don't know I locked the door. I told them I had to get something and would be right back." She shuddered. "They may try the door any moment and find out."

It felt like hours, but only minutes had passed when Lyric heard the iron-shod hooves ringing against the cobbles, followed by heavy, creaking wheels. She strained to see around the tree. Banners waved gaily from both sides of the carriage, the same as those carried by Carlton's guards when they'd gone on their horseback tour of the city. One for Graceen, one for Rasmus's household. She hurried out, Noni in her wake. She'd never been so happy to see a conveyance in her entire life.

Hanseth pulled the matching black horses in their silver-studded harnesses to a halt in front of them and waved a salute while a second, familiar-looking man climbed down and turned to face her.

"Good day, Your Highness," he said, a broad grin on his swarthy face. "It appears we'll be traveling together again, if it pleases you."

"Captain Monteith!" Lyric said, delighted. "It is so very good to see you again. I cannot think of anything I'd like more."

"Very good, my lady. We should be on our way, then. I hear we're in a bit of a hurry." He reached for the carriage door, then paused as the sound of clattering hooves and heavy wheels sliding on the cobblestones reached everyone's ears at once.

"Stop! Stop, I say!" The horses of the second carriage, eyes wide with frenzy, nearly crashed into the rear of their carriage. A voice Lyric knew only too well cursed the driver. "I told you to head them off, fool!"

"Get them into the carriage, Monteith," Hanseth ordered.

Monteith opened the carriage door and reached for Lyric.

"Quickly, my lady." He didn't have to tell her twice. She scrambled into the carriage and made room for Noni, but before the maid could get in, Celeste stormed around from behind their carriage.

"That girl's not going anywhere!" she screamed, pointing a shaking finger at Lyric. "She is under her grandfather's protection, and he has given no permission for her to leave his home."

In spite of her racing heart, Lyric was shocked at the housekeeper's appearance. The graying hair, normally neat as a pin, flew wildly about the woman's head and her face was livid.

From the driver's seat on top of the carriage, Lyric heard Hanseth's firm but calm voice. "Her Highness has been invited to the castle by the prince himself. Duke Foxmir gave his permission, madam."

"Not without the guards. Where are they? Get her out of that carriage!" In a frenzy, Celeste shoved Noni out of the way, knocking her to the ground. She tried to push past Monteith as well, but the burly captain was as solid and unmoving as an oak tree.

"Madam," Monteith ordered. "Control yourself."

Panting, Celeste stood back and Lyric hoped the woman would return to her senses. For a moment it appeared she had. When Celeste spoke again, she no longer shrieked.

"If you do not return the girl to me immediately, you will be responsible for causing war between Graceen and the kingdom of Malacar. This girl is promised to King Ralt. She was kidnapped by rebels from Tressalt, and the king wants his bride back."

"You lie!" Lyric gasped, her own fury exploding. "I was never promised to Ralt! My father told him *no.*"

"Your father?" The glee on Celeste's face bordered on demonic. "I'm afraid your father changed his mind, something you would have discovered sooner if you had not been *kidnapped*." She rolled her eyes. "He gave his word very clearly to King Ralt, in writing—just before he died."

CHAPTER 36: RAMPAGE

Lyric fell back against the carriage seat, the words a knife twisting in her heart.

It wasn't true. The woman was evil—she'd proven it over and over. Now she was lying about this horrible thing for her own monstrous purposes.

But Celeste no longer paid her any heed. She continued to shout orders, but not at Lyric or the people with her. To her horror, Lyric saw four black-garbed men flood around her carriage from the back. One carried a bow, arrow nocked, pointed upward to where Hanseth sat in the coachman's seat. The other three had swords drawn.

Celeste looked up at Hanseth and cackled like a mad woman.

"Perhaps you can see reason now, my lords? Give me the girl and go on your way and all will be well. Otherwise, my friends will cut you down where you stand."

Lyric's vision blurred and her mind refused to focus, but one thing she understood—they were outnumbered. If Hanseth and Monteith didn't turn her over to Celeste, they would be killed and she would be captured. She couldn't let that happen. Monteith still blocked her carriage door, while behind Celeste on the cobblestones, Noni sat clutching Lyric's rucksack, fumbling with the tie.

"Madam," Hanseth said, "this is a complicated situation. Let us go to the castle so that Prince Carlton and Duke Foxmir can straighten things out."

Celeste shook her head, dark eyes flashing, derision in every muscle.

"Oh, I don't think so, sir. You had your chance to play nice at the beginning. You're too late. These are the terms. You give us the girl, you get to live. If you don't—" here she held up her hands in mock dismay, "—you won't!"

"There's no need for anyone to die," Lyric said hoarsely. "I'm coming out."

"No, my lady." Monteith placed a large hand on the carriage door, holding it closed. "You mustn't go with them."

"I'm not sitting here while they kill you both." She tried to force the door open but couldn't budge it.

Monteith leaned in closer. "You must have faith, my lady. Hanseth and I will find a way out of this."

Lyric shook her head, wanting to contradict him, but before she could speak, movement behind Celeste caught her eye. Noni had staggered to her feet just a few steps behind the housekeeper, her hands quietly at her side. Even at this distance, Lyric could see the fire in the girl's eyes. What was she doing?

"No talking!" Celeste screeched. "Get out of the way now! I want that—"

Lyric screamed, but too late. Noni had leapt forward, Lyric's jewel-handled dagger raised high. She plunged it toward the housekeeper's back, but at the last instant, Celeste spun about. The Akyldi blade sliced deep into the woman's shoulder.

Lyric heard a *whoosh* and saw surprise in Noni's lovely eyes as a black-feathered arrow slammed into her chest. She stumbled back, stood for a moment, staring at the arrow. Then she sagged and dropped to the ground.

Monteith whirled and flung his dagger with dizzying speed. The black-clad bowman collapsed and the swordsmen leapt forward to the attack. One fell immediately, a green-feathered arrow in his throat.

Hanseth had loosed his own bow.

The second swordsman, following too close, tripped over his companion's body and crashed to the earth.

The remaining attacker dropped his sword and held up his arms. "Peace!"

Monteith stepped forward and scooped up the man's sword. "Malacarian, are you?"

When the man didn't answer, Monteith smashed a meaty fist against the side of his head. The man dropped without a sound.

Hanseth jumped down from the top of the carriage and bent over to look through the window at Lyric. "Are you well, Your Highness?"

All she could do was stare.

He stared back, concern in his eyes, then turned to face the carnage before them. Monteith was wrapping rope around the two surviving attackers. Celeste had slumped to the ground, her face pale as milk, dark blood staining her neat housekeeper's gown.

"Tie her up," Hanseth ordered.

"Happy to," Monteith growled, then looked past the woman to where several servants peered nervously out the door of the mansion. "You, there," he called. "Come out here and clean her up. No one will hurt you."

"Noni?" Lyric's throat felt dry beyond reason, as if she'd been swallowing dust for days.

Hanseth whirled to her. "Yes, Your Highness? How can I help you?"

"Noni." She pointed a shaking finger at the maid. "Is she ...?"

He looked to where Noni lay on the ground next to Celeste, Lyric's open rucksack lying between them. "I'll find out," he said gently and strode across the cobblestones.

Ignoring the bleeding housekeeper, he went down on one knee beside Noni. He put a hand on her heart, next to the arrow shaft, and waited. After a long moment, he looked back at Lyric, his gaze compassionate, and shook his head.

She turned away from the sight, slumping against the cushions of the carriage, closing her eyes. She'd already known. No one could survive such a wound. Surely Hanseth had known as well, but she'd had to ask, had to be sure.

The helpful, desperate maidservant was past saving.

"Your Highness?"

Hanseth stood outside the carriage, holding her rucksack in one hand and the sheathed dagger in the other. She looked into his eyes and saw kindness. "These are yours?"

When she nodded, he opened the carriage door and set the bag on the floor by her feet, the dagger lying on top.

"I'm very sorry," he said softly. "About your father. And the girl." He gestured to where a group of servants crowded around Noni and Celeste.

She felt tears burning behind her eyelids.

"I am, too." Turning away from him, she crumpled across the carriage seat onto her side. Pulling her knees up to her chest, she wrapped her arms around them, and allowed the tears to flow. She wept for Noni. She wept for her father.

She wept for herself.

Raised voices outside the carriage sometime later forced her to sit up, to face the world that could be cruel beyond measure. She wasn't finished with her tears—perhaps she never would be—but she must set them aside. If Celeste had spoken truly—if her father had indeed journeyed to that place from which no one returned—then she was the rightful ruler of Tressalt. She owed it to her people to shake off her grief and do what must be done.

Wiping the last of her tears away, she looked out the carriage window. Near at hand, Hanseth was questioning old Brandar, her grandfather's coachman. Beyond them, across the cobbled drive between the carriage and the mansion's front door, Celeste sat next to the two surviving attackers. All three were bound and gagged. Celeste's shoulder was swathed in bandages.

To their right, blankets covered three silent forms. A lump rose in her throat again but she forced it down and looked back at the coachman, whose voice was raised in agitation.

"I tell you, sir, it was not my fault. I didn't know what she was about. She's in charge of the household staff, you know. We have to obey—"

"You are not in trouble." Hanseth interrupted. "Just tell me what happened."

Brandar gave a frightened, sidelong glance at Celeste as if the woman still had power to harm him, even captive and bound as she now was.

"Brandar?" Hanseth prompted.

"Yes, sir." The grizzled coachman pulled his gaze away from the housekeeper. "Those men are from Malacar, sir. I've had to take her to meet them before, but she's always said I mustn't tell Duke Foxmir. See, she knows I've a fondness for the drink, sir, and she said she'd tell his lordship, and I'd lose my post, if I didn't do as she said."

"The Malacarians, Brandar?" Hanseth was clearly tiring of the old man's babble.

The coachman ran a hand across his perspiring forehead, then wiped the hand on his trousers.

"Yes, sir. Well, sir, we've never brought the Malacarians back with us into the city, you know, only met with them out where they've been blocking the Merchant Way these last weeks. But today, she goes into the tent where their leader sits, and a bit later they both come back out, and he's red-faced and cursing. He calls those four big blokes and says that if she knows what's good for her, she better make sure the young lady there—Princess Lyric, I mean—"

He bowed to Lyric and Hanseth turned and swept his eye quickly over her before looking back at Brandar.

"I heard him say Princess Lyric better not get away and he's sending those four soldiers to make sure she doesn't. Mistress Celeste was in a right state and she made me whip up the horses and race them all the way here, then told me to drive right in front of the king's carriage. I didn't want to do it, sir. Really, I didn't." The old man ran his hand through his thinning hair. "But Mistress Celeste said—"

"Yes." Hanseth held up a hand. "I know the rest of it."

After a moment, the old man dropped his gaze to the ground, scuffing his boots on the cobblestones.

"Well, sir, if I may be so bold," he said after a moment. "Mayn't I take the horses back to their stable and get them out of their harness? They're fearful upset and all sweaty. I'm afraid they'll colic for sure."

"Yes, yes." Hanseth waved an arm. "Go on with you, but don't go far. When the king's men get here, they may have more questions for you."

"I'm sorry, miss." The coachman turned his watery eyes to Lyric. "Truly, I am. But I was afraid—" He waved his hand toward the housekeeper.

Lyric could only stare. Brandar had known her since she was a small child visiting her grandfather's country estate with her mother, yet he could betray her like this. The drunken sot cared more about his horses than the grandchild of his employer. In light of everything else that had happened this day, this betrayal should be mild.

But it wasn't.

With many thanks and as many bows, the coachman hurried back to his four-legged charges.

Lyric climbed out of the carriage and stepped over to Hanseth. "Where's Monteith?"

"He's gone off to look for one of the patrols, to send word to the castle about what's happened here." He cocked his head, then peered over his shoulder toward the street. "And here he is now."

Following his gaze, she saw Monteith, accompanied by a mounted soldier, striding toward them.

The horse soldier dismounted but stayed where he was while Monteith came on. He bowed to her.

"A message has been sent to the castle, Your Highness, telling the prince what has happened and asking for assistance. This is Sergeant Thom." He gestured to the soldier behind him. "He'll stay here and watch this lot with me until the prince sends someone to take over. I trust this meets with your approval?"

"Of course, Captain. Thank you for seeing to it."

He nodded. "If you want my advice, my lady, you and Hanseth had better be leaving soon. I'll meet you at the house as soon as I can get there. When Duke Foxmir hears about what's happened, he'll be back in no time."

Hanseth stepped forward. "You are still determined to set out, are you not, Your Highness? I have my orders from the prince, but if you've changed your mind—"

Lyric shook her head. "I have not changed my mind. We must go immediately but there is one thing I must do first. Come with me, both of you." She pivoted on her heel and marched over to where Celeste sat.

The housekeeper stared at her, eyes narrowed in fury. Lyric stared back, untouched by the woman's rage or her wounds.

"I will speak to you this one last time. If you are wise, you will answer and tell the truth. Why have you done this?" She gestured to Hanseth. "Remove the gag."

The guard stepped forward and pulled the cloth from the woman's mouth.

Celeste's face contorted.

"You think you're so high and mighty, *Princess!* But you're nothing, nothing at all. Prince Ralt's men came to me weeks ago. They knew you would come whimpering to your grandsire. I was offered more money than I've ever seen in my life, and I was glad to take it."

Lyric's rage was near to exploding. This had all been about money? Noni's death? She swallowed the anger and forced herself to go on. "And did Prince Ralt's men also do something to King Rasmus?"

The woman smirked. "Probably. They didn't tell me but *King* Ralt has powerful help, magical, if you know what I mean, and is determined to get what he wants, though why he would want you—"

"Be still!" Lyric ordered. "I have one more question— where is the child Jiddy?"

Celeste rolled her eyes. "He's locked up in a storage closet on the first floor. You may get away now, *Princess*"— she fairly spat the word—"but you won't get far. Ralt's men will have you before this time tomorrow. You're a fool, if you think—"

"Replace the gag." Lyric spun on her heel and strode to the carriage.

Moments later, she sat alone in the coach as Hanseth turned the horses out the gate and clattered away from her grandfather's house.

CHAPTER 37: REUNION

They drove through the busy city streets for an hour before arriving at a small, nondescript house in a neighborhood full of small, nondescript houses. Hanseth jumped down to open the carriage door for her. She took his hand and stepped slowly out. She was stiff and sore, as if she'd been through a murderous brawl herself, rather than merely witnessing one. Before they reached the house, the front door flew open and a figure clad in faded riding attire raced down the path to meet them.

"Oh, my lady!" Becca slid to a stop in front of her. "You're finally here!"

Lyric looked up and narrowed her eyes, trying to find the right words.

"I am glad to see you." Her voice sounded strange, like it belonged to someone else. She shook her head.

Becca's brow furrowed, a quizzical expression on her freckled face. She glanced at Hanseth, then back at Lyric. "What's wrong, my lady?"

Hanseth looked at Lyric questioningly before turning to Becca. "Your mistress has had a bad experience at Duke Foxmir's home. Let's take her inside, shall we?"

Amira and Quinn met them at the door. Amira's silver eyes swept over Lyric as Hanseth led her to an upholstered chair.

"Something is amiss, lady," Amira said. "What is it?"

Seeing the concern in the eyes of each of these dear friends, Lyric felt the grief swelling through her once more. She inhaled deeply, steadying herself.

"We were attacked outside my grandfather's home by men of Malacar. Celeste, the housekeeper, was involved. A maidservant—" She stopped. Gripped her stomach against the pain. Forced herself to say the awful words. "A young girl who helped me after you were taken was killed. And my father is dead."

Becca burst into tears. Amira and Quinn stood, heads bowed, sorrowing and silent. Hanseth remained at her side, glancing back and forth between them all.

For a long time, no one spoke. Then Lyric took a deep, shuddering breath.

"This doesn't change anything. We must go on. We've only discovered, once again, just how cruel our enemy is. He—they—must be stopped. I hope you agree."

Amira's gaze held kindness. "I am sorry you have seen such grief so early in this journey. For us, though, there is no solution to this evil but going forward."

Becca sniffled, dabbing at her eyes with a cloth. "Whatever you think best, my lady. I go wherever you go." She gulped, then looked at Lyric, eyes wide. "But ... if your father the king is dead, then ... you are Queen, my lady. Er, Your Majesty."

Lyric shivered and crossed her arms over her chest. She didn't want to be Queen—she wanted her father back. Ultimately, it didn't matter what she wanted. An enemy sat upon her throne. She forced a smile.

"Oh, no. I am not ready for such name changes. Can we just be thankful we are together again for now? Titles can wait. I am so glad to see you all. We have been separated too long and have much to tell each other. Come, sit with me."

Hanseth excused himself to care for the horses while the rest sat together in the small house, at first in comfortable silence, then little by little catching up on the happenings of the last several days. They spoke of light, humorous things. Quinn told of a neighboring child who had kicked a ball into their yard. When he had handed the ball back, the child had run away screaming. "We thought it best if Quinn and I remained inside after that," Amira said.

Hanseth came inside, and Lyric told of the irrepressible Princess Demesne and the Great Horse Race in the park. Becca made sandwiches and brought tea.

They did not speak of the attack at Duke Foxmir's. They did not speak of King Sander's death.

The afternoon sun slanted low through the mullioned window when Monteith and another rider arrived, leading five saddled horses. Lyric was pleased to see Prince Carlton had sent the gray mare Moonbeam for her use, but was surprised by the number of horses. Why so many? Before she could ask, Monteith handed her a sealed parchment.

Carlton had written:

> *I was so very sorry to hear of your loss. In this, I am in a position to sympathize, more so than many. We never discussed this, but as I am unable to accompany you on this journey, I am sending Hanseth and Monteith with you. They are under orders to assist you in every possible way. I wish I could do more, but I have my own gates to protect. Please know that my thoughts are with you.*

She lifted her gaze to where the two soldiers were speaking quietly together while adjusting saddles on the riding horses. Again, hot tears demanded release. She'd never considered asking Carlton for such aid, but these two men would be invaluable help.

Almost as good as—but no. She shook her head, gritting her teeth. Marek was far away. Maybe he would come back to her someday, and maybe he wouldn't.

Maybe he couldn't.

She ran her hands roughly up and down her arms, trying to stave off the chill that coursed through her. Whether Marek came for her or not, the path before her was clear.

Even so, she sighed. What would he do when he learned his king was dead? Would he see his duty as completed? Would he ride away and never look back?

Marek's king. Her father. Pain shot through her heart, and she knew that nothing on this earth would take it away.

The sun hovered just above the western hills and the city streets were nearly vacant when they left the house, setting out on horseback for the city's northern gate. The rider who had come with Monteith drove the carriage back to the castle while they rode north. There was little conversation among them, no bright banners announcing them as they rode.

The houses and shops finally petered out and across a large, empty field loomed the northern gate. It was an exact replica of the southern gate they'd come through, also accompanied by Captain Monteith, just a week earlier. A lump swelled in Lyric's throat as she remembered her grandfather breaking past the border guards and racing to meet her.

He had treated her abominably most of the time she'd been in his home, but she'd never doubted that he loved her, even now. But it was a love that didn't recognize boundaries, a love that refused to listen. Someday, perhaps, she'd see him again and make him understand.

Monteith led the way through the hulking gate, under the iron portcullis.

"Getting a late start, Captain," one of the gate guards said. "Best keep an eye open and an arrow nocked. You never know what you might run into out there."

"That's a fact." Monteith nodded and rode on, the rest of the company following.

The main road veered left immediately and led back to the Merchant Way in the west. They, however, continued north on a smaller track that ran through several miles of grassy plain and into the forest. She had heard Monteith discussing the route with Quinn and Amira. Not only would this way be less traveled and, therefore, less likely to be watched, but a day's travel, once they entered the forest, would bring them to the valley where Venuzia was to meet them.

Not once on their journey had Lyric been tempted to look behind her, but now she did. The mighty walls of the city, thirty feet high and ten feet wide in places and guarded by hundreds of soldiers along its vast circumference, seemed impenetrable. But Ralt came with a wizard's power. Would the gates hold? She shivered, hoping against hope Carlton was right—that this beautiful city would have the strength to stand against whatever the renegade prince brought with him.

They'd covered scarcely a quarter of the distance along the path to the forest when the last blazing shred of the sun dropped behind the purple western hills. A moment later, a booming thud echoed across the miles. Lyric didn't have to look back to know what had happened.

The gate to the city was closed.

A cool breeze arose with the twilight as they rode on. It caressed Lyric's skin, ruffled her hair. The full moon rose in the east as the horses carried them ever nearer the forest's edge. The gray mare, Moonbeam, lifted her head, pricking her ears forward. Lyric followed the horse's gaze and became aware of an odd, sizzling sound filling the air around them. It was like meat cooking over a hot fire but with no smell. Frowning, she lifted her hand and pressed it to her heart, seeking the reassurance of the opal stone.

Ahead of her, Quinn pulled his horse to a halt and hissed, "Stop! Everyone."

Hanseth, next to Quinn, wheeled his horse around just as an arrow flew out of the spreading darkness and sank into the skirt of his saddle. "Ambush! Get back to the city!"

In an instant, all six horses raced as one back toward the city gate. The animals were frenzied and out of control. Lyric lifted her reins, trying to restrain her horse and gain some modicum of control, but Moonbeam clenched the bit in her teeth and plunged forward. Beside her, Becca's mount was running wild, eyes wide with fright. Bouncing crazily in her saddle, Becca pulled on the reins, trying to guide the horse, to slow it, but to no avail. The horse fought back, yanking its head violently, pulling the reins out of Becca's hands, and surged past Lyric and Moonbeam. Only as the horse cut in front of her did Lyric see the arrow embedded in the animal's haunch.

"Stop!" she cried but nothing could be heard over the earth-shaking thunder of the stampeding horses. What was wrong with them? Becca's horse, crazed with pain and the frenzy that gripped them all, didn't see the large stone in its path. It hit the stone, stumbled, and Becca flew over its head, somersaulting in mid-air. She slammed to the ground. The horse leapt over Becca's prone body and raced away.

"No!" Lyric screamed, yanking on Moonbeam's reins with all her strength. The rest of her companions had disappeared into the dusk, carried away by their frantic horses. Somehow, she managed to wrest control from Moonbeam. She circled the gray mare back to Becca. Flinging herself from the saddle, she ran to where the girl lay crumpled on the ground. Moonbeam raced away after the others.

Lyric knelt beside Becca, vaguely aware that the sizzling sound still surrounded them. She gently shook Becca's shoulder. *Please be all right!* The girl's eyes were closed and she did not move. Heart throbbing, Lyric leaned over and pressed her ear against Becca's chest. A strong, cadenced beat echoed through her rib cage.

Becca moaned, and Lyric sat back, relief flooding through her. Then she heard the thunder of more galloping hooves. Her terror assuaged, her rational mind returned, and she knew their danger. Their attackers were in front of her, somewhere in the darkness. Her companions were behind them.

Which group galloped toward them now?

Becca struggled to sit up, but Lyric pressed her back. "Sshh. Stay down."

Lyric peered into the deepening twilight. The galloping horses came from the direction of the forest. She gulped. Eight horsemen moved toward them through the shadows of the night, stopping a scant twenty-five yards away. The enemy, then.

"That's the one," a hoarse voice muttered. "Doesn't look like she's hurt. Grab her quick." All eight pressed their steaming horses toward them.

Where were her companions? Terror gripped her as the attackers drew near.

Two of the men leapt from their horses and strode toward her and Becca, swords in hand. "Come along, Your Highness," one of them crooned. "Time to get you back to King Ralt."

The other chuckled. "Your crown awaits you."

"No!" Lyric scooted back, reaching for her dagger, remembered, heart sinking, that it was in her pack, attached to her saddle. Heart pounding, her thoughts flew. She could run. Maybe somehow, she could escape.

No. She couldn't, wouldn't leave Becca.

She could see them approaching, hear them laughing. Her heart throbbed, except—it wasn't her heart. Hardly knowing what she did, she pulled the glowing gemstone from under her tunic. She clenched it in her fist, felt its weight, its heat. She raised the stone high, baring her teeth, and hissed at the men.

"Stop, I say. I command you to leave us alone."

The two men paused, glanced at one another, then chuckled. "Sure, Your Highness. We'll leave you alone." They resumed their relentless march, striding toward the women across the uneven ground.

Until they weren't.

Lyric narrowed her gaze, not understanding what she was seeing. It was as if the leering men had walked into an unseen wall. One of them fell, but scrambled quickly to his feet, looking from side to side, as if wondering what had hit him. The other stumbled backward, looking as bewildered as his companion.

A hot tingling flared through Lyric's raised arm, from the hand that held the stone all the way to her shoulder. She didn't understand it.

But at some deeper level, she knew. She must keep her hand raised, gripping the opal stone, and deny these men what they wanted.

They would not have her. They would not take her to Ralt. She would hold them back all night, if she had to. "*No!*"

And suddenly she realized she didn't have to hold them back any longer. Arrows sliced through the air from behind her, and the two men fell. Horses bolted past her and Becca, and the remaining attackers fled.

Only then did she let her hand fall.

She collapsed.

CHAPTER 38: WARRIOR QUEEN

"Princess Lyric—can you hear me?"

Through the shadows that jostled for space in her tired mind, Lyric thought she recognized the voice. It was quiet and authoritative, and she knew she should answer it, but she didn't seem to have control of her voice.

"What's the matter with her?" Another voice, also familiar, but fearful. "You said she wasn't injured, so why won't she wake up?"

Cool fingers moved lightly across her forehead, smoothing her hair away from her face. "She's had a shock," the calm voice said. "She'll awaken when she's ready."

"She had a lot of shocks today," came a less familiar voice. Deep, masculine. "But what was happening when we rode up? I've never seen anything like it. It was like—"

"Like she was holding the enemy at bay," the voice with quiet authority said.

Lyric forced her eyes open. "That's impossible." She pushed the cool hand away from her forehead—it was Amira's—and struggled to sit up. "I don't understand. How could such a thing happen?"

"My lady!" Becca squealed with delight. "Thank goodness you're better!"

"Yes," she began, then, faltering, looked around at the faces of her concerned friends. Amira and Becca were seated on the ground next to her. Hanseth stood nearby, holding the reins of two of the horses. Another form—it must be Quinn—held two other horses and stood with his back to the group, peering into the darkness. High above, the full moon shone directly over their heads, casting them all in shadow.

She turned back to Amira and was ashamed to hear the tremor in her own voice as she spoke.

"I don't understand. Those men were coming for us, and my arm was tingling and—" She halted and gulped, unable to put her confusion into words. "They just ... stopped."

In the moonlight, Amira's silver eyes glinted kindly at her. "I am not certain, Lady. But we don't need to know all right now. It will be best if we find a place of safety before we speak more fully. Are you hurt?"

Lyric sucked the rich, summer air deep into her lungs, trying to steady herself. She moved her head from side to side, rolled her shoulders.

"I am not injured."

But she was afraid, more afraid than she'd been in a very long time. Despite the warmth of the evening, gooseflesh broke out on her arms and neck. She reached over and grasped Amira's hand. "I must know what's happening. Tell me."

The Akyldi woman gazed at her thoughtfully.

"As I said, I do not know for sure. There are rumors, hints, in some of the ancient texts that the gemstones sometimes exhibit strange behavior. The occurrences are inconsistent, not always manifesting to each bearer. Whether it is the stone itself or its connection with the bearer is also not known. And—" Amira hesitated, then went on slowly, "—according to many of the texts, the opal stone is the most mysterious of them all."

"Mysterious? Why?" Lyric released Amira's hand and sat back. Her mind whirled, and questions without number demanded answers, but the sound of galloping hooves burst through her thoughts. She flinched, peering anxiously into the darkness.

"Do not fear the bestowal of the gift," Amira said, resting her hand lightly on Lyric's shoulder, "or the approach of the rider. It's Captain Monteith returning from the city."

She nodded, trying to relax, but she wasn't entirely successful until the horses came to a stop nearby. A moment later, Monteith's sturdy form came into view.

"I am glad to see you up, Your Highness," he said, bowing. "You gave us a scare. Are you well?"

"I am well, Captain," she told him, though not as well as she could wish. "Where have you been?"

"I went back to the gatehouse to tell the guard about the attack. They will send someone to retrieve the bodies in the morning. I told them we believed them to be more Malacarians, but the prince will want to know for certain."

Bodies? She shook her head, trying to find clarity in her muddled mind. The men who had ambushed them? Of course.

"Yes, they were from Malacar. One of them spoke of taking me back to Prince Ralt. Only ... they call him King Ralt now." The thought made her wince. She tried to shake off her revulsion to sound more queenly, more regal. "Were all the attackers accounted for?"

"Yes." Monteith nodded grimly. "We believe we got them all." He looked over his shoulder. "I've also conscripted one of their horses—the best of the lot, or I'm no horseman—to replace Miss Becca's poor beast. I left that one with the guard at the gate. He'll probably heal up fine once they get that arrow out."

"Begging your pardon, Your Highness." Hanseth had moved into the circle. "We need to be going ourselves. There's a place about an hour's ride into the forest where we can rest for the night, if you're fit to travel."

"I am fit," Lyric said, struggling to her feet. She had no desire to stay in the unguarded plain any longer than they already had. Her head still spun, but she shook off the dizziness and faced Becca. "What about you, madam? Are you fit to travel?"

The girl's eyes sparkled. "Yes, ma'am. I'll be sore in the morning, but I've no broken bones." Suddenly, she reached forward and grasped Lyric's hand, held it between both of hers. "You came for me and stood over me like a mother bear, my lady! You could have left me, but you didn't. You stayed with me." Her eyes filled with tears.

Lyric was embarrassed and spoke more roughly than she normally would, because Becca's words echoed her own thoughts during the attack.

"Of course I stayed. We women of Tressalt are far from home. We must stick together."

"One more thing," Quinn said softly.

It had been so long since she'd heard him speak, Lyric had almost forgotten his presence. She turned to the Akyldi scout. "Yes?"

"I think Princess Lyric deserves an explanation," Quinn said. "She and her servant were left alone in grave danger, while we, who have sworn to protect her, raced away." He stepped forward and knelt before her. "I am very sorry for having failed you, my lady. I did not control my horse. I pray you find it in your heart to forgive me."

Lyric's eyes widened. "Get up, Quinn. You have nothing to be forgiven for."

"He's right," Hanseth said. "I've never before been mastered by my horse as I was this evening. I do not know what got into him—it was as if there was ill magic in the air—but it matters not. My prince set me the task of seeing to your safety, and I failed. Both you and him." He stepped forward and knelt beside Quinn.

Monteith and Amira made to join them but Lyric stamped her foot.

"Stop it, all of you. Quinn, Hanseth—get up!"

When all were on their feet, facing her, Lyric raked both hands through her hair and glared at them.

"Thank you, all of you. You can't know how much it means to me to have you all with me on this journey.

But—" She raised her hand. "You are not my servants—not even you, Becca." She waved at the astonished maid, then turned to the others. "You are my friends, my companions. Please, let us just work together to see this task through to its completion."

She paused, looking at each member of the group in turn, finally settling on Hanseth.

"You are more right than you know. There *was* an ill magic in the air tonight. I heard it, felt it. Did none of the rest of you? We were attacked, yes, but this was no normal stampede of horses. We must beware. Not all of our enemies are mortal." She saw Hanseth give Monteith a quick glance, but now was not the time for greater explanation.

She took a deep breath and in exhaling, almost shuddered. "And finally, no more kneeling, please. Quinn— you and I almost died together when the Borags attacked. Hanseth and Monteith, you two fought valiantly for me earlier today." She turned to Amira and her voice softened. "You are my sister in this task. Never bow to me. We are equals, each with our part to play."

Lyric shifted her gaze to Becca. "And I include you in this. I am so glad it was you I found in the halls of the castle that morning in Tressalt. I don't know how I would have survived this long without you." She stepped forward and embraced the girl. When she pulled back, tears glistened in both their eyes.

She turned back to the group. "Now, can we please get back on these horses and leave this forsaken place?"

It took them only moments to mount and return to the trail that led to the forest and their path to the north. Even knowing what to expect, Lyric stifled a gasp when they came upon the first body. The man was face down, an arrow lodged in his back. Which one was he? One of the two who had come for her on foot, leering? One who had stood frozen behind an invisible screen when she'd raised the stone and ordered them to stop?

Prince Carlton said the large group from Malacar was still days from the city. These men must have been part of the earlier group that had set up the blockade south of Graceen, as were the four who'd accosted them at her grandfather's home.

Even as she rode past the dead, her body gave in to the horror, and tremors claimed her. Her father was dead. Noni was dead. And all these men were dead. Would Ralt ever tire of the killing?

Why wouldn't he stop?

Because he's already come too far, an inner voice whispered. *He can't stop. He can't turn back.*

She shook off her tremors and stared up at the ivory disk of the moon. She wouldn't stop either. She wanted her kingdom back. She wanted justice.

She wanted revenge.

For her father and Noni. For Master Grimstead and Duke Solano. For Rigel, with his freckled face and bright smile. For all her countrymen who had died in defense of their land. For the women and children who were now without husbands. Without fathers.

Perhaps even for Marek, if he had not survived.

Prince Ralt had chosen his course and there was no turning back for him.

She would not turn back, either. She would find the bearers of the remaining stones of prophecy. She would convince them to join her, Amira, and Venuzia. Together they would rid Argonia of Ralt and the wizard who empowered him.

She would do this, or die in the effort.

She lifted her hand to her heart, covering the opal stone. As if in answer to her silent determination, the gemstone pulsed gently and warmed beneath her touch.

ABOUT THE AUTHOR

Dawn Shipman knew she wanted to be a writer since Mrs. Juell's 10th-grade Creative Writing class. Since then, she's written stories, poetry, plays, puzzles, quizzes, and a mass of magazine articles, including interviews, how-tos, and personal experience stories. She believes freelance writing is the ideal occupation for those who are nosy by nature and like asking people personal questions.

Dawn makes her home in the beautiful Pacific Northwest where she lives with her long-haired, IT-guy husband, a gregarious German Shepherd, two disdainful cats, and four horses–two large ones and two very small (but mighty!) ones. She loves reading, writing, riding, and traveling. Contact her at dawnshipmanfiction.com.

CONNECT WITH DAWN ...

Hey, All! Thanks so much for joining me on this journey with Lyric, Marek, Becca, and the rest. I hope you loved reading this story as much as I enjoyed writing it. If you have time, would you do me the huge favor of leaving a review on Amazon, GoodReads, or anywhere else people talk about books? It doesn't have to be long—just a few words of what you liked about it and why. Every little bit helps get the word out. I would so appreciate it. Also, track me down on my website, Facebook, or Instagram—I'd love to chat!

Find me on Facebook at Dawn Shipman, Author, and Instagram @dawnshipmanfiction

For a sneak peek at the next book in The Lost Stones of Argonia series, read on ...

QUEST OF THE QUEEN

The Lost Stones of Argonia

Book 2

PROLOGUE

Ralt, Prince of Malacar, knew his father was a wise and just king. Standing before him now, an accused criminal before his judge, Ralt hated the man as he seldom had in all his sixteen years.

"You were born to be king, my son," Torian said, his face lined with weariness. "But you cannot be king. You cannot rule others when you refuse to rule yourself."

Ralt stared into the fire in the great hearth. If not for the two burly guards flanking the dais, he'd shove his self-righteous, son of a harlot father into the flames.

No one would stop him from being king.

His father sighed and lifted a scroll from his lap. He unrolled the document—the official charges of Ralt's so-called crime.

Torian lifted his head, pain shadowing the pale eyes. "You ... *forced* that girl—Glynara. You struck her and held her down. How could you do such a thing?"

Ralt resisted the urge to shrug. Had his father always been old? Besides, she was an innkeeper's daughter—she had no right to refuse.

Torian stared at him a long moment, perhaps hoping for some sign of remorse. But the only thing Ralt regretted was being caught. It made his life so ... complicated.

The king turned back to the scroll. "As punishment for your crimes—and crimes they are—a sum of three hundred gold ferules will be taken from your inheritance and given to Glynara and her family."

Ralt glared at the old man. What was his soft-headed father thinking? Three hundred ferules were a fortune.

But the king wasn't finished. "In addition to this, for a period of one year, you will serve aboard one of our merchant ships. You will begin at the lowest level and be allowed to move up only as you prove yourself obedient and hard-working."

Now Ralt was spluttering. He, a king's son, swabbing decks and gutting fish?

His father lifted a hand. "You ship out tomorrow morning. You will be watched night and day. The captain and first mate know who you are but no one else on the crew will. To them, you will be just another prisoner, sentenced to work off your crimes rather than sitting idly in a dungeon. They will treat you accordingly if you fail to do your tasks as assigned."

Ralt took a step forward, fists clenched. "You cannot do this, Father. I refuse to go. You have no right—"

"I have every right," the king said quietly. "And I am exercising that right. There is one more thing." He nodded at a servant, who pulled open the heavy oak door leading to the outer passageway. Three men entered the room, one carrying a rope, another, a long, coiled whip. All three wore executioner's masks.

Ralt stared at his father in disbelief.

"I think it important that you know how it feels to be held against your will and forced to endure torture. Perhaps then you will gain the compassion you need to be an effective ruler." The king paused but his eyes never wavered from Ralt's. "Or perhaps not. Understand, my son, that if you do not learn these lessons to my satisfaction, you will never sit on the throne of Malacar."

The whipsman had not been gentle.

Ralt suppressed a groan as he stood before the ship the next morning. The ship that would be his home for a year.

Rage burned red before his eyes as the coarse garment he wore rubbed against the welts.

One day, his father would pay.

The sound of marching feet broke through the morning silence. Ignoring the guards who stood at his side, he turned his head—carefully—to look over his throbbing shoulder. Two dungeon guards strode toward the ship, three shackled prisoners stumbling between them.

"Hey, Zander," shouted the guard who'd been sent up that morning to retrieve Ralt. "The king's sent another one. Take him to the boatswain's mate along with the rest." The guard untied the rope that bound Ralt to himself and handed it to the lead prison guard. He did not untie the fetters that bound Ralt's wrists.

"Come on with ye." The prison guard gave a sharp jerk on the rope and Ralt stumbled forward, slipped on the wet grass, almost fell. The guard guffawed stupidly. "Let's take these fine gents over to the ship, shall we? Master Liren will have some honest work for them."

His rage burned hotter still. Did none of these moronic guards recognize him? Did they not know what he would do to them when he returned?

For he would return. Of that, there could be no doubt.

He was dragged to the ship, along with the other prisoners, and quickly discovered what the *honest work* consisted of. Gutting fish and swabbing decks, as he'd thought. Loading and unloading cargo but above all—rowing. Morning, noon, and sometimes night. The *Merryweather* was fully rigged with two immense, billowing sails, but sometimes lacked a wind to fill those sails. A light breeze would not move the ship with its heavy loads between each port. During those times, Ralt and his fellow prisoners were dumped from their hammocks in the stinking recesses of the ship's hold and ordered to the oars. Any delay brought the lash down hard. Ralt soon learned to respond quickly.

He and the three prisoners from the dungeon joined sixteen others who'd already been aboard. The work was harder than anything he'd ever done and the first three days, his body rebelled in every way. The reek of fish, the constant rolling of the big vessel on the ocean waves, and the abysmal food had him vomiting from where he sat, lashed to the oars. The prisoners on the rowing bench next to him leaned as far away as they could, and the guards laughed, calling him *pretty boy* and making bawdy suggestions about how to stop the intestinal upset.

Even the other prisoners mocked him, and the fury in him grew. Three days into the journey, he snapped. As soon as he was unshackled from the oars, he flung himself onto the back of the man in front of him, pummeling and kicking with everything he had. In moments, guards and prisoners alike surrounded the combatants, stomping their feet, hooting with laughter.

The battle was short lived. The other man, larger, tougher, and not suffering from seasickness, had been taken by surprise, but rallied immediately. A huge, meaty hand smashed into the side of Ralt's head, and he crashed to the slick wooden planks of the deck, ears ringing. Several well-placed kicks cracked his ribs and would have broken them had the boatswain's mate not shown up when he did, whip in hand.

"What's the matter with ye'?" He growled at the guards. "As pitiful as the lad is, we need him to row, unless one of you wants to take his place."

For nine months, the sea was Ralt's home, and he hated every day. Storms had frightened him at first, but he learned to look forward to the high winds that meant he didn't have to row. His hair grew long, both on his head and face. His clothes became filthy, and he stank, but no one cared. His gut adjusted to the roll and pitch of the ship, and the constant rowing made him strong. He became a powerful and cunning fighter and lost fewer and fewer battles. Sometime that year, he turned seventeen, but no one marked the date.

He counted the days until his sentence was served, and he would return to Malacar to take revenge upon the man who had stolen a year of his life.

He used his skill with words to convince first one, then others of his fellow prisoners of who he was and what awaited those who helped him—and those who didn't. As time went by, a small group of malcontents formed around him, and they devised ways to skip work and shift the blame to others for lost or destroyed items. One night, after a long day and too much rum, the boatswain's mate staggered back to his quarters and was attacked by unknown men. They threw a blanket over his head, beat him bloody, and left him senseless on the floor.

The next day, when no one would or could confess, the captain ordered that all prisoners receive five lashes.

It had been worth it.

But one evening, everything changed.

The day had been breezy and warm, and they'd seen no land for days. Due more to trickery and cunning than hard work, Ralt had been allowed freedom of the ship when not rowing and this day, stood on the deck after the evening meal. Leaning against the forecastle wall, he watched the sun sink below the western horizon. A cool breeze sprang up, and glancing astern, he saw, far to the north, a seething mass of dark clouds racing toward them.

The temperature dropped, and the sea erupted to life, slapping ever higher against the ship's weathered hull. From the tiller, the deep bass of the helmsman's voice roared. "Ahoy, Captain! Get ye out here!"

The captain, a hard-faced, gray-haired man, burst from his cabin at the stern and stared at the clouds for an instant only before bellowing, "All hands to the decks!"

In moments, the deck crawled with life. Sailors raced up the rigging to reef the sails. Hatches were battened, orders shouted. The sky turned a solid iron gray and the building wind shoved the writhing sea ever higher toward them.

Ralt stood, transfixed, as death approached. Unthinking, he reached for a line dangling from the wall behind him and secured it around his waist. The mountain of water roaring toward them towered over their main mast where sailors scampered about like monkeys, but before it could strike them down, the bow of the *Merryweather* surged upward, riding the wave to its crest. The ship bobbed at the zenith, then plunged headlong into the maelstrom.

Water crashed over the ship, and only the line wrapped about him saved Ralt from being swept into the sea. Then up popped the ship's prow, the deck at a forty-five degree angle. Screaming, men slid toward the stern, grasping for anything to hold on to.

The deck leveled, water sheeting off the ship's sides. "Get on with ye!" A big hand grabbed Ralt's shoulder and shook. "Either get out there and help or get below decks. Ye canna just stand here!"

Shaking off the sailor's hand, Ralt untied the line and headed for the ladder, but the deck was awash with seawater and the ship listed to starboard. Another monstrous wave smashed into the port side and it occurred to Ralt they were going to capsize. He would not live to avenge himself upon his father, although he supposed the king would grieve that his only son died as a result of his orders.

Still, if Ralt wasn't there to watch the suffering, it wouldn't quite count.

"Below decks, I tell ye!" The big man shoved Ralt across the drenched but momentarily level deck. Ralt raised the hatch then glanced over his shoulder to see who'd had such concern for his miserable existence. Ah, Liren—the boatswain's mate—and without his whip. Here was one he wouldn't mind seeing offered to the ocean gods, but if it was to be so, he wouldn't be around to observe. Other than rowing, he'd learned nothing about the operation of the ship in fair weather or ill.

Throwing himself down the ladder, he wrenched open the door to a tiny store room, jumped in, and slammed it closed.

By midnight, the shriek of the piercing wind filled every crevice of Ralt's mind. Sleep was impossible. Believing he couldn't be in any more danger moving about the ship than in lying low, he decided to explore other areas below deck.

He soon discovered that he, two men in the infirmary, and the cook—who doubled as the ship's healer, were the only ones below. Everyone else was topside, fighting the storm. Even the other prisoners.

Fine with him. He had no interest in being swept overboard attempting to save these swine.

For two days, the *Merryweather*—whose name now seemed a profound joke—and her crew battled the raging wind and unrelenting, battering waves. The men rested in shifts when they could, eating what the cook could manage, sleeping for only brief hours before returning to the fray.

On the third day, the captain, helmsman, and first mate huddled over the small table in the galley, hands wrapped around mugs of steaming mulled wine. Ralt stood in the shadows, watching, he supposed, unobserved. They'd lost two men that day, navigation was next to impossible. The storm had pushed them to the edge of seas no one had explored. The ship was in danger of foundering—they'd already dropped what cargo they could.

Gulping the last of his wine, the captain braced himself against the table and pushed to his feet. "Come on, lads, let's get back to it." Then he turned his haggard gaze on Ralt. "And you, there. You've been skulking about long enough. Get down to the bilge and help with the pumps."

Ralt lifted a brow then smiled coolly at the captain. "Of course, sir."

The mate growled and pulled back a fist but the captain grabbed his arm. With his own hand, he slapped Ralt hard, slamming him to the deck.

"I want you to know," the captain said, standing over him, "if we survive this devil's bash, and you live to scurry back to Malacar, that you remember just who it was who struck you." He leaned closer. "I know what you've been doing these past months. Now get down to the bilge and help those men with the pumps, or I'll throw you overboard myself."

Ralt climbed to his feet, rubbing his stinging cheek, and followed the three men across the rocking deck toward the ladder. Just as the captain reached the first step, the ship shuddered then lifted and tilted to the starboard, farther and farther. Ralt scrambled but couldn't catch himself, fell, and slid across the bucking deck. Overhead, a deafening crack of timber and snapping of cables sounded over the tumult of the storm.

"We've lost the mast!" someone shouted. "Captain—the mast is down!"

The captain and his men raced up the ladder, and even though he'd been ordered below, Ralt followed. It was daylight but the gray was unrelenting—sea, sky, the ship itself. Men on the port side fell to their knees, calling on the Maker or any other god they knew. Ralt looked and saw why. A wave—vast beyond any he'd seen—surged toward the ship, rearing higher and higher.

It struck them broadside.

The world upended and he slid down the tipping deck. He flailed his arms and legs, grasping for anything to cling to. Something heavy slid across the deck, smashed into his leg.

And he was no longer attached to the ship, but free falling through the wind, into the raging sea.

Deeper and deeper, he was sucked down, until the pressure in his lungs, in his ears, his mind, threatened to tear him to pieces.

He opened his eyes and somewhere—far above, saw light. The pain in his leg was excruciating, but he used his arms and began to stroke—straining upward, reaching for the light, for the air he needed. His clothes dragged him back, pulled him down, but he fought. And fought some more.

He burst into the air, gasping, retching. The waves carried him up, down, and up again, sucking him below the surface time and again, snatching away the air. Each time, he fought his way up, stole back the air, clung to life.

But he couldn't hold on forever. He'd swallowed too much water, dizziness overtook him, and he couldn't feel his left leg. He did the only thing he could. He rolled onto his back, did his best to keep his head above water, and let the sea carry him where it would. Time passed—he didn't know how much time—but when he'd caught his breath and the wind-stricken waves seemed somewhat smaller, he turned his head, scanning the ocean around him, the sky above. He couldn't see the *Merryweather*. If it had survived, it was far away now, but finally, *finally*, the wind was calming, the waves diminishing. His clothes weighed him down and he struggled to remove them. The tunic was easy enough but he could do nothing with his breeches or the boot on the foot of the injured leg.

Panting, he lay back on the sea that was now gentle, soothing. How could the storm have blown itself out so quickly? The solid gray mass of clouds that had imprisoned the sky for the last three days broke apart. Blue appeared in the sky and to the west, a shaft of sunlight burst through the remaining clouds. The crystalline sea quieted, turning into a living tapestry of indigo and ivory.

Ralt had never been given to flights of fancy, but after the raging storm of the last days, the change seemed almost instantaneous. Magical, even.

He let the sea carry him on, comforted now by its kindly embrace. Sometime later, he felt it gather itself beneath him and push him forward on little rollers of surf. Turning his head, he saw the last thing he expected.

Land.

A sandy, glistening beach curved around him. Unfamiliar trees waved leaves of blue and gold, silver and mauve. And even more surprising—a tall man with long white hair stood on the shore, unmoving, as the sea brought Ralt to him. The man tipped narrowed, ancient eyes down to stare at him.

"Welcome to my island, Prince Ralt." A smile played across thin, cruel lips. "I am called Lothar. I think we may be of help to one another."

CHAPTER ONE

TEN YEARS LATER

The king of Tressalt sat at the table in his private chambers. His back was to Lyric but she could see he held a quill in one hand, and his head, with its mane of burnished bronze hair, was bent over a scroll spread before him. The decadent odor of something rich and sweet wafted from a mug next to the scroll. *Dark chocolate from the southern isles?* The scent made her mouth water and her stomach rumble.

"What are you drinking, Papa?" She skipped across the bearskin rug to the king's side. "It smells divine!"

He didn't answer. She put her hand on his shoulder and shook gently. "Papa?"

His head slumped forward and slowly, so slowly it seemed an eternity, he slid off the carved oak bench and rolled onto his back on the bear's pelt. Deep green eyes, frozen in death, stared sightlessly at her.

She screamed and jolted upright, fighting the tangled bedroll wrapped around her. Staring wildly about, she raked a hand through her knotted hair and pulled the bedroll tight around her shoulders. A small campfire cast flickering shadows across the sleeping forms of her companions. Becca lay closest to her on the forest floor, her breathing steady and undisturbed. On the far side of the fire, Hanseth and Monteith slept unmoving, one of them snoring gently. No sign of Quinn but Amira, as still as the cat she so often reminded Lyric of, sat watch between the men and the fire.

The Akyldi woman lifted a slender, silver brow. "A bad dream, Princess?"

Lyric nodded and lay back down. *A dream. Yes.* She pulled the blanket to her chin, fighting the chill of body and soul. Tremors racked her. If only the nightmare would fade with her wakefulness.

But it wouldn't.

She clenched her jaw and pressed her eyes shut. Her father was dead. Not even the light of day would change that.

An owl's mournful call floated through the trees overhead. Nearby, one of the horses stomped a hoof then blew softly through its lips.

Staring into the shadowy branches of the trees that surrounded their campsite, she forced herself to take one slow breath after another. Weariness enveloped her, pulling her into darkness, but for two days she'd been unable to sleep for more than a few hours at a time.

Two days ago, the servant girl Noni had been killed trying to defend her. Two days ago, she'd learned of her father's death. And two days ago, the Malacarians attacked and she'd fought back with a power she didn't understand and had never known she possessed.

Yesterday, they'd ridden into the forest north of Graceen and found the meadow where they were to meet Venuzia. Today, they'd waited all day but the ancient Sheever woman and her raptor steed had not appeared.

Lyric was queen now, but someone else sat upon her throne, so the title meant nothing. War had struck her homeland and followed hard on their trail. And there were six of them, *six*, wandering into an unfamiliar land, searching for beings who might or might not help them fulfill the prophecy that would stop their enemy.

Did they have any hope at all?

"You are troubled, my friend."

She stared at Amira from within her bedroll, then sighed and sat up. Clearly, she wasn't going back to sleep soon. She stood and wrapped the scratchy, wool blanket snuggly around her shoulders, then, stepping carefully over Becca, joined Amira at the fire. Lowering herself to the ground, she pulled her knees to her chest and clasped her arms around them, staring into the blaze. Her thoughts swirled with the crackling flames.

"I am very troubled."

Amira poked at the fire with a green pine branch. "I am sorry about your father."

Moisture collected behind Lyric's eyes. "I wish you could have known him."

For a time, the quiet snapping of the fire was the only sound in the tiny camp. Lyric roused herself. "That's not all that troubles me, though. This whole thing—what we're doing—how are we to accomplish it? I'm afraid, and I'm tired. I want to go home, but I have no home." She lowered her head to her knees. Whether they defeated Ralt or were defeated by him, the pain of some things would never heal.

Becca murmured in her sleep. Lyric lifted her head and glanced about the clearing. "Where's Quinn?"

"He's out—"

"Keeping watch over us?" Lyric shook her head. "Of course."

Light filled Amira's eyes, and her lips turned up at the corners. "It's what he does."

Lyric nodded, wondering about Marek. Where was he on this dark night? Would she ever see him again? Shivering, she pulled the blanket tighter. "Don't you two ever sleep?"

"We sleep. We just don't require as much rest as humans do."

Lyric glanced at Monteith and Hanseth. How much did they know? Prince Carlton knew the Akyldi were not human, but had he told his soldiers before assigning them to her?

Amira followed her gaze, seemed to read her thoughts. "I think it's safe. These are good men who are loyal to you. Still, it is not a truth we share gladly with others." She grinned broadly, exposing the sharp canine teeth.

"I hate it when you do that," Lyric complained then grinned, surprised and pleased that anything this night could make her smile.

Amira flashed her normal, mild Akyldi smile. "I know."

The night breeze, heavy with the scent of pine, sent fingers of chill air probing through Lyric's blanket. She inched closer to the dancing flames. "I'm also very disturbed about my new-found *gift*. It doesn't matter how powerful it is if I don't know how to use it." She frowned and glanced at her friend. "I stopped those men with the power of my words alone."

The Akyldi woman stood, reached for a small log and dropped it onto the fire. Sparks shot upward into the darkness. Amira watched until the brightness winked out then returned to her seat next to the pine tree. "Your words and the power of the opal stone. And yes, it is wise to approach such gifts with care. With such power comes great responsibility."

Lyric shivered, picked up the branch Amira had discarded and prodded the burning firewood. Her father had explained that truth to her a dozen times—the intertwining of power and responsibility. She was quite sure, though, he hadn't been thinking of a power such as this.

That didn't make the premise less true.

"You were going to tell me more about the gemstones. Do they all impart unusual powers?"

Amira shook her head. "So much is not known and much that may have been known once was lost after the Great War."

Lyric jabbed at the fire, frowning. "You must know something. What about my stone? You said something about it being mysterious."

"That may have been too strong a word." Amira removed the jasper pendant from within her tunic, stared into its ruddy surface thoughtfully. "When trying to understand the gemstones, it's best to begin with their purpose. The Maker created the six races and placed us in Argonia, then gifted each race with a Sentinel to teach and guide us. The gemstones were the conduits, the connectors between each race and its Sentinel. And a means of communication between the races."

Lyric sighed. "Yes, I know that part."

Amira lifted a brow, smiled. "If the gemstones had other powers or purposes at the beginning, that information is lost. All we know is what has come down to us from later generations and only about the opal stone. But they are only stories, and as I said, even those are inconsistent."

Lyric scowled at her friend. "This is not helping. What about—"

Amira raised a hand. "Here is what I do know. During the Great War, it became apparent that Lothar wanted all of the gemstones. It is not known why he wanted them. Whether he hoped to control the peoples through the stones, to destroy the connection between the other Sentinels and their people, or for some other reason, we do not know."

She paused, rubbing a finger lightly across the gleaming red stone. "According to the oldest manuscripts, much of the destruction that occurred during the Great War was due to Lothar's lust for the stones. Thousands upon thousands died trying to save their kingdoms and keep the stones out of his power." She sighed. "Many later scholars believe the reason for the prophecy was so the gemstones themselves would bring about his destruction."

Another log on the fire splintered and cracked, shooting sparks skyward. Lyric flinched. Lothar had desired the gemstones even before the prophecy, and now they were the key to his demise. She sighed. Of course, he wanted them.

And suddenly she remembered being accosted by Prince Ralt during the Solstice Ball. The eagerness in his eyes as he reached for her necklace. "I have a friend who's told me to search for just such *heirlooms*," he'd said.

Nausea swept over her. Did Lothar know she had the opal stone? Was this what fueled Ralt's search for her? The reason behind the attacks in Graceen and the assault on King Rasmus?

"Other than that," Amira went on, "the opal stone is the only one that's ever mentioned in the surviving texts. Shortly after Lothar's downfall and the recording of the prophecy, the human queen who held it sent word to our king. She reported sometimes knowing what people were going to say or do before they said or did those things. It had happened often enough and had started relatively soon after she inherited the opal that she wondered about a possible connection."

Lyric shook her head, frowning. "That's never happened to me."

Amira nodded. "Several generations ago, my people deemed it wise to ... keep a closer watch on our neighbors in Argonia."

"You began spying on us." Lyric scowled, jabbing at the burning firewood.

Amira shrugged. "Call it what you will. It was felt necessary, and I don't believe we're sorry." She offered a conciliatory smile. "At any rate, the young human queen at that time was overheard questioning her mother-in-law, from whom she'd received the stone, wondering about oddities she'd noticed."

"What oddities?"

Amira smiled. "The girl thought she'd developed the power to make people do things they didn't want to do. Especially her husband." Amira broke into her big Akyldi grin. "Her mother-in-law laughed and told her she should be happy. That most women would be thrilled with such an ability."

Lyric rolled her eyes. "And that's it? Nothing about any of the other stones?"

"Not that I know of. Just enough so that when you did what you did to the Malacarians two nights ago, I recalled these few tales."

Suddenly, as if of its own will, the bedroll Becca lay wrapped in began to writhe. An arm protruded from the blanket, followed by another, then by Becca's sandy, rumpled mop of hair as the girl sat up. She turned bleary eyes on Lyric. "Is all well, my lady? Is it time to get up already?"

"Everything's fine," Lyric whispered. "Go back to sleep."

Grappling with her blanket, Becca mumbled something incoherent, then disappeared within its folds.

"To answer your earlier concern," Amira said. "There is no guarantee the power you experienced with your stone will show itself again. But I will work with you, if you like, to see if you can acquire control."

Lyric covered her mouth, trying to suppress a mind-numbing yawn. Yes, if there was any way to learn to control the power of the opal stone, she must do it. That ability might make all the difference in this war.

But not now.

She stood, gathering the blanket around her. "Thank you, but I must sleep now." She gave a faint smile. "We humans require more rest than do you Akyldi." Stepping over Becca's prone body, she moved back to her bedroll. What the morrow would bring, she could no longer fret over. Arranging the blankets about her, she closed her eyes and passed immediately into deep, dreamless slumber.

Made in the USA
Monee, IL
30 April 2022

95671747R00201